# Institutional Satire in Dickens' Fiction

# Institutional Satire in Dickens' Fiction

Satyendra Prasad Singh

ATLANTIC
PUBLISHERS & DISTRIBUTORS (P) LTD

Published by

**ATLANTIC**

**PUBLISHERS & DISTRIBUTORS (P) LTD**

7/22, Ansari Road, Darya Ganj,
New Delhi-110002
Phones : +91-11-40775252, 23273880, 23275880, 23280451
Fax : +91-11-23285873
Web : www.atlanticbooks.com
E-mail : orders@atlanticbooks.com

Branch Office
5, Nallathambi Street, Wallajah Road,
Chennai-600002
Phones : +91-44-64611085, 32413319
E-mail : chennai@atlanticbooks.com



ISBN 978-81-269-1369-5



Printed in India at Nice Printing Press, A-33/3A, Site-IV, Industrial Area, Sahibabad, Ghaziabad, U.P.

# Acknowledgements

I do feel a deep sense of gratitude to my Professor Dr. Shanker A. Dutt, in the Dept. of English, Patna University, currently Chairman, Bihar Sangeet Natak Academy for his advice and writing the Foreword to this book. I thank Atlantic Publishers and Distributors (P) Ltd., New Delhi for the care taken in the publication of the book. This book is a gift to my dear son Ayush Shikhar and my little daughter Sneha Priya who will hopefully read it some day.

**Satyendra Prasad Singh**

# Foreword

There is an inexhaustible wealth of critical reading on Dickens' oeuvre that is a testimony to his importance as a writer. He responded with discerning sensitivity to the transformation of Britain into urbanized society, the hardships and human degradation that followed both in life and death. Public bodies instituted for administration and structured forms of living were, as Engel Monroe writes, "immoral, inefficient, stupid, unfeeling, and perhaps worse, aesthetically unheroic. Wherever institutions touch, people are corrupted, acquiring a corporate, collective, or administrative view of life, rather than an individual human view". Dickens mediated between the desirable and the deplorable, scripting his world view with irony, caricature, humour and occasionally anger. This constituted his satiric vision that Satyendra Prasad Singh writes about in his book *Institutional Satire in Dickens' Fiction*.

Using a substantial body of non-literary co-texts, the author takes us on a journey through the corruption and inhumanity in numerous institutions: Administration, Judiciary, Religion, Politics, Commerce and Education guided by Utilitarianism that privileged material advantage of the greatest number over moral and spiritual needs; quantity over the quality of happiness. These institutions played an active role in the creation and consolidation of power relations, 'interpellation' subjects, hailing them to be willing accomplices to their own subordination. Dickens' satire often manifests as a literary equivalent of the pictorial caricature incisively focusing on institutions as a contested site for recruitment and resistance.

This book promises to be of worth to readers and academics who cherish Dickens and study and critique him for relevance, in his times and ours.

**Dr. Shanker A. Dutt**
Professor of English, Patna University, and
Chairman, Bihar Sangeet Natak Akadamy

# Preface

The mediation between the ideal perception and the real, one which constituted the representation of 19th century social reality grew out of comprehensive and complex experiences—profound and painful—relating to law and justice, administration, education, politics and religion. The continuing distress of social injustice has been satirised by Dickens with a rare blend of horror and irreverent comedy. Thus Mortomn Danwen Zabul studies the undivided imagination as a "fable of human society at a point of crisis". The "cruelty of institutions", as Lionel Trilling calls it, forms a sustained thematic context for the satire, which covers a great part of English life. Dickens' contextualised injustices and abuses whose victims—the circumstantially disadvantaged—were portrayed and exploded substantially conveying a deeper totality. In doing so, his institutional satire in its textual exploration gave wider publicity, quite inimitably to numerous social truths and its corresponding abuses. The distress of the victims was made more poignant because of the credulity they were endowed with and that is what transforms an occasional abuse into criminality.

Dickens turned to fiction in order to unravel the "reality of naked truths" as Forster terms it. He reveals through contextualising the naked truth as a stage where vulnerable characters experience the harsh world and the interactive process becomes the foundation of satire. It mirrors a world in need of correction.

The social conscience of a sensitive writer outraged by the despicable aberration of an ideal in the furtherance of human greed is perhaps nowhere more significant than in the portrayal of his favourite world of the child. In the dehumanised humility of the victims, of the fictional narratives, the narration assumes the devastating power of Dickens' satire.

This book intends to examine and analyse the ideological apparatus that causes so much of human suffering and read Dickens in the tradition which began with Archilocus and shaped its contemporary form. It is my endeavour to make a thorough study of institutions that have become corrupted, inefficient, cruel and immoral. The particular terms are defined and described in detail.

This book will be useful to students of English literature of Indian Universities. Some of the books of Dickens like *David Copperfield, Oliver Twist, Bleak House, Great Expectations, Hard Times, Dombey and Son*, etc. are prescribed in our universities and the book throws immense light on the key themes of Dickens' novels. It will also be helpful to researchers on Dickens as it includes substantial research material and critical analysis.

**Satyendra Prasad Singh**

# Abstract

Institutions are public bodies which are structured by human beings for a codified form of living. Such institutions as schools, workhouses, solicitors' offices and courts of law, business houses, churches, prisons, government departments, circuses, etc. appear prominently in most of Dickens' novels. Its positive presence constrains and distorts human life. These institutions are "immoral, inefficient, stupid, unfeeling.... Wherever institutions touch, people are corrupted."

The institution is an apparatus through which either through repressive means, or more effectively through ideological manipulation, society is controlled by the powerful few whose interests these institutions serve. The sensitive human and social consciousness of Dickens responded to the "most odious and absurd in despotism or in oligarchy" by placing human action within the historicised co-text. It is the constant mediation between the two that disrupts the illusion of Victorian stability and unfolds a satiric vision. When it is critically determined that "satire is an art form in which the theme is exaggerated to the point of ridicule in order to expose the insufficiencies in individuals, systems and institutions thereby suggesting a betterment", Dickens' response to the co-text of the magnitude of misery in his life and times holds up a mirror to our social conscience as a critique of the past which may be read as a contemporary warning which cries out for remedy.

The Poor Laws, Imprisonment for Debt, the Court of Chancery, the harshness of mill owners, the stupidity of Parliament, the inefficiency of the government, the inadequacy of the police as well as the school, the observance of Sunday and Mammon-worship are Dickens' subjects of satire.

Dickens' satire on English administration of the Victorian England is reflected in the alarming situation of crime prevalent in English social life. He exposes child kidnapping and stealing of clothes of children in *Dombey and Son* and pick-pocketing and theft in *Oliver Twist*. In *Great Expectations* and *Oliver Twist*, Dickens exposes the failures and inefficiency of the police. In *Martin Chuzzlewit*, he ridicules the worthless and careless magistrates for failing to squelch the mob. He ridicules the evils of the new Poor Law by satirising the inhumanity, cruelty and indifference of the workhouse authorities to the sufferings of the paupers in *Oliver Twist*. The sparseness of diet offered to the inmates of the workhouse is subjected to Dickens' bitter satire. He depicts the inefficiency and inaction of the Civil Service in *Little Dorrit*. He exposes the faulty, expensive and delayed administration of justice in *Bleak House*. In Bardell vs. Pickwick case in *Pickwick Papers*, Dickens ridicules the pompous procedures of the court trial. Mr. Justice Stareleigh's manners and appearance expose the distortion and monstrosity of the system. In *David Copperfield*, Dickens attacks the hypocrisy of proctorship and considers it a theatrical performance. The iniquity of the criminal law, made for their own benefit by the privileged class is attacked in *Great Expectations*.

Dickens believes in an ideal of toleration and reasonableness in religion derived from the tradition of Milton and Locke—champions of free religious conscience. The perversion of true religious spirit among the Methodists and Evangelists is satirised in *Pickwick Papers* as is Sabbatarianism in *Little Dorrit*. In the manner of Carlyle, Dickens holds the radically Protestant view that nothing interfered more with 'true' religion than the contemporary fetishism of "Rituals, Liturgies, Creeds, Hierarchies", "which obscured the divinely ordained duty to act righteously and serve one's fellow men". Dickens shows the failure of Christianity to act as a Social Gospel by exposing the religious hypocrisy of Victorian society in *Oliver Twist*. He presents the inadequacy of church to fulfil the serving role of the religious institution. Dickens ridicules the sectarian intolerance in *Barnaby Rudge*. He dislikes religious bigotry and attacks overenthusiasts to form a counteracting force sustaining reason and common sense. He satirises Little Bethelism, the narrow and cheerless religion in *The Old Curiosity Shop*.

Dickens' most energetic satire is directed against practitioners of religion and such ecclesiastical figures as Chadband in *Bleak House*, Reverend Mr. Stiggins in *Pickwick Papers* and Melchisedech Howler in *Dombey and Son*. He casts his satirical net in Murdstone in *David Copperfield*, Pecksniff in *Martin Chuzzlewit* and Mrs. Varden and Miss Miggs in *Barnaby Rudge*. Dickens shows the pseudo benevolence of the false philanthropic missions of religious missionarics by ridiculing Mrs. Jellyby and Mrs. Pardiggle in *Bleak House*.

Dickens detests the working of parliamentary democracy of contemporary England. Politics seemed to Dickens "nothing more than complicated and extravagant ceremony". In *Pickwick Papers*, he decries the pomp and show, the absurd rivalry of the political parties, the farce election campaign and the unfair election. In *Bleak House*, he attacks the political corruption, the parliamentary intrigue and the party game of the politicians. In *Martin Chuzzlewit* and *Nicholas Nickleby*, he attacks the incompetent politicians. In *Little Dorrit*, he ridicules the corrupt politicians acting as swindlers. In *Our Mutual Friend*, he digs at the foolish and vainglorious politicians. He satirises the terrific upheaval of the Chartists in *The Old Curiosity Shop*.

In *Dombey and Son*, the very ideas that money can buy anything and human relations are conducted on the sound principles of hard commerce are jeered. Love, not business, is the only basis for human relationships. In *Dombey and Son*, the attack is not really on business but on "a poor outmoded kind of business mentality that carries its standards over into areas where they are even less useful and more ruinous than they are in business". In *Our Mutual Friend*, Dickens satirises the taste of the veneering world regarding shares. In *Martin Chuzzlewit*, he ridicules people who recognize money as the only yardstick of value. The measurement of things by its cash value denigrates all things and persons to nothingness.

The main tenets of utilitarianism include the exposure of all institutions to the tests of rational utility in the interests of the greatest happiness of the greatest number. *Hard Times* attacks the institutions that stunt love, imagination and life. Dickens calls upon the utilitarians to cultivate in people "the utmost graces of the fancies and affections to adorn their lives so much in need of ornament".

Dickens detests cruelty, inefficiency and repression in education. In *Dombey and Son*, he laughs at the Charity schools as the students are tormented by people and the teacher. The Blimber system is devastatingly cruel and its forcing system results in the stultification of students. In *Bleak House*, Dickens attacks the public school curriculum as it does not cater to the natural bent of the student. In *Hard Times*, he satirises the utilitarian system of education in which the inculcation of facts is the sole aim and imagination is suppressed. He holds that "the proper education of children must take into account their moral development, which it should foster through their fancy and love of life". In *Our Mutual Friend*, Dickens attacks the ragged school system. In *Great Expectations*, he satirises the bad academic activity of the amateurish dame school and its incompetent and tyrannical teacher, Mr. Wopsley's great aunt. In *David Copperfield*, Murdstone uses cruelty to teach David. Salem House represents the degrading institution of the nineteenth century. Mr. Creakle is a cruel, incompetent and hypocritical teacher. In *Nicholas Nickleby*, Dickens jeers Dotheboys Hall that keeps stunted, hopeless and vicious boys. Squeers is hypocritical, guile and greedy, ignorant and torturing. This novel assaults those cheap seminaries where "starvation is taught gratis".

The very purpose of Dickens' institutional satire is to excite our sympathy for the aggrieved and suffering in all sections of society. He directs our attention to the helpless victims of untoward circumstances or a vicious system. The volume and extent of the social evils are very much alarming during the Victorian age. With a reformist zeal, Dickens attacks the harshness and the lack of sympathy of the law and the cruel treatment meted out to the children. He intends to draw the attention of the administrators of the country to redress and solve those evils.

# Contents

*Acknowledgements* ........ *v*

*Foreword* ........ *vii*

*Preface* ........ *ix*

*Abstract* ........ *xi*

1. Social Matrix of Victorian England: Dickens' Response to this World and His Satiric Vision ........ 1

2. Administration and Judiciary ........ 46

3. Religion and Its Practitioners ........ 137

4. Politics, Commerce and Utilitarianism ........ 180

5. Education ........ 228

6. Conclusion ........ 265

*Bibliography* ........ 281

# Social Matrix of Victorian England: Dickens' Response to this World and His Satiric Vision

1

Institutions are public bodies which are structured by human beings for a codified form of living. Institutions of all types appear prominently in most of Dickens' novels. These include schools, banks, workhouses, shops, solicitors' offices and courts of law, business houses, churches, prisons, government departments, gentlemen's clubs, hospitable public houses, circuses and theatres, hotels and lodging houses, etc. Formally constituted or informally created, institutions provide a focus for the different actions and reactions of the characters. Its positive presence constrains and distorts human life into a variety of unexpected shapes. Individuals are forced to exercise extra-ordinary and fantastic ingenuity to preserve the flow of spontaneous life under such pressures. These institutions are "immoral, inefficient, stupid, unfeeling, and perhaps worst of all, aesthetically unheroic. Wherever institutions touch, people are corrupted, acquiring a corporate, collective, or administrative view of life, rather than an individual humane view."[1]

The Poor Laws, Imprisonment for Debt, the Court of Chancery, the harshness of Mill-owners, the stupidity of Parliament, the inefficiency of the Government, the inadequacy of the police and the school, the observance of Sunday and Mammon-worship are Dickens' subjects of satire.

The institution is an apparatus through which either through repressive means or more effectively through ideological manipulation, society is controlled by the powerful few whose interests these institutions serve. The sensitive human and social consciousness of Dickens responded to the "most odious and absurd in despotism or in oligarchy"[2] by placing human action within the historicised co-text. It is the constant mediation between the two that disrupts the illusion of Victorian stability and unfolds a satiric vision. When it is critically determined that "satire is an art form in which the theme is exaggerated to the point of ridicule in order to expose the insufficiencies in individuals, systems and institutions thereby suggesting a betterment"[3], Dickens' response to the co-text of the magnitude of misery in his life and times holds up a mirror to our social conscience as a critique of the past which may be read as a contemporary warning which cries out for remedy.

Britain, during the first half of the nineteenth century, transformed into an urbanised society. Prior to this, half of its population lived in the countryside. There was hardship and life was miserable for the rural unemployed. They came to London from outside in search of work. They came from all the counties of England into the Great Wen, the Oven, the Fever Pateh. They came from Ireland too. "Some found work, some were consigned to the workhouse (it was popularly believed that the London workhouses were strictest in the country, well earning their nicknames as 'Bastilles') but there was also a floating population of vagrants and homeless drifters (it was estimated that in 1850 there were some fifteen to twenty thousand of them) who slept in alleys or beneath the new railway arches."[4] What primarily tempted people to London was a sense that "something was going on: theatres, music halls, brightly lit streets, huge crowds, hubbub in the streets".[5] The population of London increased from one million at the beginning of the century to 4.5 million (approx.) by its end.

Due to the oversized population of the city, there was a remarkable increase in crime. London was never the safest of places and there was "nothing like the rate of crime which now afflicted the Victorians—'one newspaper in 1867 estimated that in London there were 1,00,000 persons who live by plunder'."[6] In this vast city there were several 'no go' areas such as in Bermondsey, Whitechapel, Stepney, Bethnal Green, Seven Dials, Lambeth, Southwark, Holborn and Westminster where the new Metropolitan force never approached. Before 1820 Anthony Trollope's two elder brothers heard stories of various wicked regions, where the bandit bands of the city consorted and passed outlaw lives. They heard accounts of "Saffron Hill 'where it was said all the pocket handkerchiefs stolen by all the pickpockets in London were to be seen exposed in a sort of unholy market'."[7] There were many slums of Whitechapel, Rotherhithe, Houndsditch and Bethnal Green, Southwark and Spitalfields, and in St. Giles, here whole courts were "inhabited by gang of criminals, their women and their children; where holes were cut through walls and ceilings, into cellars and out of roofs so that a man wanted by the police might soon escape; where brothels, lodging houses, rat-pits and skittle-grounds were entirely given over to the custom of criminals."[8]

Crime was not only the morbid concern of the newspaper addict, it was a burning social problem. In Dickens' early years, "crime was formidably common and unchecked; pocket-picking, for instance, was then a highly organised major industry. On this ground alone, the Gaol and the Gallows were bound to occupy him, along with the School, the Workhouses, and other such central social institutions."[9]

By 1851, 23,62,000 people inhabited London in the most overcrowded conditions "and 'suitable housing did not exist', records the social historian, Kitson Clark, 'and the additional numbers were crammed into every nook and cranny from attic to cellar of old decaying property...with little or no access to light and air'."[10] London's infrastructure was deeply affected due to this massive population and the insufficient domestic sanitation and public sewerage caused contamination and disease. Overcrowding caused widespread infection. The problems became serious owing to lack of information and scientific knowledge about the sources and nature of infection. Medical men, bureaucrats, lawyers and politicians tried to solve the problem but it proved futile.

Till mid-1860's, half of the population of London depended on water piped directly from the Thames. In this river, 200 open sewers flowed and the Thames was known as a 'vast open cloaca'. Since, this river was the source of water, untreated sewage emerged from the brown water of the standing taps or the kitchen pipes. No main drainage was constructed in the capital till 1865 and the water from the sinks and the closets passed down through old sewers and into the Thames and drained into enormous cesspools under the houses and the courts of the city. In the poorer quarters, the problem was grim. There was not "enough water to wash, or to clean whatever small rooms they possessed, and one inspector in 1847 noted that 'the filth (by which he meant principally excrement) was lying scattered about the rooms, vaults, cellars, areas and yards, so thick, and so deep, that it was hardly possible to move through it'."[11] In 1843, London's houses were 'jerrybuilt' and there was no system of ventilation or drainage. London was a source of pestilence, a breeding ground of disease.

Londoners of the river banks used water from the Thames and the Lea. In an official report on Nuisances (July 1849), it was revealed that such sewers were "pumped annually into the Thames more than seven million cubic feet of sludge on the northern bank and nearly two and a half million on the southern. The authorities on the latter side pumped 'puddle' not only into but out of the river, taking it from opposite the outfall of the Ranelagh sewer"[12] (Sludge or 'residuum' is oozy mud and it includes dung and offal of all kinds). The report further stated that the subsoil of London was sodden with seventeen million cubic feet of decaying residuum due to the regular use of domestic cesspools.

The West End Squares was situated on leaky sewers and ejected bad smells. There were cesspools for two hundred and eighty-two houses on nine acres of ground near the Oxford Street. The lower tenements of the notorious Rookery of St. Giles were over brimmed with their sewage. There was a network of cesspools beside the Abbey and it caused fever in Westminster. In Buckingham Palace, Queen Victoria became the victim of wretched ventilation and the threat of drainage smells. There were also Mr. Boffin's profitable mounds in many areas and garbage of all kinds was deposited on these for sale to manufacture bricks and manure.

The city burial grounds were full with corpses and they emitted 'noxious' gases. In Clare Market by Drury Lane above

1200 bodies were buried in the same vault between 1823 and 1824, and one grave digger at other site described: "I have been upto my knees in human flesh by jumping on the bodies so as to cram them into the least possible space at the bottom of the graves in which fresh bodies were afterwards placed."[13] In 1839, George Alfred Walker described the horrible condition of forty-three metropolitan burial grounds. Within two hundred yards in Clement's Lane off the Strand, there were four burial grounds. Walker noted that the living breathed on all sides an atmosphere impregnated with the odour of the dead. In 1843, Edwin Chadwick made a Parliamentary enquiry into the interment in towns and described in the report the possible risks to public health from the graveyards and from the delays in burying the dead. He commented on the nature of London's problem that overcrowding had left the city's churchyards tiered with coffins like geological or archaeological strata. His statistics indicated the horror: "In the metropolis, on spaces of ground which do not exceed 203 acres, closely surrounded by the abodes of the living, layer upon layer, each consisting of a population numerically equivalent to a large army of 20,000 adults, and nearly 30,000 youths and children, is every year imperfectly interred. Within the period of the existence of the present generation, upwards of a million of dead must have been interred in these same spaces."[14]

Chadwick also described the risk of infection: "A layer of bodies is stated to be about seven years in decaying in the metropolis: to the extent that this is so, the decay must be by the conversion of the remains into gas, and its escape as a miasma, of many times the bulk of the body that has disappeared."[15] In some poor and crowded districts, the smell of the decomposing dead mixed up with the smell of the sewerage. A person living in the vicinity of a graveyard has serious menace on the health. Mr. Barnett, the medical officer for the parish of Stepney, came across alarming incidence effecting serious risk to health: "Some years since a vault was opened in the churchyard and shortly after one of the coffins contained therein burst with so loud a report that hundreds flocked to the place to ascertain the cause. So intense was the poisonous nature of the effluvia arising therefrom, that a great number were attacked with sudden sickness and fainting, many of whom were a considerable period before they recovered their health."[16]

The vaults and burial grounds connected to Brunswick chapel, Limehouse, were crowded with dead. When a grave happened to be opened during the summer months, the stench was most noxious. "In one case it is described to have produced instant nausea and vomiting, and attacks of illness are frequently inputed to it. Some say they have never had a day's good health since they resided so near the chapel ground."[17] Edwin Chadwick noted in his report on the Sanitary Condition of the Labouring Population of 1842: "The annual loss of life from filth and bad ventilation are greater than the loss from death or wounds in any wars in which this country has been engaged in modern times."[18]

By 1880, Thomas A. Welton reported to the Statistical Society of London that the mortality rate had decreased by 25 per cent over the twenty-five-year period. According to him, the zymotic diseases such as Scarlatina, Typhus, Typhoid, and Typhinia and lungs diseases were the biggest killers. Fifteen years before, the Journal of the Statistical Society commented on the 25th annual report of the Registrar General. The rate of infant mortality was high during 1850-60. More than half the deaths of the children (5-10) years group were caused by the zymotic diseases and the rest by Scrofula, Tabes, Phthisis, Hydrocephalus and 'diseases of the brain and lungs'. Consumption proved to be the main killer in the age group (10-15) years overtaking fevers and diptheria. Small pox was the main killer in the age group (15-25) years but half the deaths of young women were attributed to consumption and child birth. In 1839, the population was approximately two million and there were 45,277 funerals in London, and 21,471 of them were of children under ten years age. The rate of mortality for infants was 150 in every 1000 births and it dropped to 138 in every 1000 births in 1901-05. Edwin Chadwick's estimation was that £6-8 million was saved for funeral expenses out of £24 million deposited in savings banks in 1843.

Typhus and Typhoid were endemic in London, Glasgow and some of the northern manufacturing cities. Typhus spread in 1848, 1856 and 1861. In 1831-32, Cholera first appeared in England and emanated from Jacob's Island, long famous as one of the vilest slums of London. One newspaper considered this spot as 'the very capital of Cholera'. It occurred more seriously in September 1848 and killed 52,293 people in 1849. It appeared repeatedly in the mid-summer of 1853, causing 20,097 deaths in England and Wales. Cholera spread in July 1865 fourth time and killed 14,378 men and women, 5548 in London.

Between November and December of 1847, "500,000 people were infected with typhus fever out of a total population of 2,100,000, for example, and it seemed to many people that London was indeed becoming what The Lancet described as a 'doomed city'. The average age of mortality in London was 27, while that for the working classes was 22."[19] Scarlet fever appeared in malignant form in Dublin in 1931, crossed to England in 1840 and occurred epidemically in 1844 and 1848. Smallpox killed approximately 12,000 people annually during the years 1837-40. When the Vaccination Act was enforced, the figure dropped to 5,000 per annum in the U.K. Diptheria was endemic too. Because of the appalling living conditions — "sewerage in the drinking water and so on, most people felt sick virtually all the time they were in London."[20] The slum landlords and jerrybuilders saved space by crowding families into single rooms and underground cellars and saved money by the use of cheap and insufficient building material. They did not construct drains and when provided it oozed into the water supply.

The first Public Health Act was passed in 1848. Edwin Chadwick, Secretary to the Poor Law Commissioners, was instrumental in the passing of the Act. He realised the facts: "The prisons (he wrote) were formerly distinguished for their filth and bad ventilation; but the descriptions given by Howard of the worst prisons he visited in England (which he states were among the worst he had seen in Europe) were exceeded in every wynd in Edinburgh and Glasgow inspected by Dr. Arnott and myself. More filth, worse physical suffering and moral disorder than Howard describes are to be found amongst the cellar populations of the working people of Liverpool, Manchester or Leeds and in large portions of the Metropolis."[21]

The Public Health Act of 1848 was not properly carried out by the municipalities for next twenty years. In the 'seventies', the Local Government Board was established to enforce the law and Joseph Chamberlain, the social-reforming mayor of Birmingham, was a very important figure to bring a new age. Now the Municipalities were elected bodies and produced public benefits more. But still the condition was not encouraging till the 'seventies' as a result of building and sanitary reform in England. Lord Shaftesbury was campaigning for better housing conditions and he described in *The Times* of 1 April 1851, of the squalor in the cheap lodging houses of London.

During the middle years of the century, Lord Shaftesbury established some model lodging houses totally immune from Cholera and this encouraged Parliament to pass an Act for the inspection of common lodging houses in 1851. The window tax was also repealed the same year. John Lucas remarks: "In his Second Sanitary Report to the City of London (1850) Sir John Simon speaks of the 'pestilential heaping of human beings' into slums, where disease is forever within the circle;...because Death so largely confronts these poor orphans of civilisation."[22] Dr. Simon's report on the Sanitary Condition of the City, presented to the Commissioners of Sewers, was reviewed in *The Times* on 31st December 1850 and 2 January 1851: "That the main conditions which constitute the unhealthiness of towns are definite, palpable, removable evils; that dense over-crowding of a population; that intricate ramification of courts and alleys, excluding light and air; that defective drainage; that the products of organic decomposition; that contaminated water and a stinking atmosphere are distinct causes of disease and death...that each is suspectible of abatement or removal, which will at once be followed by diminution of its alleged effects upon the health of the population."[23]

*The Times*, in its leading article, on 4 September, 1851, reported as established fact that in English towns generally half the attainable period of life is "lost to all who are born.... This loss of life is in no degree attributable either to the situation, soil, or climate of a locality, or to the density of a population, or to the employments generally prevailing.... The destroying agent is typhus fever, generated by localised filth and excessive moisture.... Bad drainage and immoderate dampness—that is to say, too little water where it is needed, and too much where it is out of place, are the generating elements."[24]

In the years 1856-59, three medical officers of health, in three parishes of London composed:

> The main cause to which we must attribute the high mortality is the close packing and overcrowding which exists throughout the district...overcrowding and disease mutually act and react upon each other.
>
> The overcrowding of dwellings is one of the most frequent sources of sickness and decay at all ages.
>
> Perhaps there is no single influence to which a human being is exposed more prejudicial to his health than overcrowding in rooms the air of which cannot be perpetually and rapidly changed.[25]

Medical observers shared with sanitary and social reformers the firm, and justified belief, that the slums of the cities provided a breeding ground for contagious disease. The Thames, which had always functioned "as London's main artery of traffic as much as its chief sewer, had become, by the 1850s, an offensively rank carrier of infection".[26]

In 1858, the Second Annual Report of the Medical officer to the Strand asks to dismiss from our minds of the idea, that sanitary improvements consist exclusively in works of drainage and of water supply. Overcrowding is without doubt the most important, and the most difficult problem with us to deal. Houses and streets may be drained most perfectly. The district may be paved and lighted so well as to excite the jealous envy of other local authorities. New thoroughfares may be constructed and every house in the district may be furnished with a constant supply of pure water. The Thames may be embanked and all entrance of sewerage into that river intercepted. But so long as "twenty, thirty, or even forty individuals are permitted, it might almost be said compelled—to reside in houses originally built for the accommodation of a single family or at most two families, so long will the evils pointed out in regard of health...continue to exist almost unchecked."[27]

The condition of the highly skilled and conscious members of the working class improved by the measures taken for sanitation. But a large section of the community remained untouched. By the 1860's their unions had begun to acquire a reputation for respectability, but as one economic historian has pointed out, the position of the poorest was very different. When they struck, "their strikes were broken in detail.... They subsisted darkly and violently in the slums of the cities, which for all Chadwick's battles were still squalid and insanitary."[28] Chadwick's famous sanitary report was presented in 1842. Six years later, in 1848, the Public Health Act was passed. But this was a mere poor reflection of the measure Chadwick and other sanitary reformers worked for.

Dickens is very much alive in treatment of the matters of sanitary condition in his novels and in the *Household Words*. He advocated to the Metropolitan Sanitary Association for a proper supply of water for the masses. He asked: "Give them a glimpse of heaven through a little of its light and air."[29] He denounced the window tax in the *Daily News* and the same was repealed in 1852. London became a fog bound city and glass could not illumine the room. The horror of a 'London particular', as this sooty, suffocating plague was called, Dickens wrote of this in the opening chapter of *Bleak House* whose first section in serial form appeared just before the Smoke Nuisance (Metropolis) Act was passed in 1852. This mounted some restrictions over factories.

In *Bleak House*, Dickens decided to frighten people if they would not listen to argument. He warned the rich population that 'the slime and pestilential gas' of the slum (Tom-all-Alone) would work to the very highest order of the society and diseases would be the best killers there. He, as main speaker, at the first anniversary banquet of the Metropolitan Sanitary Association, demanded fervently for 'Searching Sanitary Reform'. He maintained that Education and Religion can do nothing unless the path is paved for their ministrations by cleanliness and decency. He warned his listners that disease produced by appalling living condition would not remain limited to East End, its place of origin. He cautioned the comfortable and lax people who tried to ignore the problem: "It is certain that the air from Gin Lane, will be carried, when the wind is Easterly, into May fair, and that if you once have a vigorous pestilence raging furiously in Saint Giles, no mortal list of Lady Patronesses can keep it out of Almack's."[30] Dickens used his journalism to popularise abuses as conditions leading to the deaths of 159 children from cholera in the Tooting workhouse. He was also in regular contact with Henry Austin, general secretary of the Board of Health and Edwin Chadwick, the sanitary reformer. Dickens actively appealed for funds for the extension of the Great Ormond Street Hospital for sick children, founded in 1852.

Dickens made journeys through slums with his friends and visited some lodging-houses there. In "To Working Men" in *Household Words*, October 7, 1854, he wrote about the sufferings of the urban slum-dwellers and Govt.'s indifference to the improvement of the condition of the poor. He delivered a speech on 9 February, 1858, as President at a dinner organised to get financial help from the public for the Hospital for Sick Children: "The spoilt children whom I must show you are spoilt children of the poor in this great city—the children who are, every year, for ever and ever, irrevocably spoilt out of this breathing life of ours by tens of thousands, but who may in vast numbers, be preserved, if you, assisting and not contravening the ways of Providence, will help to save them."[31]

Dickens discussed the problem of sanitation in *Dombey and Son* as a warning to the danger of neglecting slum evils. He subscribed to the Health of Towns Association for the concern of Cholera. Overcrowding, bad drainage, contaminated water and emerging diseases were topical subjects. Dickens attacked the terrible picture of Jacob's Island in *Oliver Twist*. In *David*

*Copperfield* also, he talks of the sanitary question. "It was in *Household Words*, for example, that there appeared a description of a city churchyard which was no more than a 'cholera Nursery' as well as a report on the 'mental ignorance and neglect' which afflicted the labouring classes."[32]

There was a marked improvement in the police forces during the Victorian Age. The system of parish-constables and watchmen, inherited from Tudor times, was modified during the mid-eighteenth century by efficient local units such as the Bow Street Runners and Patroles, and The Thames River Police. Sir Robert Peel's great institution of the civilian police with their truncheons, blue coats and top hats (later replaced by helmets) was applied to the Metropolitan area in 1829. This police force was known as the Metropolitan Police. "The doyen of English Constabularies, it soon also became their model, for again legislation followed the families pattern: Permissive Acts for establishing municipal and county police forces were followed by compulsory Acts, with the Government gaining fuller control through an inspectorate backed by financial sanctions."[33] The people fond of liberty, property and personal safety liked the effective 'Bobbies' of London. By 1856 every county and borough was required to employ "a police force, half local, half national in its administration, discipline and finance. The days of the inefficient watchman of the Dogberry and Verges type were gone by for ever; person and property were well guarded at last without any sacrifice of freedom, and mobs and meetings could be dealt with, punctually and quietly, without calling on armed force as at Peterloo."[34] There was a general view that the New Police were more efficient and diligent and less corrupt than the previous police force. The early decades of Scotland Yard, were free from charges of corruption but in 1877, the 'de Goncourt Case' maintained that the most senior members of the Detective Department were involved in a fraudulent race gang and the public confidence in the police was badly shaken.

The criminal prisons of England were inefficient and corrupt. Excluding a few crown establishments—the Tower of London, the Hulks and Millbank Penitentiary, the prisons were under the control of local county and civic authorities and varied as per the local visiting Magistrate's diligence, good sense and policy. Prisons Acts were nominally enforced and thus the prisons were ignored with impunity. Howard's work in the late eighteenth century led his admirer build and administer prisons of a better type under his inspiration. But the Victorian penal reformer, Matthew Devenport Hill said that with the exception of changes in cleanliness, ventilation and drainage, the seed sown by Howard did not grow. During the first three decades of the century, various kinds of barbarity, laxity and mal-administration existed in the prisons and cleanliness, ventilation or drainage was not adequately facilitated in them. Many gaolers were affected by bribery and sold different kinds of privileges. They connived at escapes and trafficked at large profits in the stores of illicit goods entering the gaol. Male and female prisoners were frequently kept in the same prison or in the same building or in the same room. The officials were involved financially or otherwise in the sexual harassment of the female prisoners. Work was either non-existent or treadmill or oakum-picking, the favourite of prison-governors was in practice in the gaol. "Some prisons, on the other hand, taught trades or were highly organised factories, either with a view to the permanent benefit of the prisoners or to relieve the rates by making a profit from their work."[35]

This absurd system of prison administration was transformed by the Prison Acts of 1823 and 1835. The 1823 Act, framed and enacted by a Government, as a prison-reform measure, was a great improvement but it failed being limited in scope and due to lack of machinery for inspection and enforcement. A magistrate said back in 1793: "It is not so much for want of good laws, as from their inexecution, that the state of the prisons is so bad."[36] In 1835, the Home Secretary was given power to appoint Prison Inspectors. In 1836, the Prison Inspectors detailed their First Report with a devastating account of the prison, in which he stressed the people's duty to mark the evils of the system, being in disastrous operation in the gaol of Newgate for a long period. According to them, the classification-system, was totally ineffective. The Association of Prisoners of all ages, and of every shade of guilt, in one indiscriminate mass, was a frightful feature of the system in magnitude, and the most pernicious in effect. Another evil was the utter absence of all employment for the prisoners. The Inspectors proposed a complete change of system, including rebuilding the prison. They appended an architect's plan, but nothing was done till 1858-61. One observer remarked: "It was still, in 1850, 'one of the worst hot-beds of vice and moral disease in London', with little or no employment or instruction, and the untried still consorting with the convicted."[37]

Coldbath Fields and Tothill Fields were local prisons under the control of the Middlesex Magistrates. They were meant for minor offenders with sentences from one week to three years. The former was situated in Clerkenwell, the most vicious part of London, with the highest murder rate and the densest criminality. The latter was in the 'Devil's Acre'—'the moral plague-spot of the whole kingdom' and behind the Houses of Parliament. Coldbath Fields had a terrible reputation. Sir Francis Burdett's exposure led to temporary reforms. The prison soon returned to its bad ways, and "lived up to its nickname of 'The Bastille' (abbreviated in criminal slang to 'The steal'). But by the late 1820s it was more conspicuous for its inefficiency and corruption than for its toughness. Parliament was told in 1828 that the Middlesex gaols were actually increasing in iniquity, vilely overcrowded, grossly disorderly, and in a state of incredible filth."[38] In 1829, Chesterton became the Governor of Coldbath Fields. The previous Governor was forced to resign on the charges of conniving at the escape of prisoners.

Coldbath Fields was completely corrupt, unhealthy and uncomfortable and Chesterton, a former army officer, was appointed to raise its moral and social tone. He commented on his predecessors and on the state of the prison: "They had, ...held that their primary obligation consisted in feathering their own nests, and at the same time enriching their subordinates.... The whole machinery of the prison, ...'betokened the most appalling abuse; and I found everything around me stamped with iniquity and corruption. The best acquainted with the prison were utterly ignorant of the frightful extent of its demoralisation.' The officers conspired to maintain the iniquities of this 'sink of abomination' because they made a profit of seven or eight shillings in the pound on the vast illicit commerce which was conducted in the prison."[39]

The more powerful prisoners helped the gaolers in resisting the reforms as this measure would end their power, profit and comfort. The criminal 'yardsmen' took extra two shillings in the pound on the goods which entered the prison, besides turnkey's large commission. The serious effects of the 'tobacco barons' existed on a large scale. Every kind of contraband entered the prison and was hidden in the caches. Chesterton on inspection of the Infirmary one night, found that the mattresses were filled with merchandise and the beds by the physically fit prisoners.

Dickens had the grim experience of the prisons. At the age of twelve, he used to go to visit his father in the Marshalsea. "He was a prison haunted man from the apprentice years in journalism to those of the established master. Penal reform was urgently needed and found vigorous support from one who had been so closely acquainted with the follies and cruelties of the gaols."[40] In *Pickwick Papers*, Dickens made his protest at the squalor of the broken lives while reporting conditions in the Fleet Prison. The horrors of confinement became the background of *Little Dorrit* and the gaol is a continuing symbol of a world in bondage to stupidity and greed in this novel. Dickens described the conditions as he saw them as a reporter.

The whole period of the Victorian age was marked by interest in religious questions. As a result of Puritan ethos, the age was deeply influenced by seriousness of thought and self-discipline of character. This 'seriousness' affected the 'agnostics' who challenged the dogmas of Christianity in the last part of the Victorian age. The 'agnostics' were successful due to Darwinism and the discoveries of science. The 'High Church Movement' originated by Evangelicals had the strain of Puritanism. Mr. Gladstone, an Anglo Catholic, appealed to his Non-conformist followers and they considered life as a branch of personal religion.

Throughout the last seventy years of the nineteenth century, the real strength and felicity of the Victorian age was derived from the self-discipline and self-reliance of the individual Englishman and sprung from Puritan traditions to which Wesleyan and Evangelical movements gave another lease of life. Evangelicalism was one of the important factors in the making of the Victorians. G.M. Young observed that an average Victorian "found himself at every turn controlled and animated by the imponderable pressure of the Evangelical discipline."[41] According to David Newsome, Evangelicalism was "perhaps the most formative power behind the eminence of eminent Victorians."[42]

It originated in the middle of the eighteenth century as a protest against the prevailing attitude towards religion and morality. But it was in the first half of the nineteenth century that its influence was observed on many Victorians. People of early Victorian age reared in the Evangelical tradition were asked to rise against the vice and immorality, obscenity and vulgarity of social and individual life. Due to the Evangelical influence, the philanthropists of the time worked against drunkenness and public immorality. The Vice Society, founded in 1787, endeavoured to enhance the levels of public morality. It also asked the Government to interfere with public indecency and the ban of publication and sale of obscene articles, pictures and materials. The society urged people to be religious and to observe the Sabbath strictly.

Evangelicalism set the model of specific pattern of family life. Children, brought up in evangelical atmosphere were taught the gospels of truthfulness, seriousness and unselfishness. They were forbidden to practice gluttony, to read light books and to wear costly clothes. These 'new puritans' hated illicit and illegal sexual passion. Evangelicalism disliked the aristocratic ideas and its glorification of bourgeois values. It celebrated the virtues of simple living, hard toil and moral decency. Evangelical Christianity devoted to personal salvation was a force hostile to the worldly pleasures. The extreme wing of Evangelicalism categorically denunciated amusements. One prominent Sabbatarian leader observed: "Nothing is to be done which is merely for amusement or for gain. To saunter in the public walks when the gay and worldly scene necessarily unfits the mind for devotion—to read the public journal, or other works which are not religious, to read and to write letters upon business, or any other common topics—to pay idle visits—to engage in frivolous conversation at home or elsewhere...must be contrary to the Christian's duty of the Lord's day."[43] Another commented: "Thousands have ascribed their religious declension, and subsequent ruin, to Sunday Walks."[44]

The Sabbatarian movement, a well organised pressure group, sought moral reform through legislation. The Sabbatarian organisations made widespread publicity, petition campaigns and caused parliamentary bills to promote restrictions on Sunday of drinking hours, trade, travel, rights of assembly, postal delivery, band concerts in public parks and other Godless activities.

A Sunday holiday was looked upon as a heinous scene: "In Scotland, nothing profane was tolerated on a Sunday; even whistling and fishing were denounced as 'great crimes', every windowshade in Edinburgh was pulled down on Sundays, turning it into a 'city of whited sepulchres'. With nothing to do outside of church, for many Sunday became an 'intolerable burden', a mockery of our high state of civilisation."[45] The specifically evangelical influence was widely diffused and fashionable in church circles. The 'low churchmen' (Evangelicals), were strong enough to enforce, both by law and custom, 'Sabbath Observance'. This was the condition during the middle decades of the century.

The 'seventies' and 'eighties' had been a period of puritanism in ethical and sexual ideas. The popular heroes of the period were religious men such as Livingstone, the African explorer and missionary; General Gordon, the soldier-philanthropist, Lord Shaftesbury and Mr. Gladstone. To these men, life was the service of God. The older and more definite religious beliefs meaningful to them, were being attacked by the 'Agnostics' who were also puritan in feeling and outlook. Huxley defied the clergy at the meeting of the British Association in Oxford like Luther at Worms. Leslie Stephan and John Morley refused to compromise with the dogmas in the spirit of Puritanism.

The Puritan attitude to life and conduct was inculcated by the Bible religion of the Victorians and the Anglo-Catholic religion. The Anglo Catholic religion grew out of the Oxford Movement of the 'thirties' and was represented by Gladstone and Salisbury. This religion was powerful among the parish clergy. The Anglo-Catholic influence caused a less strict observance of the 'Sabbath' than Evangelicals. There was a gradual modification of the 'English Sunday'. Many families stressed on 'Sunday reading' of serious but not necessarily religious books. The novels and magazines were forbidden for one day and great classical literature such as *The Bible, Pilgrim's Progress* and *Paradise Lost*, in addition to more secular poetry and history, were to be used. Modified Sunday observance of the Bible reading and family prayers were common till the end of the century.

English religion was dominating in the middle of the nineteenth century. But there were weaknesses in its foundations. The movement of scientific discovery undermined the belief in the verbal inspiration of the Bible and was common to the Non-conformists, to the Church Evangelicals and to High Churchmen like Bishop Samuel Wilberforce and Mr. Gladstone. Charles Darwin's scientific researches led him to conclusions not consistent with the narrative of the early chapters of Genesis which was a part of the English Bible. The whole idea of evolution and of 'man descended from a monkey' was totally inconsistent with existing religious ideas of creation. Naturally the religious world took up arms to "defend positions of dateless antiquity and prestige. Naturally the younger generation of scientific men rushed to defend their revered chief, and to establish their claim to come to any conclusion to which their researches led, regardless of the ancient traditions of the Church. The strife raged throughout the 'sixties', 'seventies' and 'eighties'. It came to involve the whole belief in the miraculous, extending into the borders of the New Testament itself. The 'intellectuals' became more and more anti-clerical, anti-religious and materialistic under the stress of the conflict."[46]

There was no fixed working hours in the mills and factories during the boyhood and youth of Dickens. So, it was of utmost importance to the working people to enjoy Sunday outside for their health and happiness. But there was little liberty to enjoy Sunday and the further bondage was sought by Sir Agnew measures. The workers got tired by their six long days. They were very much poor and so they could not make regular excursions into the country. They had not even the opportunity of games or sports if they crossed from the slums and mean streets to the front of the town. The churches and chapels were open along with taverns and gin-palaces.

Dickens denounced the Sabbatarians, who compelled the jaded working people to opt liquor as alternative to loafing: "You hold out no inducement, you offer no relief from listlessness, you provide nothing to amuse his mind, you afford him no means of exercising his body. Unwashed and unshaven, he saunters moodily about, weary and dejected. In lieu of the wholesome stimulus he might derive from nature, you drive him...to the gin-shop as his only resource; and when, reduced to a worse level than the lowest brute in the scale of creation, he lies wallowing in the Kennel, your saintly law givers lift up their hands to heaven, and exclaim for a law which shall convert the day intended for rest and cheerfulness into one of universal gloom, bigotry, and persecution."[47]

Sir Andrew's Sabbath Observances Bill aroused Dickens to write *Sunday Under Three Heads* and many other pieces in response to proposals for new restrictions on Sunday activities. The author's anger sparked off also by the conduct of the Bishop of London in detailing on 'the vicious addiction of the lower classes to Sunday excursions'. The Dickensian wrath was directed at the Established Church as at the Melchizedek Howlers in the Chapels. The odious Sunday Observance Bill claimed to save the workers from 'sacrificing their comforts, health, religious privileges and conscience'. It prohibited the employment of any of them in public transport and catered with heavy penalties for breach of these orders. Simultaneously, it exempted from its discipline a whole army of domestic servants, engaged in the preparation of meals and for all the outings of the rich in their own carriages. Timothy Sparks noted: "The Baronet's dinner must be cooked on Sunday, the Bishop's horses must be groomed, and the Peer's carriage must be driven. So, the menial servants are put utterly beyond the pale of the grace unless indeed, they are to go to heaven through the sanctity of their masters, and possibly they might think even that rather an uncertain passport."[48]

The Bill did not come into action and Dickens contributed much to this win. The coaches and cabs used to ply for fares on Sundays. The popular tea-gardens were open for refreshment. But there were no Sunday games or sports. Galleries and museums were closed on Sundays and there was no half-holiday on Saturday and no bank holidays. Still people occupied the gin.

Legislation to stop military band concerts in public parks occasioned a defence of music as 'a rational, cheerful, innocent amusement for the tens of thousands of overworked humanity'. Dickens contributed $10 to a fund to support private band concerts in place of forbidden military band concerts. During the parliamentary discussion of a bill to restrict the availability of drink on Sundays, it was argued that the working classes were 'very much in the condition of children' and needed the assistance of the law in their struggles with temptation. Dickens authored an essay 'The Great Baby' in which he protested drinking. The Sabbatarian legislation to close the Post office invited Dickens' wrath. He considered this action as a part of a campaign to spread gloom on the Lord's Day. He launched a defence of the right of the people to amusements.

Dickens responded to the problem of leisure with stinging satire. Besides such well-known set pieces in his fiction as the description of the maddening boredom of an English Sunday in *Little Dorrit* and the address to the Brick Lane Branch of the United Grand Junction Ebenezer Temperance Association by the canting drunkard Mr. Stiggins in *Pickwick Papers*, he used his journalism as a forum for the support of amusements for the people. From the early *Sunday Under Three Heads*, to the late 'Great Drunkery Discoverly' which he helped his son Charley to prepare for *All The Year Round* in 1869, he counter attacked against specific attempts to restrict the pleasures of the poor.

Drunkenness and heavy expense on drink was also a major evil of the city life during the Victorian age. It was the reason for crime and the ruin of families. This ugly scene of English Society was shown by the great caricaturists from the times of Hogarth's *Gin Lane* to George Cruikshank's prints of *The Bottle* and *The Drunkard's Children* (1847-48). The Total Abstinence or *Teetotalism* was a movement against this evil of English social life. The 'Blue Ribbon Army' made a vigorous attack on the drinking habits of all the sections of the society. The takers of the total abstinence were to pledge in the face of the world to keep the promise and they wore the blue ribbon on their breasts. In the 'seventies' the Temperance Movement, sought to shorten drinking hours, provide alternative attractions to drink or prohibit its consumption altogether.

The proper and moderate use of wine and beer were encouraged by amusements and occupations such as reading, music, playing and watching organised games, bicycling, country and seaside holidays, etc. These things controlled the dullard's itch for the bottle in the cupboard and lowered down the attractions and choice of the 'gin palace'. The brewing companies were frightened and the public houses were made more decent to sale other things. "And Belfour's Licensing Act of 1904 at length found a practical method of reducing the excessive number of houses of sale."[49]

The Poor Law was one of the most difficult problems of the 19th century England. From 1817 onwards, the British Parliament made attempts to reform the Old Law. The Old Law was framed during the governance of Queen Elizabeth and was known as the 'allowance system'. It proved to be disastrous to the independence, the industrial habits and the morals of the rural labourers. The possession of either legitimate or illegitimate children provided a claim to extra financial assistance. People understood that the present state of pauperism in the beginning of the 19th century would go beyond agricultural labourers to industrial workers as well.

The New Poor Law of 1834 replaced the Old Law. Ivor Brown observes: "This allowed workers to draw a dole for themselves and families varying according to the price of bread. This was paid for out of the local rates. It was obviously a subsidy to employers who could thus keep down wages at other people's expense. The ending of that injustice without a sufficient rise in wages meant bitter hardship for the poor. The able-bodied had to work in penury; if there was no food for their dependants they could go into the workhouse controlled by boards of guardians who were often chiefly guarding the tax-payers and determined to spend as little as possible on the inmates. In that they succeeded. The national burden of Poor Relief was rapidly reduced. The paupers paid for that by the miserable accommodation and strictly regulated diet which awaited them if they 'went inside'."[50]

The New Poor Law was also meant for the removal of ills of the Old Law. For the able-bodied men, in place of the weekly allowance, it now made a provision for work. It intended to take care of the aged, the sick, and the truly indigent. For this purpose it made a "strict segregation of the different classes of paupers, and the care of them, preferably, in different institutions."[51]

The Poor Law made a distinction between the really poor and helpless and pretending persons to be poor. The new Poor Law was aimed primarily at the 'able-bodied' pauper, and "it sought to eliminate, what Dickens calls the 'professional pauper' by administering a workhouse test; that is, if an able-bodied pauper wanted relief, he would have to receive it within the confines of a workhouse under conditions less attractive than those prevailing on the outside. This test would assure that only those who were truly helpless would apply."[52] The Poor Law Amendment Act of 1834 construed that no decent person would accept poor relief. But practically the workhouse kept the idler, the drunkard, the prostitutes and the aged, ill, infirm and the foundling. The children were not educated or educated badly and they were to live in the company of doubtful persons. They led a life of slavery at the same time.

The condition of the agricultural labourer, in the South, was miserable during the 'thirties' and 'hungry forties'. With the introduction of the New Poor Law of 1834, the poor workers in field and factory were badly affected as the 'workhouse test' was introduced for public relief and outdoor relief was abolished. It was a very cruel measure over the Speenhamland policy of granting the poor rate in aid of wages. This Speenhamland policy had pauperised the employed worker and kept wages down and ruined the ratepayers. The commissioners worked on the principle that the workhouse must be less attractive than the employment in the field and the factory. They were bound not to raise the attractiveness by introducing a minimum wage. So they tried to lower the standard of the workhouse life.

G.M. Trevelyan writes about the administration of New Poor Law of 1834: "It was pure Benthamism, a combination of the elective with the bureaucratic principle, as advocated in Bentham's 'Constitutional Code'. The three Government Commissioners (bureaucrats representing the Central Government) are to lay down the rules for Poor Law administration and to see they are enforced. But the actual people to administer these rules are local elective bodies—the Board of Guardians. Every 'union' of parishes is to be administered by a 'Board of Guardians of the Poor', to be elected by all the ratepayers. Both the centralised bureaucrats at the top, and the democratically elected boards of guardians in the localities are the Benthamite substitute for the old methods of Government by country gentleman acting as unpaid Justices of the Peace."[53]

The working class in town and country took the New Poor law as bitterly tyrannical. The harshness of the law, in separation of families, inculcated in the rural poor a distaste for Benthamite improvement. Even the burst of activity over pauper children in 1849-50 was "largely prompted by fear and shame. For in 1848 Drouet's vast baby farm at Tooting, where, 1400 children were kept together with awful overcrowding, had an outbreak of cholera in which many children died; and the details revealed at the inquests once more brought the Poor

Law Authorities unwelcome fame."[54] Dickens comments on the New Poor Law in the postscript to *Our Mutual Friend*: "But that my view of the Poor Law may not be mistaken or misrepresented, I will state it. I believe that there has been in England, since the days of the STUARTS, no law so often infamously administered, no law so often openly violated, no law habitually so ill-supervised. In the majority of the shameful cases of disease and death from destitution, that shock the public and disgrace the country, the illegality is quite equal to the inhumanity and known language could say no more of their lawlessness."[55]

The workhouses were like the prisons. The central inhumanity of the 1834 Poor Law amendment lay in their attempt to make conditions within "the workhouses less tolerable—'less eligible' in the official terminology—than the outside world of work in a time of general economic depression. The workhouses were intended to be as like prisons as possible, with the separation of the sexes and families into male and female wards, strict discipline and a diet worse, according to Dickens, than in prison."[56] Outdoor relief was terminated as it was based on poor rate and considerable increase in this created more paupers. The Old Law operated on local level through the Justices of the Peace. Relief under this law worked to the advantage of local authority, the land owning employers and their agents during the times of hardship and distress. But they lost their power in the changed scenario.

Dickens considered the poor law brutal and ridiculed its National Commissioner, its boards of guardians and officials. 'Bumbledom' indicated a complete system of workhouse incarceration which the Act was putting into force. In *Oliver Twist*, Dickens attacked the No. 1 Dietary authorised by the commissioners and considered it to be a dismal fare, limited and starchy.

The fabulous wealth and manufacturing power of England in the first half of the nineteenth century produced a new middle class and a raw industrial proletariat. They wanted a new system of education according to their need. No Government before Gladstone's in 1870 proposed for state education because of the fear of battle of rival denominations in this regard and the Church as well as Dissent's fight over the question of religious teaching. The state began in 1833 to make a grant of twenty thousand pounds a year for school buildings of voluntary societies. An Educational Committee of the Privy Council was established to distribute the allowance and it had a permanent secretary and a system of inspection of the state-aided schools.

The English state left the people to be educated by private religious charity. There was no sufficient arrangement for the primary education of the people. G.M. Young has noted that in the thirties of the nineteenth century, a survey of elementary education pointed out to serious contemporaries a profoundly disquieting picture. "Most of the school-buildings were far from good, and in nearly all the cases, thoroughly bad. The teachers were also neither qualified nor competent."[57]

The secondary education developed with the growth of the 'Public School System'. Three types of secondary schools existed in the beginning of the century. The 'public schools' had a classical curriculum and were ill disciplined but fashionable. They existed at Eton, Manchester and Harrow and at few other places. The unfashionable dissenting middle class went to the private academies for a scientific and modern education. The discipline was better at this type of secondary school. The Grammar schools were in a bad condition due to sheer negligence and corruption: "The seven or eight hundred grammar schools in the tradition of Dotheboys Hall in *Nicholas Nickleby*, Dr. Blimber's Academy in *Dombey and Son* and Salem House, run by Mr. Creakle in *David Copperfield* were already in existence in different parts of England. It is true that those institutions made some provisions for the education of the sons of the tradesmen, rich farmers and lower gentry, but they failed to satisfy the middle classes because they were responsible for the appearance of the worst-educated industrialists and professional men of the late Victorian period. For this, to meet the interests of the middle classes in the 'thirties of this century in the industrial areas of Birmingham, Sheffield, Leicester and Hull several schools were founded by the individual efforts of either factory owners or well-to-do townsmen, or of some religious groups or bodies."[58]

The public school was a fashion statement. The great educational reformer of the 'thirties Dr. Thomas Arnold, Head master of Rugby from 1828 to 1842, was instrumental in popularising the public schools. His emphasis on religion and chapel services, his monitorial system and his largely successful efforts to suppress bullying, drinking, profligacy and the worst indiscipline of the old 'beer garden' type of Public Schools, established an example. His academic proposals, supported and strengthened by his broad theology, his advocacy of a union between the Anglicans and Non-conformists and his eagerness to meet the wants of the great manufacturing towns and districts, were sponsored by the middle class. The boys of middle class homes were sent to this type of institution in great numbers and it was believed that they would be instructed in qualities like self-discipline, public spirit, vigour and manliness of character. These schools in the middle of the century fed the Oxford and Cambridge Universities, and also the newly founded London University (1834) with a large number of students, constituting the two major groups of the English middle classes—the clergyman and the lawyers. Organised games developed and assisted popularising the Public School. "The 'middling orders of society' found in the reformed Public School the door of entrance for their sons into the 'governing class'. The old landed gentry, the professional men and the new industrialists were educated, together, forming an enlarged and modernised aristocracy, sufficiently numerous to meet the various needs of government and of leadership in Victoria's England and Victoria's Empire."[59] The 'Public Schools' were a grand success but it had certain limitations. They were very much limited to the Classics and could not fulfil the total needs of the age. Intellect was less developed in such a school. The upper, the upper-middle and the professional classes under Public Schools were alienated from the rest of the nation. The expense of a Public School was higher than the Grammar School and Day School and a great burden was imposed on the middle class.

The year 1870 was epoch-making in English education. Education was the chief battle ground of religious denominations. No government, Whig or Tory could set up a national system of education due to the fear of Dissenters or the Established Church and English education suffered during the mid-Victorian period. A network of Voluntary Schools was spread in the country due to religious and sectarian zeal and was paid for by the private subscription. This religious and sectarian zeal frightened off both the political parties to solve the education problem on a national level. Primary education was given to people by the Voluntary Schools conducted on Church principles. The Voluntary Schools known as National Schools, were founded by the (Anglican) National Society. They were given meagre allowance by the state since 1833. Gladstone's Bill of 1870 doubled the state grant to the Church Schools and the Roman Catholic Schools. The publicly controlled schools called the Board Schools were to be paid out of the Local Rates and they were to be governed by elected School Boards. In National Schools, church teaching was allowed but the Act prohibited the use of catechism or formulary distinctive of any denomination in religious teaching in the New Board Schools. The Dissenters charged the state for perpetuating the Church Schools of the villages. In the villages, there was only Church Schools for children while in the towns there were Board and Voluntary Schools. The Church schools were brought under County of Country Councils by the Belfour's Act of 1902.

By the Act of 1870, England obtained a system of universal primary education. During 1870-90, the average school attendance increased from one and a quarter million to four and a half million and the expense on every child was doubled. The state could not adopt sufficient steps for secondary education. The School Boards have single town or village as their's jurisdiction. They have not wide educational outlook and the battle of church and Dissent was personal and intense due to their parochial character. There was no provision for school scholarship to go for universities. The Belfour's Education Act of 1902 made up the defects of the Act of 1870. This Act was inspired by Sir Robert Morant, a public servant. This Act gave power to elected County Councils and to certain large Borough Councils for primary and secondary education and abolished the School Boards. The elected County Council and the certain large Borough Councils performed their tasks through Education Committees. They had larger area and broader views and thus beneficial to Primary and Secondary Education. The Act proved an effective ladder to the universities. The Education Acts of 1870 and 1902 made England able to compete in the coming age of machinery. But the popular education failed to meet the rural needs and speeded up the rural exodus. It produced a vast population of reading public but not worthy masses. They were the victim of sensations and cheap taste. The quality of literature and journalism lowered down because they were to reach the millions of half educated and quarter educated people. The standard set by the small highly educated persons was replaced by the standard of the majority.

Further an official return, "made in 1889, gives over 40,000 children in the London Board Schools, or nearly 10 per cent of the number on the roll, as habitually attending in want of food, to which the number returns from voluntary schools add about 11,000 in the same condition. Puny, pale-faced scantily clad and badly shod, these small and feeble folk may be found sitting limp and chill on the school benches in all the poorer parts of London."[60]

Dickens attacked the evil conductment of schools such as the notorious Dotheboys Academy in *Nicholas Nickleby*. He had shown the world mostly bad schools treating child as a sort of human hopper in to which facts so defied by Mr. Gradgrind in *Hard Times* could be thrown. He introduced modern ideals of education where the standards and tests were utilitarian and inhuman. He exposed the vicious elements and principles of the schools, at a time when England's education system including its clash of private and public methods and tyranny of religious interference was a chaos. "But prevailingly, and with the instinct of a born reformer, guiding him, Dickens dealt his sledge-hammer blows against the Gradgrinds, and Squeers of the educational world, in the pictures he drew of no less than eight and twenty schools."[61]

Dickens drew the pictures of abuse of childhood by the educational system. The school became an intellectual hot-house in which an unnatural forcing process was in operation. He, as a significant pedagogic leader, introduced on English soil of the Kindergarten reform.

Dickens saw the boy in the Ragged School 'with burning cheeks and great gaunt eager eyes' who had nothing in the world except a 'bottle of physic'. During his wanderings through the slums of London, Dickens visited the Ragged Schools conducted by young workers. Such institution imparting free education to the poor, was spreading in the country. A Ragged School in the Field Lane, Holborn was conducted by Samuel Starey. He appealed to Miss Coutts for support. Dickens arranged to visit the school in response to her request. He was moved and excited and wrote Miss Coutts a letter praising the school. He made plans to improve the institution. "He asked Starey to find out how much it would cost to install a large trough or sink, with a good supply of running water, soap and towels."[62] He had no doubt that Miss Coutts would do whatever he asked her in the matter. Dickens offered to write on Ragged Schools for the *Edinburgh Review*.

Industry was the important component of the social matrix of Victorian England. Its growth affected the various walks of social life of the Victorians. During the first half of the nineteenth century, the power of the industrial system grew. Chimneys smutted the sky and killed grass and trees. Chemical waste made the streams dirty. The exposed and gloomy tenements appeared like a blight over the countryside. There was row upon row of feeble houses and consisted three quarters with no lavatory. Thousands of human beings were pushed into damp rooms and cellars. Heaps of excrements and domestic refuse drained into ditches, the only source of drinking water to people. The owners of the factories violated the Ten Hours Bill. They selfishly defied sanitary regulations in unventilated workrooms, and they did not accomplish fencing of the dangerous machinery. "The philosophy of the industrialists savagely denied that they had any duty to their employees except to pay them the wage established by the law of supply and demand, and insisted that the prosperity of the country depended upon high profits and cheap labour. The industrial system established a tyranny all the deadlier because it professed to be based upon scientific laws inherent in the very structure of society."[63]

When the Reform Bill of 1832 was passed, a terrible agitation of the factory workers emerged in the Industrial North. The factory hands were fighting against the hard condition of factory life, especially the working hours. In Yorkshire, the agitation was carried on by a Radical and Tory coalition. All parties took part in the agitation at Westminster. The popular drive behind this movement came from factory population, mostly Radicals. The Tory country gentlemen were not hostile to the movement. The Squires denounced the evils of factory employment. In 1833, the British empire stopped the children's labour in the textile industries at home. Lord Althorp's Factory Act of 1833 legally limited the working hours of children and young persons. Factory inspectors were appointed to enforce the Factory Act. They possessed the power of entry into the factories.

The Ten Hours Bill (1847) limited the working hours of women and youths in textile factories and thus stopped work after ten hours. In Parliament liberals such as Melbourne, Cobden and Bright were against the Bill whereas Russell, Palmerston and Macaulay were in favour of the Bill. Among the conservatives, Peel opposed the Bill and the protectionist Squires voted in favour of the Bill. "But the man who finally carried the Bill through the House of Commons was Fielden, the largest cotton spinner in England; and the man who told with him in the lobby had passed from the position of worker to that of employer in the same industry."[64] The Bill had created a heated controversy but fulfilled the aspirations of the employees.

The Reform Bill of 1832 was extension of the Franchise. The Factory Acts of 1833 and 1847 governed the conditions and hours of all the branches of industry. The factory system was transformed into an instrument to create average material conditions for the labourer. "Robert Owen's vision of decent conditions of life for factory hands, which he had embodied in his own New Lanark Mills, was destined in the course of a hundred years to be made the standard for the greater part of the industrial world. And the decisive first steps were taken in 1833 and 1847, during the period which it is usual to condemn as obsessed by the doctrine of laissez faire."[65]

There was appalling conditions of female and child labour in the coal mines. By the Lord Shaftesbury Mines Act of 1842, underground employment of women and of children under ten was prohibited. By the Act of 1850, adult males were protected by a Mines Inspectorate. The state finally intervened in the safety in the mines. The gross ill-usage of little boys as sweeps, by the manufacturers who found it cheaper to drive them through the soot-choked chimneys than to use a long brush, was a great evil. In 1875, Shaftesbury obtained the passing of an Act to forbid this practice in England.

Utilitarianism was a middle class movement to advance the interests of the capitalists. This movement was inspired by the writings of Jeremy Bentham, James Mill and John Stuart Mill. They were political philosophers and pleaded liberal and progressive measures. As economists, they advocated the idea of the unhindered growth of capitalism. There was the formative influence of Benthamite utilitarianism and political economy on the life and thought of Victorian middle class.

Utilitarianism in ethics and politics aimed at practical efforts to improve the conditions of human life on rational principles. A utilitarian philosopher was materialistic and opposed to any type of social tyranny and injustice. He was the champion of individual freedom. "From the economic point of view he had firm conviction in Free Trade, unlimited freedom to competition, capitalism and 'laissez faire', i.e., the non-interference of the state in the individual life. He believed that by the observance of these economic principles the resources of the country could be properly utilised, its wealth could be increased and the greatest good of the greatest number achieved."[66]

The tenets of utilitarianism suited the taste and liking of the capitalists of Victorian England. The industrialists and big businessmen of Victorian England believed that they were the pillars of the society. They felt that the unhindered growth of capitalism would do maximum good to the people. The utilitarian believed that the ills of the society can be remedied by individual efforts. The Victorian middle class also believed in the individual philanthropy of the capitalist manufacturers. As the Victorian capitalists wanted the maintenance of cheap labour and freedom from Government interference in economic life, they did not want any philanthropy exercise from the Government. Many alms-houses and orphanages of Victorian England were established by the surplus wealth of the industrial manufacturers and it showed the practice of private charity. The middle class had the conviction that the sincere efforts on the part of the individuals can improve the condition of the society and can remedy the sufferings of the distressed and the exploited.

There was the gradual rise in the total tonnage of British shipping. It increased from 2.5 to 4 million tons during 1827-48. The overseas trade became increasingly prosperous along with the commerce and industries. The historians of nineteenth century commercial life recorded that the middle of the century was the age of coal and iron. According to them, it was also the age of cotton. The major part of a businessman's capital was invested in cotton and textile industries and the businessman was much benefited. The advancements in the fields of trade and industry prepared "England by the end of 1850 a really formidable economic force in international commerce."[67] According to G. Kitson Clark, she was established in the centre of a vast network of world trade. The large accumulation of capital in the hands of the trading manufacturing class made them to think that they were the very pillars of society. The mill owners, shippers, traders, bankers and financiers became power loving.

According to G.M. Trevelyan, sail was substituted by steam and wood by iron in the British Mercantile service during the forties. In 1847, steamships were few and small and

Britain recorded a total tonnage of 1,16,000 out of three million tons of the whole merchant service. In the fifties and sixties, the, ocean going ships were run by steam and they were built of iron first and then of steel. The change occurred due to English iron and steel manufacturing. In 1848, Britain manufactured half the pig-iron of the world. It was trebled in the next thirty years. The West of Scotland, Staffordshire, Wales and the North-Eastern of Tyneside and Middlesbrough were the regions of iron production. "The Californian and Australian gold discoveries ushered in a great period of expanding trade of which England, by her lead over other countries both in commerce and industry, was able to reap the principle benefit in the middle years of the century. In 1870, the volume of the external trade of the United Kingdom exceeded that of France, Germany and Italy together and was between three and four times that of the United States."[68]

Free trade increased shipping and overseas trade of Britain. In the eighties, the coastal trade was greater in cargo tonnage than the overseas commerce and it included a large part of home consumed coal. In 1885, a third of the world's sea-going ships were British and they included four-fifths of the world's steamships. The fast going 'Clippers' were British and in 1885, the tonnage under sail was similar to 1850s but steam tonnage grew by four millions. The oceans of the world were the highways of Britain. The tonnage of the port of London "was sixty per cent greater than that of the Mersey, though Liverpool, dealing in Lancashire's cotton, exported more British goods than the capital."[69] The Thames and Mersey docks were constructed in the eighties. The railways increased the overseas trade. Whitby, Lancaster, Ayr and other small harbours followed Fowey, Chester and Cinque ports. Barrow and Grimsby became great due to the railways in the last half of the 19th century. Southampton revived and Cardiff passed Newcastle as the world's greatest coal exporter. Tyneside, during the days of Armstrong's Elswick, increased strongly.

There was the growth of the Limited Liability Company and municipal trading. The large impersonal control of capital and industry enhanced the numbers and value of shareholders as a class. They were a class having irresponsible wealth and detached from the land and the duties of the landowner and the responsible management of business. America, Africa, India, Australasia and parts of Europe were being developed by the British capital during the nineteenth century. The British shareholders were enriched by industrialisation. "Towns like Bournemouth and Eastbourne sprang up to house large 'comfortable' classes who had retired on their incomes, and who had no relation to the rest of the community except that of drawing dividends and occasionally attending a shareholders' meeting to bully the management. On the other hand, 'shareholding' meant leisure and freedom which was used by many of the later Victorians for the highest purposes of a great civilisation."[70]

The increasing power and organisation of the Trade Unions, in the skilled trades, made the workers able to meet the managers of the companies on equal terms. The strike and lock-out in the factories enabled the two parties to respect their strength and to know the value of negotiation. It was practically necessary to protect the Trade Union Rights against the law and thus labour was brought into politics to form a party. Trade Unions and combinations to increase wages was legalised by the legislation of 1825. Unfortunately, in 1867, in the Boilermakers' case, Judges headed by the Lord Chief Justice passed a judgement that unions, being 'in restraint of trade', were illegal associations. The Reform Bill of 1832 gave the workers Parliamentary Franchise and now they could mount constitutional pressure on politicians for the remedy of their grievances. "Consequently Gladstone's Act of 1871 restored to unions the right to exist on favourable terms, and Disraeli's Act of 1875 legalised 'peaceful picketing'."[71]

The Trade Union Movement spread from skilled to unskilled trades during London dockers strike led by John Burns in 1889. Trade unionism spread to most trades and most regions of England and it became a powerful weapon of defence for workers' wages. In 1901, the Judges pronounced the work of former Parliament in regard to Trade Unionism illegal. This

Taff Vale decision provoked the formation of Labour Party in Parliament in the beginning of the new century and the Act of 1906 secured to the Trade Unions highly privileged exemption from legal action.

The period between the two first Reforms Bills (1832-67) was the 'age of coal and iron'. This age was also known as the 'Railway age'. There was a remarkable progress in the construction of railway and steamship between 1830 and 1850 and consequently the English nation recorded an "expansion of the heavy industries, mining and textiles. The first great success of steam railway was registered in 1830 when there was the inauguration of the new Manchester and Liverpool railway by the Duke of Wellington and it took approximately forty years more for the construction of an additional 15,620 miles of railway lines. The booming expansion of railways in England almost throughout the nineteenth century brought about many significant changes in the commercial and public life of the English nation."[72]

The Railways opened out new vistas for the carriage of goods and a new means of passenger traffic. It served the rapidly growing industrial centres, and facilitated the transport of raw materials and finished products. The personal mobility was facilitated along with the conveyance of newspapers, magazines and mail, including, novels, to the booksellers. The coming of the Railway doomed the canals as well as the stage coaches. The short local lines in the coal districts were developed during 1836-37 and 1844-48, the two periods of railway investment. Majority of the railroad investors and promoters, during the thirties, were Dissenters and Quakers of the Midlands and the North—Peases, Croppers, Sturges. The Bradshaw's Railway Time Table was issued in 1839.

The London and Birmingham Railway began in 1834. During the forties, the 'railway mania' engrossed the people of England. "And within a few years, the 'railway mania' was at its height, covering acre upon acre of London with iron rails, platforms, shunting yards and engine sheds, repair shops and ticket offices, refreshment rooms and coal bunkers and displacing hundreds of thousands of its inhabitants. Almost twenty thousand people were obliged to abandon their homes by the building of the line from the London and Birmingham's depot to its terminal station in Euston Square alone; and most of them, unwilling to move far away, crowded into already overpopulated areas nearby, adding yet another problem to the continuing tragedy of the London poor."[73]

The railway mania created a tendency to invest money in fake or unsuccessful railway companies. George Hudson, the Railway king, was the leader. The more foolish part of the public was cheated but a large residuum of successful new lines survived. Hudson was a swindler, but scored his mark across the face of England. Great Britain had about 2000 miles of railway lines in 1843 and 5000 miles in 1848. The means of transporting heavy goods and long distance travelling was railways. The canals, after a service of half a century, were mostly ruined and many of them were bought by railway companies. Main roads did not exist as the chief means of transport. The posting inns and postilions did not exist and the public mail coach and heavy family coach of the aristocratic class disappeared. 'Landau', the light 'Victoria', the homely four wheeler and the democratic omnibus ran in the streets of London. In the countryside the gig, the wagonette, the pony cart and the dog cart used to ply. Horse traffic was subsidiary to railways. Byroads increased in number. Long journeys were not carried on by road and the great highways were deserted.

Railways gave an opportunity to the social inferiors of the Victorian people to mix freely with their social superiors. It was the symbol of change in Victorian England. The great symbol of the change, in Dickens' fiction as in the "history of the period, is, as House points out, the development of the railways: they made, more quickly and more thoroughly, than it is easy for us to imagine, a new England, as the institution of an efficient Metropolitan Police Force made a new London...but the coach, and pedestrianism for those who could not afford the coach, gave way before the train with its first, second, and third class compartments, its much greater speed and its much greater cheapness. And the arrival of the train quite literally changed the face of England; which is why it is so powerful a symbol of change in *Dombey and Son*."[74]

The Reform Act of 1832 was made to assist the industrial and commercial lords to gain power and influence in the politics of England and to restrain the dominance of the British peerage and manorial lords. It was a middle-class movement for electoral reforms. "By redistributing the constituencies and by giving the propertied class the power to vote, the Act of 1832 effected an increase in the number of the electorate, approximately 5,00,000 before 1832, by about half by the Act of 1832. The enhancement in the number of voters gave more power and prestige to the men who represented the manufacturing and commercial interests of contemporary society."[75] Dickens worked as a Parliamentary reporter and he attended the debates on the Reform Bill. He was disillusioned with everyday practice of politics and did not appreciate the complicated apparatus of Government.

Neglect and ill-usage of children was prevalent in the Victorian society. The streets of the slums were the only playground of the city children. Few of them went to schools till 1870. They had no Play Centres. The Society for the Prevention of Cruelty to Children was founded only in 1884. The nineteenth century saw the gradual disuse of "cruel flogging of boys, which educational reformers had deplored in vain for ages past."[76] In vast areas of London and other cities "there was no open spaces within the reach of the children, whose only playground outside the school yard was the hard and ugly street. To millions the divorce from nature was absolute, and so too was the divorce from all dignity and beauty and significance in the wilderness of mean streets in which they were bred, whether in the well-to-do suburb or the slum."[77]

The Crimean War was fought during 1854-56 between an alliance of British and French forces against the Russians. Britain showed its catastrophic incompetence in the conduct of the campaign. "The utter breakdown of the Commissariat and Medical Service, though partly due to sheer ignorance of what the campaign involved was due more to the cumbrous machinery which seemed to exist only for the purpose of delaying orders. The medical supplies lying unopened on the dock and the cargo of cabbages thrown into the sea were adequate examples how not to do it."[78] Fourteen thousand were alive, five thousand fit for service out of the army of fifty-four thousand sent to Russia. The gross incompetence of the War Office during the Crimean War was exposed by the sufferings of the sick and the wounded.

The early Victorian Whitehall was the nest of sloth and jobbery. Dickens ridiculed in *Little Dorrit* the incompetence of the Tite Barnacles. "They are unforgettably satirised as they dismissed enquiries, circumlocuted, declined to be precipitated and met demands for 'something to be done' with a masterly display of 'How not to do it'."[79] Dickens was not opposed to the centralisation of administration but chiefly to lack of co-ordination that led to inefficiency, muddle and human misery in the Crimean War. *Household Words* also took up the cause of reform, attacking the administration of Lord Palmerston.

The satire on Circumlocution Office is depicted in *Little Dorrit*. "The extent and vehemence of his criticism of the civil service give the book a more precise political orientation than his other novels have. Still, it cannot be said that the political motif dominates while he directly attacks government administration in his periodical articles, in the novel he uses it as one type of human weakness among several, and extends his satire to include English society as a whole."[80]

In 1855, Austen Henry Layard, a fiery liberal M.P. and a friend of Dickens asked his help for reform of the British administration as he saw its failures during the Crimean War. In June 1855, Layard's motion for Civil Service Reform was defeated in Parliament. Then, Administrative Reform Association was founded to create public opinion for the reform. Dickens took active part in the formation of this society. He became a subscribing member and took the chair at a meeting of the Association at Drury Lane on June 27 and delivered his best public speeches. He was at the height of his power when he created the factual fiction of the Barnacles and thrashed the appointment system in *Household Words* and in *Little Dorrit*.

The workers were dissatisfied with the Reform Act of 1832 and started a political campaign for a complete democratic charter. It was active between 1838 and 1848. This chartist agitation was led by Lovett of the London Working Men's Association and Feargus O' Connor. Lovett believed in legal and constitutional agitation and Feargus O' Connor was prepared to advocate violence. The charter which they put forward "contained six demands: annual Parliaments, manhood suffrage, vote by ballot, equal electoral districts, payment of members of Parliament, and the abolition of the property qualification for members."[81] This was a moderate programme and four points were accepted.

The middle class gained wealth and money and these made them self-conceited. They did not pay attention to the socially and economically inferiors. Capital was controlled by them and made them proud and haughty, narrow and insular. Thus, to the Victorian middle class, Mammon was the only God to be sincerely worshipped. "The middle class desire for money led the Victorians to cultivate such habits as a Dombeyan pride in possession, exhibitionism and a certain debasement in taste."[82]

Material progress created social security and a self-satisfied, boastful generation was formed. The average educated Victorians in the industrial and urban areas became self-satisfied. They were, to quote Matthew Arnold, mainly interested in "a life of jealousy of the Establishment, disputes, tea-meetings, openings of chapels, sermons."[83] This sort of smugness or self-complacency of the age was termed 'Podsnappery' by Dickens.

As the poverty and misery of the urban poor increased, the number of philanthropic organisations also grew in number to eradicate them. In 1851, 536 philanthropic societies were operating in London. Then, no government organised or urban help was available to the people. So such societies filled the vacuum.

Dickens took active part in the amelioration of social conditions. He was associated with Angela-Burdett Coutts' Urania Cottage, the home for reforming prostitutes, and with her plans for a model housing project in Nova Scotia Gardens, the most notorious region of Bethnal Green. "The idea of the home was to take off the streets any woman who sincerely wished to escape from such a life, clean up their manners and morals, and ship them off to the colonies."[84]

Dickens acted as chairman of an administrative committee from 1847 to 1858 and supervised it. He finalised as to who was to be admitted to the reformatory home. He advised the resident superintendent on discipline, training and everyday management and made all the necessary arrangements for sending them overseas.

Dickens' satire, says Philip Collins, is among the finest in literature. It is not as deeply inflicting as that of Voltaire or Swift nor as crushing as Hobbes' but it "is pointed enough for its purpose, and has none of the bitter, withering tincture which forms so large a portion of satire in general; and it is done in that style that one might easily suppose an individual under the lash laughing at it himself, and feeling its deep truth at the same time.... And this satire is also more powerful, for when a man makes us writhe, we are more apt, with roused feelings, to attack him than to think of reforming ourselves, as was the case with Cobbett; he shocked the prejudices of people too abruptly —told them they were fools in too plain a manner, to make them feel so."[85]

Dickens' best humorous writing is faintly linked with Augustan satire by his use of mock-heroics. In the manner of Hogarth, he takes a keen and practical view of life in depicting the ludicrous side of human nature, "and rendering its follies more apparent by humorous exaggeration—'peculiarly skilful in his management of details, throwing in circumstances which serve not only to complete the picture before us, but to suggest indirectly antecedent events which cannot be brought before our eyes."[86] But unlike Hogarth, he does not possess least agreeable qualities—cynicism and coarseness. There is no touch of misanthropy in his satire and no coarseness in his descriptions. His works reflect the pictures of humble life.

In creating characters, Dickens is tolerant and many-sided. As a satirist, he is intolerant and one-sided. Unlike other satirists, he has a wonderful power in individualising abuses in persons. Juvenal, Dryden and Pope are keen satirists of character. But they are comparatively ineffective in the art of concealing their moral purpose under an apparently dramatic form. Dickens' individualising power is strong and as a satirist he simply personifies his personal opinion.

Dickens feels all the wrongs that are committed, and the vices that are practised. He avenges himself by ridicule. He does not paint but punishes. In fact, he is gloomy like Hogarth. He makes us burst with laughter by the buffoonery of his invention and the violence of his caricatures. He brings his characters to absurdity.

Dickens is very much interested in social satire and comic incident to give more space to moral action. According to Barbara Hardy, The power of *Pickwick Papers* lies in its comedy. Dickens is weak in his use of comedy of humours but very strong in comic wit, joke and anecdote. He is very successful in his combination of the comic and the macabre. Barbara Hardy writes: "Dickens' comedy needs the stiffening either of satire or of the macabre, and where his comedy is neither satiric nor dark it is always least successful.... The strength of *Pickwick Papers* lies in grotesque or satiric comedy that is toughened, blackened, and enlarged in context; its weakness lies in horseplay and comic character that is muted, mild, and cut-off from the realities it pretends to mock."[87]

Dickens plays with horseplay and makes it satirical in the political scenes of Eatanswill, the social scenes of Bath and the religious and marital aggressions arising out of Tony Weller's widder hating humour. The Wellers give Dickens the satirical point of view within the novel, a requirement of his comedy. *The Pickwick Papers* has a brilliant comic spirit with his exuberant satire. There are splendid satire on the lawyers. The powerful sketches of satire show Dickens' mastery of linguistic parody and caricature.

In *Martin Chuzzlewit*, there are brilliant comic scenes and a great deal of satire, linguistic humour and farce. There is the thematic connection between the social satire and the individual type of selfishness. "The great satirist can turn to gross sentimentality with his left hand knowing what his right hand is doing."[88] In *Oliver Twist*, the pathos is contrasted with the institutional satire of workhouse officialdom. Satire and sick humour flourish in Dickens' comic prototypes.

## NOTES

1. Monroe Engel, *The Maturity of Dickens*, Harvard University Press, Cambridge, Massachussetts, 1967, p. 92.
2. Alan Shelston, *Charles Dickens, Dombey and Son*, and *Little Dorrit*, Macmillan, Basingstoke, Hampshire, 1985, p. 119.
3. Shanker A. Dutt, Lecture, *Refresher Course in English*, Academic Staff College, Patna University.
4. Peter Ackroyd, *Dickens' London: An Imaginative Vision*, Headline, London, 1987, pp. 17-18.
5. *Ibid.*, p. 103.
6. *Ibid.*, pp. 18-19.
7. Humphry House, *The Dickens World*, Oxford University Press, London, New York, Toronto, 1942, p. 43.
8. E.W.F. Tomlin, *Charles Dickens 1812-1870*, Weidenfeld and Nicholson, London, 1969, p. 84.
9. Philip Collins, *Dickens and Crime*, Macmillan & Co. Ltd., London, New York, St. Martin's Press, 1962, p. 2.
10. Peter Ackroyd, *op. cit.*, p. 103.
11. *Ibid.*, p. 19.
12. E.W.F. Tomlin, *op. cit.*, p. 163.
13. Peter Ackroyd, *op. cit.*, p. 20.
14. Andrew Sanders, *Charles Dickens: Resurrectionist*, Macmillan, London, 1982, p. 12.
15. *Ibid.*
16. *Ibid.*, p. 13.
17. *Ibid.*
18. *Ibid.*, p. 3.
19. Peter Ackroyd, *op. cit.*, p. 20.
20. *Ibid.*, p. 126.
21. G.M. Trevelyan, *English Social History*, Orient Longman, Bombay, 1968, p. 529.

22. John Lucas, *Charles Dickens: The Major Novels*, Penguin Books, Harmondsworth, Middlesex, 1992, p. 76.
23. A.E. Dyson, *Dickens: Bleak House, A Casebook*, Macmillan, London, 1969, pp. 118-19.
24. *Ibid.*, p. 119.
25. Alexander Welsh, *The City of Dickens*, Clarendon Press, Oxford, 1971, p. 16.
26. Andrew Sanders, *op. cit.*, p. 7.
27. Peter Ackroyd, *op. cit.*, pp. 127-28.
28. Grahame Smith, *Dickens: Money and Society*, University of California Press, Berkeley and Los Angeles, 1968, p. 145.
29. E.W.F. Tomlin, *op. cit.*, p. 165.
30. Kate Flint, *Dickens*, The Harvester Press, Brighton, Sussex, 1986, p. 24.
31. Debiprasad Bhattacharya, *The Middle Class in Dickens*, Minerva Associates, Calcutta, 2000, p. 35.
32. Peter Ackroyd, *Introduction to Dickens*, Mandarin Paperbacks, London, 1992, p. 123.
33. Philip Collins, *op. cit.*, p. 8.
34. G.M. Trevelyan, *op. cit.*, pp. 530-31.
35. Philip Collins, *op. cit.*, p. 6.
36. *Ibid.*
37. *Ibid.*, p. 32.
38. *Ibid.*, p. 54.
39. *Ibid.*, p. 55.
40. E.W.F. Tomlin, *op. cit.*, p. 150.
41. Debiprasad Bhattacharya, *op. cit.*, p. 31.
42. *Ibid.*
43. Paul Schlicke, *Dickens and Popular Entertainment*, Unwin Hyman, London, Boston, Sydney, Wellington, 1985, p. 10.
44. *Ibid.*
45. *Ibid.*, p. 198.
46. G.M. Trevelyan, *op. cit.*, p. 566.
47. Ivor Brown, *Dickens in His Time*, Thomas Nelson & Sons Ltd., London, 1963, p. 176.
48. *Ibid.*, pp. 176-77.
49. G.M. Trevelyan, *op. cit.*, p. 571.

50. E.W.F. Tomlin, *op. cit.*, pp. 154-55.
51. Debiprasad Bhattacharya, *op. cit.*, p. 46.
52. Alexander Welsh, *op. cit.*, p. 95.
53. G.M. Trevelyan, *op. cit.*, pp. 538-39.
54. Humphry House, *op. cit.*, p. 100.
55. Allan Grant, *A Preface to Dickens*, Longman, London, New York, 1984, p. 60.
56. *Ibid.*
57. Debiprasad Bhattacharya, *op. cit.*, p. 48.
58. *Ibid.*, p. 30.
59. G.M. Trevelyan, *op. cit.*, p. 520.
60. Grahame Smith, *op. cit.*, p. 146.
61. Richard Burton, *Charles Dickens*, Folcroft Library Edition, Folcroft PA, 1977, pp. 272-73.
62. Edgar Johnson, *Charles Dickens: His Tragedy and Truimph*, Penguin Books, New York, London, 1986, p. 255.
63. *Ibid.*, p. 405.
64. G.M. Trevelyan, *op. cit.*, p. 543.
65. *Ibid.*, p. 544.
66. Debiprasad Bhattacharya, *op. cit.*, p. 34.
67. *Ibid.*, p. 29.
68. G.M. Trevelyan, *op. cit.*, p. 534.
69. *Ibid.*, p. 559.
70. *Ibid.*, p. 573.
71. *Ibid.*, p. 574.
72. Debiprasad Bhattacharya, *op. cit.*, p. 27.
73. E.W.F. Tomlin, *op. cit.*, p. 96.
74. Walter Allen, *The English Novel*, Penguin Books, Harmondsworth, Middlesex, 1991, p. 170.
75. Debiprasad Bhattacharya, *op. cit.*, p. 29.
76. *Ibid.*, p. 546.
77. *Ibid.*, p. 579.
78. Humphry House, *op. cit.*, p. 187.
79. E.W.F. Tomlin, *op. cit.*, p. 148.
80. J.C. Reid, *Charles Dickens, Little Dorrit, Edward Arnold*, London, 1967, p. 12.

81. Ivor Brown, *op. cit.*, p. 25.
82. Debiprasad Bhattacharya, *op. cit.*, p. 37.
83. *Ibid.*, pp. 36-37.
84. K.J. Fielding, *Charles Dickens: A Critical Introduction*, Longmans, Green & Co., London, New York, Toronto, 1958, p. 105.
85. Philip Collins, *Dickens the Critical Heritage*, Routledge and Kegan Paul, London, 1971, p. 67.
86. *Ibid.*, p. 72.
87. Barbara Hardy, *The Moral Art of Dickens*, The Athlone Press of the University of London, London, 1970, pp. 84-85.
88. *Ibid.*, p. 118.

# Administration and Judiciary

2

## ADMINISTRATION

Dickens has joined a people's political agitation, the Administrative Reforms Association and he has contributed articles to *Household Words* in which he has attacked the government's incompetence. According to Forster, Dickens has continued to write the utter reality of the truth. The institution of penal administration in Victorian England receives the novelist's attention and because of its gross and deplorable insufficiencies the perspective mediation between what exists in reality and what it ought to be by implication.

The criminals have posed much danger in London. The city has had 'no-go' areas in its rookeries and slums. One lakh persons have lived by plunder in 1867. Child kidnapping and stealing the child's clothes has been common. In *Dombey and Son*, Florence, the daughter of the proud business giant, Mr. Dombey, accompanies Polly Toodle and Susan Nipper on Paul's visit to Staggs' Garden. In a moment of confusion, Florence is separated from them and is swept up in the seemy side of London's underworld:

> The old woman took her by the wrist, and said, 'I'll show you.' She was a very ugly old woman, with red rims round her eyes, and a mouth that mumbled and chattered of itself when she was not speaking. She was miserably dressed, and carried some skins over her arm. She seemed to have followed Florence some little way at all events, for she had lost her breath; and this made her uglier still, as she stood trying to regain it: Working her shrivelled yellow face and throat into all sorts of contortions.[1]

A very frightened Florence is swept down the street described as 'black' and 'solitary'. The hag introduces herself as Mrs. Brown, adding with the venal touch to Dickensian irony 'Good Mrs. Brown'. They go by some very seedy places, such as brick-fields and Tile-yards. Then the old woman turns down a dirty lane filled with the mud in deep black ruts in the middle of the road. She stops before a shabby little house and opens the door with a key she takes out of her bonnet. She pushes the child before her into a back room, with a great heap of rags of different colours lying on the floor. There is no furniture at all. The walls and ceiling are quite black. Mrs. Brown knows Florence Dombey's identity. Formalities done it is time for professional attention:

> 'I want that pretty frock, Miss Dombey', said Good Mrs. Brown, 'and that little bonnet, and a petticoat or two, and anything else you can spare. Come! Take'em off.'

Florence obeyed, as fast as her trembling hands would allow; keeping, all the while, a frightened eye on Mrs. Brown. When she had divested herself of all the articles of apparel mentioned by that lady, Mrs. B. examined them at leisure, and seemed tolerably well satisfied with their quality and value.

'Humph!' she said, running her eyes over the child's slight figure, 'I don't see anything else-except the shoes. I must have the shoes, Miss Dombey.'[2]

Poor Little Florence takes them off quickly, only too glad to conciliate Mrs. Brown. The old woman then produces some abject substitutes from the bottom of the heap of rags, together with a shabby girl's cloak and the crushed remains of a bonnet picked up from some ditch. In this poor clothing, she instructs Florence to dress herself making it a prelude to her release. The child complies with increased readiness. In hurriedly putting on the bonnet, her hair gets entangled. "Florence was so relieved to find that it was only her hair and not her head which Mrs. Brown coveted, that she offered no resistance or entreaty, and merely raised her mild eyes towards the face of that good soul."[3]

Mrs. Brown's physical attributes and mannerisms suggest her menacing action. She is ugly and frightening like any evil witch in fairy story or legend.

Good Mrs. Brown watches the beautiful hair of Florence like a great black spider and is prepared to cut them off. Her luxuriant hair, is to be scissored and sold by Mr. Brown. The terrible scissors passes over her head and thus she is exposed to fatal danger. Her vulnerability is filled with nightmare horror. A dreadful adult waving a deadly weapon over a helpless child takes place "like a frozen delirium elsewhere in his writings, most notably in *Oliver Twist* and *David Copperfield*. It is Dickens' most intense icon of ferocious adult aggression against innocent childhood."[4] Good Mrs. Brown recalls her distant daughter's long hair and finally stops. At the time of release, she insists Florence not to go home but to her father's office in the city. Mrs. Brown prevents the injunction with horrible threats telling her that she is "now going to lead her to a public street whence she could inquire her way to her friends. But she cautioned her, with threats of summary and deadly vengeance in case of disobedience,... and these directions Florence promised faithfully and earnestly to observe."[5]

The alarming condition of crime in nineteenth century England is reproduced in the novel. Images of violence or symbols of terror are frequently textualised both as social realism as well as for a clearly defined satiric purpose. The loose and inefficient administration, both civil and penal were responsible for the vulnerability of its victims. This was particularly true of children who were its most poignant victims.

The crime of kidnapping in English social life is exposed for social censure in *Oliver Twist* too. Mr. Brownlow sends Oliver to return some books and to make a payment to the bookseller. He has five-pound note in his jacket pocket, books under his arm and a new suit of clothes on his back. In the way, he is surprised to be addressed as dear brother. Nancy stops him by having her arms thrown tight around his neck. She tells everyone that he is her younger brother. Oliver cries out and struggles for his escape but in vain. Bill Sikes tears the books from Oliver's grasp and strikes over his head. Dickens portrays:

> Weak with recent illness, stupefied by the blows and the suddenness of the attack, terrified by the fierce growling of the dog and the brutality of the man, and overpowered by the conviction of the bystanders that he really was the hardened little wretch he was described to be—what could one poor child do? Darkness had set in, it was a low neighbourhood; no help was near; resistance was useless. In another moment he was dragged into a labyrinth of dark narrow courts, and forced along them at a pace which rendered the few cries he dared to give utterance to wholly unintelligible.[6]

Thus Oliver is kidnapped by Nancy and Bill Sikes and he is brought back to Fagin's gang. Dickens satirically shows the rising crime of Victorian England and he has serious concern for an efficient administration to check them.

Fagin runs a company for pick-pocketing and theft in London. Oliver is brought to this gang by Artful Dodger. Artful Dodger, Charley Bates and Oliver go out to steal handkerchief. Mr. Brownlow is pick-pocketed by this gang:

> What was Oliver's horror and alarm as he stood a few paces off, looking on with his eyelids as wide open as they would possibly go, to see the Dodger plunge his hand into the old gentleman's pocket, and draw from thence a handkerchief; to see him hand the same to Charley Bates; and finally to behold them both running away round the corner at full speed.[7]

Handkerchiefs were stolen by thieves in England. There were regions where shops were established to buy and sell these handkerchiefs. Dickens writes of such shops in Saffron Hill:

> In its filthy shops are exposed for sale huge bunches of second hand silk handkerchiefs, of all sizes and patterns; for here reside the traders who purchase them from pick-pockets. Hundreds of these handkerchiefs hang dangling from pegs outside the windows or flaunting from the door-post; and the shelves, within, are piled with

> them.... It is a commercial colony of itself—the emporium of petty larceny; visited at early morning and setting-in of dusk by silent merchants, who traffic in dark back-parlours, and who go as strangely as they come. Here the clothesman, the shoe-vamper, and the rag-merchant display their goods, as sign-boards to the petty thief; here stores of old iron and bones, and heaps of mildewy fragments of woollen stuff and linen, rust and rot in the grimy cellars.[8]

Oliver is lured by the members of Fagin's gang to join it. Charley asks Oliver to put him under Fagin and Dodger advocates to make a fortune thus. Oliver is further tempted by Dodger:

> Fagin will make something of you, though, or you'll be the first he ever had that turned out unprofitable. You'd better begin at once; for you'll come to the trade long before you think of it, and you're only losing time, Oliver.
>
> Master Bates backed this advice with sundry moral admonitions of his own; which, being exhausted, he and his friend Mr. Dawkins launched into a glowing description of the numerous pleasures incidental to the life they led, interspersed with a variety of hints to Oliver that the best thing he could do would be to secure Fagin's favour without more delay, by the means which they themselves had employed to gain it.[9]

The alarming situation of crime is hinted above and the law and order situation is shown bad during the Victorian London.

In *Oliver Twist*, a theft is schemed by Fagin at Chertsey. Bill Sikes, Toby Crackit, both the housebreakers take Oliver on the expedition of burglary. Although Oliver does not want to go to steal, the housebreakers drag him to the house for the purpose of robbery. The shutter of the house is opened by Bill and Crackit and they have the motive to push Oliver into the house through a window. Dickens describes:

> It was a little lattice-window, about five feet and a half above the ground, at the back of the house, which belonged to a scullery, or small brewing-place, at the end of the passage. The aperture was so small that the inmates had

> probably not thought it worthwhile to defend it more securely; but it was large enough to admit a boy of Oliver's size, nevertheless. A very brief exercise of Mr. Sikes's art sufficed to overcome the fastenii g of the lattice, and it soon stood wide open also.[10]

Giving Oliver a dar k lantern, Bill Sikes puts him in the house through the window. Oliver goes upstairs and wants to alert the family. But they are roused by noise and shout at him from the stairtop. Bill fires his own pistol after men and drags the boy up. Oliver is hit and so he bleeds. Dickens is very thoughtful of the rising crime of theft in Victorian England and he is very serious regarding the loose administration of the contemporary Britain.

At another place in *Oliver Twist*, Mr. Bumble and Mrs. Bumble go to a particular place for an interview with Monks. Dickens writes about the locale: "This was far from being a place of doubtful character; for it had long been known as the residence of none but low and desperate ruffians, who, under various pretences of living by their labour, subsisted chiefly on plunder and crime."[11] Dickens shows that there were such places in contemporary Britain inhabited by the criminals and they created danger to the social life of England.

Noah Claypole and Charlotte come to London to make an illegal fortune. They stay at the Three Cripples, a pub and one of the haunts of Fagin. The former is interested in emptying pockets, women's ridicules, houses and mail-coaches and banks. Fagin overhears them and agrees to set them on work for a payment of twenty pounds. Noah asks the Jew to provide him a pretty work without more risk, as being at home. The latter recommends that there is a good deal of money made in snatching bags and parcels of the old ladies and running round the corner. Noah replies that it cannot serve his purpose as the old ladies holter out a good deal and scratch sometimes. Then the Jew prescribes:

> 'The kinchins, my dear', said the Jew, 'is the young children that's sent on errands by their mothers, with six pences and shillings; and the lay is just to take their money away—they've always got it ready in their hands—and then

> knock'em into the kennel, and walk off very slow, as if there was nothing else the matter but a child fallen down and hurt itself....' 'To be sure it is', replied Fagin; 'and you can have a few good beats chalked out in Camden-town, and Battlebridge, and neighbourhoods like that, where they're always going errands, and you can upset as many kinchins as you want any hour in the day.'[12]

Through all these crimes prevalent in English social life, the novelist expresses serious concern over the inefficient administration of England. Dickens is the champion of a shared ethical initiative based on an awareness of the socially embedded nature of human existence. "The writer's absorption with crime, in a rogues' gallery of every shade from Bill Sykes and Jonas Chuzzlewit to Montague Tigg and Wackford Squeers, is not simply Newgate Calendar sensationalism, but a concern with murder, fraud and cruelty as deliberate transgressions against this mutuality."[13]

England was policed by the old system of parish constables and watchmen before 1829. The Fielding brothers, Henry and John, improved the safety of London during 1750-80, by establishing the Bow Street Runners and Patroles. Thames River Police increased the size of all these efficient police forces. Although London had a comparatively efficient police force, there were shocking inadequacies in administration. There was a huge amount of undetected crime and the crisis of Gordon Riots of 1780 exposed the inadequacies of the police. Dickens considered these disorders as the product of faulty criminal laws, incompetent prison regulations and the bad police. He satirises the inefficiency of the police administration of England in *Oliver Twist* and *Great Expectations*.

In *Great Expectations*, Bow Street Runners police is sent to Kent to investigate the assault upon Mrs. Joe Gargery. The Constables, and the Bow-street men from London arrive about the house for a week or two, to investigate the case. Dickens presents his sardonic observation of the Bow Street Runners:

> They took up several obviously wrong people, and they ran their heads very hard against wrong ideas, and persisted in

trying to fit the circumstances to the ideas, instead of trying to extract ideas from the circumstances. Also, they stood about the door of the Jolly Bargemen, with knowing and reserved looks that filled the whole neighbourhood with admiration; and they had a mysterious manner of taking their drink, that was almost as good as taking the culprit. But not quite, for they never did it.[14]

The pretentious professionalism of the Bow Street men carefully caricatured through the juxtaposition of images of time taken as surrogacy for efficiency accompanied by blandering acts such as to detain the wrong people, to adjust circumstances to the ideas and mysterious way of drinking. Such are the stylistic devices used to satirise the failures and pathetic insufficiency of the police.

In *Oliver Twist*, the Bow Street Runners are called to Chertsey after Bill Sikes and his gang break the house. Blathers and Duff, investigate the case. The former asks the master of the house about the circumstances of the robbery. Mr. Losberne recounts them at great length. Messrs. Blathers and Duff look very knowing and exchange a nod. Blathers opins that he cannot say anything certain untill he sees the place. But he considers that the robbery is not executed by a yokel and Duff too affirms this. Mr. Losberne makes it plain and clear that this attempt is not made by a countryman. Blathers asks about the boy that the servants are talking on. Mrs. Losberne says that one of the frightened servants chooses to take it into his head that he is something to do with this attempt to break into the house. Blathers finds this correct, nods his head and plays carelessly with the handcuffs. He wants to know the identity of the boy and asks about his home and his accounts.

Mr. Losberne replies that he knows his complete history. But, presently, he asks the police to see the place where the thieves have made their attempt. Mr. Blathers is of the opinion that it is better to inspect the premises first, and examine the servants afterwards and that is the usual way of doing business.

Messrs. Blathers and Duff, attended by the native constables, Brittles and Giles, go into the little room at the end of the passage and look out at the window. Afterwards, they go round by way of the lawn and look in at the window. They are given candle to inspect the shutter and a lantern to trace the foot-steps. After that, they are provided pitchfork to poke the bushes with. Blathers and Duff clear the room and hold "a long counsel together, compared with which, for secrecy and solemnity, a consultation of great doctors on the knottiest point in medicine would be mere child's play".[15]

The police fails to discover the thieves. The Bow street policemen investigate and report that the robbers are experts. They manage to conclude that the thieves are professionals from the city, and they are helped by a boy they put through a window:

> 'Well, master', said Blathers, entering the room, followed by his colleague, and making the door fast before he said any more. 'This warn't a put-up thing.'...
>
> 'We find it was a town hand', said Blathers, continuing his report, 'for the style of work is first-rate'...
>
> 'There was two of 'em in it', continued Blathers; 'and they had a boy with 'em; that's plain from the size of the window. That's all to be said at present.'[16]

In *Bleak House*, Bucket is based on Inspector Field of the Metropolitan Police. Dickens admires his detective skill. He is not blinded by his admiration to Bucket's compromised moral position. The Inspector tries to set things pleasant in accordance with his duty. He offers the distressed genuine sympathy and consolation. But his duty always comes first and he is devoted to the truth. Bucket is not beyond arresting an innocent man, for if he turns out to be guilty, Bucket will collect the reward of a hundred guineas. The most that can be said for Bucket "is that this strategy for survival does work, even if he is left morally compromised, and so he makes the near best out of the almost impossible situation in which the people of *Bleak House* find themselves."[17]

Dickens presents the Lord Mayor as a grotesque and farcical figure, both cynical and abjectly servile. The latter does not act because of the great persons being involved in the riots.

The historical descriptions also emphasise the inertia and cowardice of the London authorities, but they do not turn the "chief magistrates into mere Dickensian automatons of the most deplorable type."[18]

Dickens had much contempt for magistrates. The magistrates are the instruments of Government. The public order is restored by force. The Government had only methods of repression by force and intimidation through the law. In *Martin Chuzzlewit*, when Mr. Pecksniff has dismissed Tom Pinch, social correction in adulthood is produced in the form of verbal caricature:

> Oh late-remembered, much-forgotten, mouthing, braggart duty, always owed, and seldom paid in any other coin than punishment and wrath, when will mankind begin to know thee! When will men acknowledge thee in thy neglected cradle, and thy stunted youth, and not begin their recognition in thy sinful manhood and thy desolate old age![19]

A magistrate is produced as careless and worthless, inimical to the call and ethics of duty, a rare "country gentleman and brave a squire, had you no duty to society, before the ricks were blazing and the mob were mad; or did it spring up, armed and booted from the earth, a corps of yeomanry full-grown!"[20]

The Government does not endeavour to prevent the causes of riot and it does not make efforts to suppress the riot after its outbreak. The riot can be put down by firm action in the beginning. Unfortunately, it increases in magnitude because of the failure of the shy and ignorant magistrates to act with decision. The riots can be "halted only with great bloodshed."[21]

The Speenhamland policy offered allowances-top-up-wages for those workers whose earnings were below a certain standard. But the authorities maintained that this policy encouraged employers to provide low wages as they knew that their employees or labourers would seek relief from the state. The Poor Law Amendment Act, 1834 tried to sort out this loophole. By this law, it was ruled that no 'outdoor' relief would be given to low-paid or unemployed labourers. Relief was to be given within the confines of the workhouse. The claimant had to pass the 'workhouse test' to prove himself or herself a pauper. The government had the opinion that the law would decrease unemployment. Able-bodied unemployed men would have to get a job or starve. It was meant that the law would encourage all employers to pay the subsistence wage and would lower the poor rate from which the wage-supplement had been paid and would stop the pauper from breeding in idleness because once in the workhouse he would be parted from his wife.

The workhouses were constructed to provide work for the unemployed. But the condition in workhouses was extremely bad. In *Oliver Twist*, Dickens points out the evils of the New Poor Law by satirising the poor houses or workhouses: "The intended reform of the new Poor Law, far from accomplishing its purpose either broke or brutalised the spirit of its victims."[22]

The workhouses were the seats of Church wardens and overseers. They were the instigators and perpetuators of the bad establishment. The human spirit is systematically suppressed for subjection. Dickens attacks the guardians of the parish-unions under the new law with full strength and ferocity. He shows theirs inhumanity and negligence to the sufferings of the poor. He criticises the Benthamite principle, the calculation of 'less eligibility' of the 1834 Poor Law Amendment Act.

Oliver is to be dispatched to a branch workhouse where there is not sufficient food or clothing supplied. The superintendent of the workhouse is a poor woman whose slim resources spur her enterprise. She half-starves babies in care of the parish and pockets part of the money provided to feed them. Dickens mocks at the particulars about the superintendent. She is convinced that seven pence-halfpenny's worth per week can manage a good round diet for a child to fill its stomach comfortably. The grotesque and black humour is evident. Oliver is likely to be starved or smothered or crushed to death by mere accident. Parish children are often ignored in turning up a bedstead. They are scalded to death during washing. The board makes periodical visits to the farm. The children are neat and clean. It is hoped that this system of farming "would produce any very extraordinary of luxuriant crop. Oliver

Twist's ninth birthday found him a pale thin child, somewhat diminutive in stature, and decidedly small in circumference."[23] Dickens satirises the inhuman cruelty inflicted on children under the workhouse system. He challenges the scientific economy underlying the new Poor Laws.

Dickens condemns the management of the workhouse. He also condemns the principles behind the law. The members of the Board of Governors are very sage, deep, philosophical men. They discover that poor people like the workhouse. It is a regular place of public entertainment for the poorer classes. It is a tavern and a public breakfast, dinner, tea, and supper are available throughout the year with payment. In this brick and mortar elysium, there is all play and no work. To set things right, the members establish the rule that all poor people are given the alternative of being starved by a gradual process in the house, or by a quick one. For the elimination of the poor, they contract with the water-works to provide an unlimited supply. They arrange with a corn-factor to supply periodically small quantities of oatmeal. They issue three meals of thin gruel a day, with an onion twice a week, and half a roll on Sundays. They kindly undertake to divorce poor married people. The relief is inseparable from the workhouse and that frightens people.

Dickens is very critical about the clothes of all the paupers, "which fluttered loosely on their wasted, shrunken forms, after a week or two's gruel. But the number of workhouse inmates got thin as well as the paupers; and the board were in ecstasies."[24]

Oliver is born in a workhouse of the Old Law. When he comes back from Mrs. Mann's, the New Law is into force and the Board is set up. The new 'Bastilles' are also notorious. Dickens points out that the Board of Guardians is responsible for stunting the physical and mental growth of the poor orphans. They treat the boys like drudges and deny them all human cares. They make such provisions as to accelerate the process of starvation and thus their extinctions. Dickens attacks the new system to provide the only divorces available in England. It gives heavy expense to the parish in burying its victims. But the reduced number of those seeking relief delights the Board.

The sparseness of workhouse diet given to the inmates of the workhouse is also hinted in *Oliver Twist*. Low diet is the unique feature of the New Poor Law. Dickens' description of low diet is a significant satire on the commissioners approved dietaries. His portrayal of Oliver demanding more gruel is allegorical presentation of institutional disgrace of the English society. It is also a satire on the increasing complaint that the diet approved by the commissioners is not sufficient to feed the paupers.

The dining room of the boys is a large stone hall. There is a copper at one side of the room. The master with one or two women, ladle the gruel at mealtimes. Each boy finds one porringer. During great public celebration, he gets two ounces and a quarter of bread besides. The bowls are never required to be washed. The boys polish them with their spoons to shine. They sit staring at the copper, with eager eyes, as if to devour the very bricks of its composition. They suck their fingers to catch up any stray splashes of gruel. Oliver Twist and his companions suffer the tortures of slow starvation for three months. Lastly they become voracious and wild with hunger. The tall boy hints darkly to his companions, that unless he is provided another basin of gruel per diem, he may some night happen to eat the weak boy who sleeps next to him. A council is held to decide who shall walk up to the master after supper that evening and ask for more; and it falls to Oliver Twist.

In the evening, the gruel is served out. The gruel disappears. Oliver is desperate with hunger, and reckless with misery. He rises from the table; and advances to the master with basin and spoon in hand. He says alarmed at his own temerity: 'Please, sir, I want some more.'[25]

The master turns very pale. He gazes in stupefied astonishment on the small rebel for some seconds. Then he clungs for support to the copper. The assistants are paralysed with wonder, and the boys with fear. The master aims a blow at Oliver's head with the ladle. He pinions him in his arms, and shrieks aloud for the beadle. The board sits in solemn conclave. Mr. Bumble rushes into the room in great excitement. He addresses the gentleman in the high chair, and horrified at the temerity of Oliver's utterance reveals shock and disbelief: 'That boy will be hung,' said the gentleman in the white waistcoat. 'I know that boy will be hung.'[26]

Oliver is ordered into instant confinement. A bill is next morning pasted on the outside of the gate, offering a reward of five pounds to anybody who takes Oliver Twist "who wanted an apprentice to any trade, business, or calling."[27]

Oliver's request for more gruel is actually "a direct satire upon the dietary provisions for the inmates of workhouses, and suggests that Dickens was deliberately attacking 'what *The Times* called BENTHAMITE cant'."[28] Humphry House notes that there is an element of exaggeration in Dickens' description of the quantity of meals for the workhouse children. But, though a bit exaggerated, necessary for satire, it is "no falsification of the actual position prevailing in the workhouses."[29]

The inhumanity of the episode is brought to sharp focus by the fine equilibrium between the tragic and the comic, a device mastered by Shakespeare and Chaplin. It is the contrast that brings the suffering to sharp relief as Dickens satirises the cruelty and inhumanity suffered by the poor under the New Poor Law.

The cruelty of the board is seen when it decides to send Oliver Twist to sea: "The board, in imitation of so wise and salutary an example, took counsel together on the expediency of shipping off Oliver Twist in some small trading vessel bound to a good unhealthy port; which suggested itself as the very best thing that could possibly be done with him; the probability being that the skipper would flog him to death, in a playful mood, some day after dinner, or would knock his brains out with an iron bar; both pastimes being, as is pretty generally known, very favourite and common recreations among gentlemen of that class. The more the case presented itself to the board, in this point of view, the more manifold the advantages of the step appeared; so they came to the conclusion that the only way of providing for Oliver effectually was to send him to sea without delay."[30]

When Oliver is brought to Mr. Sowerberry, the undertaker, his wife sets before him victuals. Oliver takes the food ferociously and Dickens satirises the philosopher who recommend bad foodstuffs to others:

> I wish some well-fed philosopher, whose meat and drink turn to gall within him, whose blood is ice, whose heart is iron, could have seen Oliver Twist clutching at the dainty viands that the dog had neglected. I wish he could have witnessed the horrible avidity with which Oliver tore the bits asunder with all the ferocity of famine. There is only one thing that I should like better and that would be to see the philosopher making the same sort of meal himself, with the same relish.[31]

When Noah abuses Oliver at the place of Sowerberry. The latter seizes him by the throat and gives him a heavy blow. Bumble, the workhouse beadle, is called on. He explains to Mrs. Sowerberry: 'Meat, ma'am, meat', replied Bumble, with stern emphasis. 'You've overfed him, ma'am, You've raised a artificial soul and spirit in him, ma'am, unbecoming a person of his condition; as the board, Mrs. Sowerberry, who are practical philosophers, will tell you. What have paupers to do with soul or spirit? It's quite enough that we let'em have live bodies. If you had kept the boy on gruel, ma'am, this would never have happened.'[32] Dickens satirises that beadle advocates for only gruel given to the paupers. The board only wants to keep body not spirit in the paupers. According to beadle, when Oliver is given sufficient food, his spirit has grown and so he makes a heavy blow to Noah.

The workhouse administration is not set to safeguard the health of the paupers but to worsen it. Dickens makes a caricature and laughs at the insecure methods adopted by the board to move the paupers. It is ironical to say that it is cheaper to move than to bury: 'That's when they're ill, Mrs. Mann', said the beadle. 'We put the sick paupers into open carts in the rainy weather, to prevent their taking cold'.... 'The opposition coach contracts for these two, and takes them cheap', said Mr. Bumble. "They are both in a very low state, and we find it would come two pound cheaper to move'em than to bury'em—that is if we can throw'em upon another parish, which I think we shall be able to do, if they don't die upon the road to spite us."[33]

Mrs. Mann, the farmer of infants, asks beadle to look to little Dick. The porochial child has become too weak as if a 'scarecrow'. Dickens describes the effect of workhouse administration with sarcasm:

> The child was pale and thin, his cheeks were sunken, and his eyes large and bright. The scanty parish dress—the livery of his misery—hung loosely on his feeble body; and his young limbs had wasted away, like those of an old man.[34]

Mrs. Corney, matron of the workhouse, asks the beadle whether he considers out-of-door relief a very bad thing. Mr. Bumble opines that out-of-door relief is the parochial safeguard when it is properly managed. Dickens attacks this irregular system with raillery: "The great principle of out-of-door relief, is, to give the paupers exactly what they don't want; and then they get tired of coming'...'that's the great principle; and that's the reason why, if you look at any cases that get into them owdacious newspapers, you'll always observe that sick families have been relieved with slices of cheese'."[35]

The dehumanised government and administrative machinery is satirised in the depiction of Mrs. Thingumming in *Oliver Twist*. She is a nurse and she is not interested in nursing the dying mother of Oliver Twist. But she is engaged in taking the contents of the gin bottle. Bumble, the workhouse master, is an instance of savage comedy in Dickens, a grotesque figure rendered ridiculous. He is "any unimaginative and corrupt bureaucratic underlying in any system of society to whom power is given, seen from the point of view of the victim."[36]

In 1839, half of the funerals in London occured for children under ten years age. Child mortality was the great evil of the early nineteenth century. But this could have been avoided if proper sanitation had been introduced by the administration. In his periodical, Dickens criticised the horrors of urban sanitation leading the poor to a 'poisoned life'. During 1851, he delivered a speech to the Metropolitan Sanitary Association. In this speech, he talked of the stinking wind which carries disease from the poorer to the richer pockets of the city. In *Household Words*, Dickens described a city churchyard as a 'Cholera Nursery'. The sanitary question is an important ingredient in Dickens' fiction.

In *Bleak House*, smallpox spreads in Tom-all-Alone's. This slum provides a pestilential ground for the living. It is a black, dilapidated street and it has tumbling tenements "reeking with foul stains and loathsome smells, dripping with dirty rain, and sheltering within its ruined walls a human vermin that crawls and coils itself to sleep in maggot numbers on the rotting boards of its floors among fetid rags."[37] Tom-all-Alone's possesses creeping moisture and resultant disease. There is a close connection between the vermin breeding on the wretches in this slum and the wretches infesting its tenements. They are deadly parasites. *Bleak House* not merely gives frightful instances of slums and pauper graveyards; the novel describes "how they contaminate high and low alike; that disease is no respecter of class."[38]

The brickmakers hovels near St. Albans are reinforced by the rat-infested pauper's graveyard. Here, Captain Howden and Jo are buried and Lady Dedlock dies. This is based on the notorious graveyard of St. Martin's-in-the Fields. Dickens describes the disease bearing pollutions on the night of Krook's death. This is a "fine steaming night to turn the slaughter-houses, the unwholesome trades, the sewage, bad water, and burial grounds to account, and give the Registrar of Deaths some extra business."[39] Overcrowding, bad drainage and contaminated water engender diseases.

Dust is a factor responsible for pollution, with a house falling. In Tom-all-Alone's, there has been a crash twice and each time a house has fallen with a cloud of dust. These accidents have made "a paragraph in the newspapers, and have filled a bed or two in the nearest hospital. The gaps remain, and there are not unpopular lodgings among the rubbish. As several more-houses are nearly ready to go, the next crash in Tom-all-Alone's may be expected to be a good one."[40]

Tom-all-Alone's houses are without a pane of glass, without a window-frame, with the bare blank shutters tumbling from their hinges and falling into parts, "the iron-rails peeling away in flakes of rust; the chimneys sinking in; the stone steps to every door (and every door might be Death's door) turning stagnant green; the very crutches on which the ruins are propped, decaying."[41] Due to moisture, iron rusts and stone turns to green and causes disease.

Dickens writes in *Bleak House*, "A reeking little tunnel of a court gives access to the iron gate—with very villainy of life in action close on death, and every poisonous element of death in action close on life—here, they lower our dear brother down a foot or two: here, sow him in corruption, to be raised in corruption: an avenging ghost at many a sick bedside: a shameful testimony to future ages, how civilisation and barbarism walked this boastful island together."[42] Dickens shows that our dear brother is lowered down in the tunnel. His grave is the very tunnel itself. Dickens further describes: "For a time there were some dungeon lights burning, as the lamp of Life burns in Tom-all-Alone's; heavily, heavily, in the nauseous air, and winking—as that lamp, too, winks in Tom-all-Alone's—at many horrible things."[43] There is nauseous air and it causes winking of life.

A.E. Dyson comments: "Hence the stress upon slums as a breeding-ground of disease, crime and political subversion; of plagues that would reach from the foul courts of London right to the mansions of the great. The cholera struck London in 1848, and again when *Bleak House* was being written (it was almost unknown there until 1832, when its appearance was greeted by some opponents of Reform as a sign). By having his heroine infected with smallpox, however, Dickens recognises dangers inherent in virtue itself in our fallen world."[44]

Jo lives in the slum of Tom-all-Alone's. His body has a horrible stench that Lady Dedlock cannot bear. He dies of neglect, malnutrition and disease and the narrative consists in the accusation with sad notes: "Dead, your Majesty, Dead, my lords and gentlemen. Dead, Right Reverends and Wrong Reverends of every order. Dead, men and women, born with Heavenly compassion in your hearts. And dying thus around us everyday."[45]

Inspector Bucket at Mr. Tulkinghorn's behest takes Snagsby, the law stationer and makes a journey to Tom-all-Alone's. This is based on Dickens' journey to St. Giles Rookery with Inspector Field. Dickens describes the unhygienic condition of the place resulting in recurrent deaths. Mr. Snagsby passes along the middle of a villainous street, undrained, unventilated, deep in black mud and corrupt water and reeking with smells. Branching from this street and its heaps of ruins, are other streets and courts so infamous that Mr. Snagsby sickens in body and mind, and feels as going, into the infernal gulf. Bucket asks Mrs. Snagsby to draw off a bit as a kind of shabby palanquin is borne towards them, surrounded by a noisy crowd and he means that the fever comes up the street. Mr. Bucket cooly asks Darby, the constable, about a line of stinking ruins. The latter replies that all of them are fever houses and there "for months and months, the people 'have been down by dozens,' and have been carried out, dead and dying, 'like sheep with the rot.' Bucket observing to Mr. Snagsby as they go on again, that he looks a little poorly, Mr. Snagsby answers that he feels as if he couldn't breathe the dreadful air."[46]

*Bleak House* is the most significant investigation of the manifold effects of disease on urban life in the nineteenth century. An unspecified contagious disease, like Esther's scars, smallpox, symbolises the real destructiveness caused by the rottenness of society. Dickens, being unspecific, is able to exploit "a more general Victorian concern with fever. The contemporary concern was well founded, for fevers, even those loosely diagnosed as 'brain fever' and likely to be the result of mental as much as physical disease, regularly reached epidemic proportions in the middle years of the century."[47]

In *Oliver Twist*, Dickens describes the prevalence of measles in the town. Sowerberry, the undertaker deals in coffins. Oliver is apprenticed to this trade and gains experience. Due to measles, many children attain their deaths. Dickens writes: "The oldest inhabitants recollected no period at which measles had been so prevalent, or so fatal to infant existence; and many were the mournful processions which little Oliver headed, in a hat-band reaching down to his knees, to the indescribable admiration and emotion of all the mothers in the town."[48]

When Oliver escapes Sowerberry, he goes to London with John Dawkins. Oliver finds the place very much dirty. Dickens describes: "A dirtier or more wretched place he had never seen. The street was very narrow and muddy, and the air was impregnated with filthy odours."[49]

In *Oliver Twist*, Jacob's Island, is a watertide area of decaying warehouse and tenements. It is beyond Dockhead, in the Borough of Southwark and surrounded by a muddy ditch six or eight feet deep and fifteen or twenty wide, known as Folly Ditch. The neighbourhood is also the filthiest place. The ways leading to this place smells and possess offensive sights. Dickens writes:

> Crazy wooden galleries common to the backs of half a dozen houses, with holes from which to look upon the slime beneath; windows broken and patched, with poles thrust out on which to dry the linen that is never there; rooms so small, so filthy, so confined, that the air would seem too tainted even for the dirt and squalor which they shelter; wooden chambers thrusting themselves out above the mud, and threatening to fall into it, as some have done; dirt-besmeared walls and decaying foundations; every repulsive lineament of poverty, every loathsome indication of filth, rot, and garbage;—all these ornament the banks of Folly Ditch.[50]

Dickens hints the filthy and confined houses unsuitable for health. It is due to the lack of proper heed paid by the health authorities.

Dickens writes in *David Copperfield* of the neighbourhood near Golden Square that a building is 'decayed and dirty'. He, also, describes the bad ventilation and 'common dust-heap'. "The city has become 'unsound and even unsafe'."[51]

In *Dombey and Son*, Dickens gives a very blunt warning against the dangers of neglecting slum evils. The slum can infect the whole of society with disease. The magistrate or judge admonish the unnatural outcasts of society. They scold them for being unnatural in brutal habits, unnatural in want of decency, unnatural in losing and confounding all distinctions between good and evil; unnatural in ignorance, in vice, in recklessness, in contumacy, in mind, in looks, in everything. But the condition of the good clergymen or doctor, is no better. His life is imperilled as every breath he draws goes down into their dens, lying within the echoes of our carriage wheels and daily tread upon the pavement stones. There is the world of odious sights—millions of immortal creatures. There is the polluted air, foul with every impurity that is so poisonous to health and life. Offended, sickened, and disgusted, man makes a channel by which misery and death alone can enter. Any simple plant, or flower, or wholesome weed, cannot have its natural growth, or put its little leaves off to the sun in this foetid bed. The ghastly child, with stunted form and wicked face, hold forth on its unnatural sinfulness, and laments its being, so early, "far away from Heaven—but think a little of its having been conceived, and born and bred, in Hell!"[52] Dickens lashes the bad and miserable condition of sanitation through this description.

In different fashions, Balzac in *Les Employes* (1836) and Trollope in *The Three Clerks* (1858) discuss government service. Dickens, like these nineteenth century novelists, gives public administration as the fictional background to his novel, *Little Dorrit* (1857). He attacks the universal system of jobbing and favouritism introduced into the public service by Sir Charles Trevelyan and Sir Stafford Northcote. His creation of Circumlocution Office in *Little Dorrit* is a bitter satire on English administration. Edgar Johnson and Jack Lindsay consider that "the Circumlocution Office is a correct exposure of the evils of capitalist administration."[53]

Dickens' indictment of the ponderous inertia of the Circumlocution Office concerning the general administration of the country is prompted by the bureaucratic negligence of the conditions of the soldiers on the battlefield of Crimea. The Roebuck Report of June 18, 1855 on the distressing condition of the British Army declared that the British soldiers "were exposed...to all the sufferings and inconveniences of cold, rain, mud, and snow, on the high ground, and in the depth of winter. They suffered from fatigue, exposure, want of clothing, insufficient supplies for the healthy, and imperfect accommodation for the sick."[54] The condition of the military hospital at Scutari was miserable. The hospital had no healthy and hygienic atmosphere and there was no adequate arrangement of beds, towels, soaps, brooms, trays and laundries for the wounded soldiers.

*Little Dorrit* is a satire on the Circumlocution Office. Dickens is shocked by the inefficiencies of the civil service. William Howard Russell's articles in *The Times* described in detail the appalling suffering of wounded British soldiers in the Crimea. No sufficient preparations were made for the care of wounded. There were not sufficient surgeons. There were no dressers and nurses. There was not even linen to make bandages. Alexander Welsh comments on the satire against the Circumlocution Office that it is concerned with Dickens' exaggerated feelings of being on the point of national disaster: "The Crimean debacle was offensive to the degree that one believed...in the superior advance of civilisation in England."[55] According to him, the satire is directed not against bureaucracy but against its negligence.

Dickens wrote numerous articles in the *Household Words* on the administrative insensitivity of the British Government. In an article namely "Red Tape", Dickens presented the lethargic behaviour of English bureaucracy:

> Your public functionary who delights in Red Tape...is the peculiar curse and nuisance of England. Iron, steel, adamant,

can make no such drag-chain as Red Tape. An invasion of Red Ants in innumberable millions, would not be half so prejudicial to Great Britain, as its intolerable Red Tape.

Your Red Tapist is everywhere. He is always at hand, with a coil of Red Tape, prepared to make a small official parcel of the largest subject. In the reception room of a Government office, he will wind Red Tape round and round the sternest deputation that the country can send to him. In either House of Parliament he will pull more Red Tape out of his mouth, at a moment's notice, than a conjuror at a Fair. In letters, memoranda, and dispatches, he will spin himself into Red Tape, by the thousand yards.... He will measure, from Downing Street to the North Pole, or the heart of New Zealand, or the highest summit of the Himalaya Mountains, by inches of Red Tape.... He has but one answer to every demonstration of right, or exposition of wrong, and it is. 'My good Sir, this is a question of Tape.'[56]

The Circumlocution Office is the result of Dickens' observation of the government officials' extreme trust and dependence upon red tape during the Crimean War. Dickens' speech on administrative reform is an attack on the governments' indifference to the British soldiers at Crimean War: "The power of Nobody is becoming so enormous in England, and he alone is responsible for so many proceedings, both in the way of commission and omission; he has so much to answer for, and is so constantly called to account."[57]

According to Dickens, the hand of this surprising person in the late war is wonderful. He leaves the tents behind. He leaves the baggage behind. He selects the worst possible ground for encampments. He provides no means of transport. He kills the horses. He paralyses the commissariat. He knows nothing of the business he professes to know and monopolises. He destroys the English Army. Nobody gives out the famous unroasted coffee. Nobody makes the hospitals more horrible. Nobody occasions all the terrible confusion of Balaklava harbour. Nobody orders the deadly Balaklava cavalry charge. The non-relief of Kars is the work of Nobody and Nobody justly and severely suffers for that infamous transaction.

In Civil matters, Nobody is active. A Civil office breaks down, in Nobody's department. A dispatch of the greatest moment is sent to a minister abroad, during the serious crisis and nobody reads it. British subjects are offended in a foreign land and nobody interferes. The loyal subjects of England, at a distance, want to exchange political, commercial, and domestic intelligence with the people and nobody stops the mail. The government, with all its powerful means and appliances, is constantly beaten and left behind by private enterprise and it is due to Nobody's fault.

The anger and disgust with the bureaucracy is obvious in the novel *Little Dorrit*. Dickens shows his contempt for officialdom in the description of Circumlocution Office. He describes how Tite Barnacle and his family administered the government departments according to the grand principle of 'How not to do it.' The novel is a satiric exposure of some of the realities of the government.

In *Little Dorrit*, Carlyle's various offices are put together in the mysterious Circumlocution Office. The office procedures serve as a mask for indifference and privilege. The toadies running the Circumlocution Office are mainly responsible for the science of 'How not to do it.' The satire of *Little Dorrit* "is directed against the monopoly of administrative power in the hands of a few, the injustice of this monopoly and its impracticality for a modern nation. Barnacles, as the name suggests, are merely parasites."[58]

The Circumlocution Office is a government department symbolising all government departments. It is a complex system of jobbery and nepotism as a result of intermarriages between the Barnacle and Stilt-stalking families and the posts given to their descendants. Dickens had Fitzjames Stephen family in mind while describing this bitter satire.

The circumlocution office is the most important department under government. No public business is performed without the acceptance of the circumlocution office. To do the plainest right or to undo the plainest wrong is quite impossible without the express authority of the Circumlocution Office. "If another

Gunpowder Plot had been discovered half an hour before the lighting of the match, nobody would have been justified in saving the Parliament until there had been half a score of boards, half a bushel of minutes, several sacks of official memoranda, and a family-vault full of ungrammatical correspondence, on the part of the Circumlocution Office."[59]

The glorious establishment involves the difficult art of governing the country. The circumlocution office with all the public departments in the art of perceiving—HOW NOT TO DO IT performs the multiple works of the government.

Dickens satirises this machinery of administration which is not quick about its action. He ridicules the routine and rule based role of the bureaucracy. He bitterly expresses the strange inclination of the circumlocution office not to work with smooth efficiency and promptness as desired.

Dickens shows that the administrative insensitivity of the Circumlocution Office has approval from Parliament: "It is true that the debates of both Houses of Parliament the whole session through, uniformly tended to the protracted deliberation; How not to do it. It is true that the royal speech at the opening of such session virtually said, My lords and gentlemen, you have a considerable stroke of work to do, and you will please to retire to your respective chambers, and discuss, How not to do it."[60]

Dickens is very much critical on the honourable ministers who support the slow process of work of the bureaucratic machinery. Sometimes, parliamentary questions are asked about its inaction. Even parliamentary motions are laid or threatened by members holding that the real aim of government is How to do it. Then the noble lord, or right honourable gentlemen defend the Circumlocution Office, by telling that "the Circumlocution Office not only was blameless in this matter, but was commendable in this matter, was extollable to the skies in this matter."[61]

Dickens talks of the Barnacle in *Little Dorrit*. Lord Decimus Tite Barnacle, rises to official heights with the mighty idea that he asks Lords that he is yet to be told that it behoves a minister of this free country to set bounds to the philanthropy, to cramp the charity, to fetter the public spirit, to contrast the enterprise, to damp the independent self-reliance, of its people..., in the great art How not to do it. When any ill-advised member of either house tries How to do it by bringing in a Bill to do it, the Bill is dead when Lord Decimus Tite Barnacle, rises up in his place, and repeats the very idea through which he has promoted himself to the official peak.

Mr. Barnacle of the Circumlocution Office is introduced as the magnificent example of the despicable and stupid acts regarding the administrative machinery. Messrs Tite Barnacle and Stiltstalking are the representatives of the twenty or thirty permanent under secretaries and heads of department. The public affairs is executed by them and meanness, folly and vulgarity are their special attributes.

The most successful piece of institutional portraiture is Dickens' presentation of the Civil Service, the citadel of ease and privilege. Dickens delineates a very funny satirical exposition of Tite Barnacle:

> He had a superior eye-glass dangling round his neck, but unfortunately had such flat orbits to his eyes, and such limp little eyelids, that it wouldn't stick in when he put it up, but kept tumbling out against his waistcoat buttons with a click that discomposed him very much.[62]

The eyeglass and the limp little eyelids ridicule the pretence and feebleness of this ruling class. The extra comic detail is endowed in the flat orbits of the eyes. The language exactly follows upper-class vagueness accompanied by the mannerism of the clicking eye-glass. "Light comedy is not an end in itself; the lightness here suggests the silliness and frivolity of what is described. The levity is part of reproach and bitter criticism."[63]

*How not to do it* is the great study and object of public departments and professional politicians round the circumlocution office. Every new premier and every new government assuming the office considers something necessary to be done but very soon they discover How not to do it. When a general election is over, every returned man who spoke during canvass because it has not been done, asserted and pledged that it is to be done, begins to devise, How it is not to be done.

The Circumlocution Office goes on mechanically, with its perfect wheel of statesmanship, How not to do it, in motion. This Office is down upon any ill-advised public servant going to do it or seeming to be in remote danger of doing it due to accident, with a minute, and a memorandum, and a letter of instructions. It is "this spirit of national efficiency in the Circumlocution Office that had gradually led to its having something to do with everything."[64]

Dickens shows that the art of perfection is 'How not to do it' achieved by the Circumlocution Office. He satirises the Circumlocution Office that has lost its efficiency. The government ministers are made inactive by the inertia of the Civil Service. This system, inert and wrong-headed, paralyses all features of science, defence, social service, government and arts. The wretched clients wait in halls, glass cases, fire proof passages. They meet office juniors who does not know the cases in hand but he has the knowledge of something of some business and by office seniors they are referred to the office and go to sections and are given forms with assurance that nothing anyone does will ever achieve anything.

The bureaucrats of the Circumlocution Office are Barnacles. Arthur Clennam makes an enquiry of the nature of debt of Mr. Dorrit which has put him into the Marshal sea prison. Mr. Barnacle replies that the Circumlocution Department may have possibly recommended. He cannot say that some public claim against the insolvent estate of a firm or co-partnership belonging to this person shall be enforced. The case may have been, during official business, referred to the Circumlocution Department for its consideration. The Department may have begun, or confirmed, a Minute making that recommendation.

Arthur Clennam is readmitted to the presence of Barnacle Junior and asks him that he wants to know the case. The latter remonstrates that he must not come into the place to know. Then Arthur Clennam asks Barnacle Junior of the precise nature of the claim of the crown against a prisoner for debt,

Mr. Dorrit. The latter threatens the former that he comes to the authority without prior appointment. But Arthur repeats his case. Then Barnacle Junior stares at him until his eye-glass falls out and scolds Arthur that he possesses no right to come to this sort of move. He, then, inquires whether it is public business and the suitor replies in affirmative. He advises him to try the Secretariat Department and asks him to consult Jenkins and the mashed potato messenger, Mr. Wobbler. Arthur goes to Mr. Wobbler and asks him about the case and Mr. Wobbler replies:

> 'Cann't inform you', observed Mr. Wobbler, apparently to his lunch.
>
> 'Never heard of it. Nothing at all to do with it. Better try Mr. Clive, second door on the left in the next passage.'
>
> 'Perhaps, he will give me the same answer.'
>
> 'Very likely', 'Don't know anything about it', said Mr. Wobbler.[65]

Dickens shows that Arthur Clennam is not given information of his enquiry by the circumlocution office regarding Dorrit's debt. He goes from one official to another to know but he is disappointed.

The role of the Court of Chancery is played by the Circumlocution Office and the governing-class family of Barnacles. Dickens has created a great satire on all aristocratic bureaucracies, "with its repertoire of the variations possible within the bureaucratic type and its desolating picture of the emotions of a man being passed on from one door to another."[66]

In *Little Dorrit*, the 'symbolic labyrinth' is the circumlocution office. It has closely linked halls, offices, passageways, and levels of authority Arthur Clennam and Daniel Doyce wander hopelessly. They fill out numerous forms and make "appeal after appeal without coming any closer to a satisfactory answer to their question."[67]

Like Kafka's hero, Daniel Doyce experiences like a criminal when he is connected to the Circumlocution Office, the labyrinthine prison changed into an institution of government. Product of the "irresponsibility and greed of the upper class, with its legion of parasitical Barnacles', the circumlocution office can imprison a man in its endless corridors and miles of Red Tape as securely as any Marshalsea or as any moral flaw."[68]

The satirical presentation of the Barnacles and the labyrinth of the Circumlocution Office is striking because ruling castes are not shown as monsters. They are charming, amiable and easy going, with their upper-class mannerisms, their relaxed casualness. The Young Barnacle tells Clennam that he must not come to the office to know.... This horrible utterance is "part of Dickens' superb creation of what A.O.J. Cockshut calls 'lazy, humane, selfish, privileged people, sheltering behind a weak barricade of minutes and forms.' According to Mr. Cockshut, Dickens was showing how all this lovable absurdity "could have consequences that were harsh and irrevocable."[69]

Dickens indicts that the business of the country is done very slowly and the inventors and projectors of improvements are treated with neglect. Dickens writes:

> 'Have you ever heard of any proprietor or inventor who failed to find it all but inaccessible, and whom it did not discourage and ill-treat?'
>
> 'I cannot say I ever have.'
>
> 'Have you ever known it to be beforehand in the adoption of any useful thing? Ever known it to set an example of any useful kind?'
>
> 'I am a good deal older than my friend here,' said Mr. Meagles, 'and I'll answer that Never.'[70]

David Doyce, Arthur Clennam's business partner, an ingenious smith and engineer, is entangled in the cobweb of public administration and fails to get a patent for his invention.

Thus, the Circumlocution Office has the "power to strangle any patent at birth by preventing its application to public use. Thus, once more, it has the power to put a man in prison, but no notion why it has done so, and no intention of doing, anything to get him out again."[71] Inefficiency, is only one of

Mr. Dickens's charges against the government. "Neglect of useful inventions and gross corruptions are thrown in by way of makeweight."[72]

The Circumlocution Office symbolises the coterie rule of a group of ignorant, muddle-headed and self-centered persons.

## JUDICIARY

Dickens had substantial experience of the Court of Chancery in his youth as a shorthand writer and journalist. He himself filed suits against persons who had pirated his works and he felt the pain of the Chancery proceedings. In 1844, he tried to stop publication of a plagiarism of *A Christmas Carol*, but finally dropped the suit against the bankrupt pirates. He failed to gain the costs from the offenders. In 1850, he wrote in *Household Words* an scathing article "The Martyrs of Chancery." *Bleak House* is his most energetic criticism of Chancery. His grievances against the Court of Chancery are expressed: "Complaints had been made of the Court of Chancery; of its dilatory proceedings; of the enormous expense which is entailed on its suitors.... It was beyond a doubt...the greatest grievance of the nation.... It was confidently asserted by persons of great weight that there were depending in that court 23,000 cases, some of which had been going on for five, ten, twenty and thirty years! that there had been spent therein thousands of pounds, to the ruin, nay, utter undoing, of many families!... that what was ordered in it one day was contradicted the next, so that in some cases there had been 500 orders or more; and that, at last, when the purses of clients began to be emptied, and their spirits a little cooled, then, by a reference to some gentleman in the country, the cause came to be suddenly ended! In one word, that the Court of Chancery was not better than "a mystery of wickedness and a standing cheat."[73]

The Chancery was old-fashioned, collapsing and parasitical. The legal functionaries lived upon the delays, obscurities and cost of litigation. Human beings were the victim of the slow and cruel process of Chancery: "It destroyed the souls and bodies of those who became involved (often through no more active intent than by being named as beneficiaries in contested wills) in its machinery."[74]

Chancery abuse had become a major topical issue during 1851. *The Times* contained a leading article on Ist January 1851 on the Court of Chancery and the columnist observed: "We believe that the time is rapidly approaching when the public necessities and the public will must triumph over the inertia of an antiquated jurisprudence and the obstacles raised by personal or professional interest...the community suffers...from a confused mass of laws, from costly and dilatory procedure, and from an inadequate number of Judges.... This opinion has now become so strong and universal in the country that active measures for the reform of the law...are becoming the test by which a large proportion of the Liberal party are disposed to try the sincerity and the capacity of their present leaders. We would crowd our columns day after day with the remonstrances which are addressed to ourselves, especially with reference to the present state of the Court of Chancery."[75] The writer points out the inertia, the confusion, the costly and delayed processes, and the vested interests hindering reform.

In *The Times*, 24 December, 1850 issue, there was a more powerful protest: "If a house be seen in a peculiarly dilapidated condition, the beholder at once exclaims, 'Surely that property must be in Chancery'; and the exclamation very correctly expresses the popular opinion as to the effect of legal proceedings generally upon all property which unluckily becomes the subject of litigation in any shape.... Success and defeat are alike fatal to litigation."[76] The same sentiment occurs as a staple motif: "The lingering and expectant suitors waste their lives as well as their substance in vain hopes, and death robs them of their wished-for triumph, if ruin have not already rendered it impossible."[77]

Reflections of the Chancery show that there were utmost difficulties in litigation. The public hated it and everybody was seriously affected by its working. It was commonly perceived as a 'terror', a 'devouring gulf', a 'den' from which no footsteps returned. "Ask why such a family was ruined, why the representatives of a wealthy man are wanderers over the face of the earth, why the butlers, and housekeepers, and gardeners of the kindest master in the world, in spite of ample legacies in his will, are rotting on parish pay, why the best house in the street is falling to decay, its windows all broken, and its very dross disappearing, why such a one drowned himself, and another is disgraced—you are just as likely as not to hear that a Chancery suit is at the bottom of it. There is no word so terrible to an Englishman as this. An honest, industrious man...will turn pale and sick at heart at the bare mention of Chancery. A suit in that court is endless, bottomless and insatiable."[78]

Robert Lowe, leader-writer, later Chancellor of the Exchequer, traced a suit introduced in 1815 in the Court of Chancery and after the passage of thirty-six years, a considerable period of time, the suit still exists: "When this old suit was new, the counsel who have succeeded to its management were probably babes in arms, and the judge before whom it is heard a truant school boy. Since the parties first applied to this dilatory tribunal for the determination of their rights three Monarchs have succeeded to the aged Prince in whose reign it was commenced.... The occupant of every throne in Europe, and every prominent office in the English Church & state, has been changed, but still the inexorable Chancery suit holds on its way, permanent in the midst of never ending change, the only immutable thing in an era of restless transition."[79]

It embittered the lives of those engaged in the 'hereditary curse' which "a suit in equity on the present system hands down to the children who are to inherit it. We leave our suits to our children just as we bequeathed to them too often our mental peculiarities and bodily infirmities. The little plaintiffs and defendants grow up for the benefit of Chancery; and she adopts them as naturally as they succeed to us."[80]

*Pickwick Papers, Oliver Twist* and *David Copperfield* express satiric digs on the corrupt and rotten legal system of Victorian England. *Bleak House* especially notes the weaknesses of the Court of Chancery with its special technique of obstruction. The wickedness of the Court of Chancery is the part of the greater evil of the British legal system. "It was, for example, the arbitrary division between Courts of "Law" and Courts of "Equity"—between actions in the Court of Common Pleas, and pleadings at the Chancery Bar—with their incompatible modes of procedure and rules of evidence—which gave the Court of Chancery its peculiar powers of working mischief. And behind the whole legal system, maintaining it and protecting it from all innovation, was the whole governing system of the country—the system which was defended and upheld by the Boodle Party no more than, or less than, by the Buffer Party—the system which in the opinion of Sir Leicester Dedlock and his swarm of parasitical cousins, could not be altered in any iota except for the worse, or without risk of opening the floodgates of revolution and anarchy."[81]

In *Bleak House*, Dickens' indictment against the Court of Chancery in particular and against the lawyers in general is severe. It shows the slyness and cunning wisdom of the legal practitioners. The theme of legal injustice is also taken up in *Oliver Twist* as Dickens introduces the figure of Mr. Fang, the police court magistrate. Dickens suggests Mr. Fang as worthless and incompetent repository of justice. The public was attentive to the improper delays, endless and huge costs, counter suits, appeals and complex process of the Court of Chancery. A case was brought to notice by Shutton Sharpe on Chancery Delays at Lord's Select Committee on Administration of Justice 1840. The case was lodged in 1832 but it was not finalised till 1840. Jarndyce and Jarndyce in *Bleak House* indicates the entanglements of vested interests and institutions encouraged by legal procedures. The Court of Chancery supported greed, hindered generous action and obstructed men's progress.

Both Dickens and Kafka started their careers in law. Dickens acted as an office boy for lawyers. He then opted reporting in Doctors' Commons. For him, the court looked like a chapel and "monkish attorneys" muddled wills and testaments there. These ecclesiastical courts were established by the side of St. Paul's. Kafka studied law and worked as a clerk. In *Bleak House* and *The Trial*, Dickens and Kafka discussed odd religious courts and "the central theme of both novels is the machinery of law crushing everybody and everything which comes under its wheels, the victim realising all its horrors without understanding its mechanism."[82]

In *Pickwick Papers*, Dickens makes a mighty protest against the English legal system by creating the dishonest figures of Dodson and Fogg. In Bardell vs. Pickwick case, he presents the vain pomposity and superficiality of the guardian of law. He humorously portrays Sergeant Buzfuz and Mr. Justice Stareleigh. He shows that Mr. Pickwick is enmeshed in the baffling nets of the law due to the idiocy and shrewdness of the legal officials.

Dickens satirically presents Doctors' Commons in *David Copperfield*. *Bleak House* presents the fog imagery. It suggests something that chokes and obfuscates like the iniquity of Jarndyce suit affects the characters of *Bleak House*. The sooty London fog envelopes the whole England and it stands for the obstructive procedures and outmoded institutions and selfish interests. The fog symbolises Chancery, and Chancery represents the complete web of clotted antiquated institutions that restrain England. The Lord High Chancellor with a fogging glory round his head implies the sinister distortions of the spirit and structure of justice in the late 18th Century England:

> On such an afternoon, if ever, the Lord High Chancellor ought to be sitting here—as here he is—with a foggy glory round his head, softly fenced in with crimson cloth and curtains, addressed by large advocate with great whiskers, a little voice, and an interminable brief, and outwardly directing his contemplation to the lantern in the roof, where he can see nothing but fog. On such an afternoon, some score of members of the High Court of Chancery bar ought to be—as here they are—mistily engaged in one of the ten thousand stages of an endless cause, tripping one another up on slippery precedents, groping knee-deep in technicalities, running their goat-hair and horse-hair warded heads against walls of words, and making a pretence of equity with serious faces, as players might.[83]

Later the Chancery shockingly spreads to include the entire country. Dickens writes in *Bleak House*, "This is the Court of Chancery; which has its decaying houses and its blighted lands in every shire; which has its worn-out lunatic in every madhouse, and its dead in every churchyard; which has its ruined suitor, with his slipshod heels and threadbare dress, borrowing and begging through the round of every man's acquaintance; which gives to monied might, the means abundantly of wearing out the right; which so exhausts finances, patience, courage, hope; so over throws the brain and breaks the heart; that there is not an honourable man among its practitioners who would not give—who does not often give—the warning, 'Suffer any wrong that can be done to you, rather than come here!'"[84]

Dickens digs heavily at the Court of Chancery. The images that construct it are those of neglected architecture. The character of the suitor foregrounded against this setting is that of lunatic and he is in the madhouse. The suitor suffered much and he is dead in the churchyard. The decrepit architecture and financial ruin of the suitor run parallel. It exhausts finances, patience, courage and hope and destroys the brain and heart. The practitioners of the Court of Chancery warn the comers to suffer the harm done but not to visit the court for justice. Jarndyce vs. Jarndyce not only enmeshes innocent and remote people at the present time but it has a terrible history. Despite of all the Lord Chancellors and interminable arguments and counter arguments of advocates the suit still lingers on:

> Jarndyce and Jarndyce drones on. This scarecrow of a suit has, in course of time, become so complicated, that no man alive knows what it means. The parties to it understand it least; but it has been observed that no two Chancery lawyers can talk about it for five minutes, without coming to a total disagreement as to all the premises. Innumberable young people have married into it; innumberable old people have died out of it. Scores of persons have deliriously found themselves made parties in Jarndyce and Jarndyce, without knowing how or why; whole families have inherited legendary hatreds with the suit. The little plaintiff or

> defendant, who was promised a new rocking-horse when Jarndyce and Jarndyce should be settled, has grown up, possessed himself of a real horse, and trotted away into the other world. Fair wards of court have faded into mothers and grandmothers; a long procession of Chancellors has come in and gone out; the legion of bills in the suit have been transformed into mere bills of mortality; there are not three Jarndyces left upon the earth perhaps, since Old Tom Jarndyce in despair blew his brains out at a coffee-house in Chancery Lane; but Jarndyce and Jarndyce still drags its dreary length before the court, perennially hopeless.[85]

The frustrating delay in the administration of justice is satirically represented. Jarndyce and Jarndyce is continuing for long. The prototypes of this unending case is numerous. Philip Hobsbaum writes: "One instance, cited by Edgar Johnson, was the Day Case, which at the time of Dickens's writing had been going on for seventeen years, had involved at any given time between seventeen and forty lawyers, and had already incurred costs of $70,000. Even more long-drawn-out was the Jennings case, which crawled on throughout the nineteenth century, from seventeen years before Dickens's birth to forty-five years after he died, amassing as it went, costs of over $250,000!"[86]

But Edgar Johnson is of the view that Jarndyce and Jarndyce is the original of the Jennings case: "Jarndyce and Jarndyce was suggested by the notorious Jennings case, involving the disputed property of an old miser of Acton who had died intestate in 1798, leaving almost $1,500,000. When one of the claimants died in 1915 the case was still unsettled and the cost amounted to $250.00."[87] The Chancery as an institution has no any real social role. From this centre of social anarchy emanate mysteries and confusions to engulf the remotely concerned people with it. If the single case of Jarndyce and Jarndyce can spread evil far and wide, the total of evil caused by the whole court of Chancery may be greater no doubt:

> How many people out of the suit, Jarndyce and Jarndyce has stretched forth its unwholesome hand to spoil and corrupt, would be a very wide question...no man's nature has been made better by it. In trickery, evasion,

> procrastination, spoliation, botheration, under false pretences of all sorts, there are influences that can never come to good.... The receiver in the cause has acquired a goodly sum of money by it, but has acquired too a distrust of his own mother, and a contempt for his own kind.... Shirking and sharking, in all their many varieties, have been shown broadcast by the ill-fated cause; and even those who have contemplated its history from the outermost circle of such evil, have been insensibly tempted into a loose way of letting bad things alone to take their own bad course, and a loose belief that if the world go wrong, it was, in some off-hand manner, never meant to go right.[88]

Dickens shows that Jarndyce and Jarndyce has evil influences. It seems a terrible game, infecting with unreality the people coming into its contacts. It is fatally pervasive and its "dominance are such that those influenced by it are forced to view at least part of their world through its distorted and cloudy mirror."[89]

In *Bleak House*, Krook, nicknamed the Lord Chancellor, and his rag and bone shop is a parody and deadly caricature of Chancery: "KROOK, RAG AND BOTTLE WAREHOUSE.... In all parts of the window were quantities of dirty bottles, blacking bottles, medicine bottles, ginger-beer and soda-water bottles, pickle bottles, wine bottles, ink bottles: I am reminded by mentioning the latter, that the shop had, in several little particulars, the air of being in a legal neighbourhood, and of being, as it were, a dirty hanger on and disowned relation of the law.... There was a little tottering bench of shabby old volumes, outside the door, labelled 'Law Books', all at 9d. Some of the inscriptions I have enumerated were written in law-hand, like the papers I had seen in Kenge and Carboy's office, and the letters I had so long received from the firm. Among them was one, in the same writing, having nothing to do with the business of the shop, but announcing that a respectable man aged forty-five wanted engrossing or copying to execute with neatness and despatch: Address to Nemo, care of Mr. Krook within.... A little way within the shop-door lay heaps of old crackled parchment scrolls, and discoloured and dog's-eared law-papers. I could have fancied that all the rusty keys, of which there must have been hundreds huddled together as old iron, had once belonged to doors of rooms or strong chests in lawyers' offices. The litter of rags tumbled partly into and partly out of a one-legged wooden scale, hanging without any counterpoise from a beam, might have been counsellors' bands and gowns torn up. One had only to fancy, as Richard whispered to Ada and me while we all stood looking in, that yonder bones in a corner, piled together and picked very clean, were the bones of clients, to make the picture complete."[90]

The parallels are further emphasised through the staple images of disrepair 'wasting away and going to rack and ruin' and a dark rusty muddle, all rust and cobwebs: "You see I have so many things here", he resumed, holding up the lantern, "of so many kinds, and all, as the neighbours think (but they know nothing), wasting away and going to rack and ruin, that that's why they have given me and my place a christening.... And I have a liking for rust and must and cobwebs. And all's fish that comes to my net. And I can't abear to part with anything I once lay hold of (or so my neighbours think, but what do they know?) or to alter anything or to have any sweeping nor scouring, nor cleaning, nor repairing going on about me. Tha'ts the way I've got the ill name of Chancery. I don't mind. I go to see my noble and learned brother pretty well everyday, when he sits in the Inn. He don't notice me, but I notice him. There's no great odds betwixt us. We both grub on in a muddle. Hi, Lady Jane!"[91]

The passage illustrates with startling realism the two tier correspondence between settings and contexts on the one hand and the persons who preside over and gain from it on the other. There is a sustained likeness between Krook's shop and the Chancery and Krook and the Lord Chancellor. As chancery, Krook does not part with somebody when it is taken in catch. Both deal in a muddle. Dickens sharpens the point still more when he writes:

> A large grey cat leaped from some neighbouring shelf on his shoulder, and startled us all.

> 'Hi! show 'em how you scratch. Hi! Tear, my lady!', said her master.
>
> The cat leaped down, and ripped at a bundle of rags with her tigerish claws, with a sound that it set my teeth on edge to hear.
>
> 'She'd do as much for any one I was to set her on', said the old man. 'I deal in cat-skins among other general matters, and hers was offered to me. It's a very fine skin, as you may see, but I didn't have it stripped off! That warn't like Chancery practice though, says you![92]

The feline presence is represented as cruel and fierce. It is a bad, destructive tearing force: "The Court of Chancery is representative not only of corruption and social decay, but is itself symbolised by the junk shop kept by Krook, known as 'Lord Chancellor' and his savage cat expressive of 'strict statutes and most biting laws'."[93]

Law infects and brings down the people coming into contact with its terrible system. Krook talks to the wards in Jarndyce that Tom Jarndyce visited Krook often. Tom was restless and strolled about when the case was on. He forbade the little shopkeepers to keep in the Chancery. Dickens writes of Tom's observation of the Chancery: "For," says he "it's being ground to bits in a slow mill; it's being roasted at a slow fire; it's being stung to death by single bees; it's being drowned by drops; it's going mad by grains."[94]

Tom Jarndyce is so fed up with his case that he blows his brains out. Krook describes: "He came in at the door", said the old man, slowly pointing an imaginary track along the shop, "on the day he did it—the whole neighbourhood had said for months before, that he would do it, of a certainty sooner or later—he came in at the door that day, and walked along there, and sat himself on a bench that stood there, and asked me (you'll judge I was a mortal sight younger then) to fetch him a pint of wine. 'For', says he, 'Krook, I am much depressed; my cause is on again, and I think I'm nearer judgement than I ever was.'" I hadn't a mind to leave him alone; and I persuaded him to go to the tavern over the way there, t' other side my lane

(I mean Chancery Lane); and I followed and looked in at the window, and saw him, comfortable as I thought in the arm-chair by the fire, and company with him. I hadn't hardly got back here, when I heard a shot go echoing and rattling right away into the inn. I ran out—neighbours ran out—twenty of us cried at once, "Tom Jarndyce."[95]

Krook gives an account of sufferings in Chancery and consequent suicide of Tom Jarndyce. The cousins sum up a dialogue that is a heavy blow on the Court of Chancery. To them it was a shock to come into the inheritance of a protracted misery:

> 'Quite an adventure for a morning in London!' said Richard, with a sigh. 'Ah, cousin, cousin, it's a weary word this Chancery!'
>
> 'It is to me, and has been ever since I can remember', returned Ada. 'I am grieved that I should be the enemy—as I suppose I am—of a great number of relations and others; and that they should be my enemies—as I suppose they are; and that we should all be ruining one another, without knowing how or why, and be in constant doubt and discord all our lives. It seems very strange, as there must be right somewhere, that an honest judge in real earnest has not been able to find out through all these years where it is.'
>
> 'Ah, cousin!' said Richard. 'Strange, indeed! all this wasteful wanton chess-playing is very strange. To see that composed Court yesterday jogging on so serenely, and to think of the wretchedness of the pieces on the board, gave me the headache and the heartache both together. My head ached with wondering how it happened, if men were neither fools nor rascals; and my heart ached to think they could possibly be either. But at all events, Ada—I may call you Ada?'[96]

Ada is very much critical of the sufferings of the chancery. The preceeding images of muddles and cobwebs permeates to the obfuscation of truth, which it is ironically the business of the legal system to unravel: "What rightly distresses Ada is the realisation that merely by being born they are enemies in the struggle for existence which the laissez faire society of course did nothing to mitigate; hence the stress laid on the fact that the wide variety of people concerned in the Jarndyce case have been born into it willy-nilly, and, like Miss Flite's symbolic birds, 'die in prison'."[97] Richard gets a headache and heartache due to the evil influences of the Court of Chancery. Jarndyce's own account is devastating. He talks of Jarndyce and Jarndyce: "A certain Jarndyce, in an evil hour, made a great fortune, and made a great Will. In the question how the trusts under that Will are to be administered, the fortune left by the Will is squandered away; the legatees under the Will are reduced to such a miserable condition that they would be sufficiently punished if they had committed an enormous crime in having money left them; and the Will itself is made a dead letter...ever ends. And we can't get out of the suit on any terms, for we are made parties to it, and must be parties to it, whether we like it or not. But it won't do to think of it! When my great uncle, poor Tom Jarndyce, began to think of it, it was the beginning of the end!"[98]

Everybody is given copies of the court's proceedings. Cart loads of papers are accumulated. Questions are sent to Equity and Law but both are unable to do something without the solicitor and the counsel of the both parties. The process is going on but never ends. Dickens satirises the lengthy and expensive course of administration of Justice. Jarndyce terms the practice of Chancery as 'Wiglomeration':

> 'More Wiglomeration', said he. 'It's the only name I know for the thing. He is a ward in Chancery, my dear. Kenge and Carboy will have something to say about it; Master Somebody-a-sort of ridiculous Sexton, digging graves for the merits of causes in a back room at the end of Quality Court, Chancery Lane will have something to say about it; Counsel will have something to say about it; the Chancellor will have something to say about it; the Satellites will have something to say about it; they will all have to be handsomely fee'd, all round, about it; the whole thing will be vastly ceremonious, wordy, unsatisfactory, and expensive,

and I call it, in general, Wiglomeration. How mankind ever came to be afflicted with Wiglomeration, or for whose sins these young people ever fell into a pit of it, I don't know; so it is.'[99]

Dickens, through Laurence Boythorn, projects his deep detestation and anger for the Chancery. The Chancery court has such heavy corruption that it cannot be reformed. Laurence Boythorn converses with Jarndyce and his outburst of contempt at the mention of Chancery is thus narrated by Dickens:

> "There never was such an infernal cauldron as that Chancery, on the face of the earth!", said Mr. Boythorn. "Nothing but a mine below it on a busy day in term time, with all its records, rules, and precedents collected in it, and every functionary belonging to it also, high and low, upward and downward, from its son the Accountant-General to its father the Devil, and the whole blown to atoms with ten thousand hundred-weight of gun-powder, would reform it in the least."[100]

Rick who is a ward in Jarndyce and Jarndyce, is very much interested in the case. Under the influence of Chancery he becomes careless. He is caught up in a vast mechanical system of which he is a helpless victim:

> These were my thoughts about Richard. I thought I often observed besides, how right my guardian was in what he had said; and that the uncertainties and delays of the Chancery suit had imparted to his nature something of the careless spirit of a gamester, who felt that he was part of a great gaming system.[101]

For Rick Carstone, the Chancery is not only an oppressive social institution capable of reform but it is also a curse upon the human condition. Irrational, and run by an enormous machinery of dehumanised creatures "this monstrous collection of debris asserts itself upon the suitor before the court-born into the case or thrust into it—with the promise of a total resolution that it cannot help but frustrate a bright future that it cannot help but blight. Its monumental absurdity that promises the clarity of order attracts irresistibly, feeds slowly and long, destroys utterly. It functions as this more than social evil, as this sphinx, for Rick, for Miss Flite, for Gridley, and for countless others, even as such symbols of the Court as Krook and Mr. Tulkinghorn considerably exceed mere human dimensions."[102]

When Rick is entangled deeply in the case and goes to lawyers for advice, his nature changes. He begins to mistrust and suspect John Jarndyce. The latter complains of this to Esther and infers that this is not his fault. It is due to the chancery suit. Dickens writes:

> 'Is it possible, Guardian', I asked, amazed, 'that Richard can be suspicious of you?'
>
> 'Ah, my love, my love', he said, 'it is in the subtle poison of such abuses to breed such diseases. His blood is infected, and objects lose their natural aspects in his sight. It is not his fault.'
>
> 'But it is a terrible misfortune, Guardian.'
>
> 'It is a terrible misfortune, little woman, to be ever drawn within the influences of Jarndyce and Jarndyce. I know none greater. By little and little he has been induced to trust in that rotten reed, and it communicates some portion of its rottenness to everything around him.'[103]

The rottenness of the case infiltrates the very characters of human beings who are unfortunate to be connected to it. When Esther says to her guardian, John Jarndyce that little experience will teach Richard what a false and wretched thing Chancery is. Then John Jarndyce replies:

> 'We will hope so, my Esther', said Mr. Jarndyce, '.... There are not many grown and matured men living while we speak, good men too, who, if they were thrown into this same court as suitors, would not be vitally changed and depreciated within three years—within two—within one. How can we stand amazed at poor Rick? A young man so unfortunate', ...'cannot at first believe (who could ?) that Chancery is what it is. He looks to it, flushed and fitfully, to do something with his interests, and bring them to some

settlement. It procrastinates, disappoints, tries, tortures him; wears out his sanguine hopes and patience, thread by thread; but he still looks to it, and hankers after it, and finds his whole world treacherous and hollow.'[104]

It is a continued verbal attack on the Court of Chancery. Rick, is caught in the chancery's net and emphasizes that Chancery taints everybody with no hope of exemption. He says to Esther:

> 'Come, sister, come', said Richard, a little more gaily, 'you will be fair with me at all events. If I have the misfortune to be under that influence, so has he. If it has a little twisted me, it may have a little twisted him, too. I don't say that he is not an honourable man, out of all this complication and uncertainty; I am sure he is. But it taints everybody. You know it taints everybody. You have heard him say so fifty times. Then why should he escape?'[105]

According to Rick Carstone, Chancery has evil influences on everybody. It develops into a metaphysical entity, "reflecting the nature of existence as much as the legal tangles and abuses of Victorian England."[106] Richard is reduced to a scarecrow due to the evil influences of Jarndyce and Jarndyce. John Jarndyce observed Richard at dinner slovenly in dress, careless in manners, often relapsing into dull withdrawals. His eyes which were once blue and merry had waned to an exhausted restlessness. The perceptible transformation signified "a ruin Richard's youth and youthful beauty had all fallen away."[107]

Jarndyce and Jarndyce is heard in the court at Westminster. Richard and Esther are attending the court. Everything goes on smoothly. Though Esther's eyes underneath lurks the roughness of the suitors' lives and deaths; she observes the trapping of formality and ponders on the waste and want, the representative misery and the perpetual deferment of hope. This polite show continues calmly with the observation of the protocol of respectability "to behold the Lord Chancellor, and the whole array of practitioners under him, looking at one another and at the spectators, as if nobody had ever heard that all over England the name in which they were assembled was a bitter jest: was held in universal horror, contempt, and indignation: was known for something so flagrant and bad, that little short of a miracle could bring any good out of it to anyone: this was so curious and self-contradictory to me, who had no experience of it".[108] Esther, sitting where Richard had put her, observes and listens to the proceedings enveloped in a sense of unreality. The only human being who could make any sense of it was "poor little Miss Flite, the madwoman, standing on a bench, and nodding at it."[109]

Dickens' satire in this illustration is double edged. While the Chancery continues under the satiric manner there is the other edge of satire directed at all those who acquiesce and collaborate to support this institution. In doing so, the people actively participate in the acquiescence to their own subordination and the continuation of status quo.

John Jarndyce talks of the unreasonableness and injustices of the Jarndyce and Jarndyce case in the Court of Chancery. Richard is still delusioned. John Jarndyce tells Esther: 'Ah, Dame Trot, Dame Trot!' returned my guardian, 'what shall we find reasonable in Jarndyce and Jarndyce! Unreason and injustice at the top, unreason and injustice at the heart, and at the bottom, unreason and injustice from beginning to end—if it ever has an end—how should poor Rick, always hovering near it, pluck reason out of it? He no more gathers grapes from thorns, or figs from thistles, than older men did, in old times.'[110]

There is gross corruption and delay in the administration of justice. It is quite surprising that Richard confided in Jarndyce and Jarndyce. The monumental suit in the Chancery is brought to close:

> 'Mr. Kenge', said Allan, appearing enlightened all in a moment. 'Excuse me, our time presses. Do I understand that the whole estate is found to have been absorbed in costs?'
>
> 'Hem! I believe so', returned Mr. Kenge. 'Mr. Vholes, what do you say?'
>
> 'I believe so', said Mr. Vholes.

'And thus the suit lapses and melts away?'

'Probably', returned Mr. Kenge. 'Mr. Vholes?'

'Probably', said Mr. Vholes.[111]

A long suit finally ends but it is not valuable to the wards in Jarndyce. "The only event in the Court of Chancery that proves to have significant consequences for the people outside is the cessation of Jarndyce and Jarndyce when the whole property in dispute has been consumed in legal costs. But this is itself a conclusion reached by the stern requirements of economics rather than by the arcane logic of the law. Chancery affects men's lives the way God does, not by direct intervention in human affairs, but by commanding belief or disbelief."[112] The Jarndyce suit is finally reduced to a single image: the tons of paper "recording the endless processes of the trial which are dumped in the courtroom".[113]

The interminable case of Jarndyce and Jarndyce receives the status of monster capable of swallowing up generations of people passing its ways: "The one great principle of the English law is, to make business for itself. There is no other principle distinctly, certainly, and consistently maintained through all its narrow turnings. Viewed by this light it becomes a coherent scheme, and not the monstrous maze the laity are apt to think it. Let them but once clearly perceive that its grand principle is to make business for itself at their expense, and surely they will cease to grumble."[114] The sweeping indictment of the whole legal system of Great Britain is thus a major achievement of Dickens in *Bleak House*: "Urged by such a ruthless theory, which had been born in a solicitor's office and an obsolete ecclesiastical court, the novelist yielded more than once to the temptation of turning his fiction into a weapon of attack against the law and the legal system of his country."[115]

Mr. Vholes, the lawyer, represents the vested interests of a corrupt society and so the privileged defend and patronise his interest: "Now you cannot afford—I will say, the social system cannot afford—to lose an order of men like Mr. Vholes. Diligent, persevering, steady, acute in business. My dear sir, I understand your present feelings against the existing state of things, which I grant to be a little hard in your case; but I can never raise my voice for the demolition of a class of men like Mr. Vholes."[116]

The nineteenth century society consisted of two broadly defined classes, the exploiters and the exploited, and chancery is a paradigm of that society. "Conversation Kenge may use that 'respectable man' Mr. Vholes as a means of defending the excesses of the system, but we have a pretty shrewd idea that it is not Mr. Vholes' well being with which he is mainly concerned."[117] The respectability of Mr. Vholes has been mentioned strongly as an example before Parliamentary committees and has been said repeatedly in private talks in private conversation. Mr. Vholes' respectability is cited by the forces of reaction, as a reason for blocking all efforts for reform of the English Law:

> So in familiar conversation, private authorities no less disinterested will remark that they don't know what this age is coming to; that we are plunging down precipices; that now here is something else gone; that these changes are death to people like Vholes; a man of undoubted respectability, with a father in the Vale of Taunton, and three daughters at home. Take a few steps more in this direction, say they, and what is to become of Vholes's father? Is he to perish? And of Vholes's daughters? Are they to be shirt-makers or governesses? As though, Mr. Vholes and his relations being minor cannibal chiefs, and it being proposed to abolish cannibalism, indignant champions were to put the case thus: Make man-eating unlawful, and you starve the Vholeses![118]

Dickens undermines the concept of the respectable man in Victorian society with its ethics of economic cannibalism. The blocking of reforms in English Law is indicated through the sarcasm of Mr. Vholes for maintaining the balance of social harmony.

The argument regarding the nature of English institution is developed with sardonic wit from the fact that Mr. Vholes is so respectable that he cannot be sacrificed: "But the law is only the archetype of those vested interests that plunder society under the guise of being society, that strangle the general welfare, that grow fat on the miseries of the poor. It is one of the instruments that give 'monied might the means abundantly of wearing out the right,' the visible symbol behind which lurk the forces of greed and privilege spinning their labyrinthine webs of corruption."[119] Dickens clearly shows that the Chancery Court against which his attack is levelled is not only attacked in itself. It is attacked still more as a type and a symbol of the whole wrong embodied in the archaic and rotten constitution of society. Dickens compares this wrong to "cannibalism practised on a vaster and more horrible scale."[120] *The Times* had renewed the complaints of the chancery commission, Russell, the Prime Minister, brought out a Bill on the subject,' but it proved to be totally inadequate. Hobsbaum points out: "So Noodle and Doodle aid and abet the grubbing and grinding lawyers; and they all succeed in bringing about the state of affairs that includes Poor Jo, Tom-all-Alone's and the wards in Jarndyce."[121]

Lady Dedlock of Chesney Wold has also a chancery suit related to her land which is supervised by Mr. Tulkinghorn. There is the usual repetition of the staple motifs of delay and expense: "Sir Leicester has no objection to an interminable chancery suit. It is a slow, expensive, British, constitutional kind of thing. To be sure, he has not a vital interest in the suit in question, her part in which was the only property my Lady brought him; and he has a shadowy impression that for his name—the name of Dedlock—to be in a cause, and not in the title of that cause, is a most ridiculous accident. But he regards the Court of Chancery, even if it should involve an occasional delay of justice and a trifling amount of confusion, as a something, devised in conjunction with a variety of other somethings, by the perfection of human wisdom, for the eternal settlement (humanly speaking) of everything. And he is upon the whole of a fixed opinion, that to give the sanction of his countenance to any complaints respecting it, would be to encourage some person in the lower classes to rise up somewhere-like Wat Tyler."[122]

When Richard, Ada and Esther are about to leave the Court of Chancery, they are confronted by a little eccentric woman, Miss Flite:

> 'Oh!' said she. 'The wards in Jarndyce! Very happy, I am sure, to have the honour! It is a good omen for youth, and hope, and beauty, when they find themselves in this place, and don't know what's to come of it.'
>
> 'Mad!' whispered Richard, not thinking she could hear him.
>
> 'Right! Mad, young gentleman', she returned so quickly that he was quite abashed. 'I was a ward myself. I was not mad at that time', curtseying low, and smiling between every little sentence. 'I had youth and hope I believe, beauty. It matters very little now. Neither of the three served or saved me. I have the honour to attend court regularly. With my documents. I expect a judgement. Shortly. On the Day of Judgement. I have discovered that the sixth seal mentioned in the Revelations is the Great Seal. It has been open a long time ! Pray accept my blessing.[123]

Dickens uses ornithological images relating to Miss Flite's possessions to narrate the chancery victimhood. She keeps a number of linnets and larks in cages that symbolise the victims of chancery. Dickens tells the painful human condition in a chancery world through these birds: "I began to keep the little creatures", she said, "with an object that the wards will readily comprehend. With the intention of restoring them to liberty. When my judgement should be given. Ye-es!"[124]

The trial in the Court of Chancery is long and justice is delayed and the birds have short period of life so they are dying in imprisonment. Death in reality parallels a symbolic death at the Chancery. Miss Flite is however not entirely certain of the Dickensian devices of the literal and the symbolic. There seems the fair possibility that the symbolic may mimic the literal and that she may become the fate of her imprisoned birds: 'I positively doubt sometimes, I do assure you, whether while matters are still unsettled, and the sixth or Great Seal still prevails, I may not one day be found lying stark and senseless here, as I have found so many birds!'[125] The touch of horror is given when Krook, the nick-named Lord Chancellor adds:

> 'When my noble and learned brother gives his Judgement, they're to be let go free', said Krook, winking at us again. 'And then', he added, whispering and grinning, 'if that ever was to happen—which it won't—the birds that have never been caged would kill'em.'[126]

The enemy of the birds, the feline image of the twin Lord Chancellor, is "the Law, and we are confirmed in, or reminded of this identification when we get to Mr. Vholes".[127] Miss Flite speaks of the Court of Chancery as a final cause drawing men to their destruction by means of its irresistible magnetic attraction:

> 'There's a cruel attraction in the place. You can't leave it. And you must expect'.... It's the Mace and Seal upon the table.
>
> What could they do, did she think? I mildly asked her.
>
> "Draw," returned Miss Flite. "Draw people on, my dear. Draw peace out of them. I have felt them even drawing my rest away in the night. Cold and glittering devils!"[128]

Of her own case Miss Flite narrates: "First, our father was drawn—slowly. Home was drawn with him. In a few years, he was a fierce, sour, angry bankrupt, without a kind word or a kind look for any one. He had been so different, Fitz-Jarndyce. He was drawn to a debtor's prison. There he died. Then our brother was drawn—swiftly—to drunkenness. And rags. And death. Then my sister was drawn. Hush! Never ask to what! Then I was ill, and in misery; and heard, as I had often heard before, that this was all the work of Chancery. When I got better, I went to look at the Monster. And then I found out how it was, and I was drawn to stay there."[129]

Miss Flite warns the wards in Jarndyce of their possible ruin by the Court of Chancery:

> I am a little rambling. But I have noticed. I have seen many new faces come, unsuspicious, within the influence of the

Mace and Seal, in these many years. As my father's came there. As my brother's. As my sister's. As my own. I hear Conversation Kenge, and the rest of them, say to the new faces, "Here's little Miss Flite. O you are new here; and you must come and be presented to little Miss Flite!" "Very good. Proud I am sure to have the honour!" And we all laugh. But, Fitz-Jarndyce, I know what will happen. I know, far better than they do, when the attraction has begun. I know the signs, my dear. I saw them begin in Gridley. And I saw them end. Fitz-Jarndyce, my love, speaking low again: "I saw them beginning in our friend the Ward in Jarndyce. Let someone hold him back. Or he'll be drawn to ruin."[130]

Dickens discusses the meaningless delays and complicated procedures of the Court of Chancery that leads to the ruin of the half-insane and illiterate Krook—a victim of the legal system—who always poses to be the Lord Chancellor, the frustrated Miss Flite, driven half crazy and Richard who depends a lot on the verdict and finally pays the penalty by undergoing psychological and moral deterioration. Richard dies on learning that the Jarndyce and Jarndyce has collapsed. Miss Flite restores her birds their liberty. She has given up expecting a judgement in her favour. She realises that there is no justice obtainable in this world.

The Gridley case is based on an actual case in Staffordshire sent to Dickens by W. Challinor on 11 March, 1852. The original case is about a small farmer who disputed a Will to decide the part of a legacy his brother had received in advance. It was "made public by a disinterested person who was professionally acquainted with the whole of the monstrous wrong from beginning to end."[131]

Gridley is in the process of self-destruction:

'Mr. Jarndyce', said Gridley, with a rough sort of salutation, 'You bear your wrongs more quietly than I can bear mine. More than that, I tell you—and I tell this gentleman, and these young ladies, if they are friends of yours—that if I took my wrongs in any other way, I should be driven mad!

> It is only by resenting them, and by revenging them in my mind, and by angrily demanding the justice I never get, that I am able to keep my wits together.' 'It is only that', he said, speaking in a homely, rustic way, and with great vehemence. 'You may tell me that I over-excite myself. I answer that it's in my nature to do it, under wrong, and I must do it. There's nothing between doing it, and sinking into the smiling state of the poor little mad woman that haunts the court. If I was once to sit down under it, I should become imbecile.'[132]

Gridley has sorrowful experiences of the Courts of Equity. He is pained for twenty-five years. In the court, he is made the butt of jests by other occupants of the court. His wit is solid because he is resenting and revenging the wrongs in his mind. He is an innocent victim of chancery. He narrates the origin and process of the case:

> 'I am one of two brothers. My father (a farmer) made a Will, and left his farm and stock, and so forth, to my mother, for her life. After my mother's death all was to come to me, except a legacy of three hundred pounds that I was then to pay my brother. My mother died. My brother, sometime afterwards claimed his legacy. I, and some of my relations, said that he had had a part of it already, in board and lodging, and some other things. Now mind! That was the question, and nothing else. No one disputed the Will; no one disputed anything but whether part of that three hundred pounds had been already paid or not. To settle that question, my brother filing a bill, I was obliged to go into this accursed Chancery; I was forced there, because the law forced me, and would let me go nowhere else. Seventeen people were made defendants to that simple suit! It first came on, after two years. It was then stopped for another two years, while the Master (may his head rot off!) inquired whether I was my father's son—about which there was no dispute at all with any mortal creature. He then found out that there were not defendants enough—remember, there were only seventeen as yet! but that we

> must have another who had been left out; and must begin all over again. The costs at that time—before the thing was begun!—were three times the legacy. My brother would have given up the legacy, and joyful, to escape more costs. My whole estate, left to me in that will of my father's, has gone in costs. The suit, still undecided, has fallen into rack, and ruin, and despair, with everything else—and here I stand, this day! Now, Mr. Jarndyce, in your suit there are thousands and thousands involved where in mine there are hundreds. Is mine less hard to bear, or is it harder to bear, when my whole living was in it, and has been thus shamefully sucked away?'[133]

Gridley's case is delayed and the suit has exhausted his costs. He complains of his treatment in an interminable chancery suit which is driving him bad. But to his utter dismay, he is caught in a great mechanical system which in many ways anticipates the bureaucratic image and existential futility of Franz Kafka:

> The system! I am told, on all hands, it's the system. I must n't look to individuals. It's the system. I mustn't go into court, and say, "My Lord, I beg to know this from you—is this right or wrong? Have you the face to tell me I have received justice, and therefore am dismissed?" My Lord knows nothing of it. He sits there to administer the system. I mustn't go to Mr. Tulkinghorn, the solicitor in Lincoln's Inn Fields, and say to him when he makes me furious, by being so cool and satisfied—as they all do; for I know they gain by it while I lose, don't I?—I mustn't say to him, I will have something out of someone for my ruin, by fair means or foul! He is not responsible. It's the system. But if I do no violence to any of them, here—I may! I don't know what may happen if I am carried beyond myself at last!—I will accuse the individual workers of that system against me, face to face, before the great eternal bar![134]

Gridley has become violent due to the generation of abject futility by the Court of Chancery. His temperament undergoes transformation as he engages in socially and institutionally unacceptable conduct to suffer custody but it seems therapeutically cathartic in some ways:

> Mr. Jarndyce,...! I am violent, I know. I ought to know it. I have been in prison for contempt of court. I have been in prison for threatening the solicitor. I have been in this trouble, and that trouble, and shall be again. I am the man from Shropshire, and I sometimes go beyond amusing them—though they have found it amusing, too, to see me committed into custody,.... I tell them, that if I did restrain myself, I should become imbecile. I was a good-enough-tempered man once, I believe. People in my part of the country say they remember me so; but, now, I must have this vent under my sense of injury, or nothing could hold my wits together. "It would be far better for you, Mr. Gridley", the Lord Chancellor told me last week, "not to waste your time here, and to stay, usefully employed, down in Shropshire", "My Lord, my Lord, I know it would", said I to him, "and it would have been far better for me never to have heard the name of your high office; but unhappily for me, I can't undo the past, and the past drives me here!"[135]

He comes to George to fire shots to keep his wits together. George describes Gridley's conduct to John Jarndyce: "Why, the man was so badgered, and worried, and tortured, by being knocked about from post to pillar, and from pillar to post",... that he got out of sorts. I don't believe he had any idea of taking aim at anybody; but he was in that condition of resentment and violence, that he would come and pay for fifty shots, and fire away till he was red hot. One day I said to him when there was nobody by, and he had been talking to me angrily about his wrongs, "If this practice is a safety-valve, comrade, well and good; but I don't altogether like your being so bent upon it, in your present state of mind; I'd rather you took to something else." I was on my guard for a blow, he was that passionate; but he received it in very good part, and left off directly.[136]

In a manner reminiscent of Swift, Dickens presents colourful and varied lawyers with an insight that is essentially satiric. Man lives in the expectation of justice and his desire of it has created the law, but human nature, in practice, has produced lawyers with vested interests. The immoral role of lawyers is evident when John Jarndyce tells Esther about Jarndyce and Jarndyce:

> The Lawyers have twisted it into such a state of bedevilment that the original merits of the case have long disappeared from the face of the earth. It's about a Will, and the trusts under a Will—or it was, once. It's about nothing but Costs, now. We are always appearing, and disappearing, and swearing, and interrogating, and filing, and cross filing, and arguing, and sealing, and motioning, and referring, and reporting, and revolving about the Lord Chancellor and all his satellites, and equitably waltzing ourselves off to dusty death, about Costs. That's the great question. All the rest, by some extraordinary means, has melted away.[137]

A prime representative of the profession Mr. Vholes is given Dickensian touches of exaggeration and diminution. The very name indicates a rodent and it undermines riverbanks. It embodies the prejorative associations of the shady tricks of card games. Mr. Vholes is thus narrated:

> Mr. Vholes (was) a sallow man with pinched lips that looked as if they were cold, a red eruption here and there upon his face, tall and thin, about fifty years of age, high-shouldered, and stooping. Dressed in black, black-gloved, and buttoned to the chin, there was nothing so remarkable in him as a lifeless manner, and a slow fixed way he had of looking at Richard.[138]

Richard is entangled in Jarndyce and Jarndyce and Vholes is to assist at his ruin. He has come to take him back to London to watch the action in the court. The performative art situates the predatory in the aesthetics of a ritual. It is carefully constructed gothic image forebooding in the warm darkness with the road hedged and lined with looming trees. Against this backdrop that approximates conditions of painting, the foregrounded action is that of a performance: ensnaring a prey through charm:

> Mr. Vholes, quite still, black-gloved, and buttoned up, looking at him as if he were looking at his prey and charming it. I have before me the whole picture of the warm dark night, the summer lightning, the dusty track of road closed in by hedgerows and high trees, the gaunt pale horse with his ears pricked up, and the driving away at speed to Jarndyce and Jarndyce.[139]

Richard and Vholes together express on a small scale the complete nature of Chancery. The former has his faith in wealth and has conviction in the court's capacity to fulfil his wishes. Through such dependence the court is sustained: "Vholes is given further employment and hope turns to despair. The victim is willing and becomes prey to the life-devouring predator."[140] Vholes is seen by Dickens as a ravenous flock of birds of prey: "an avaricious tribe of extortioners making an unsavoury living out of what was, in effect, 'essentially a form of considered and organised oppression' dedicated to one great principle—'to make money'."[141]

Mr. Vholes is a representative figure of corrupt, dishonest and greedy lawyer. His only delight is to exploit his clients. Richard sits in the chamber of his lawyer and Mr. Vholes looks at Richard with a gaze. The predatory feline image further amplifies the narrative: "Mr. Vholes, after glancing at the official cat who is patiently watching a mouse's hole, fixes his charmed gaze again on his young client, and proceeds in his buttoned-up-half-audible voice, as if there were an unclean spirit in him that will neither come out nor speak out."[142]

Vholes is so insensitive and Richard is 'wasting away beneath the eyes of this adviser.'[143] J.H. Miller comments: "But he is slowly consumed by his vampire like lawyer, Vholes, just as the Jarndyce and Jarndyce is entirely consumed in costs."[144] When the two processes are, complete, Vholes gives a gasp showing that he has swallowed the last bit of his client. In the name of looking the interests of his client Richard, Mr. Vholes thwarts him and satisfies his self-interest. He is the product of a materialistic society where generosity and honesty are restricted and where men work for making money only.

In the judicial system, the judges, jury, magistrates, the judicial officers, lawyers and barristers are Dickens' object of satire. Justice Stareleigh and the magistrate Nupkins are presented as comic pictures of laughter and fun. Mr. Tulkinghorn, solicitor to the Court of Chancery and legal adviser to Lord Leicester, is an agent of destruction. He manipulates his employers, hates his clients, possesses insatiable desire for power and thus tries to expose and humiliate Lady Dedlock. He is a treacherous and disloyal fellow and the blackness of his mind is revealed by his black dress:

> One peculiarity of his black clothes, and of his black stockings, be they silk or worsted is, that they never shine. Mute, close, irresponsive to any glancing light, his dress is like himself. He never converses, when not professionally consulted. He is found sometimes, speechless but quite at home, at corners of dinner-tables in great country houses, and near doors of drawing-rooms.[145]

Mr. Tulkinghorn "carries family secrets in every limb of his body, and every crease of his dress".[146] The imagery of dust shows the nullity of this solicitor: "Plenty of dust comes in at Mr. Tulkinghorn's window, and plenty more has generated among his furniture and papers. It lies thick everywhere. When a breeze from the country that has lost its way, takes fright, and makes a blind hurry to rush out again, it flings as much dust in the eyes of Allegory as the law or Mr. Tulkinghorn, of its trustiest representatives may scatter, on occasion, in the eyes of the laity."[147] F.R. Leavis states: "Actually, the only extraordinary thing about him, is the contrast between his public self and the private self, that inner self which drives him; and which his innocuous public self makes him seem, negligible to his employers, the revelation of his private staff is terrifying to those who like Lady Dedlock stand in his way or arouse his antipathies."[148] Dickens describes Mr. Tulkinghorn with a sense of sarcasm and uses diabolic symbolism to unravel his personality.

A comic trial of Bardell vs. Pickwick is described in *Pickwick Papers*. Talking about Bardell vs. Pickwick, Philip Hobsbaum writes: "The judge in the case Mr. Justice Stareleigh, is all too close to his original, Sir Stephen Gazelee. Even more remarkable is the basis for the prosecuting attorney. The serjeant Buzfuz of the case was based on a Serjeant, Bompas-described by one of his contemporaries as stout, sandy, and forceful in his efforts to press his point upon a jury. The plot-material derived from a different but equally usable source: the celebrated Norton-Melbourne case, which Dickens himself reported in twenty-six columns the month before he wrote his fictional version. Mr. Norton had brought an action against the Prime Minister, Lord Melbourne, for 'criminal conversation' (namely adultery) with his wife. The evidence was so trivial and the testimony so corrupt that the jury returned an acquittal without leaving the box."[149]

Mr. Pickwick arranges lodging in Mrs. Bardell's apartment. Once he requests his amorous widowed land lady to send her son away. He then inquires her whether to keep two people requires much greater expense than to keep one. His declaration of his intention of hiring a manservant is taken by his landlady as a proposal of marriage. Mrs. Bardell faints in the arms of the bewildered Pickwick. At the same time, his friends Tupman, Winkle and Snodgrass arrive to visit him. Mr. Pickwick advocates his innocence before his friends. They concur in all his excuses but do not believe him. Then he receives a letter from a couple of sharp-practising attorneys, Dodson and Fogg, informing him that they are asked by Mrs. Bardell to begin an action against him for breaking the promise of marriage. Pickwick gets the intelligence that the act is the conspiracy of Dodson and Fogg.

The appearance and manners of Justice Stareleigh displays the distortion and monstrosity of the judicial system. He is described comically as short and fat. The abutting of high and low diction is an assault on the pomposity of the judge. He "rolled in, upon two little turned legs, and having bobbed gravely to the bar, who bobbed gravely to him, put his little legs underneath his table, and his little three-cornered hat upon it; and when Mr. Justice Stareleigh had done this, all you could see of him was two queer little eyes, one broad pink face, and somewhere about half of a big and very comical-looking wig."[150] The satiric vision operates in two distinct ways in *Bleak House* and *The Pickwick Papers.* In the former the exaggeration to expose is achieved through dark and gloomy images. In the latter the ludicrous is achieved to expose: "The judge had no sooner taken his seat, than the officer on the floor of the court called out 'Silence!' in a commanding tone, upon which another officer in the gallery cried 'Silence!' in an angry manner, where upon three or four more ushers shouted 'Silence!' in a voice of indignant remonstrance."[151]

The court must be grave. But it is just a show, a mere cosmetic facade and Dickens makes a jest of court trial. The pompous procedures of the court is mocked. Everything is topsy turvy. A shout for commotion is a mockery of the court trial. It is a paradox that the court is mistaken for more talk when silence descends on the court. Buzfuz speaks a lot and pauses for breath. His face becomes crimson. The vacuity of the whole affair is shown when there is silence in the court: "The silence awoke Mr. Justice Stareleigh, who immediately wrote down something with a pen without any ink in it. Nothing will come of nothing."[152] Justice Stareleigh is sleeping when the proceeding of the court is going on. He looks profound to impress that he always thinks deeply when his eyes are shut. Dickens makes a caricature of the irresponsibility and incompetence of the judge and the irregular trials of the court. "Dickens was generally thought to have caught exactly, in *Pickwick Papers*, the tones and mannerisms of Mr. Justice Gazelee, who was indeed very deaf, very short, and comically pompous and eccentric. These traits—already (according to Denman's biographer) 'an endless source of amusement to the Bar'—Dickens 'immortalised, and scarcely caricatured,...under the punning sobriquet of Mr. Justice Stareleigh.'"[153]

Incompetent jurymen are appointed to take part in the trial and to help in the verdict:

> 'I know I ought to do, if I got on as well as I deserved, but I don't, my Lord,' answered the chemist.

> 'Swear the gentleman,' said the judge, peremptorily.
>
> The officer had got no further than the 'You shall well and truly try,' when he was again interrupted by the chemist.
>
> 'I am to be sworn, my Lord, am I?' said the chemist.
>
> 'Certainly, sir,' replied the testy little judge.
>
> 'Very well, my Lord,' replied the chemist, in a resigned manner.
>
> 'Then there'll be murder before this trial's over; that's all. Swear me, if you please, sir'; and sworn the chemist was, before the judge could find words to utter.[154]

The caricature of Stareleigh as a literary device is expressed as "an admirable likeness of an ex-judge, who, with many valuable qualities of head and heart, had made himself a legitimate object of ridicule by his ludicrous explosions of irritability on the bench."[155] The court converses that only ten out of twelve jurymen are present. Orders are passed to manage any two and a green grocer and a chemist are brought before the judge. The chemist takes a plea that he has left his shop unattended and so the uninformed boy can sell oxalic acid for Epsom salts and laudanum for Senna:

> 'I beg this court's pardon', said the chemist, who was a tall, thin, yellow-visaged man, 'but I hope this court will excuse my attendance.'
>
> 'On what grounds, sir?', said Mr. Justice Stareleigh.
>
> 'I have no assistant, my Lord,' said the chemist.
>
> 'I can't help that, sir', replied Mr. Justice Stareleigh. 'You should hire one.'
>
> 'I can't afford it, my Lord,' rejoined the chemist.
>
> 'Then you ought to be able to afford it, sir,' said the judge, 'reddening; for Mr. Justice Stareleigh's temper bordered on the irritable, and brooked not contradiction.'[156]

Dickens makes a travesty of the judicial system. The disorganized character of the court procedure is shown ridiculous and the court with the spectators and interaction between the bar and bench and witnesses are comically presented. The judge calls and notes down Snubbin's assistant Mr. Phunkey as Mr. Monkey. Winkle's christian name creates confusion and leads to immense laughter. Winkle, as a witness, is asked by the judge:

> 'What's your Christian name, sir?' angrily inquired the little judge.
>
> 'Nathaniel, sir.'
>
> 'Daniel,—any other name?'
>
> 'Nathaniel, sir—my Lord, I mean.'
>
> 'Nathaniel Daniel, or Daniel Nathaniel?'
>
> 'No, my Lord—only Nathaniel, not Daniel at all.'
>
> 'What did you tell me it was Daniel for, then, sir?' inquired the judge.
>
> 'I didn't, my Lord,' replied Mr. Winkle.
>
> 'You did, sir,' replied the judge with a severe frown. 'How could I have got Daniel on my notes, unless you told me so, sir?'[157]

Nathaniel is taken as Daniel, Mrs. Cluppins as Truppins, Jupkins and Muffins. The confusion regarding these names is jests on the court's stupidity. Dickens' description of the distortions in the system of justice changes from the collective symbolic scenes to individual perceptions and in this act human snobbery and hypocrisy are pointed out.

Serjeant Buzfuz, the chief advocate for Mrs. Bardell uses histrionics like smiting the table with a tremendous thumb. He is not interested in the factual content of the case. Dickens' forceful argument in the court is a satire on the rhetoric of insincerity and language of blackmail. Buzfuz describes the death of Mrs. Bardell's husband very emotionally. The comic description and rhetorical blackmailing of the judge is accomplished:

> "The plaintiff, gentleman", continued Serjeant Buzfuz, in a soft and melancholy voice, "the plaintiff is a widow; yes, gentlemen, a widow. The late Mr. Bardell, after enjoying, for many years, the esteem and confidence of his sovereign,

as one of the guardians of his royal revenues, glided almost imperceptibly from the world, to seek elsewhere for that repose and peace which a custom-house can never afford."[158]

Serjeant Buzfuz with his intelligent and clever pleading creates sympathetic effects on the jurymen. He pleads that for two years Pickwick has continued to live regularly at Mrs. Bardell's house. Mrs. Bardell, during this period, has waited on him, attended to his comforts, cooked his meals, looked out his linen for the washerman. She has darned, aired and prepared it for wear. She has enjoyed his fullest trust and confidence. Many times, he has given half pence, and on some occasions even six pences, to her little boy. Sometimes, he has patted the boy on the head. He has inquired the boy whether he has won any alleys tors or commoneys lately. He has asked the boy whether he will like to have another father. About a year ago, Pickwick has suddenly begun to absent himself from home, for long period of time, with the intention of gradually breaking off from my client. Buzfuz explains further: "But I shall show you also, that his resolution was not at that time sufficiently strong, or that the charms and accomplishments of my client prevailed against his unmanly intentions; by proving to you, that on one occasion, when he returned from the country, he distinctly and in terms, offered her marriage: Previously however, taking special care that there should be no witness to their solemn contract; and I am in a situation to prove to you, on the testimony of three of his own friends, most unwilling, witnesses gentlemen—most unwilling witnesses—that on that morning he was discovered by them holding the plaintiff in his arms, and soothing her agitation by his caresses and endearments."[159]

Mr. Buzfuz, very cunningly, establishes the proposal of marriage offered by Pickwick to Mrs. Bardell. Although it is a lie, but the attorney makes it believe by his powerful and sympathetic pleading. Dickens satirises both attorneys and the court that is made to administer justice to the people. He laughs at the high legal ingenuity of Mr. Buzfuz. The climactic point of a farcical absurdity is attained when two innocuous chits are established as loveletters of Mr. Pickwick to

Mrs. Bardell. The first is related to his requirements as a lodger and the second is just an intimation of his absence. Mr. Buzfuz says that two letters have passed between the parties and they are written in the handwriting of the defendant. These letters bear language of affectionate attachment. They are secret communications. They are penned in the most glowing language and the most poetic imagery. These letters that are to be viewed with a cautious and suspicious eye as they are intended, by Pickwick, "to mislead and delude any third parties into whose hands they might fall." Let me read the first: "Garraway's, twelve o'clock. Dear Mrs. B—Chops and Tomato sauce. Yours, Pickwick." Gentlemen, what does this mean? Chops and Tomato sauce! Yours, Pickwick! Chops! Gracious heavens! and Tomato sauce! Gentlemen, is the happiness of a sensitive and confiding female to be trifled away, by such shallow artifices as these? The next has no date whatever, which is in itself suspicious. "Dear Mrs. B; I shall not be at home till tomorrow. Slow coach." And then follows this very remarkable expression. "Don't trouble yourself about the warming-pan." The warming pan! Why, gentlemen, who does trouble himself about a warming-pan? When was the peace of mind of man or woman broken or disturbed by a warming-pan, which is in itself a harmless, a useful, and I will add, gentlemen, a comforting article of domestic furniture? Why is Mrs. Bardell so earnestly entreated not to agitate herself about this warming-pan, unless (as is no doubt the case) it is a mere cover for hidden fire—a mere substitute for some endearing word or promise, agreeably to a preconcerted system of correspondence, artfully contrived by Pickwick with a view to his contemplated desertion, and which I am not in a condition to explain? And what does this allusion to the slow coach mean? For aught I know, it may be a reference to Pickwick himself, who has most unquestionably been a criminally slow coach during the whole of this transaction, but whose speed will now be very unexpectedly accelerated, and whose wheels, gentlemen, as he will find to his cost, will very soon be greased by you!"[160]

Very intelligently, Buzfuz presses the point to the jury that Mr. Pickwick had made a proposal of marriage to Mrs. Bardell.

The pleonastic doublet is used by Buzfuz to the messages sent by Pickwick to Mrs. Bardell. The lawyer manipulates these innocent notes and thus external reality disappears. Buzfuz feigns outrage at Pickwick's vile cryptogram about "Chops and Tomato Sauce." He then probes the sexual innuendos of "slow coach", a symbol of Pickwick's dilatory courting and "Don't trouble yourself about the warming pan" suggests "a mere cover for hidden fire". Pickwick "might never have fallen victim to this mockery of justice; but once arraigned, he faces the final debasement of poetic impulse he has never understood, in the law's ironic imputation of metaphorical language where, manifestly, there was no such intent."[161]

Buzfuz demands heavy punishment for Pickwick from the court. Witnesses are bullied in *Bardell vs. Pickwick*. Winkle as a witness is cross-examined by Mr. Skimpin. Mr. Winkle replies that it is quite impossible for him to say how many times he has seen Mrs. Bardell. Then he is asked if he has seen her twenty times. He replies that he has seen her more than twenty times. Then he is asked whether he has seen her a hundred times. He is asked whether he cannot swear that he has seen her more than fifty times. He is asked whether he does not know that he has seen her at least seventy-five times. He is warned that he should better take care of himself, and mind what he is about. The witness having been by these means reduced to the requisite ebb of nervous perplexity, the examination continues as follows:

> 'Pray, Mr. Winkle, do you remember calling on the defendant Pickwick at these apartments in the plaintiffs' house in Goswell Street, on one particular morning, in the month of July last?'
>
> 'Yes I do.'...
>
> 'Now, sir, tell the gentlemen of the jury what you saw on entering the defendant's room, on this particular morning. Come; out with it, sir; we must have it, sooner or later.'
>
> 'The defendant, Mr. Pickwick, was holding the plaintiff in his arms, with his hands clasping her waist,' replied

Mr. Winkle with natural hesitation, 'and the plaintiff appeared to have fainted away.'

'Did you hear the defendant say anything?'

'I heard him call Mrs. Bardell a good creature, and I heard him ask her to compose herself, for what a situation it was, if anybody should come, or words to that effect.'

'Now, Mr. Winkle, I have only one more question to ask you, and I beg you to bear in mind his lordship's caution. Will you undertake to swear that Pickwick, the defendant, did not say on the occasion in question, "My dear Mrs. Bardell, you're a good creature; compose yourself to this situation, for to this situation you must come," or words to that effect?'

'I-I didn't understand him so, certainly,' said Mr. Winkle, astounded at this ingenious dove-tailing of the few words he had heard, 'I was on the staircase, and couldn't hear distinctly; the impression on my mind is.'[162]

Mr. Phunky examines Mr. Winkle in a smooth and complacent manner asking whether Pickwick's conduct toward the opposite sex has ever led him to believe that he has ever contemplated matrimony:

'Oh no; certainly not,' replied Mr. Winkle.

'Has his behaviour, when females have been in the case, always been that of a man, who, having attained a pretty advanced period of life, content with his own occupations and amusements, treats them only as a father might his daughters?'

'Not the least doubt of it,' replied Mr. Winkle, in the fulness of his heart. 'That is-yes-oh. yes-certainly.'

'You have never known anything in his behaviour towards Mrs. Bardell, or any other female, in the least degree suspicious?' said Mr. Phunky, preparing to sit down; for Serjeant Snubbin was winking at him.

'N-n-no,' replied Mr. Winkle, 'except on one trifling occasion, which, I have no doubt, might be easily explained.' ...Amid the profound silence of the whole court, Mr. Winkle

> faltered out, that the trifling circumstance of suspicion was Mr. Pickwick's being found in a lady's sleeping apartment at midnight; which had terminated, he believed, in the breaking off of the projected marriage of the lady in question, and had led, he knew, to the whole party being forcibly carried before George Nupkins, Esq., magistrate and justice of the peace, for the borough of Ipswich![163]

Winkle, as a witness, is forced by the oratory of the attorneys to speak up in the plaintiff's favour. Garret Stewart comments on the manipulation of circumstancial evidence: "That circumstantial evidence which we are to find is every bit as fictitious as Sam's stories, and not nearly so credible."[164]

Serjeant Buzfuz asks Sam how he has not seen Mrs. Bardell in the arms of Mr. Pickwick. He browbeats him:

> 'Do you mean to tell me, Mr. Weller', said Serjeant Buzfuz, folding his arms emphatically, and turning half-round to the jury, as if in mute assurance that he would bother the witness yet: 'Do you mean to tell me, Mr. Weller, that you saw nothing of this fainting on the part of the plaintiff in the arms of the defendant, which you have heard described by the witnesses?'

'Certainly not', replied Sam. 'I was in the passage till they called me up and then the old lady was not there.'

'Now, attend, Mr. Weller', said Serjeant Buzfuz, dipping a large pen into the inkstand before him, for the purpose of frightening Sam with a show of taking down his answer. 'You were in the passage, and yet saw nothing of what was going forward. Have you a pair of eyes, Mr. Weller?'[165]

Sam Weller reveals in the court that the ladies have talked about Dodson and Fogg taking the case (*Bardell vs. Pickwick*) on speculation:

> 'Do you remember going up to Mrs. Bardell's house, one night in November last?'
>
> 'Oh yes, very well.' ...'Oh, you did get a talking about the trial,' said Serjeant Buzfuz, brightening up with the anticipation of some important discovery. 'Now what

> passed about the trial; will you have the goodness to tell us, Mr. Weller?'
>
> 'Vith all the pleasure in life, sir,' replied Sam. 'Arter a few unimportant observations from the two wirtuous females as has been examined here today, the ladies gets into a very great state o' admiration at the honourable conduct of Mr. Dodson and Fogg-them two gen'l'men as is settin' near you now.' This, of course, drew general attention to Dodson and Fogg, who looked as virtuous as possible.
>
> 'The attorneys for the plaintiff,' said Mr. Serjeant Buzfuz. 'Well! They spoke in high praise of the honourable conduct of Messrs Dodson and Fogg, the attorneys for the plaintiff, did they?'
>
> 'Yes,' said Sam, 'they said what a wery gen'rous thing it was o' them to have taken up the case on spec, and to charge nothing at all for costs, unless they got'em out of Mr. Pickwick.'[166]

Dickens, remarkably, exposes his satiric technique. A judge works on the notion that if one is right, then the other is wrong. It is a fact that can be easily inferred by a simple person but it is commonly uttered by a judge. So it gives ludicrous effect:

> Mr. Justice Stareleigh summed up, in the old-established and most approved form. He read as much of his notes to the jury as he could decipher on so short a notice, and made running comments on the evidence as he went along. If Mrs. Bardell were right, it was perfectly clear that Mr. Pickwick was wrong, and if they thought the evidence of Mrs. Cluppins worthy of credence they would believe it, and, if they didn't, why they wouldn't. If they were satisfied that a breach of promise of marriage had been committed, they would find for the plaintiff with such damages as they thought proper; and if, on the other hand, it appeared to them that no promise of marriage had ever been given, they would find for the defendant with no damages at all. The jury then retired to their private room to talk the matter over, and the judge retired to his private room, to refresh himself with a mutton chop and a glass of sherry.[167]

The verdict is in favour of Mrs. Bardell. Dickens writes:

'Gentlemen,' said the individual in black, 'are you all agreed upon your verdict.'

'We are,' replied the foreman.

'Do you find for the plaintiff, gentlemen, or for the defendant?'

'For the plaintiff.'

'With what damages, gentlemen?'

'Seven hundred and fifty pounds.'[168]

The inimitable *Bardell vs. Pickwick* trial creates the picture of the bad tempered and incompetent Mr. Justice Stareleigh. It also displays the quite enough absurdity of Sergeant Buzfuz. "The bullying of Mr. Winkle and the other witnesses, and the consequent perversion of truth and justice, place in a strikingly ludicrous: The absurd and odious effects of the English law of evidence and its practice."[169] The action against Pickwick for breach of promise of marriage, is "one of the most acute and pointed satires upon the state and administration of English law that ever appeared in the light and lively dress of fiction."[170]

Dickens' satire of the judicial magistrates is another attack on the system of justice. These magistrates are concerned with the maintenance of law and order and with the conduct of legal proceedings. Mr. Nupkins, the magistrate and his subordinates are attacked. Mr. Pickwick comes in contact with Mr. Nupkins and a legal farce follows. Sam acts as an instrument of ridicule on the brutality of society: 'This is a wery impartial country for justice.... There ain't a magistrate goin' as don't commit himself, twice as often as he commits other people'.[171] George Nupkins, the principal magistrate is an impressive personality frowning with majesty and boiling with rage. The lady reports to the magistrate of the possibility of a bloody duel at Ipswich, and she blames Pickwick and Tupman behind this. The magistrate calls Mr. Jinks, Mr. Muzzle, Mr. Grummer and there is a show of pompous magisterial authority.

Mr. Nupkins knows the King's officers' authority and discusses the constitutional maxim and considers duelling prohibited by Magna Charta. His total ignorance of history and administration is no doubt bureaucratic conceit. The magistrate treats duelling a greater breach of peace:

> "This is even more unconstitutional" said the magistrate, "this is even a greater breach of the peace, and a grosser infringement of his Majesty's prerogative. I believe duelling is one of his Majesty's most undoubted prerogatives, Mr. Jinks."
>
> 'Expressly stipulated in Magna Charta, sir', said Mr. Jinks.
>
> 'One of the brightest jewels in the British crown, wrung from his Majesty by the Barons, I believe, Mr. Jinks?' said the magistrate.[172]

Mr. Nupkins, the magistrate is shown funny for his utter disregard of the procedure of criminal prosecution. He asks Grummer and Jinks to utter the many charges against Pickwick and his partymen. When dinner is ready, he is to pronounce his summary judgement. When Pickwick stakes a claim to be heard, Mr. Nupkins agrees on clerk's suggestion but threatens previously. Dickens attacks the system of English justice through Grummer. Mr. Grummer is ordered to arrest Pickwick and Tupman. He has little concern for the civil rules of law and justice. There is a protest from the Pickwickians:

> 'This is a private room, sir. A private room.'
>
> Mr. Grummer shook his head, and replied, 'No room's private to his Majesty when the street door's once passed. That's law. Some people maintain that an Englishman's house is his castle. That's gammon.'
>
> The Pickwickians gazed on each other with wondering eyes.
>
> 'Which is Mr. Tupman?', inquired Mr. Grummer. He had an intuitive perception of Mr. Pickwick; he knew him at once.
>
> 'My name's Tupman', said that gentleman.
>
> 'My name's Law'; said Mr. Grummer.
>
> 'What?' Said Mr. Tupman.
>
> 'Law', replied Mr. Grummer, 'law, civil power, and exekative; them's my titles; here's my authority.'[173]

The Sergeants Inn—the court for obtaining the legal document (habeas corpus) is satirised by Dickens. Mr. Pickwick goes to this court with his attorney Perker to obtain the document for being forwarded to the jail. He is shocked to see the swarming hordes of professional bailers and the shabby touts roaming to be a guarantor in a case. He encounters these people earning their livelihood by falsehood and perjury. Pickwick is told by Perker that the man around him is a bail, no doubt:

> 'A what!' exclaimed Mr. Pickwick.
>
> 'A bail', replied Perker.
>
> 'A bail!'
>
> 'Yes, my dear sir—half a dozen of 'em here. Bail you to any amount, and only charge half a crown. Curious trade, isn't it?' said Perker, regaling himself with a pinch of snuff.
>
> 'What! Am I to understand that these men earn a livelihood by waiting about here, to perjure themselves before the judges of the land, at the rate of half a crown a crime!' exclaimed Mr. Pickwick, quite aghast at the disclosure.[174]

Dickens shows the reality of the naturalisation of perjury in the legal system: "Why I don't exactly know about perjury, my dear sir, replied the little gentleman. 'Harsh word, my dear sir, very harsh word indeed. It's a legal fiction, my dear sir, nothing more."[175] The barristers, clients, pimps and touts of the commissioners of the Insolvent Court at Lincoln Inn are presented by Dickens with realism and irony. The badly lighted and ill ventilated rooms and the sight of the commissioners of the Insolvent Court in their twigs with little greasy desks and dirty look are pathetic descriptions. It is a haunting place for the destitute shabby-genteel people in London. The court is shown as a pub. It has the stench of spirit and liquor. Dickens writes:

> The steams of beer and spirits perpetually ascend to the ceiling and, being condensed by the heat, roll down the walls like rain; there are more old suits of clothes in it at one time, than will be offered for sale in all Houndsditch in a twelve month; more unwashed skins and grizzly beards

> than all the pumps and shaving-shops between Tyburn and Whitechapel could render decent, between sunrise and sunset.[176]

Dickens presents the Insolvent Court possessing expertise in seediness. The indigent barristers have no fixed offices and run business either in the parlours of the public houses or in the yards of the prisons.

Dickens records his eloquent protest against the English legal system by depicting the dubious figures of Dodson and Fogg in *Pickwick Papers*. Pickwick talks of Dodson and Fogg by referring to his Pickwick vs. Bardell case: "It's a conspiracy...'a base conspiracy between these two grasping attorneys, Dodson and Fogg. Mrs. Bardell would never do it;—she hasn't the heart to do it;—she hasn't the case to do it'. Ridiculous-ridiculous.... It's a vile attempt to extort money."[177] Dickens laughs at Messrs Dodson and Fogg and they represent organised dodging and planned confusion or obfuscation of reality and a legally sanctioned plunder of the gullible people. Both are astute and shrewd. The dual partners in law provoke already hurt and irascible Pickwick. Pickwick calls them swindlers, thieves and rascals and later makes an assault on them. They have the sole aim to involve Mr. Pickwick into further damages for defamation and assault: "...added Mr. Fogg. Go on, sir, do go on. You had better call us thieves, sir; or perhaps you would like to assault one of us. Pray do it, sir, if you would, we will not make the smallest resistance. Pray do it sir."[178] Pickwick is Dickens' textual device for institutional satire and accuses those who are resources: "You are a well-matched pair of mean, rascally, pettifogging robber."[179]

Mr. Perker is a dodging and fogging agent of legal chicanery. He possesses the diabolical and pragmatic way of legal argument: "We have only one to adopt, my dear sir,... cross examine the witnesses, trust to Snubbin's eloquence; throw dust in the eyes of the judge; throw ourselves on the jury."[180]

Serjeant Snubbin is a legal quibbler. He is a past master in trebling the court business and so he prolongs the case: "Gets treble the business of any man in court-engaged in every case."[181] Dickens suggests the dishonest ethics of Snubbin's legal profession through his ill-washed dress, unkempt face and slovenly style of personal appearance and costume. Mr. Snubbin's dishonesty is shown through the lawyer's ignorance of the case of his client, Mr. Pickwick.

Sampson Brass, the lawyer in *The Old Curiosity Shop* is legal adviser to Quilp and he is 'one of her Majesty's attorneys of the Courts of King's Bench and Common Pleas at Westminster and a solicitor of the High Court of Chancery. He is presented as obsequious, rapacious, double dealers, perjurers and suborners of evidence: 'This Brass was an attorney of no very good repute from Bevis Marks in the City of London, he was a tall meagre man, with a nose like a wen, a protruding forehead, retreating eyes, and hair of deep red.... He had a cringing manner, but a very harsh voice, and his blandest smile were so extremely forbidding, that to have had his company under the least repulsive circumstances, one would have wished him to be out of temper that he might only scowl.'[182] The remarkable aspect of Sampson's villainy is his dishonesty. He plays the second fiddle to satisfy his master.

Sally Brass is the clerk to her own brother lawyer Sampson Brass. She is a partner in various kinds of crimes and inhumanity, perjury, false evidence, devilish inhuman brutality. She has no feminine graces and looks like ugly Shakespearean witch. She is her brother's confidential plotter and intriguer. Both brother and sister devise illegal means to earn money. They are wrangling over the issue of the induction of Kit as a new clerk. Daniel Quilp's identification of Law with Miss Sally Brass is quite satirical: 'Is that my Sally?' croaked the dwarf, ogling the fair Miss Brass, "Is it Justice with the bandage off her eyes, and without the sword and scales? Is it the Strong Arm of the Law? Is it the Virgin of Bevis?"[183]

In *David Copperfield*, the eponymous hero's friend Steerforth, shares a sour view of Doctor's Commons. David's aunt, Betsey Trotwood wants him to be a proctor and David asks Steerforth the meaning of a proctor. According to Steerforth, a proctor is a "monkish attorney". He practices in some faded courts in Doctors Commons. He is a type of judicial functionary like solicitors of the Courts of Law and Equity. Dickens lashes the hypocrisy and 'gentility' of proctorship and considers it nothing but theatrical performance, a pantomime: "They are like actors: Now a man's a judge, and now he is not a judge; now he's one thing, now he's another, now he's something else, change and change about; but it's always a very pleasant profitable little affair of private theatricals presented to an uncommonly select audience."[184] "Copperfield's experience of Doctors' Commons again acts as a reprise of Dickens' own work in that nest of courts and legal men...and, of course, Copperfield's work as a shorthand reporter in the Houses of Parliament is a direct transcription of the novelists' anonymous service in that capacity."[185]

When David is apprenticed to Jerkins and Spenlow to become a proctor in the Doctor's Commons, he finds that it is a happy hunting-ground of the legal touts and hangers-on. He finds a number of hangers-on and outsiders about the Commons, who, without being proctors themselves acts as middle-men. They get work done by real proctors, who lend their names in consideration of a share in the spoil. These touting law gentlemen sometimes collide as their's interests clash. Dickens laughs at the mockery and corruption and orderliness of Doctors' Commons "and there were a good many of these, too.... Kidnappers and inveiglers were planted in all the avenues or entrance to the Commons, with instructions to do their utmost to cut off all persons in mourning, and all gentlemen with anything bashful in their appearance, and entice them to the offices in which their respective employers were interested.... The conflicting interests of these touting gentlemen being of a nature to irritate their feelings, personal collisions took place; and the Commons was even scandalised by our principal inveigler (who had formerly been in the wine trade, and afterwards in the sworn brokery line) walking about for some days with a black eye. Any one of these scouts used to think nothing of politely assisting an old lady in black out of a vehicle, killing any proctor whom she inquired for, representing his employer as the lawful successor and representative of that proctor, and bearing the old lady off (sometimes greatly affected) to his employer's office."[186]

The judicial system is attacked once more in *David Copperfield* when the presiding judge is satirised: "Blinking over a little desk like a pulpit desk, in the curve of the horse-shoe, was an old gentleman, whom, if I had seen him in an aviary, I should certainly have taken for an owl, but who, I learned, was the presiding judge."[187]

David asks his senior lawyer Mr. Spenlow to define the true character of his professional business. Mr. Spenlow describes that in the litigation of a disputed Will of thirty or forty thousand pounds the advocate could make a good share through long arguments at every trial and through a series of evidence of interrogatory and counter interrogatory proceedings. His definition is ironical and a bitter exposure of English justice:

> It was the most conveniently organised place in the world.... For example you brought a divorce case, or a restitution case, into the Consistory. Very good. You tried it in the Consistory. You made a quiet little round game of it, among a family group, and you played it out at leisure. Suppose you were not satisfied with the Consistory, what did you do then? Why, you went into the Arches. What was the Arches? The same court, in the same room, with the same bar, and the same practitioners, but another judge, for there the Consistory judge could plead any court-day as an advocate. Well, you played your round game out again. Still you were not satisfied. Very good. What did you do then? Why, you went to the Delegates. Who were the Delegates? Why, the Ecclesiastical Delegates were the advocates without any business, who had looked on at the round game when it was playing in both courts, and had seen the cards shuffled, and cut, and played, and had talked to all the players about it, and now came fresh, as judges to settle the matter to the satisfaction of everybody! Discontented people might talk of corruption in the Commons, closeness in the Commons and the necessity of

reforming the Commons, said Mr. Spenlow solemnly, in conclusion; but when the price of wheat per bushel had been highest, the Commons had been busiest, and a man might lay his hand upon his heart, and say this to the whole world,—"Touch the Commons, and down comes the country!"[188]

The world of *Great Expectations* is a world where the underprivileged by birth are shown to be constantly victimised, antagonised, beggared by their social superiors. They are further crushed by an unfairly repressive legislation. The iniquity of the criminal law, made for their own benefit by the privileged class, is dramatically underlined when Magwitch tells Pip and Herbert how he, the underdog and Compeyson are tried together but sentenced separately according to their manners, looks, accomplishments and circle of acquaintances. Magwitch and Compeyson are put in the dock. The latter looks, with his curly hair and his black clothes and his white pocket-handkercher. The former looks a common sort of wretch. When the prosecution opens and the evidence is put short, it bears heavy on Magwitch and light on Compeyson. When the evidence is given in the box, Magwitch always comes forward. His money is always paid. It is calculated that he works the thing and so he will get the profit. But, when the defence comes on, the counsellor for Compeyson says to lord and gentlemen, that two persons are side by side. The younger is well brought up. The elder is ill brought up. The younger is seldom seen in these transactions, and only suspected. The elder is always seen in them and always with his guilt brought home. And when it comes to character, Compeyson has attended the school. His school fellows are not in this position. He is not known by witnesses in such clubs and societies. To Magwitch, he is tried before, is known up hill and down dale in Bridewells and Lock-Ups. And when it comes to speech-making, Compeyson can speak to them with his face dropping every now and then into his white pocket-handkercher and with verses in his speech too and Magwitch can only say to gentlemen that man at his side is a most precious rascal.

When the verdict comes, Compeyson is recommended to mercy on account of good character and bad company and Magwitch is treated as guilty. When Magwitch says to Compeyson that once out of the court, he will smash his face, the latter prays the Judge to be protected, and gets two turn-keys. "And when we're sentenced, ain't it him as gets seven year, and me fourteen, and ain't it him as the Judge is sorry for, because he might a done so well, and ain't it me as the Judge perceives to be a old offender of wiolent passion, likely to come to worse?"[189]

This is based on the famous trial scene in Paul Clifford in which the hero, speaking in self-defence before his judges-puts society in the dock: "I hesitate not to tell you, my lord! Judge— to proclaim to you, gentleman of the jury that the laws which I have broken through my life. I despise in death? Your laws are but of two classes; then one makes criminals, the other punishes them. I have suffered by the one—I am about to perish by the other. My lord, it was the turn of a straw which made me what I am. Seven years ago, I was sent to the House. I was sent to the House of correction for an offence which I did not commit; I went thither, a boy who had never infringed, a single law—I came forth, in a few weeks, a man who was prepared to break all laws!... The laws themselves caused me to break the laws...your legislation made me what I am! and it now destroys me, as it has destroyed thousands, for being what it made me!... Let those whom the law protects consider it a protector; when did it ever protect me? When did it ever protect the poor man? The government of a state, the institutions of law, profess to provide for all those who 'obey'. Mark! a man hungers—do you feed him? He is naked, do you clothe him? If not, you break your covenant, you drive him back to the first law of nature, and you hang him, not because he is guilty, but because you have left him naked and starving."[190]

*Barnaby Rudge* exposes Dickens' disgust for the practice of hanging many people for slight offences. He discusses the notorious case of Mary Jones, hanged in 1771 for shoplifting. Her husband has been press-ganged and her children have been starving. "Hugh the Bastard's mother, abandoned by her aristocratic seducer, and hanged at Tyburn, with her six-year old son looking on, for passing forged notes, is a fictional variant on Mary Jones, and Hugh's participation in the Riots is, in part, his revenge against a society which could commit such an outrage."[191]

The slow, and irresponsive judiciary is ridiculed in *Oliver Twist*. For example, the court room scene with the two magistrates—one nearly half blind and dozing off behind the desk and the other reading a newspaper and pulling the other man's sleeve—is a satire on the conduct of justice in Dickens's contemporary Britain. Oliver is brought to the magistrate's court. He is being sent as an apprentice to Gamfield, the chimney sweep. The magistrate cross-questions and this is satire on the silly and insensitive judge:

> 'Well', said the old gentleman. 'I suppose he is fond of chimney sweeping?'
>
> 'He dotes on it, your worship', replied Bumble, giving Oliver a sly pinch to intimate that he had better not say he didn't.
>
> 'And he will be a sweep, will he?' inquired the old gentleman.[192]

Mr. Fang, the police magistrate is satirised in *Oliver Twist*. His manner of administering justice is funny. His dirty court is for summary justice. "His face was stern and much flushed. If he were really not in the habit of drinking rather more than was exactly good for him, he might have brought an action against his own countenance for a libel, and have recovered heavy damages."[193] Mr. Fang considers the plaintiff as accused. This bumbling magistrate inflicts insults on Mr. Brownlow, the respectable gentleman. This man has arrived to this court to supply true details and to save Oliver from the clutches of law:

> "Officer!" said Mr. Fang, throwing the paper on one side, "what's this fellow charged with?"
>
> "He's not charged at all, your worship", replied the officer. "He appears against the boy, your worship."[194]

Mr. Fang deals hard with Oliver in the dock. He is insensitive and inhumane. He treats Oliver as a vegabond, a hardened scoundrel. He rejects his feeble prayer for a glass of water as stuff and nonsense. He considers his fainting fit as a deliberate shamming and pronounces sentence of three months hard labour. Dickens observes:

> "Stuff and nonsense!", said Mr. Fang, "don't try to make a fool of me."
>
> "I think he really is ill, your worship", remonstrated the officer.
>
> "I know better", said Mr. Fang.
>
> "Take care of him, officer", said the old gentleman, raising his hands instinctively, "he'll fall down."
>
> "Stand away, officer", cried Fang; "let him, if he likes."

Oliver availed himself of the kind permission, and fell heavily to the floor in a fainting fit. The men in the office looked at each other, but no one dared to stir.

> "I knew he was shamming", said Fang,... "Let him lie there; he'll soon be tired of that."
>
> "How do you propose to deal with the case, sir?", inquired the clerk in low voice.
>
> "Summarily", replied Mr. Fang. "He stands committed for three months—hard labour, of course."[195]

Norris Pope comments: "The mistreatment of juveniles at the hands of unqualified magistrates is intended as serious social criticism, as is the viciousness and stupidity of the police magistrate Fang—though the latter portrait illustrates the fact that Dickens was often most comic when he was also most serious (Victorian readers clearly understood that Fang was meant to suggest the metropolitan magistrate A.S. Laing, who was finally removed from the bench in January 1838, six months after the publication of Dickens' caricature)."[196]

In *Oliver Twist*, Artful Dodger is involved in the pick-pocketing case. He is produced before the magistrate for stealing a snuff box. This juvenile delinquent asks an explanation for the violation of privileges:

> "Hold your tongue, will you?", said the jailer.
>
> "I'm an Englishman, ain't I?", rejoined the Dodger; "where are my privileges?"
>
> "You'll get your privileges soon enough", retorted the jailer, "and pepper with 'em."
>
> "We'll see wot the Secretary of State for the Home Affairs has got to say to the beaks, if I don't", replied Mr. Dawkins.[197]

Artful Dodger asks the magistrate to dispose of the case and the charge of pick-pocketing is considered by him as defamation of his character. He declines to plead in his own defence and this is indictment on the English justice:

> "Do you mean to say anything, you young shaver?"
>
> "No", replied the Dodger, "not here, for this ain't the shop for justice, besides which, my attorney is a-breakfasting this morning with the Wice-President of the House of Commons; but I shall have something to say elsewhere, and so will he, and so will a wery numerous and 'spectable circle of acquaintance as'll make them beaks wish they'd never been born, or that they'd got their footmen to hangem' up to their own hat-pegs afore they let 'em come out this morning to try it on upon me."[198]

Dickens underlies the fact that justice operates in class terms. "The perception that justice is a class matter becomes essential to the pattern of *Oliver Twist*, and because of it life's terrible disorders break in upon that enclosed world of fiction where justice can operate with rare impartiality."[199]

The Fleet Prison in *Pickwick Papers* illustrates the sheer inhumanity that is practiced upon human beings and it becomes a powerful instrument of abject debasement. "So strong is the urge in Dickens to treat transgressions against the laws of Nature (if not of Nations) that he is led to illustrate the wickedness of imprisonment for debt so powerfully that the comic tone preserved by a genuinely sentimental writer dealing with such a scene (like Goldsmith showing Dr. Primrose in prison for debt) is lost."[200]

As Mr. Roker leads Mr. Pickwick into the prison, he passes through a narrow, dirty and low gallery and crosses through the hall flight "which appeared to lead to a range of damp and stone vaults, beneath the ground, and those, I suppose, are the little cellars where the prisoners keep their small quantities of coals. Unpleasant places to go down to; ...'you don't really mean to say that human beings live down in those wretched dungeons'."[201] The binary order of living is articulated by Mr. Roker. It is not only that prisoners have to live down there, but that they die down there as well. The particular class of lawbreakers among whom Mr. Pickwick finds himself in the Fleet are debtors. In selecting this "class of offender rather than another for him to encounter, one of Dickens' reasons was, of course, that he considered the English laws of his day concerning debt to be monstrously unjust and sending his fictional hero there gave him an opportunity for satirical exposure of a real social abuse."[202]

The unhygienic atmosphere of the Fleet Prison in *The Pickwick Papers* is described. The prison is dirty and hazardous for the human beings: "The only vermin in the room in which he is put is a dingy-looking fly which crawls over his pantaloons; the atmosphere, which in reality was poisonous, strikes him merely as 'intolerably close,' except in the coffee-room gallery where the smell of tobacco smoke is 'perfectly suffocating'."[203] A young woman, with a child in her arms, who seemes scarcely able to crawl, from emaciation and misery, walks up and down the passage in conversation with her husband, who has no other place to see her in. As they pass Mr. Pickwick, he hears the female sob; and once she burst into such a passion of grief, that she is compelled to lean against the wall for support, while the man takes the child in his arms, and tries to soothe her.

Mr. Pickwick's heart is really too full to bear it, and he goes upstairs to bed. The warden's room is very uncomfortable. In decoration and convenience it is several hundred degrees inferior to the common infirmary of a country gaol. Pickwick satisfies himself, "by mathematical calculation, that the apartment was about equal in annual value to the freehold of a small street in the suburbs of London."[204]

In *Pickwick Papers*, the other grave aspect of the prison is detailed. Mr. Pickwick looks into the room which is filthily dirty, and smells intolerably close. There is no vestige of either carpet, curtain, or blind. There is not even a closet in it. There are remnants of loaves and pieces of cheese, and damp towels, and scrags of meat, and articles of wearing apparel, and mutilated crockery, and bellows without nozzles, and toasting-forks without prongs. They present somewhat of an uncomfortable appearance when "they are scattered about the floor of a small apartment, which is the common sitting and sleeping room of three idle men."[205] If a prisoner has money, he can find anything. He can find a good room and he can take wine. The condition of the penniless debtor is atrocious as like the chancery prisoner. The lot of the penniless debtor is worse than the convicted criminal. The convict is fed gratis by the state but the penniless debtor is to subsist on the charity of the fellow prisoners or die of starvation: "There were no regular rations of food. When they had pawned almost all the clothing in which they had arrived they were left to beg and to starve."[206]

Dickens describes the sufferings of the penniless prisoner and arraigns the abominable system in *Pickwick Papers*. The poor side of a debtor's prison is that in which the most miserable and abject class of debtors are confined. A prisoner upon the poor side, pays neither rent nor chummage. His fees, upon entering and leaving the gaol, are reduced in amount. And he becomes entitled to a share of some small quantities of food. The food is provided out of the trifling legacies made by charitable persons in their wills. "Until within a very few years past, there was a kind of iron cage in the wall of the Fleet Prison, within which was posted some man of hungry looks, who, from time to time, rattled a money-box, and exclaimed in a mournful voice, 'Pray, remember the poor debtors; pray, remember the poor debtors.' The receipts of this box, when there were any, were divided among the poor prisoners; and the men on the poor side relieved each other in this degrading office."[207]

The seriousness of these realities is made explicit when Pickwick is imprisoned for debt in the Fleet. In 1837, debtors have not been suspended in an iron cage on the Fleet Wall to appeal for alms, the condition of such prisoners has been still questionable: "We still leave unbolted in the leaves of our statute book, for the reverence and admiration of succeeding ages, the just and wholesome law which declares that the sturdy felon shall be fed and clothed, and that the penniless debtor shall be left to die of starvation and nakedness. This is no fiction."[208]

The imprisonment of Pickwick affords an opportunity of depicting the interior of a debtor's prison and the manifold evils of that system. When his compassionate spirit no longer endures the spectacle of suffering and wretchedness, in the Fleet he locks himself in his room for three months. He says: "My head aches with these scenes, and my heart too. Henceforth I will be a prisoner in my own room."[209]

In *Great Expectations*, the Newgate Prison of London is introduced to Pip. He is invited by some half-drunk minister of justice to hear a trial. He declines the proposal, but engages himself to the offer of a glimpse of the courtyard: "Where the gallows was kept, and also where people were publicly whipped, and then he showed me the Debtors' Door, out of which culprits came to be hanged: heightening the interest of that dreadful portal by giving me to understand that 'four on' em' would come out at that door the day after-tomorrow at eight in the morning, to be killed in a row. This was horrible, and gave me a sickening idea of London."[210]

Pip visits Newgate Prison in 1830. He says that it has been visiting time "when Wemmick took me in; and a potman was going his rounds with beer; and the prisoners, behind bars in yards, were buying beer, and talking to friends; and a frouzy, ugly, disorderly, depressing scene it was."[211]

Dickens points out that the prisons have been much neglected in 1830. The luxury of the prisons of 1860s is deplored. When Pip emerges from the gaol he feels tainted, contaminated and soiled. He says: "I beat the prison dust off my feet as I sauntered to and fro, and I shook it out of my dress, and I exhaled its air from my lungs."[212] Dickens has never doubted that the old unreformed gaols have been a shocking scandal. The Newgate of the late eighteenth century appears in both his historical novels, *Barnaby Rudge* and *A Tale of Two Cities*. The bad criminal laws and the bad prison regulations have fostered the growth of the worst people of London who has supported the Gordon Riots. "The trials of Charles Darnay at the Old Bailey is preface by a similar attack on criminal laws and penal system of the 1770s."[213] Newgate has been a very bad place and many sorts of immorality have been practiced here. This prison has bred serious diseases too.

In *Little Dorrit*, a new dimension of prison is discussed where oppression within oppression is shown. In Marseilles, there is a villainous prison. One of its chambers is a repulsive place that even the obtrusive stare blinks at it. It is left to such refuse of reflected light as it can find for itself. Two men are within the melancholy prison. The chamber contains also rats and other unseen vermin, in addition to the seen vermin. It receives such light as it gets through a grating of iron bars fashioned like a pretty large window by means of which it can be always inspected from the gloomy staircase. "A prison taint was on everything there. The imprisoned air, the imprisoned light, the imprisoned damps, the imprisoned men, were all deteriorated by confinement. As the captive men were faded and haggard, so the iron was rusty, the stone was slimy, the wood was rotten, the air was faint, the light was dim. Like a well, like a vault, like a tomb, the prison had no knowledge of the brightness outside; and would have kept its polluted atmosphere intact in one of the spice islands of the Indian Ocean."[214]

Graphic animal images of rats and vermin combine with the gloom of unventilated darkness and create a sepulcheral atmosphere of despairing humanity within. It penetrates and taints all before it. The exposition of humanity is further accentuated with the aid of contrasts: The world within and the world outside. "Marseilles has been a tainted place, but a place of refuge; the prison is now its tainted heart. Here, the arrows of light cannot penetrate; but their absence brings no relief. The very air is constraint and degradation; if the church brought a welcome escape from too much whiteness, too much staring, the dungeon is final, intolerable dusk. And, like Tom-all-Alone's, the dungeon dominates, reducing its inmates, good or evil, to verminous brutes."[215]

## NOTES

1. Valerie Purton, *Charles Dickens, Dombey and Son, Everyman*, J.M. Dent, London; Charles E. Tuttle, Vermont, 1997, pp. 69-71.
2. *Ibid.*, p. 72.
3. *Ibid.*, p. 73.
4. Harry Stone, *Dickens and the Invisible World*, Macmillan, London, 1980, p. 181.
5. Valerie Purton, *op. cit.*, p. 73.
6. Introduction and Notes by Ella Westland, *Oliver Twist, Charles Dickens*, Wordsworth Classics, Hertfordshire, 2000, p. 96.
7. *Ibid.*, p. 60.
8. *Ibid.*, p. 161.
9. *Ibid.*, p. 118.
10. *Ibid.*, pp. 142-43.
11. *Ibid.*, p. 241.
12. *Ibid.*, p. 283.
13. *The Times Literary Supplement*, TSL Education Ltd., London, Feb. 4, 2000, p. 9.
14. Margaret Cardwell, *Charles Dickens, Great Expectations*, Oxford University Press, New York, 1994, pp. 119-20.
15. Ella Westland, *op. cit.*, p. 195.
16. *Ibid.*, pp. 196 97.
17. F.S. Schwarzbach, *Dickens and the City*, University of London, The Athlone Press, London, 1986, p. 139.
18. Sylvere Monod, *Dickens the Novelist*, University of Oklahoma Press, Norman, 1967, p. 194.
19. Chuzzlewit Martin, *Charles Dickens*, Wordsworth Classics, Hertfordshire, 1994, p. 457.

20. *Ibid.*, p. 458.
21. Monroe Engel, *The Maturity of Dickens*, Harvard University Press, Massachussetts, Cambridge, 1967, pp. 102-03.
22. Debiprasad Bhattacharya, *The Middle Class in Dickens*, Minerva Associates, Kolkata, 2000, p. 46.
23. Ella Westland, *op. cit.*, p. 6.
24. *Ibid.*, p. 11.
25. *Ibid.*, p. 12.
26. *Ibid.*, p. 14.
27. *Ibid.*
28. Peter Ackroyd, *Introduction to Dickens*, Mandarin Paperbacks, London, 1992, p. 50.
29. Debiprasad Bhattacharya, *op. cit.*, p. 47.
30. Ella Westland, *op. cit.*, p. 22.
31. *Ibid.*, p. 27.
32. *Ibid.*, p. 43.
33. *Ibid.*, p. 108.
34. *Ibid.*, p. 109.
35. *Ibid.*, pp. 147-48.
36. Walter Allen, *The English Novel*, Penguin Books, Harmondsworth, Middlesex, 1991, p. 167.
37. Jacob Korg, *Twentieth Century Interpretations of Bleak House*, Prentice Hall, Englewood Cliffs, N.J., 1968, p. 29.
38. Graham Storey, *Charles Dickens: Bleak House*, Cambridge University Press, 1987, p. 7.
39. Andrew Sanders, *Charles Dickens: Bleak House*, Everyman, J.M. Dent, London; Charles E. Tuttle Vermont, 1994, p. 403.
40. *Ibid.*, p. 201.
41. *Ibid.*, p. 90.
42. *Ibid.*, p. 139.
43. *Ibid.*, p. 568.
44. A.E. Dyson, *The Inimitable Dickens*, Macmillan, London, New York, St. Martin's Press, 1970, p. 180.
45. Andrew Sanders, *op. cit.*, pp. 588-89.
46. *Ibid.*, p. 284.
47. Andrew Sanders, *Charles Dickens: Resurrectionist*, Macmillan, London, 1982, p. 6.

48. Ella Westland, *op. cit.*, p. 36.
49. *Ibid.*, p. 50.
50. *Ibid.*, pp. 329-30.
51. Alexander Welsh, *The City of Dickens*, Clarendon Press, Oxford, 1971, p. 15.
52. Valerie Purton, *op. cit.*, p. 623.
53. Michael Slater, *Dickens, 1970*, Chapman and Hall, London, 1970, p. 138.
54. Debiprasad Bhattacharya, *op. cit.*, p. 54.
55. John Lucas, *Charles Dickens: The Major Novels*, Penguin Books, Harmondsworth, Middlesex, 1992, p. 102.
56. Debiprasad Bhattacharya, *op. cit.*, pp. 54-55.
57. Philip Hobsbaum, *A Readers' Guide to Charles Dickens*, Thames and Hudson, London, 1972, p. 190.
58. Alexander Welsh, *op. cit.*, p. 45.
59. Harvey Peter Sucksmith, *Charles Dickens, Little Dorrit*, Oxford, At the Clarendon Press, 1979, p. 100.
60. *Ibid.*, p. 101.
61. *Ibid.*, p. 102.
62. *Ibid.*, p. 104.
63. Barbara Hardy, *Charles Dickens, The Writer and His Work*, Profile Books Ltd., Windsor, Berkshire, England, 1983, p. 79.
64. Harvey Peter Sucksmith, *op. cit.*, p. 101.
65. *Ibid.*, p. 110.
66. Alan Shelston, *Charles Dickens: Dombey and Son* and *Little Dorrit*, Macmillan, Basingstoke, Hampshire, 1985, p. 145.
67. J.H. Miller, *Charles Dickens: The World of His Novels*, Harvard University Press, Cambridge, Massachussetts, Oxford University Press, London, 1959, p. 233.
68. *Ibid.*, p. 234.
69. J.C. Reid, *Charles Dickens: Little Dorrit*, Edward Arnold, London, 1967, p. 34.
70. Harvey Peter Sucksmith, *op. cit.*, p. 177.
71. Philip Hobsbaum, *op. cit.*, p. 193.
72. Philip Collins, *Dickens the Critical Heritage*, Routledge & Kegan Paul, London, 1971, p. 370.
73. Sylvere Monod, *Dickens the Novelist*, University of Oklahoma Press, Norman, 1967, p. 392.

74. Angus Wilson, *The World of Charles Dickens*, Martin Secker & Warburg, London, 1970, p. 231.
75. A.E. Dyson, *Dickens Bleak House*, Macmillan Press Ltd., Houndmills, Basingstoke, Hampshire and London, 1969, p. 112.
76. *Ibid.*
77. *Ibid.*
78. *Ibid.*, p. 114.
79. *Ibid.*, p. 115.
80. *Ibid.*
81. T.A. Jackson, *Charles Dickens: The Progress of a Radical*, People's Publishing House, New Delhi, 1990, p. 81.
82. Mark Spilka, *Dickens and Kafka: A Mutual Interpretation*, Dennis Dobson, London, 1963, p. 199.
83. Andrew Sanders, *op. cit.*, p. 4.
84. *Ibid.*, pp. 4-5.
85. *Ibid.*, pp. 5-6.
86. Philip Hobsbaum, *A Reader's Guide to Charles Dickens*, Thames and Hudson, London, 1972, p. 163.
87. Jacob Korg, *Twentieth Century Interpretations of Bleak House*, Prentice Hall, Englewood Cliffs, N.J., 1968, p. 23.
88. Andrew Sanders, *op. cit.*, p. 6.
89. Grahame Smith, *Dickens, Money and Society*, University of California Press, Berkeley and Los Angeles, 1968, p. 136.
90. Andrew Sanders, *op. cit.*, pp. 47-48.
91. *Ibid.*, pp. 49-50.
92. *Ibid.*, p. 50.
93. K.J. Fielding, *Charles Dickens: A Critical Introduction*, Longman, Green and Co., London, New York, Toronto, 1958, p. 124.
94. Andrew Sanders, *op. cit.*, p. 51.
95. *Ibid.*
96. *Ibid.*, p. 56.
97. F.R. Leavis/Q.D. Leavis, *Dickens: The Novelist*, Chatto and Windus, London, 1970, p. 231.
98. Andrew Sanders, *op. cit.*, p. 89.
99. *Ibid.*, p. 91.

100. *Ibid.*, p. 109.
101. *Ibid.*, p. 208.
102. Jacob Korg, *op. cit.*, p. 104.
103. Andrew Sanders, *op. cit.*, p. 447.
104. *Ibid.*, p. 448.
105. *Ibid.*, p. 478.
106. Jacob Korg, *op. cit.*, p. 104.
107. Andrew Sanders, *op. cit.*, p. 745.
108. *Ibid.*, p. 314.
109. *Ibid.*, p. 315.
110. *Ibid.*, p. 738.
111. *Ibid.*, p. 785.
112. Jacob Korg, *op. cit.*, p. 33.
113. *Ibid.*, p. 49.
114. Andrew Sanders, *op. cit.*, p. 497.
115. Sylvere Monod, *op. cit.*, p. 19.
116. Andrew Sanders, *op. cit.*, pp. 497-99.
117. Grahame Smith, *op. cit.*, p. 137.
118. Andrew Sanders, *op. cit.*, p. 499.
119. Jacob Korg, *op. cit.*, p. 24.
120. T.A. Jackson, *op. cit.*, p. 83.
121. Philip Hobsbaum, *op. cit.*, p. 163.
122. Andrew Sanders, *op. cit.*, p. 13.
123. *Ibid.*, p. 32.
124. *Ibid.*, p. 52.
125. *Ibid.*, pp. 52-53.
126. *Ibid.*, p. 184.
127. F.R. Leavis/Q.D. Leavis, *op. cit.*, p. 130.
128. Andrew Sanders, *op. cit.*, pp. 452-53.
129. *Ibid.*, p. 453.
130. *Ibid.*
131. Debiprasad Bhattacharya, *The Middle Class in Dickens*, Minerva Associates, Kolkata, 2000, p. 53.
132. Andrew Sanders, *op. cit.*, pp. 195-96.
133. *Ibid.*, p. 196.

134. *Ibid.*, p. 197.
135. *Ibid.*
136. *Ibid.*, p. 313.
137. *Ibid.*, p. 88.
138. *Ibid.*, p. 485.
139. *Ibid.*, pp. 486-87.
140. Joseph Gold, *Charles Dickens: Radical Moralist*, University of Minnesota Press, Minneapolis, 1972, p. 190.
141. Christopher Hibbert, *The Making of Charles Dickens*, Longman, London, 1967, p. 98.
142. Andrew Sanders, *op. cit.*, p. 501.
143. *Ibid.*, p. 743.
144. J.H. Miller, *Charles Dickens: The World of His Novels*, Harvard University Press, Cambridge, Massachusestts, Oxford University Press, London, 1959, p. 201.
145. Andrew Sanders, *op. cit.*, pp. 11-12.
146. *Ibid.*, p. 148.
147. *Ibid.*, p. 279.
148. F.R. Leavis and Q.D. Leavis, *op. cit.*, p. 218.
149. Philip Hobsbaum, *op. cit.*, p. 33.
150. David Ellis, *The Pickwick Papers: Charles Dickens*, Wordsworth Classics, Hertfordshire, 2000, p. 437.
151. *Ibid.*
152. Garret Stewart, *Dickens and the Trials of Imagination*, Harvard University Press, Cambridge, Massachussetts, 1974, p. 71.
153. Philip Collins, *Dickens and Crime*, Macmillan & Co. Ltd., London, New York, St. Martin's Press, 1962, p. 182.
154. David Ellis, *op. cit.*, p. 438.
155. Philip Collins, *Dickens the Critical Heritage*, Routledge and Kegan Paul, London, 1971, p. 61.
156. David Ellis, *op. cit.*, p. 438.
157. *Ibid.*, p. 448.
158. *Ibid.*, pp. 440-41.
159. *Ibid.*, p. 444.
160. *Ibid.*, pp. 444-45.
161. Garret Stewart, *op. cit.*, pp. 72-73.
162. David Ellis, *op. cit.*, pp. 449-50.

163. *Ibid.*, pp. 451-52.
164. Garrett Stewart, *op. cit.*, p. 71.
165. David Ellis, *op. cit.*, p. 454.
166. *Ibid.*, p. 455.
167. *Ibid.*, p. 456.
168. *Ibid.*, pp. 456-57.
169. Philip Collins, *op. cit.*, p. 54.
170. *Ibid.*, p. 74.
171. David Ellis, *op. cit.*, p. 321.
172. *Ibid.*, p. 312.
173. *Ibid.*, pp. 313-14.
174. *Ibid.*, p. 529.
175. *Ibid.*
176. *Ibid.*, p. 560.
177. *Ibid.*, pp. 233-34.
178. *Ibid.*, p. 256.
179. *Ibid.*, p. 697.
180. *Ibid.*, p. 400.
181. *Ibid.*, p. 399.
182. *The Old Curiosity Shop: Charles Dickens*, Wordsworth Classics, Hertfordshire, 1995, pp. 73-74.
183. *Ibid.*, p. 212.
184. Adrienne E. Gavin, *David Copperfield, Charles Dickens*, Wordsworth Classics, Hertfordshire, 1999, p. 295.
185. Peter Ackroyd, *Introduction to Dickens*, Mandarin Paperbacks, London, 1992, p. 118.
186. Adrienne E. Gavin, *op. cit.*, pp. 479-80.
187. *Ibid.*, *op. cit.*, p. 302.
188. *Ibid.*, p. 332.
189. Margaret Cardwell, *Charles Dickens, Great Expectations*, Oxford University Press, New York, 1994, p. 347.
190. Anny Sadrin, *Great Expectations*, Unwin Hyman, London, 1988, pp. 62-63.
191. Philip Collins, *op. cit.*, p. 221.
192. Introduction and Notes by Ella Westland, *Oliver Twist, Charles Dickens*, Wordsworth Classics, Hertfordshire, 2000, p. 19.
193. *Ibid.*, p. 65.

194. *Ibid.*
195. *Ibid.*, p. 67.
196. Norris Pope, *Dickens and Charity*, Macmillan, London, 1978, p. 160.
197. Ella Westland, *op. cit.*, p. 290.
198. *Ibid.*, p. 291.
199. John Lucas, *The Melancholy Man: A Study of Dickens' Novels*, Methuen & Co. Ltd., London, 1970, p. 23.
200. John Gross and Gabriel Pearson, *Dickens and the Twentieth Century*, Routledge & Kegan Paul, London, 1962, p. 45.
201. David Ellis, *op. cit.*, p. 534.
202. Martin Price, *Dickens: A Collection of Critical Essays*, Prentice Hall, Englewood Cliffs, N.J., 1980, p. 79.
203. Christopher Hibbert, *op. cit.*, p. 60.
204. David Ellis, *op. cit.*, p. 540.
205. *Ibid.*, p. 551.
206. Ivor Brown, *Dickens in His Times*, Thomas Nelson & Sons Ltd., London, 1963, p. 66.
207. David Ellis, *op. cit.*, p. 554.
208. Kate Flint, *Dickens*, The Harvester Press, Brighton, Sussex, England, 1986, p. 38.
209. David Ellis, *op. cit.*, p. 599.
210. Margaret Cardwell, *op. cit.*, p. 164.
211. *Ibid.*, p. 257.
212. *Ibid.*, p. 261.
213. Philip Collins, *op. cit.*, p. 31.
214. Peter Sucksmith Harvey, *Charles Dickens, Little Dorrit*, Oxford, Clarendon Press, 1979, pp. 3-5.
215. A.E. Dyson, *The Inimitable Dickens*, Macmillan, London, New York, St. Martin's Press, 1970, p. 207.

# 3 Religion and Its Practitioners

Although his novels are filled with churches and his world peopled with divines of all theological hues, Charles Dickens rejects formal Christianity after his childhood. In his view, Anglicanism has become spiritually moribund. Likewise, Catholicism, stressing dogma to the detriment of good deeds, undermines Christian action. Evangelicalism, emphasising the Old Testament and the individual's sense of sin seems to "fragment the Christian Community and to neglect the New Testament's moral code."[1]

In the light of evangelical and dissenting criticism, Dickens inserts a general apology in the 1847 Preface to *Pickwick Papers* first cheap edition: "Lest there should be any well-intentioned persons who do not perceive the difference (as some could not, when OLD MORTALITY was newly published), between religion and the cant of religion, piety and the pretence of piety, a humble reverence for the great truths of Scripture and an audacious and offensive obtrusion of its letter and not its spirit in the commonest dissensions and meanest affairs of life, to the extraordinary confusion of ignorant minds, let them understand that it is always the latter, and never the former, which is satirised here. Further, that the latter is here satirised as being, according to all experience, inconsistent with the former, impossible of union with it, and one of the most evil and mischievous falsehoods existent in society—whether it establish its headquarters, for the time being, in Exeter Hall, or Ebenezer Chapel, or both."[2]

Dickens' contemporaries consider his religious iconoclasm as a blasphemous attack on Christianity. His irreverent presentation of clergyman such as Stiggins, and Chadband, religious humbugs like Mrs. Jellyby and Mrs. Pardiggle evokes hostile response from his critics. Many of the divines and reviewers call him 'sneerer and vilifier' of religion. *The Dublin Review* blames him for his libel against the Catholic religion. The high Church *Christian Remembrancer* notices 'mere pagan sentimentalism' in his works. Thomas Arnold, a tolerant advocate of the Broad Church theology fails to admire the real spirit of Dickens' attack on religious hypocrisy. Majority of his detractors miss to observe that Dickens wants to demolish not religion but the cant and perversion of religion. His satire on the cant of religion angers some people. His admirer, a methodist minister in Philadelphia complains to Dickens in 1867 that 'the satirical dress' clothed to his religious characters such as Stiggins, Chadband and Mrs. Clennam leads the young and uncultivated to respond to the strictest type of christian conduct with suspicion. Dickens contradicts the point of the clergyman and expresses his true sense of satire. He intimates that it is an age of great religious activity. There is immense enthusiasm for the common cause of Christianity, but especially more for the success of particular denominations. Competition with zeal leads to the engagement of irregular persons as christian teachers. He makes an effort to check this tendency and doing thus a good service to real truth.

Dickens' pitiless belittlement of the religious deviations fills the traditional and orthodox people with doubt and his religious implications evoke unfriendly reaction. All his reviewers and critics of the time fail to understand that Dickens never presents his religious view. He does not indulge in any theological discussion of the formal elements in Christianity.

In his novels, Dickens satirises the various forms of Christianity describing church rituals. His account of Paul's christening is superbly produced in his novel *Dombey and Son*. Holy Baptism is a sacrament deeply communal and takes place in the Sunday Worship Service. It celebrates the child's entry into the earthly christian community and at the same time the kingdom of God. Little Paul is brought to the Church. The place is chilly and earthy. The tall covered pulpit and reading desk; the gloomy empty pews lying under the galleries and lost in the shadow of the great grim organ; the dusty matting and cold stone slabs; the ghastly free seats in the aisles; and the damp corner by the bell-rope, where the black trestles used for funerals are hidden along with some shovels and baskets, and a deadly looking coil of rope; the strange, distinctive bad smell and the very pale light present a cold and dismal scene.

There is a wedding going on in the Church and it looks dismal. In the vestry the fire is smoking and a very old over worked and low paid attorney's clerk is searching. He is running his forefinger down the parchment pages of a big register gorged with burials. Over the fireplace is a ground plan of the vaults underneath the Church. Mr. Chick skims the literary part of it loudly and so enlivens the company. He reads the reference to Mr. Dombey's tomb in full and the marriage is performed too. Dickens attacks the Church as it accomplishes the matrimonial rites but Mr. Chick refers to Mrs. Dombey's tomb and attorney's clerk goes through the burial register.

After sometimes, a wheezy little pew-opener afflicted with an asthma, summons them to the font. She is fit for the churchyard and not for the Church. She, due to her infirmity, and so that the marriage party does not forget her, goes about the building coughing like a gampus. The clerk (the undertaker) comes up with a jug of warm water. He pours it into the font uttering something and takes the chill off. Then the clergyman, an amiable and mild-looking young curate and a tall figure, appears in full white dress. Paul rents the air with his cries, to see the ghastly sight. He is heard under the portico, during the rest of the ceremony, now fainter, now louder, now hushed. The attention of two ladies are distracted. Mrs. Chick is continuously deploying into the centre aisle, to send out messages by the pew opener and Miss Tox keeps her Prayer—book open at the Gunpowder Plot, and she, now and then, reads responses from that service.

Mr. Dombey remains impassive and perhaps assists in making it cold. The young curate smokes at the mouth as he reads. The clergyman delivers (very unaffectedly and simply) the closing exhortation, relative to the future examination of the child by the sponsors. "The register signed, and the fees paid, and the pew-opener (whose cough was very bad again) remembered, and the beadle gratified, and the sexton (who was accidentally on the door-steps, looking with great interest at the weather) not forgotten, they got into the carriage again, and drove home in the same bleak fellowship."[3]

Dickens describes the christening of Paul comically and satirically. Miss Tox's murmuring responses from the Gunpowder plot at the christening is a 'malice in...points of faith'.[4] When the ritual is over, its culmination is the clinking of coin—the clergyman, the pew owner, the beadle and the sexton all are remembered. The ritual of cash payment is done and the exchange of gifts is performed. The Church is a baptism mill, a marriage mill, and a funeral mill. One rite follows the other and the ministrants only collect coins at each round. In a Mammon worshipping age, "the church too has become unfeeling, and its rituals—organs of forgetting rather than remembering the dead, marital duty, or God's Commandments—only encourage the general spiritual amnesia."[5]

Dickens indicates the failure of Christianity as a Social Gospel by presenting the religious hypocrisy of English society in 19th century England in *Oliver Twist*. Oliver is interviewed by the Board when he returns from the branch workhouse:

> 'I hope you say your prayers every night', said another gentleman in a gruff voice; 'and pray for the people who feed you, and take care of you like a Christian.'
>
> 'Yes, Sir', stammered the boy. 'The gentleman who spoke last was unconsciously right. It would have been very like a Christian, and a marvellously good Christian, too, if Oliver had prayed for the people who fed and took care of him. But he hadn't, because nobody had taught him.'[6]

The question asked to Oliver is the introduction of religious rhetoric. According to the Board, Oliver should be rhetorically religious. "Like a Christian" in this context means the use of the ritual form and language only so that in the novel "Christian" becomes synonymous with hypocrisy and falsehood.[7] Compliments are paid to Sikes' dog. Sikes is very much surprised to find the dog's ferocity: 'He's as willing as a Christian, strike me blind if he isn't!, said Sikes, regarding the animal with a kind of grim and ferocious approval.'[8] Charley Bates considers the dog as christian and comments on the religious hypocrisy of English people:

> 'He's an out-and-out christian', said Charley.
>
> 'This was merely intended as a tribute to the animal's abilities, but it was an appropriate remark in another sense, if Master Bates had only known it; for there are a great many ladies and gentlemen, claiming to be out-and-out Christians, between whom and Mr. Sikes's dog there exists very strong and singular points of resemblance.'[9]

Dodger also notes the animal's surly attributes leading to a description of Puritan gloom and religious bigotry.

The new Poor Law amendment has provided teaching of Bible and Catechism and appointment of Chaplains and ministers in the workhouses. The comic satirist condemns the religious hypocrisy of divine service and Bible teaching in the workhouses. He satirises the nature of benefits of religious consolation in the baby farms. Oliver Twist is treated badly in the workhouse for his offence of asking for more gruel:

> He was kicked into the same apartment every evening at prayer time and there permitted to listen to, and console his mind with, a general supplication of the boys, containing a special clause, therein inserted by authority of the board, in which they entreated to be made good, virtuous, contented, and obedient, and to be guarded from the sins and vices of Oliver Twist: Whom the supplication distinctly set forth to be under the exclusive patronage and protection of the powers of wickedness, and an article direct from the manufactory of the very Devil himself.[10]

Dickens presents soulless ritualism in the religious observance of the Christian society of his time with sardonic fun in the burial service in *Oliver Twist.* A cynical absence of sensitivity to bereavement is shown. Oliver goes with Sowerberry as he measures a pauper's corpse and attends the poor woman's funeral. Sowerberry, the pauper woman's husband, and old mother, four bearers pressed into service from the workhouse and the beadle make a group for the pauper women's funeral. Dickens observes:

> At length, after the lapse of something more than an hour, Mr. Bumble, and Sowerberry, and the clerk, were seen running towards the grave. Immediately afterwards the clergyman appeared, putting on his surplice as he came along. Mr. Bumble then thrashed a boy or two, to keep up appearances, and the reverend gentleman, having read as much of the burial service as could be compressed into four minutes, gave his surplice to the clerk, and walked away again.[11]

Dickens satirises the clergyman. As a matter of fact, the burial service cannot be shortened. Dickens does not quote any prayer book word. This shows the complete failure of the perfunctory rite to console the two wretched mourners. The Church fails to act as a fundamental office for the poor. Dickens has based his detail on a funeral he has seen in real life. One day, Marcus Stone and Dickens have been walking in Cooling. Then, Dickens has told him: "You see that church? That is where I saw a pauper's funeral in *Oliver Twist*, exactly as it is written in the book. Here is something more interesting still. A few months afterwards I received a letter from the clergyman who behaved in an unseemly way on that occasion, asking me whether I conceived it possible that such a thing could ever occur. I wrote back to him and said; 'Thou art the man'."[12]

The novelist is aware of the shortcomings of the Established Church and its representatives which propel the criticism of the inadequacy of the religious institution. The Church does not fulfil the practical, saving role demanded of it by the gospels because the narrowness and rigidity of the Evangelicals dominating the Church weakens its ability. In describing Nemo's burial near the close of 'Our Dear Brother' in *Bleak House*, Dickens reproduces the priest's lines from the burial service to compare, in Stephen C. Gill's words, 'the horror of what is going on...with the meaning of genuine Christianity.'[13] The departed our dear brother is brought to a savage abominable ground to receive the Christian burial. The burial service reflects that its meaning is totally lost. The burial liturgy should mean as a reminder of the brotherhood of all under the parentage of God.

Dickens believes in a form of Christianity which aims at improving the condition of the poor and the outcast. So, he attacks the form of religious activity of his time not helpful to the poor:

> Much mighty speech making there has been, both in and out of Parliament, concerning Tom, and much wrathful disputation how Tom shall be got right. Whether he shall be put into the main road by constables, or by beadles, or by bell ringing, or by force of figures, or by correct principles of taste, or by high Church, or by low Church, or by no Church; whether he shall be set to splitting trusses of polemical straws with the crooked knife of his mind, or whether he shall be put to stone-breaking instead. In the midst of which dust and noise, there is but one thing perfectly clear, to wit, that Tom only may and can, or shall and will, be reclaimed according to somebody's theory but no body's practice. And in the hopeful meantime, Tom goes to perdition head foremost in his old determined spirit.[14]

The condition of Tom-all-Alone's is very pathetic but no Church is able to improve its condition and hence Dickens lashes the failure of Christianity to alleviate the circumstances of the downtrodden.

Dickens reveals the distortions of the Christian Church through the religious insensitiveness of his times. Jo, the poor crossing sweeper, attends 'Inkwich' for Nemo. His evidence is turned down since he is not able to express exactly the things to be done after his death in case he tells a lie. Dickens represents here the hypocrisy of the organised religion. The Church or body of proliferating sect, demands an answer on a point of doctrine that is not settled and decided by reputed theologians and divines. Jo's refusal as a witness by the established religion shows the hollowness of the Christian society. Dickens, as a satiric thrust, attaches negative implication to the holders of organised religion. So, a doctor, in place of the clergyman, conducts the final ritual of taking the dying child through the opening of the Lord's prayer.

Dickens laughs at the forms of Christianity of the time for their failure to develop a sufficient social gospel. Many working class men of Tom-all-Alone's and Bleeding Heart Yard find the religion misfit for them. Dickens shows the insensitivity of the organised religion through the complaint of the impoverished brickmaker:

> Don't I never mean for to go to Church ? No, I don't never mean for to go to Church. I shouldn't be expected there, if I did; the beadle's too genteel for me.[15]

Dickens ridicules the introduction of class discrimination in the House of God. The discarded and the impoverished think that religion is only meant for the rich folks. Henry Mayhew's report reveals that the London Scavanger never visits any Church or Chapel. Sometimes, he has not suitable clothes. He supposes that he cannot be admitted into such fine places in any working dress. He has been once in a Church but has felt quite strange and so he has never visited again. He thinks that the Churches are fittest for rich people.

Dickens attacks the malign features of evangelicalism. Evangelicalism is defined as a doctrine of salvation by faith in the atoning death of Christ. It refuses the effectiveness of good works or the sacraments. The Evangelical Protestant lays emphasis on the completely corrupt state of human nature following the Fall, recognises the sole authority of the Bible over Church or cleric, rejects the idea that any supernatural gift is imparted by ordination. This religion has developed out of the Methodist revival in the first half of the eighteenth century, and is concerned rather with the Calvinist than the Arminian branch of that movement. At the heart "of Evangelical theology, as at the heart of Methodism, stood the doctrine of conversion, a belief in the intense and dramatic personal change which occurred when, burdened down by a sense of sin and inadequacy, one threw oneself on God's mercy and was regenerated."[16]

The subversive cockney humour sets up the basic tone of Dickens' treatment of Evangelical cant in *Pickwick Papers*. This form of humour is rooted in a long tradition of popular anti-clerical and anti-religious satire of the medieval fabliaux. This post-Reformation development has associated religion incessantly with solemnity and has continued into the nineteenth century. The new puritanism of the Evangelicals has reasserted the impropriety of laughing at godliness. After the publication of *Pickwick Papers, Eclectic Review* has warned Dickens for his endeavour of making fun of fanaticism as it may lead the young and unitiated public to find merely "cant, hypocrisy and fanaticism" in Christianity. So, for the orthodox proponents of the *Eclectic Review*, fanaticism and hypocrisy should never be jested despite their existence. Dickens has attacked this monstrosity of religion through intermingling of high seriousness and folk humour. Anti-evangelical satire is present in *Pickwick Papers*. Christ has told Nicodemus that a man cannot see the kingdom of God unless he is born again. The exchange between Sam Weller and his father about Sam's mother-in-law satirically hints the distorted notions of rebirth and resurrection:

> 'How's mother-in-law this mornin'?
>
> 'Queer, Sammy, queer', replied the elder Mr. Weller, with impressive gravity. 'She's been getting rayther in the Methodistical order lately, Sammy: and she is uncommon pious to be sure. She's too good a creetur for me, Sammy. I feel I don't deserve her.'
>
> 'Ah', said Mr. Samuel, 'that's wery self-denyin' o' you.'
>
> 'Wery', replied his parent, with a sigh. 'She's got hold o' some inwention for grown-up people being born again, Sammy; the newbirth, I thinks they calls it. I should wery much like to see that system in haction, Sammy. I should wery much like to see your mother-in-law born again. Wouldn't I put her out to nurse!'[17]

The comic interlude, presents considerable fun. The elder Weller converses with Samuel Weller that his mother-in-law is extraordinary pious and she has got the invention of being born again. She, thus, belongs to the Methodists. Dickens makes a caricature to jeer at the evangelicals. "In fact, no term had been more frequently ridiculed by eighteenth century anti-Methodists than the expression 'New Birth'."[18] Dickens has firm belief that a man seeking heaven must be born again in the good thoughts of his creator. The novelist does not accept that it is helpful for a hound to express such in a definite snuffling form of words. The anti-evangelicals has treated snuffling a highly evangelical trait. In *Pickwick Papers*, prayer meetings, the 'kiss of peace', West Indian philanthropy and confused enthusiasm for temperance are also features of evangelicalism. Humphry House comments: "A joke as broad as this on a point of doctrine, not yet connected with any sanctimoniousness in a character, and a doctrine, moreover, found so easily in the Bible, suggests a clever journalist playing up to the drunk Church-and-king mobs hired to jeer at Wesleyans or Painites, and it is one of the rare instances in Dickens's novels of that sheer cock-a-snook vulgarity which peeps out at times in his letters."[19]

The 'methodistical order' uttered by Sam Weller, is related to the 19th century religious scene. Different Christian sects and denominations, struggled and competed to hold men's souls. Methodists, Calvinist Methodists, Armenian and Wesleyan Methodists and the Evangelicals intensely discussed their own denominational and ritual subtleties. The representative Methodist preacher and the gullibility of the innocent people are described in Albert H. Lyles' book *Methodism Mocked: The Satiric Reaction to Methodism in 18th Century*. The screams, the shout, the jarring songs, the disorders and indecencies of the Methodist revival meetings are found in *The Life of Joseph Barker*: "Barker was brought up a Wesleyan and became an itinerant preacher for the New Connexion until in 1841 he turned to unitarianism, then finally returned to Methodism as a Primitive Methodist Preacher. That Dickens had Methodists in mind, and indeed quite probably the primitive Methodists, is indicated by the pineapple-rum aspect of Stigginism which reaches its climax at that meeting of Brick Lane Branch of the Limited Grand Junction Ebenezer Temperance Association. In contrast to the main body of the movement, which was more moderate about the pleasures of the flesh, the Primitive Methodists called for complete abstinence, a call which inevitably led to dramatic backslidings among weaker brother'n."[20]

The term 'Methodistical' had become synonymous with 'evangelical' for long. Before Dickens, Sydney Smith revealed the insanity of the Methodistical sect and decried the Calvinist and the Evangelical conspiracy against common sense and reasonable orthodox Christianity. The perversion of the true religious spirit among the Methodists and Evangelicals, the religious excesses and dogmatic zeal of misled matrons create domestic disagreement and conjugal dissension. Dennis Walder notes: "Some are weak vessels like Mrs. Nubbles, others are stronger, like Mrs. Mac Stinger or Mrs. Varden, or more complex portraits such as Mrs. Murdstone and Mrs. Clennam, cold and heartless examples of where evangelical rigidity might lead. But what exactly is Mrs. Weller, theologically speaking? Mrs. Nubbles and Mrs. Mac Stinger may be dissenters: Mrs. Varden, Mrs. Murdstone and Mrs. Clennam, Church of England but Mrs. Weller's Association is 'Methodistical'."[21]

Dickens shows the distortions in Christianity when Mrs. Weller realises her folly in her deathbed recantation. Elder Weller reports to his son her feelings during her illness:

> That if a married 'ooman vishes to be religious, she should begin vith dischargin' her dooties at home, and makin' them as is about her cheerful and happy, and that vile she goes to church, or chapel, or wot not, at all proper times, she should be wery careful not to conwert this sort o' thing into a excuse for idleness or self-indulgence.[22]

The expressions of Tony Weller on flocks making clothes for copper coloured people and paying no attention to flesh coloured Christians show the religious hypocrisy of false philanthropy prevalent in the Methodists and the Christians. Dickens lodges fundamental objection to the misdirection of energy among zealots.

Dickens satirises evangelical religious hypocrisy in *Pickwick Papers*. A man of topographical bent knows that Muggleton is a corporate town, with a mayor, burgesses, and freemen. A person who consults the addresses of the mayor to the freemen, or the freemen to the mayor, or both to the corporation, or all three to Parliament, learns that "Muggleton is an ancient and loyal borough, mingling a zealous advocacy of Christian principles with a devoted attachment to commercial rights; in demonstration where of, the mayor, corporation, and other inhabitants, have presented at divers times, no fewer than one thousand four hundred and twenty petitions against the continuance of negro slavery abroad, and an equal number against any interference with the factory system at home; sixty-eight in favour of the sale of livings in the Church, and eighty-six for abolishing Sunday trading in the street."[23] Dickens satirises superficial concerns, manifestably hypocritical for the negroes, factory system and the Church and Sabbatarianism.

Dickens highlights Evangelical hypocrisy. Earlier, Cobbet had done by writing an Exposure of the Pretended Friends of the Blacks in 1830. Regarding the Factory Act, Evangelicals had been on both sides. Although some men's guilty feelings over situations in England had been displaced to a concern for foreign blacks. Dickens added to the "memories of parish meetings he had reported for the Morning Chronicle, at which the 'odious and oppressive tithe system was attacked for its tendency to bring religion and its ministers into contempt (5 December, 1834). Muggleton's weakness upon the corruption of the Church (the sale of livings and ecclesiastical sinecures led to Peel Ecclesiastical Commission at this time), linked with its enthusiasm for abolishing competitive street-trading on Sundays, suggests the kind of Sabbatarianism Dickens attacks in *Sunday Under Three Heads*, a mingling of commercial and religious impulses which he felt certain lay behind Sir Andrew Agnew's notorious Bill."[24] Dickens hated Evangelicalism in its cruder, harsher and non-conformist manifestations. He also criticised other forms of religious behaviour—Puseyism, Ritualist fopperies and Roman Catholic priestcraft.

Dickens attacks sabbatarianism in his novel *Little Dorrit*. When Dickens returns to London after a visit to Paris, he faces sorrowful London of which he penned to Sir Joseph Olliffe on Sunday 25 February 1855, "the bells are making such an intolerable uproar that I can't hear myself think."[25] In *Little Dorrit*, Arthur Clennam returns to London after a twenty year of absence. Dickens presents an anti-sabbatarian pronouncement:

> It was a Sunday evening in London, gloomy, close and stale. Maddening church bells of all degrees of dissonance, sharp and flat, cracked and clear, fast and slow, made the brick-and-mortar echoes hideous. Melancholy streets, in a penitential garb of soot, steeped the souls of the people who were condemned to look at them out of windows, in dire despondency. In every thoroughfare, up almost every alley, and down almost every turning, some doleful bell was throbbing, jerking, tolling, as if the Plague were in the city and the dead-carts were going round. Everything was bolted and barred that could by possibility furnish relief to an over worked people. No pictures, no unfamiliar animals, no rare plants or flowers, no natural or artificial wonders of the ancient world all taboo with that enlightened strictness, that the ugly South Sea gods in the British Museum might have supposed themselves at home again. Nothing to see but streets, streets, streets. Nothing to breathe but streets, streets, streets. Nothing to change the brooding mind, or raise it up. Nothing for the spent toiler to do, but to compare the monotony of his seventh day with the monotony of his six days, think what a weary life he led, and make the best of it or the worst, according to the probabilities.[26]

Dickens sketches a powerful picture of the gloom of London on Sunday. There are the noisy church bells heard. There are melancholy streets and the people are sad. Every sort of amusement is forbidden. Only streets are visible all around and nothing for recreation is available on sunday. Dickens satirises sabbatarians for restricting amusement on sunday. He depicts the despair of people with Baudelairean intensity. He uses parallel key images of Baudelaire's dark city scenes. At the same time, "the depiction of London's melancholy streets in their 'penitential garb of soot', steeping 'the souls of the people who were condemned to look at them out of windows, in dire despondency'...is clearly an attack upon the contemporary worship of 'the Lord's Day'."[27] London is transformed into a vast, frightful Sunday prison, "where the succession of gloomy desolate, streets adds to the controlled impression that it is a city of plague and death. Even the church bells have become imbued with the fanatical aspirations of their sabbatarian masters, and provide a damning insight into the sabbatarian mentality."[28] The state of spiritual desolation is depicted with the complete identity between Clennam's inner condition and the London he visits on a Sunday evening. The physical horror of the place is even worse: "Fifty thousand lairs surrounded him where people lived so unwholesomely, that fair water, put into their crowded rooms on Saturday night, would be corrupt on Sunday morning."[29]

In *Little Dorrit*, Arthur Clennam listens to the last monotonous bell while he sits in the coffee-house on Ludgate Hill on the Sunday morning in London. He remembers a series of miserable Sundays. He admits that he dislikes that day. There is the dreary Sunday of his childhood. During this, he is scared out of his senses by a terrible tract which begins business with the poor child by asking him why he is going to Perdition. The poor child is not in a condition to satisfy and his infant mind, is further attracted. There is the sleepy Sunday of his boyhood. Like a military deserter, he marches to chapel by a picket of teachers three times a day, morally handcuffed to another boy. He willingly barters two meals of indigestable sermon for another ounce or two of inferior mutton at his meagre dinner in the flesh. There is the boring Sunday of his nonage. His mother, grim of face and relentless of heart, sits all day behind a Bible. The sacred book is bound in the hardest and barest boards with decorated cover and a wrathful sprinkling of red upon the edges of the leaves. This is a fortification against sweetness of temper, natural affection, and a gentle intercourse. "There was the resentful Sunday of a little later, when he sat glowering and glooming through the tardy length of the day, with a sullen sense of injury in his heart, and no more real knowledge of the beneficent history of the New

Testament, than if he had been bred among idolaters. There was a legion of Sundays, all days of unserviceable, bitterness and mortification, slowly passing before him."[30]

Dickens' taunt on the Sabbatarians is present in *Nicholas Nickleby* when the young protagonist runs across an advertisement for a sincere cook:

> Family of Mr. Gallanbile, M.P. Fifteen guineas, tea and sugar, and servants allowed to see male cousins, if godly. Note. Cold dinner in the kitchen on the Sabbath, Mr. Gallanbile being devoted to the Observance question. No victuals whatever cooked on the Lord's Day, with the exception of dinner for Mr. and Mrs. Gallanbile, which, being a work of piety and necessity, is exempted. Mr. Gallanbile dines late on the day of rest, in order to prevent the sinfulness of the cook's dressing herself.[31]

In the advertisement, it is crystal clear that for the VIP's or the rich people, dinner on Sunday is exceptionally prescribed. Dickens satirises Sabbatarians for their discrimination between rich and poor while observing the Lord's Day. In an anti-Sabbatarian pamphlet, *Sunday Under Three Heads*, a minimal orthodox shrine is pictured as a fort of intolerant zeal and ignorant enthusiasm. Dickens attacks the organised sabbatarian activity.

Dickens saw Sunday used by the upper classes as a means of oppressing the lower. His *Sunday Under Three Heads*, was written against Sir Andrew Agnew's Sunday Observance Bill in 1836 and contains that every single restriction of the Bill on travelling, shopping, amusements etc. was a restriction on the poorer classes. The rich had the provision to use the seventh day as normal and their carriages, footmen, huge meals were served by servants. But for the poor any kind of travel and enjoyment was to be criticised and forbidden because they had not the leisure or the money for such things on the other six days of the week. Sunday was organised as "another means of keeping the people down and enforcing the 'prudence' and economy already advocated by the Malthusian politicians".[32]

Dickens scorned all types of intolerance and exclusiveness. Christianity was a religion of heart for him surpassing all sectarian obstacles, a unifying faith. When the spirit of anti-Catholicism and anti-Popery transformed into a fanatic Protestant creed and it became hard to profess reasonableness and liberal respect for other sects, the novelist attacked the sectarian intolerance in his novel, *Barnaby Rudge*. He expresses his total disliking for religious fanaticism and satirises demented enthusiasts to create a positive counteracting force of goodness based on reason and common sense. His preface to the novel embodies that he did not possess sympathy with the Romish Church and was charged with being hearty always and naive anti-Papist. The true spirit of his christian faith is revealed in his vindication of the rights of Catholics to worship according to his will. Dennis Walder notes: "True Protestantism is revealed in terms of the frank and honest attitudes of the locksmith Gabriel Varden who abhors his wife's mindless anti-popery and resists as strongly as he can the general upsurge in religious fanaticism around him."[33]

Dickens abhors sectarian religious violence, the product of ignorance and gullibility of common people. Dennis the hangman, and Muster Gashford meet Hugh and admit him as a member of the Protestant Association of England. They show enthusiasm, and violent sentiments in slogans:

> 'No Popery, brother!' cried the hangman.
>
> 'No Property, brother!' responded Hugh.
>
> 'Popery, Popery,' said the secretary with his usual mildness.
>
> 'Down with everybody, down with everything! Hurrah, for the Protestant religion!'[34]

Dennis represents brutality and cynicism prevalent in the religious bigotry. He inquires Lord Gordon's men: "Are we to be under orders to pull down one of them Popish chapels or what."[35] He hates the Papists. But he is fearful that Catholics may replace hanging by boiling and roasting when they will graf power. In the manner of Swiftian irony of *A Modest Proposal* and ridiculous religious enthusiasm of the mob, Dennis, too is very sceptical that he will become jobless:

> 'Well then, look here', said the hangman. 'If these Papists gets into power and begins to boil and roast instead of hang, what becomes of my work! If they touch my work that's a part of so many laws, what becomes of the laws in general, what becomes of the religion, what becomes of the country!'[36]

Dennis has visited the Protestant Church twice and he thinks that he is blessed by God in the form of new hanging laws enacted by Parliament:

> "Did you ever go to church, Muster Gashford?"
>
> "Ever!" repeated the secretary with some indignation; "Of course."
>
> "Well", said the ruffian, "I've been once-twice, counting the time I was christened—and when I heard the Parliament prayed for, and thought how many new hanging laws they made every session, I considered that I was prayed for."[37]

Dennis opposes Papists for their complete abolition so that they do not interfere with the Protestant system of hanging:

> Now mind, Muster Gashford,... I mustn't have my Protestant work touched, nor this here Protestant state of things altered in no degree, if I can help it; I must n't have no Papists interfering with me, unless they come to me to be worked off in course of law; I mustn't have no boiling, no roasting, no frying-nothing but hanging.... In support of the great Protestant principle of having plenty of that, I'll'...a burn, fight, kill-do anything you bid me, so that it's bold and devilish—though the end of it was, that I got hung myself.[38]

Dickens paints the dark side of Protestant religious bigotry and represents the Gordon riots as an event of extreme religious zeal as well as an example of denominational factionalism.

Dickens' satire on Little Bethelism is concerned with a return to the movement against narrow, cheerless religion opened in *Sunday Under Three Heads* and *Pickwick Papers.*

He attacks the inclination of religious professors to suppress the recreation of the poor. In *The Old Curiosity Shop*, the novelist is concerned with play going and the theatre. The long tradition of satiric invective is against "puritan attitudes towards the theatre, but, as Hood suggested, a new 'zeal-of-the-land-Busy' spirit was abroad in the 1840s, with bigots 'ready to burn' picture Galleries, Museums, Literary Institutions, Her Majesty's Theatres and the people's Punch and Judy".[39]

Dickens attacks the proselytism of Little Bethelism in *The Old Curiosity Shop*. Kit Nubbles promises to his family that they shall visit Astley's play house on his holiday. But his mother objects that plays are not sinful but she is afraid of it:

> 'I know who has been putting that in your head', rejoined her son disconsolately; 'that's Little Bethel again. Now I say, mother, pray don't take to going there regularly, for if I was to see your good-humoured face that has always made home cheerful, turned into a grievous one, and the baby trained to look grievous too, and to call itself a young sinner (bless its heart) and a child of the devil (which is calling its dead father names); if I was to see this, and see little Jacob looking grievous likewise, I should so take it to heart that I'm sure I should go and list for a soldier, and run my head on purpose against the first cannon-ball I saw coming my way.'[40]

According to Kit, his mother has changed under the effect of Little Bethelism. The baby is trained to look grievous too. Kit's mother wants to make him very wretched and uncomfortable. Kit suggests to her that there is no wrong in looking cheerful. The path of his making calls upon him to be a snivelling, solemn, whispering chap, sneaking about. He expresses in a most unpleasant snuffle. "The contemptuous repetition of sound and image in 'snivelling', 'sneaking', and 'snuffle', coupled with the reiterated assertion of a 'nat'ral' right to laugh, suggests an attack not just on the anti-theatre lobby, but on a total religious attitude. Many evangelicals (popularly supposed to be flat-nosed snufflers) held that frequenting plays afforded 'a proof of the depravity of human nature beyond most other things'...an association of Christian dogma and repression peculiarly repellant to Dickens, for whom, of course, human nature is essentially good, because made by the beneficent creator, as are the 'natural' emotions of joy and pleasure."[41] Kit Nubbles detests Little Bethel Chapel and its minister and it reflects Dickens's hatred of the Chatham Chapel and the preacher officiating there.

Dickens jabs at the cant of non-conformist religion and the style of its preaching in *The Old Curiosity Shop*: 'Stay, satan, stay!' roared the preacher again. 'Tempt not the woman that doth incline her ear to thee, but hearken to the voice of him that calleth. He hath a lamb from the fold!' cried the preacher, raising his voice still higher and pointing to the baby. 'He beareth off a lamb, a precious lamb! He goeth about like a wolf in the night season, and inveigleth the tender lambs!'[42] It is the caricature stricted through the depiction of zeal combining visual and auditory exaggeration that produces the satiric effect.

Dickens knew that the year 1851 was the time of religious crisis and public anxiety caused by the establishment of the Roman Catholic hierarchy in England during the previous year. "As to what Lord John Russell called 'papal aggression', he seems to have followed the Prime Minister's lead in blaming it upon the Puseyites: 'If the universities', he wrote to Miss Coutts on 22 August 1851, had been forced to adjust themselves to the character of the times, we never should have had to bless Oxford for the intolerable enormity it has dug out of the mire."[43]

Dickens hated the Roman Catholic Church and the Oxford Movement. The party within the Anglican church had its goal to restore it to primitive Catholic roots. E.B. Pusey, the new Oxford leader, was very instrumental in this regard. Dickens derides them in his novel, *Bleak House*. Apart from Mrs. Pardiggle, the ladies who ask Jarndyce for money to house the Medieval Mary's Sisterhood are Puseyites. But the most dangerous Puseyites are the fashionable guests gathered at one of Sir Leicester Dedlock's country house parties at Chesney Wold. They have established a 'dandyism' in religion:

> There are, at Chesney Wold this January week, some ladies and gentlemen of the newest fashion, who have set up a Dandyism—in Religion, for instance. Who, in mere lackadaisical want of an emotion, have agreed upon a little dandy talk about the Vulgar wanting faith in things in general; meaning, in the things that have been tried and found wanting, as though a low fellow should unaccountably lose faith in a bad shilling, after finding it out! Who would make the Vulgar very picturesque and faithful, by putting back the hands upon the Clock of Time, and cancelling a few hundred years of history.[44]

This is an attack upon the Oxford Movement in 1852. Dickens was disgusted at the establishment of the Roman Catholic hierarchy in England in 1850. The Puseyites were responsible for this great wickedness.

For Carlyle, 'dandy' was a fond word of public disgrace and shame, the opposite of the earnest man. In the manner of Carlyle, Dickens connects the Puseyite dandies with the other group of "elegant Chesney Wold guests 'of another fashion', 'who have agreed to put a smooth glaze on the world and to keep down all its realities'."[45] The dandy part of Puseyism—the High church ritual was disliked by Dickens and Carlyle. When Dickens tells of the dandy talk of the Vulgar wanting faith in things he implicates the general failure of Anglicanism to address itself to the working-class. Dickens knew that the Religious census of 1851 recorded the low proportion of the working-class professing any religion. He also noticed the scholars of the period discovering—the radical estrangement of the working class from religion during the first half of the nineteenth century. E.P. Thomson makes the same remarks in his Making of the English Working-class. Henry Pelling wrote about E.R. Wickham's *Church and People in an Industrial City*. He approves Wickham's evidence that in Sheffield the working class did find not only difficult to go to church or chapel, but disliked to go. John Morley pointed out that 'Anglican Church was not the church of a nation, but the church of a class; not the benign counsellor and helpful protectress of the poor, but the mean serving—maid of the rich'."[46] Dickens' references to dandyism in religion in *Bleak House* focus on the church of a class.

Dickens remarks on Jo in *Bleak House*: "And there he sits, munching and gnawing, and looking up at the great Cross on the summit of St. Paul's Cathedral, glittering above a red and violet-tinted cloud of smoke. From the boy's face one might suppose that sacred emblem to be, in his eyes, the crowning confusion of the great, confused city; so golden, so high up, so far out of his reach."[47] Dickens indicates that the great cross of St. Paul's Cathedral is itself the symbol of confusion. To the working class, the church is not helpful and so the church is not appealing to the workers. The cathedral dome is out of the reach of Jo like the source of celetial light is out of the range of the dog in Kafka's fable. Dickens satirises the senselessness and uselessness of the faith of his times.

In *Great Expectations*, Pip's state of his religious and spiritual awareness is described comically: "My construction even of their simple meaning was not very correct, for I read, 'Wife of the Above' as a complimentary reference to my father's exaltation to a better world; and if any one of my deceased relations had been referred to as 'Below', I have no doubt I should have formed the worst opinions of that member of the family. Neither, were my notions of the theological positions to which my Catechism bound me, at all accurate; for, I have a lively remembrance that I supposed my declaration that I was to 'walk in the same all the days of my life', laid me under an obligation always to go through the village from our house in one particular direction, and never to vary it by turning down by the wheelwright's or up by the mill."[48] The ironic presentation of Heaven and Hell and the Catechism is a satire on conventional theology.

In *Little Dorrit*, Arthur Clennam falls victim to the gloomy theology of the *Old Testament*. Its harsh glory shows the cruelty and materialism under pious masks. Arthur's parents weigh, measure and price everything and beyond these they treat no existence. Strict people are professors of a stern religion. Their very religion is a gloomy sacrifice of tastes and sympathies and these are offered up as part of a bargain for the security of their possessions. "Austere faces, inexorable discipline, penance in this world and terror in the next—nothing graceful or gentle anywhere, and the void in my crowd heart everywhere—this was my childhood, if I may so misuse the word as to apply it to such a beginning of life."[49] In the religion of Arthur's parents, materialism is of greatest importance. The heart of the Victorian paradox is "imagined in personal terms: The paradox of an evangelical spirit which denied the world, the flesh and the devil, while compromising itself with a thorough going, dutiful materialism."[50]

Arthur Clennam's mother is the presiding genius of a kind of wicked church. She is a woman of irreligious nature. She sits at her desk as if performing at a dumb church organ. She makes a prayer that her enemies might be "put to the edge of the sword, consumed by fire, smitten by plagues and leprosy, that their bones might be ground to dust, and that they might be utterly exterminated."[51] In the ridicule of Mrs. Clennam, Dickens lashes the narrow-minded traditional concept of religion that instilled into her mind the idea of the impurity of our hearts. In *Little Dorrit*, Dickens presents formal religious profession as a mask for hypocrisy and an excuse for cruelty.

Dickens reduces the preacher or clergyman to absurdity to ridicule them. Stiggins is a religious humbug and belongs to the evangelicals. John Foster was a Baptist minister and an ardent believer in the distinguishing doctrines of evangelicalism. His commentary on the evangelical cant and humbug is excellent. His reaction to a Stiggins is significant. The religious habits of some Christians is extremely disgusting. The people dislike everything grimace, as for instance, a solemn lifting up of the eyes, artificial impulses of the breath, grotesque and regulated gestures and postures in religious exercises, an affected faltering of the voice, and, abrupt and ill-timed religious exclamations in common discourse producing an irreverent and almost ludicrous effect, though they are even benedictions to the Almighty. Foster believes that "the happiest improvement in point of veneration for genuine religion will produce no tolerance still for such habits. Nor will the dislike to them be lessened by ever so perfect a conviction of the sincere piety of any of the persons who have fallen into them."[52]

When Sam Weller goes to Dorking to meet his father and step mother, he looks at Mr. Stiggins eating greedily the richly buttered toast and swallowing the hot pine-apple rum. The priest is described with denigration:

> He was a prim-faced, red-nosed man, with a long, thin countenance, and a semi-rattlesnake sort of eye-rather sharp, but decidedly bad. He wore very short trousers, and black-cotton stockings, which, like the rest of his apparel, were particularly rusty. His looks were starched, but his white neckerchief was not, and its long limp ends straggled over his closely-buttoned waistcoat in a very uncouth and unpicturesque fashion.[53]

Dickens satirises the practitioner of religion, Stiggins in *The Pickwick Papers*. Mr. Stiggins gets on his legs and proceeds to deliver an edifying discourse for the benefit of the company. He is to deliver discourse specially for Mr. Samuel. He adjurs Mr. Samuel in moving terms to be upon his guard in the sink of wickedness into which he is fallen. He asks him to abstain from all hypocrisy and pride of heart and to follow all things exact pattern and copy of him. He concludes that like him, he is a most estimable and blameless character and all his acquaintance and friends are hopelessly abandoned and profligate wretches. He further more conjurs him to avoid the vice of intoxication which he compares to the filthy habits of swine and dangerous drugs that filchs away the memory. At this point of his discourse, the reverend and red-nosed gentle man becomes singularly incoherent and staggers to and fro in the excitement of his eloquence.

Mr. Stiggins does not desire his hearers to be upon their guard against false prophets and wretched mockers of religion. They are more dangerous members of society than the common criminal. These professors of religion cast scorn and contempt on the most sacred, and "bringing into partial disrepute large bodies of virtuous and well-conducted persons of many excellent sects and persuasions. But as he leant over the back of the chair for a considerable time, and closing one eye, winked a good deal with the other, it is presumed that he thought all this, but kept it to himself."[54] Stiggins is represented in an ironical way. His way of discourse is caricatured. He possesses hypocrisy, a trait of evangelicalism. He preaches abstinence and belongs to The Brick Lane Branch of The United Grand Junction Ebenezer Temperance Association but he, himself, is addicted to wine. With Stiggins and other members of the Association, Dickens attacks the hypocrisy of the temperance movement and expresses contempt for missionary teetotalism. Mrs. Weller and the red-nosed gentleman vent a variety of pious and holy execrations against its authors. The latter recommends a "bottle of port wine, warmed with a little water, spice, and sugar, as being grateful to the stomach, and savouring less of vanity than many other compounds. It was accordingly ordered to be prepared. Pending its preparation the red-nosed man and Mrs. Weller looked at the elder W. and groaned."[55]

Mr. Stiggins tastes the contents of the glass which Sam places in his hand. He puts his umbrella on the floor and tastes it again passing his hand peacefully across his stomach twice or thrice. He "then drank the whole at a breath, and smacking his lips, held out the tumbler for more."[56] The Parish Priest, Stiggins, is satirised mercilessly with cruel barbs of ridicule. He grunts and groans and he is dealt with pungent sarcasm. He condemns Tony Weller for his refusal to contribute to the fund of the infant Negroes in the West Indies:

> "The fact is, my young friend", said Mr. Stiggins, solemnly, "he has an obderrate bosom. Oh, my young friend, who else could have resisted the pleading of sixteen of our fairest sisters, and withstood their exhortations to subscribe to our noble society for providing the infant negroes in the West Indies with flannel waistcoats and moral pocket handkerchiefs?"[57]

Tony Weller considers it better to help people nearer the home than abroad. He is well acquainted with the fact that the contribution made by the evangelical ladies is used to pay taxes and for the comforts of the priests. Mr. Stiggins, the deputy shepherd, is a parasite and borrows money. Tony Weller tells his son Sam Weller regarding Stiggins mode of borrowing: "Borrows eighteen-pence on Monday, and comes on Tuesday for a shillin' to make it up half a crown; calls again on Vensday for another half-crown to make it five shillin' and goes on, doubling, till he gets it upto a five pound note in no time, like them sums in the 'rithmetic book 'bout the nails in the horse's shoes, Sammy."[58]

Dickens reveals the parasitism of the organised religion. Weller discusses the exploitation of female groups by the Parish priests. He narrates that Mrs. Weller and other Parish women go from door to door taking in hand blue soup-plates for paying the water rates for the deputy shepherd. Mr. Stiggins' parasitism is described with sarcasm:

> "The shepherd's water-rate!" said Sam.
>
> "Ay", replied Mr. Weller, "there was three quarters owin', and the shepherd hadn't paid a farden, not he perhaps it might be on account that the water warn't o' much use to him, for it's wery little o' that tap he drinks, Sammy, wery; he knows a trick worth a good half dozen of that, he does. Hows'ever, it warn't paid, and so they cuts the water off. Down goes the shepherd to chapel, gives out as he's a persecuted saint, and says he hopes the heart of the turncock as cut the water off, 'll be softened.... Upon this, the women calls a meetin', sings a hymn, wotes your mother-in-law into the chair, wolunteers a collection next Sunday, and hands it all over to the shepherd."[59]

The utter defeat, utter humiliation, slapping, kicking of Stiggins and immersing of his head into a horse-trough full of water show Dickens' disillusionment with the hypocrisy of all organised religions. The death of Mrs. Weller results from her sitting long and late on the damp grass in the rains for listening to the deputy shepherd. This instills in him hatred for the religion represented by Stiggins. When the priest reaches Mr. Weller's house to mourn, he is ridiculously interested to know whether Mrs. Weller has left something either for him or for the chapel:

"Do you know, young man", whispered Mr. Stiggins, drawing his chair closer to Sam, "whether she has left Emmanuel anything?"

"Who's he?" inquired Sam.

"The Chapel", replied Mr. Stiggins; "Our Chapel; our fold, Mr. Samuel."

"She hasn't left the fold nothin', nor the shepherd nothin', nor the animals nothin", said Sam, decisively; "nor the dogs neither."[60]

Mr. Weller boils with violent anger to find the priest's presence. Mr. Stiggins engages himself to full use of the bar and the kitchen of the Weller household. Then Mr. Weller becomes furious and clutches him by the collar and kicks him. He pounds him with his toy boots and forces his head in horse trough full of water. The self-seeking deputy shepherd receives baptism by total immersion in water. Dickens' hatred of such priest is expressed when he makes Weller to utter: "Send any vun o'them lazy shepherds here, and I'll pound him to a jelly first, and drownd him artervards!"[61]

Dickens presents a non-conformist humbug Reverend Melchisedech Howler in *Dombey and Son* with a brilliant rhetorical flourish: "It was not unpleasant to remember, on the way thither, that Mrs. MacStinger resorted to a great distance every Sunday morning, to attend the ministry of the Reverend Melchisedech Howler, who, having been one day discharged from the West India Docks on a false suspicion (got up expressly against him by the general enemy) of screwing gimlets into puncheons, and applying his lips to the orifice, had announced the destruction of the world for that day two years, at ten in the morning, and opened a front parlour for the reception of ladies and gentlemen of the Ranting persuasion, upon whom, on the first occasion of their assemblage, the admonitions of the Reverend Melchisedech had produced so powerful an effect, that, in their rapturous performance of a sacred jig, which closed the service, the whole flock broke through into a kitchen below, and disabled a mangle belonging to one of the fold."[62]

Rev. Melchisedech Howler is the minister of the Ranting Persuasion. He preaches in a front parlour and it sustains so heavy effect on his congregation that they begin a live dance. He is produced as an "extravagance of humour, with what a rapture of robust mirth."[63] The satiric presentation commences with the fine choice of name and includes all the characteristic features. Dickens, definitely, knows that 'Ranter' is a designation generally applied to Primitive Methodists. He also knows that it is "not uncommon for Primitive Methodists (as well as for the members of several other sects) to 'jump' or even break out into dance during religious services."[64]

Making authoritative prophecies hypocritically masqueraded as divinely inspired was another characteristic of Howler. On approaching the chapel, a neat white washed edifice, recently engaged by the Reverend, he, on very urgent solicitation, consents to give "the world another two years of existence, but had informed his followers that, then, it must positively go."[65]

Howler's flexibility regarding prophecy is explicitly linked with his financial success in the preaching business—a traditional view of evangelical motives. Itinerant preachers, critics are regularly far "more interested in worldly gain than in saving souls."[66] The most serious charge against Independent Methodists is that of trading in souls. The preachers are in a sort of trade.

Another of Dickens' religious humbug is Reverend Chadband in *Bleak House*. He is a religious hypocrite. He thrives at the expense of the poor and the ignorant to exploit under the mask of his fierce evangelical cant. He is an insensitive and a savage religious minister. Dickens uses Chadband on a prototype of 'The Reverend Mr. Irving's Orations' in *Blackwood Magazine*. Irving is a member of the 'Gormandising School of Eloquence'. Chadband bears his affected manner, raising of his hand and his bombastic speech from this prototype. He has a disgusting appearance. His oily face, stern look and fat smile are physical attributes of his moral ugliness. Dickens uses an animal imagery of a trained circus bear to multiply the pungency of his personality:

> Mr. Chadband is a large yellow man, with a fat smile, and a general appearance of having a good deal of train oil in his system.... Mr. Chadband moves softly and cumbrously, not unlike a bear who has been taught to walk upright. He is very much embarrassed about the arms, as if they were inconvenient to him, and he wanted to grovel; is very much ...putting up his great hand, as delivering a token to his hearers that he is going to edify them.[67]

As the stupid religionist, Chadband is the typical example of the mischief of cant and hypocrisy in domestic missionary work. He professes no denominational ties and has no connection with any particular chapel, meeting house or church. It shows that "he is intended to be an evangelical and that he is probably a non-conformist."[68] He confirms his stupidity in his evangelical speech which clothes hypocrisy:

> I say this brother, present here among us, is devoid of parents, devoid of relations, devoid of flocks and herds, devoid of gold, of silver, and of precious stones, because he is devoid of the light that shines in upon some of us...I ask you what is that light?... 'It is,'...'the ray of rays, the sun of suns, the moon of moons, the star of stars. It is the light of Terewth...'. Say not to me it is not the lamp of lamps. I say to you, it is. I say to you, a million times over, it is.[69]

Dickens lashes the uneducated stupid preachers of the Evangelical Methodist sects in his childish and bombastic oration on 'terewth' (truth). The habit of distending common place comparisons was deeply fixed in evangelical speech. The associations proceed from word to word and move farther from the original point of reference. The "habit of association once formed may proceed in indefinite triumph with no point of reference at all."[70] The usual language of hypocrisy, of Vulgar hypocrisy, is cant. The religious cant is an affected use of the phrases which are heard employed as suitable to evangelical truth. The hypocrite connects no distinct ideas with these phrases. The appropriate diction vanishes from Christian society, leaving the truth in its mere essence. Consequently, the pretender reduces to assume the mask of religion on the wider and laborious plan of the acquisition of an understanding of its leading principles to assign them discriminately in his own language. "Religion would therefore be seldomer dishonoured by the mockery of a false semblance."[71] Chadband uses every noun twice. His is hypocritical effort to make more of less. He uses a kind of double talk.

Frye considers Stiggins and Chadband as the greasy lout of the same kind. They have their ancestor in Ben Jonson, zeal-of-the-Land Busy. Dickens presents Mr. Chadband as a flattering and gormandising hypocrite as he evokes the divine peace on Mrs. Snagsby household: "My friends", says Mr. Chadband, "Peace be on this house! On the master thereof, on the mistress thereof, on the young maidens, and on the young men! My friends, why do I wish for peace? What is peace? Is it war? No. Is it strife? No. Is it lovely, and gentle, and beautiful, and pleasant, and serene, and joyful? O yes! Therefore, my friends, I wish for peace, upon you and upon yours."[72]

As a clergyman, Chadband likes sermonising but accomplishes it in a boring and insinuating manner. Dickens implies that such sermonising is practically useless, "although it befits a man who trades in religion."[73] The sophistic redundancies of Chadband gather to what British calls, in connection with 'Busy', the "comic deformation of logic as a means of suggesting hypocrisy."[74] Chadband's ministrations provide "fine satires on evangelical habits of extempore preaching and prayer—described by Dickens as 'piling verbose flights of stairs, one upon another...[a] style of oratory...widely received and much admired'."[75]

Dickens considers religion meaningless unless it makes a practical effort to redress the grievances of the victims of society. In Jo, he finds a representative of the ghastly, stunted children and he condemns the society's failure to provide for destitutes like Jo. He shows the inhumanity and the insensitivity of the organised religion towards the reality of social misery and human tragedy. He focalises in Chadband's discourse:

> "We have here among us, my friends", says Chadband, "a Gentile and a Heathen, a dweller in the tents of Tom-all-Alone's and a mover-on upon the surface of the earth. We

> have here among us, my friends", and Mr. Chadband, untwisting the point with his dirty thumb-nail, bestows an oily smile on Mr. Snagsby,..."a brother and a boy. Devoid of parents, devoid of relations, devoid of flocks and herds, devoid of gold and silver, and of precious stones. Now, my friends, why do I say he is devoid of these possessions? Why? Why is he?" Mr. Chadband states the question as if he were propounding an entirely new riddle, of much ingenuity and merit, to Mr. Snagsby and entreating him not to give it up.[76]

Dickens scorns evangelical cant of the Chadband type and he shows the great corruption of this heartless discourse maker as he considers Jo's parents responsible for his impoverishment and not the society: "Or put it, my juvenile friends", said Chadband, stimulated by the sound, "that the unnatural parents of this slumbering Heathen—for parents he had, my juvenile friends, beyond a doubt-after casting him forth to the wolves and the vultures, and the wild dogs and the young gazelles, and the serpents, went back to their dwellings and had their pipes, and their pots, and their flirtings and their dancings, and their malt liquors, and their butcher's meat and poultry, would that be Terewth?"[77] The animal imagery used in this bombastic preaching is wonderful.

Reverend Chadband misappropriates Scripture texts. When he addresses Jo, "My young friend, it is because you know nothing that you are to us a gem and jewel" (19.242), he reverses Proverbs 20:15 ("the lips of knowledge are a precious jewel") in order to make Jo a likely prospect for his own lessons of wisdom. When he blesses the Snagsby dwelling, "May this house live upon the fatness of the land; may corn and wine be plentiful therein, may it grow, may it thrive, may it prosper, may it advance, may it proceed, may it press forward!" (242), Dickens' allusion to Isaac's blessing meant for Esau but given to the dissembling Jacob (Gen. 27:28) revises the roles in this classic case of deception: Chadband is the false patriarch blessing other impostors as well as himself, their well-fed guest who wants another invitation.[78]

Chadband uses monstrous attempts to reconcile Jo to his Maker. He addresses the starving Jo. He details insensitively on the boy's spiritual needs. He uses metaphysical nonsense and his high sounding religious talk contains Dickensian irony:

> My young friend, says Chadband, it is because you know nothing that you are to us a gem and a jewel. For what are you, my young friend? Are you a beast of the field? No. You are a human boy, my young friend. A human boy. O glorious to be a human boy! And why glorious, my young friend? Because you are capable of receiving the lessons of wisdom, because you are capable of profiting by this discourse, which I now deliver for your good, because you are not a stick, or a staff, or a stock, or a stone, or a post, or a pillar.[79]

Chadband uses absurd cants, a distinguishing characteristic of evangelicalism. Chadbandism furnishes its audience a refuge from the truths. He discourses on the spiritual unhappiness of Jo and sorts out its causes: "Because you are in a state of darkness, because you are in a state of obscurity, because you are in a state of sinfulness, because you are in a state of bondage."[80]

Chadband has no social role because instead of removing the darkness and obscurity, he delivers a discourse to Jo and hungry Jo stands perplexed. He expounds the doctrine of natural depravity to account for Jo's sufferings. All he offers to Jo is preachment and pedantry.

At home or abroad, religious efforts having smack of hypocrisy and self-gratification aroused Dickens' anger and he showed memorably by Chadband in *Bleak House*. Chadband's language of discourse is no medium of human communion. It is no thoroughfare but an expressive dead end. He does not deliver addresses but speaks absurd soliloquies and blinds Jo to any glimmer of truth. He thus obstructs the path to salvation. In the tradition of his spiritual predecessors Stiggins in *Pickwick Papers* and Melchisedech Howler in *Dombey and Son*, Chadband is engaged in the trade of "religious forms and professions strictly for his own benefit."[81] He deals in species of exhortation treated as spiritual and to rate at a fixed value in coin. The faults of Howler and Stiggins mark the faults of Chadband. With Chadband, Dickens pointed out that evangelicals were largely recompensed for the loss of worldly enjoyment by the table's pleasures. Chadband is unlike Stiggins or Howler a monument to the ridiculous use of pious jargon. Dickens, certainly, dislikes "sanctimonious slang: 'I discountenance all obtrusive professions of and tradings in religion', he wrote to a correspondent several years later, 'as one of the main causes why real Christianity has been retarded in this world'."[82]

Mr. Chadband drinks wine but remarkably notes that it is "our sinful material nature that requires us to take 'refreshment'."[83] The extremely righteous Chadband is neither a smoking oil factory nor a vessel of the spirit of God and requires always to be filled. He is Dickens' most successful comic portrait. He fattens himself and is engaged in "preaching about the sinfulness of the human condition".[84]

In Dickens' views, missionaries were complete nuisances as they were not able to improve the place and instead made it worse. He was specially disappointed by the overseas missionary work. Mrs. Jellyby and Mrs. Pardiggle, both Christian missionaries, are ridiculed in *Bleak House.* The denigration embodies the satiric presentation of the utopian projects of religious enthusiasts like Mrs. Caroline Chisolm of his time. Dickens joins a sardonic touch in the description of Mrs. Jellyby. She is a religiously mad woman and her philanthropic mission does not permit to look into the misery at home and she looks abroad. She is very much enthusiastically busy in her African Borrioboola Gha project but neglects her own children and husband. Richard and Ada go to Mrs. Jellyby's house and they find misery and filth there. They learn her unconcern for her children. Peepy, the little child has fallen downstairs and the visitors notice the dirt:

> I made my way to the poor child, who was one of the dirtiest little unfortunates I ever saw, and found him very hot and frightened, and crying loudly, fixed by the neck between two iron railings, while a milkman and a beadle,

> with the kindest intentions possible, were endeavouring to drag him back by the legs, under the general impression that his skull was compressible by those means.[85]

Mrs. Jellyby's scheme to cultivate coffee and the natives on the banks of Niger is associated with Exeter Hall, the bastion of Victorian evangelical philanthropy that promoted the ill-fated Niger expedition of 1846. Mrs. Jellyby reports to them a great deal about Borrioboola Gha and the natives. But her daughter Caddy exposes her mother's religious obsession with a misguided philanthropy: "I wish Africa was dead!... I hate it and detest it. It's a beast!"[86]

Temperance and abolition were the chief targets of the religious moral side of Caroline Chisolm's Buxton expedition. Dickens' satirical exposure of Mrs. Jellyby made his friend Lord Chief Justice Derman, the abolitionist charge Dickens of obstructing human progress. Dickens clarified that Mrs. Jellyby's exposure was the general vice of the time—the neglect of private duties. He had an underlying fear that such steps for public charity would destroy the real course by making an impression of cant and humbug in the minds of reflecting people.

Mrs. Pardiggle in *Bleak House* is a Puseyite Philanthropist. Dickens says that these enthusiasts confuse or avoid the social issue by a distorted kind of religion. Dickens shows his contempt for her: "She was a formidable style of lady, with spectacles, a prominent nose, and a loud voice, who had the effect of wanting a great deal of room. And she really did, for she knocked down little chairs with her skirts that were quite a great way off.... She seemed to come in like cold weather, and to make the little Pardiggles blue as they followed."[87]

Mrs. Pardiggle is very happy to talk the contribution made by her children to different charity organisations. Her talkativeness shows her foolish insensitivity to human condition:

> "These, young ladies", said Mrs. Pardiggle, with great volubility after the first salutations, "are my five boys. You may have seen their names in a printed subscription list (perhaps more than one), in the possession of our esteemed

friend, Mr. Jarndyce. Egbert, my eldest (twelve), is the boy who sent out his pocket money, to the amount of five-and-three pence, to the Tockahoopo Indians. Oswald, my second (ten-and-a half), is the child who contributed two-and-nine pence to the Great National Smithers Testimonial. Francis, my third (nine), one-and-six pence-half penny; Felix, my fourth (seven), eight pence to the Superannuated Widows; Alfred, my youngest (five), has voluntarily enrolled himself in the Infant Bonds of Joy, and is pledged never, through life, to use tobacco in any form."[88]

Mrs. Pardiggle also neglects her children. Edith Summerson and Ada see her children in bad condition and there is also a fierce glimmer in their eyes. Mrs. Pardiggle considers her superiority over Mrs. Jellyby as latter's children do not share their pocket money to ridiculous charity organisations like Tockahoopo Indian or Infant Bonds of Joy. She forces her children to attend the church services and this indicates the soulless routine of chapel going and hymn-reading matrons.

Dickens points out through his indignant satiric thrust that all the Jellybys, Pardiggles and Chadbands of the world make things worse. They confuse charity to suit their own need and thus dominate and exploit the religion.

Jo's condition is miserable. He is the victim of social neglect. But Mrs. Pardiggle or Mrs. Jellyby or the Society for the Propagation of the Gospel does not make efforts for his improvement. Dickens was called not only irreligious but also anti-christian by Reverend Henry Christopherson for his satirical treatment to the Society for the Propagation of the Gospel. He ridiculed the false philanthropy of the missionary organisations having concern for people beyond the seas and avoiding the sick and the suffering at home. In *Dexter Letters*, he opined that the home mission and the foreign mission were not conducted equally, despite the home claim being stronger and more urgent of the two. He refrained from drawing the stronger comparison between the sums even expended in efforts to remove the darkest ignorance and degradation from the very doors. He found mistakes in a sincere wish to do good.

Pecksniff, in Dickens' novel *Martin Chuzzlewit*, considers himself righteous. His virtue is self-proclaimed but his hypocrisy is representative of Dickens' comic genius. A female considers him as an exceptional missionary of peace and love. But a male treats him as a trader of saintly semblances. He retains a scriptural text or moral precept with him. He believes in a special providence:

> Now, there being a special Providence in the fall of a sparrow, it follows (so Mr. Pecksniff would have reasoned), that there must also be a special Providence in the alighting of the stone or stick, or other substance which is aimed at the sparrow. And Mr. Pecksniff's hook, or crook, having invariably knocked the sparrow on the head and brought him down, that gentleman may have been led to consider himself as specially licensed to bag sparrows, and as being specially seised and possessed of all the birds he had got together.[89]

Dickens satirises Pecksniff and makes a caricature of his belief in special providence. It is considered that many national undertakings were given justifications on the same lines and hence he claims for providential favour. Of this, Norris Pope comments: "Dickens, then, could not have avoided knowing that 'special providences' had a precise and vital significance for evangelicals, just as he would have been aware that the doctrine did not add to evangelical popularity. 'The mass of the world', Lord Ashley wrote in 1848, 'are all erect against the admission of special providences; it savours, they think, of fanaticism, hypocrisy, cant'."[90]

Dickens' bitter hatred of evangelicalism in its most malignant forms does not find expression against any typical Christian doctrine. He discusses Murdstone's religion:

> The gloomy taint that was in the Murdstone blood darkened the Murdstone religion, which was austere and wrathful. I have thought, since, that its assuming that character was a necessary consequence of Mr. Murdstone's firmness, which wouldn't allow him to let anybody off from the utmost weight of the severest penalties he could find any excuse

> for. Be this as it may, I well remember the tremendous visages with which we used to go to church, and the changed air of the place. Again the dreaded Sunday comes round, and I file into the old pew first, like a guarded captive brought to a condemned service. Again, Miss Murdstone, in a black velvet gown, that looks as if it had been made out of a pall, follows close upon me; then my mother; then her husband. There is no Peggotty now, as in the old time. Again, I listen to Miss Murdstone mumbling the responses, and emphasising all the dread words with a cruel relish. Again, I see her dark eyes roll round the church when she says, 'miserable sinners', as if she were calling all the congregation names. Again, I catch rare glimpses of my mother, moving her lips timidly between the two, with one of them muttering at each ear like low thunder. Again, I wonder with a sudden fear, whether it is likely that our good old clergyman can be wrong, and Mr. and Miss Murdstone right, and that all the angels in Heaven can be destroying angels. Again, if I move a finger or relax a muscle of my face, Miss Murdstone pokes me with her prayer book, and makes my side ache.[91]

Murdstone's religion is grim. A church going is presented where Miss Murdstone pokes David during the service with her prayer book till his sides ached. She rolls her dark eyes round. David pays attention to the church service and finds that the clergyman is singing a drowsy song. He, then, observes a child making faces at him. He sees outside the porch: "and there I see a stray sheep—I don't mean a sinner, but motton—half making up his mind to come into the church."[92] Dickens satirises the identification of deeply religious with a dead ritual of a harsh and gloomy nature.

Real Christianity is religion of the Murdstones in *David Copperfield*. But the Murdstones "still remain significant as Dickens's first serious attempt to portray the gloomy and repressive side of evangelicalism in a distinctly respectable, Anglican setting."[93]

A false religious cry was raised by men who have no religion and by those who cannot divide the commonest principle of right and wrong. It spread of intolerance and persecution and it was senseless no doubt. They represented ultra-protestant bigotry: "Many of those who were banded together to support the religion of their country, even unto death, had never heard a hymn or a psalm in all their lives. But these fellows having for the most part strong lungs, and being naturally fond of singing, chanted any ribaldry or nonsense that occurred to them, feeling pretty certain that it would not be detected in the general chorus, and not caring much if it were."[94]

The depiction of religious bigotry and irrational progression of numerical strength of those that participate in such movements is observable in *Barnaby Rudge*. People not even religious participated in the anti-Catholic riots. Marcus notes: "In representing the Gordon riots as an amalgam of extreme religious zeal and primitive protest and radicalism, Dickens accentuated the similarities between the disturbance of 1780 and what he conceived to be dangerous circumstances of his own time."[95] Dickens observes that "it was a most exquisite satire upon false religious cry which had led to so much misery, that some of these (condemned rioter) owned themselves to be Catholics, and begged to be attended by their own priests."[96]

Mrs. Varden is a firm Protestant. She subdues her husband with Protestant religion. She is very sensitive of references made to God and angels in relation to human beings. Miss Miggs admires her for maintaining an angel's sweetness in her nature and Mrs. Varden reacts sharply:

> "Miggs", said Mrs. Varden, "You're profane."
>
> "Begging your pardon, mim", returned Miggs, with shrill rapidity, "such was not my intentions, and such I hope is not my character, though I am but a servant."
>
> "Answering me, Miggs, and providing yourself", retorted her mistress,..."is one and the same thing. How dare you speak of angels in connection with your sinful fellow-beings...'mere'...'worms and grovellers as we are!'"[97]

Mrs. Varden possesses enthusiastic spirit of Protestantism and engages herself again and again to moralistic preachings to an unattentive audience. Love is sinister for her and concerns the perdition and corruption of the human soul. Hugh intimates her that he owns the tenderest heart alive and loves all the ladies. Mrs. Varden scolds him for this irreligious outpourings: "Mrs. Varden opined that if he did, he ought to be ashamed of himself; such sentiments being more consistent...with a benighted Mussulman or wild Islander than with a staunch Protestant."[98] Dickens satirises the hypocrisy of this misled Protestant when she preaches the sleeping Joe Willet:

> This she proceeded to do, and finding that Mr. Willet's eyes were fixed upon her with an appearance of deep attention, gradually addressed the whole of her discourse to him, whom she entertained with a moral and theological lecture of considerable length, in the conviction that great workings were taking place in his spirit. The simple truth was, however, that Mr. Willet, although his eyes were wide open and he saw a woman before him whose head by long and steady looking at seemed to grow bigger and bigger until it filled the whole bar, was to all other intents and purposes fast asleep.[99]

Mr. Varden, her husband, advises her daughter, Dolly, to read a tale 'Blue Beared' by Charles Perrault. Mrs. Varden reacts that she cannot tolerate her child recommended for perusal of the adventures of a Turk or Mussulman. She admires Lord George Gordon's speeches. The Protestant Association is run by her. She charges Mr. Varden that he had not dropped something into the charity box except a tobacco-pipe's two little bits. She admires her daughter Dolly as she dropped ribbons and bands into the charity box. She is happy with Miss Miggs "who flung her wages, as it were, into the very countenance of the Pope, and bruised his features with her quarter's money."[100] Mrs. Varden considers any contribution to this association as a challenge to Pope for true religion. She, like Lord George Gordon's mob, believes in 'No Popery'.

Dickens attacks the misguided religious enthusiasm and hypocrisy of Mrs. Varden. She possesses zeal for Protestant religion but she is not sincere in its practical application to her daily life. She eats more but moralises her daughter Dolly to "reflect upon the voluntary sacrifices of the missionaries in foreign parts who lived chiefly on salads."[101] Dickens laughs at the hypocrisy of Mrs. Varden: "Mrs. Varden was seldom very Protestant at meals, unless it happened that they were under-done, or over-done, or indeed that anything occurred to put her out of humour. Her spirits rose considerably on beholding these goodly preparations, and from the nothingness of good works, she passed to the somethingness of ham and toast with great cheerfulness."[102]

Miss Miggs, the woman servant in Varden's housc, also practices religion on wrong principle. She scorns the whole male sex on the general principle and proposition of Protestant ethics: Fickle, false, base, scottish, inclined to perjury, and wholly undeserving. On a mysogynistic pattern, she likes the death of womankind to teach a lesson to the male sex:

> nay, her feeling for her order ran so high, that she sometimes declared, if she could only have good security for a fair, round number—say, ten thousand—of young virgins following her example, she would, to spite mankind, hang, drown, stab, or poison herself, with a joy past all expression.[103]

Dickens presents the danger of fanaticism reaching the broad masses. Miss Miggs responds to the rioters to spread her bitterness and hatred: "Simmun and gentlemen, I've been locked up here for safety, but my endeavours has always been, and always will be, to be on the right side—the blessed side—and to prenounce the Pope of Babylone, and all her inward and her outward workings, which is Pagin. My sentiments is of little consequences, I know, cried Miggs, with additional shrillness."[104] As a protestant, Miss Miggs thinks others as pagans.

In *Our Mutual Friend*, Reverend Frank Milvey is a sincere, tolerating and painstaking man of religion. Mr. Boffin, the Golden Dustman, approaches him for his assistance in getting an orphan for adoption. Both the clergyman and his wife fix their own responsibility and go to every workhouse and the Infant school in search of an orphan. This philanthropic mission brings about spurt in the prices of an orphan and Dickens satirises the religious hypocrisy of English people: "The suddenness of orphans rise in the market was not to be paralleled by the maddest records of the Stock Exchange. He would be at five thousand per cent discount at nurse making... and would go up to five thousand per cent premium before noon."[105]

## NOTES

1. Vogel Jane, *Allegory in Dickens*, The University of Alabama Press, University of Alabama, 1977, p. 22.
2. Norris Pope, *Dickens and Charity*, Macmillan, London, 1978, p. 21.
3. Valerie Purton, *Dombey and Son,* 'Everyman,' J.M. Dent, London, Charles E. Tuttle, Vermont, 1997, pp. 58-59.
4. Janet L. Larson, *Dickens and the Broken Scripture*, The University of Georgia Press, Athens, 1985, p. 89.
5. *Ibid.*, pp. 88-89.
6. Introduction and notes by Ella Westland, *Oliver Twist,* Charles Dickens, Wordsworth Classics, Hertfordshire, 2000, p. 10.
7. Joseph Gold, *Charles Dickens: Radical Moralist*, University of Minnesota Press, Minneapolis, 1972, p. 36.
8. Ella Westland, *op. cit.*, p. 98.
9. *Ibid.*, p. 116.
10. *Ibid.*, p. 15.
11. *Ibid.*, p. 35.
12. Dennis Walder, *Dickens and Religion*, George Allen and Unwin, London, Boston, Sydney, 1981, p. 54.
13. Janet L. Larson, *op. cit.*, p. 28.
14. Andrew Sanders, *Bleak House,* 'Everyman,' J.M. Dent, London, Charles E. Tuttle, Vermont, 1994, p. 568.
15. *Ibid.*, p. 100.
16. Dennis Walder, *op. cit.*, p. 18.
17. Introduction and notes by David Ellis, *The Pickwick Papers,* Charles Dickens, Wordsworth Classics, Hertfordshire, 2000, p. 281.
18. Norris Pope, *op. cit.*, p. 22.
19. Humphry House, *The Dickens World*, Oxford University Press, London, New York, Toronto, 1942, p. 114.
20. Dennis Walder, *op. cit.*, p. 39.

21. *Ibid.*, p. 35.
22. David Ellis, *op. cit.*, p. 680.
23. *Ibid.*, p. 88.
24. Dennis Walder, *op. cit.*, p. 39.
25. *Ibid.*, p. 176.
26. Harvey Peter Sucksmith, *Charles Dickens, Little Dorrit*, Oxford, At the Clarendon Press, 1979, pp. 26-29.
27. Dennis Walder, *op. cit.*, p. 176.
28. Norris Pope, *op. cit.*, p. 84.
29. *Little Dorrit,* Charles Dickens, Wordsworth Classics, Hertfordshire, 1996, p. 29.
30. Harvey Peter Sucksmith, *op. cit.*, pp. 30-31.
31. Dickens Charles, *Nicholas Nickleby, Hard Times, A Christmas Carol*, Octopus Books Ltd., London, 1983, p. 135.
32. Humphry House, *op. cit.*, p. 124.
33. Dennis Walder, *op. cit.*, p. 92.
34. Donald Hawes, *Charles Dickens, Barnaby Rudge*, 'Everyman,' J.M. Dent, London, Charles E. Tuttle, Vermont, 1996, p. 291.
35. *Ibid.*, p. 286.
36. *Ibid.*, p. 287.
37. *Ibid.*
38. *Ibid.*
39. Dennis Walder, *op. cit.*, p. 68.
40. *The Old Curiosity Shop,* Wordsworth Classics, Hertfordshire, 1995, pp. 142-43.
41. Dennis Walder, *op. cit.*, p. 68.
42. *The Old Curiosity Shop*, *op. cit.*, pp. 261-62.
43. A.E. Dyson, *Dickens, Bleak House*, Macmillan, London, 1969, p. 108.
44. Andrew Sanders, *op. cit.*, p. 146.
45. Graham Storey, *Charles Dickens, Bleak House*, Cambridge, University Press, 1987, p. 4.
46. John Lucas, *The Melancholy Man*, Methuen & Co. Ltd., London, 1970, p. 217.
47. Andrew Sanders, *op. cit.*, p. 248.
48. Margaret Cardwell, *Charles Dickens*, *Great Expectations*, Oxford University Press, New York, 1994, p. 42.

49. Harvey Peter Sucksmith, *op. cit.*, p. 20.
50. Dennis Walder, *op. cit.*, p. 185.
51. Dorrit Little, *op. cit.*, p. 36.
52. Humphry House, *op. cit.*, p. 115.
53. David Ellis, *op. cit.*, p. 344.
54. *Ibid.*, p. 591.
55. *Ibid.*, p. 589.
56. *Ibid.*, p. 590.
57. *Ibid.*, p. 346.
58. *Ibid.*, p. 347.
59. *Ibid.*, p. 348.
60. *Ibid*, p. 685.
61. *Ibid.*, p. 686.
62. Valerie Purton, *op. cit.*, pp. 202-03.
63. George Robert Gissing, *Charles Dickens: A Critical Study*, Blackie, Bombay, 1928, p. 111.
64. Norris Pope, *op. cit.*, p. 27.
65. Valerie Purton, *op. cit.*, p. 822.
66. Norris Pope, *op. cit.*, p. 28.
67. Andrew Sanders, *op. cit.*, p. 240.
68. Norris Pope, *op. cit.*, p. 128.
69. Andrew Sanders, *op. cit.*, pp. 327-28.
70. Humphry House, *op. cit.*, p. 117.
71. *Ibid.*
72. Andrew Sanders, *op. cit.*, p. 240.
73. Debiprasad Bhattacharya, *The Middle Class in Dickens*, Minerva Associates, Calcutta, 2000, p. 105.
74. Garret Stewart, *Dickens and the Trials of Imagination*, Harvard University Press, Cambridge, Massachussetts, 1974, p. 132.
75. Norris Pope, *op. cit.*, p. 131.
76. Andrew Sanders, *op. cit.*, p. 327.
77. *Ibid.*, p. 329.
78. Janet L. Larson, *op. cit.*, p. 19.
79. Andrew Sanders, *op. cit.*, p. 247.
80. *Ibid.*

81. Paul Schlicke, *Oxford Readers Companion to Dickens*, Oxford, The University Press, 1999, p. 84.
82. Norris Pope, *op. cit.*, p. 29.
83. Paul Schlicke, *op. cit.*, p. 180.
84. *Ibid.*, p. 228.
85. Andrew Sanders, *op. cit.*, p. 34.
86. *Ibid.*, p. 41.
87. *Ibid.*, p. 93.
88. *Ibid.*, pp. 93-94.
89. *Martin Chuzzlewit*, Charles Dickens, Wordsworth Classics, Hertfordshire, 1994, p. 304.
90. Norris Pope, *op. cit.*, p. 27.
91. Introduction and notes by Adrienne E. Gavin, *David Copperfield,* Charles Dickens, Wordsworth Classics, Hertfordshire, 2000, p. 48.
92. *Ibid.*, p. 18.
93. Norris Pope, *op. cit.*, p. 29.
94. Donald Hawes, *op. cit.*, p. 370.
95. Steven Marcus, *Dickens from Pickwick to Dombey*, Chatto & Windus, London, 1965, p. 175.
96. John Lucas, *op. cit.*, p. 103.
97. Donald Hawes, *op. cit.*, p. 107.
98. *Ibid.*, p. 166.
99. *Ibid.*, pp. 166-67.
100. *Ibid.*, p. 316.
101. *Ibid.*, pp. 167-68.
102. *Ibid.*, p. 167.
103. *Ibid.*, p. 57.
104. *Ibid.*, p. 483.
105. *Our Mutual Friend*, Charles Dickens, Wordsworth Classics, Hertfordshire, 1997, p. 183.

# Politics, Commerce and Utilitarianism

# 4

## POLITICS

Dickens has worked as a parliamentary reporter of *The Morning Chronicle* and *The Mirror of Parliament*. Parliament has been a talking shop and it has been a spectacle of noise and chaos. Witnessing the legislative proceedings and observing the petty politicians in English political life, Dickens has grown increasingly sceptical of the mechanics of parliamentary democracy for the nation's benefit. For Dickens, Politics have been the battle of the polling-booths. Also, he has not insisted on the immediate and wide extension of the right to vote as demanded by other Radicals. He has sought clean air instead of "fetid vapours in the streets and had only contempt for the hot air of oratory on the hustings and in the Houses of Parliament."[1]

Dickens has preferred popular government to representative government. According to him, representatives are not chosen fairly and behave quite undemocratically after their election. He has replied to a vote of thanks at the Birmingham and Midland Institute on September 27, 1869: "I will now discharge my conscience of my political creed, which is contained in two articles, and has no reference to any party or persons. My faith in the people governing is, on the whole, infinitesimal; my faith in the People governed is, on the whole, illimitable."[2]

Dickens has explained that while the hearts of the People (capital P) are sound, the heads of the people (small P) who govern are unsound. Hopes of reform has seemed to be chimerical and lawgivers are proved to be the obstructionists of the society. When Dickens has been asked to stand for Parliament, his refusal is explicit: "I believe that no consideration would induce me to become a member of that extra-ordinary assembly." ..."It appears to me that the House of Commons and Parliament altogether is become just the dreariest failure and nuisance that ever bothered this much bothered world."[3] Dickens mistrusts Parliamentary Institutions. He condemns the people who run these institutions in **American Notes**: "I do not remember having ever fainted away, or having even been moved to tears of joyful pride, at sight of legislative body. I have borne the House of Commons like a man, and have yielded to no weakness, but slumber, in the House of Lords. I have seen elections for borough and county, and have never been impelled (no matter which party won) to damage my hat by throwing it up into the air in triumph, or to crack my voice by shouting forth any reference to our Glorious Constitution, to the noble purity of our independent voters, or, the unimpeachable integrity of our independent members."[4]

Dickens' experiences in America and the United Kingdom has brought him to the conclusion that elected assemblies were inadequate as legislators and also inadequate as a means to bring public opinion to bear on the executive.

Dickens has wide experience as a parliamentary reporter and he has long connection and closeness with Carlyle. So, he looks upon the parliamentary system of government with ridicule. No doubt, he has regard for democratic rule. But like Carlyle, he does not cherish the idea that parliament should be totally abolished to welcome the benevolent despot. He attacks this system of administration because he thinks that it cannot do positive good to the people.

Dickens, in *Pickwick Papers*, presents a comic and satirical description of Eatanswill election. He turns it into a riotous farce. The Eatanswill people consider themselves of the utmost and most mighty importance. Everyman in Eatanswill, feels himself bound to unite, heart and soul, with one of the two great parties that divides the town—the Blues and the Buffs. Dickens ridicules the rivalry between two political parties: "Now the Blues lost no opportunity of opposing the Buffs, and the Buffs lost no opportunity of opposing the Blues; and the consequence was, that whenever the Buffs and Blues met together at public meeting, Town-Hall, fair, or market, disputes and high words arose between them. With these dissensions it is almost superfluous to say that everything in Eatanswill was made a party question. If the Buffs proposed to new skylight the market-place, the Blues got up public meetings, and denounced the proceeding; if the Blues proposed the erection of an additional pump in the High Street, the Buffs rose as one man and stood aghast at the enormity. There were Blue shops and Buff shops, Blue inns and Buff inns; there was a Blue aisle and a Buff aisle in the very church itself."[5] The deterioration in the democratic values had percolated down to the worst. Even over the minor issues of concern, political vendetta was triggered.

Party politics regards that it is possible for two rational people to "hold different opinions about a policy and possible for a man to be convinced by argument that his opinion has been mistaken. It also presupposes that, however widely their political opinions may differ, all voters are agreed that the goal of politics is the establishment of a just and smoothly running society. But in Eatanswill the pleasure of party rivalry and debate has become an end in itself to both parties, a closed game world, and the real goal of politics has been forgotten."[6] Dickens' invective at the politicians of his time in *Pickwick Papers* is good-humoured and mildly satirical.

In England, Dickens has seen from his boyhood that parliament has been becoming imperfect due to the initial corruption of its members through the process of election. Merit has been undermined by the social or financial influence during the electoral process. Secondly, the corruption of electioneering promises and party propaganda has destroyed the morale of an M.P. from the very beginning. Hence Dickens suspects the very sincerity and independence of its members. In *Pickwick Papers*, there are two newspapers in the town—*Eatanswill Gazette* and the *Eatanswill Independent*. The former advocates Blue principles and the latter Buffs. Honourable Samuel Slumkey, of Slumkey Hall, is the Blue candidate and Horatio Fizkin, Esq. of Fizkin Lodge, near Eatanswill, is the

Buff candidate. There is immense heat and dust about the election. There is the mockery of convassing in Eatanswill election in *Pickwick Papers*:

> A crowd of idlers were assembled in the road, looking at a hoarse man in the balcony, who was apparently talking himself very red in the face in Mr. Slumkey's behalf; but the force and point of whose arguments were somewhat impaired by the perpetual beating of four large drums which Mr. Fizkin's committee had stationed at the street corner. There was a busy little man beside him, though, who took off his hat at intervals and motioned to the people to cheer, which they regularly did, most enthusiastically; and as the red-faced gentleman went on talking till he was redder in the face than ever, it seemed to answer his purpose quite as well as if anybody had heard him.[7]

Dickens satirises the malpractices used by the parties in Eatanswill election. Mr. Pickwick, who has gone to this town to see an election, goes to Perker, Samuel Slumkey's agent, and makes an enquiry:

> 'And what are the probabilities as to the result of the contest?' inquired Mr. Pickwick.
>
> 'Why doubtful, my dear sir, rather doubtful as yet', replied the little man. 'Fizkin's people have got three-and-thirty voters in the lock-up coach-house at the White Hart.'
>
> 'In the coach-house!', said Mr. Pickwick, considerably astonished by this second stroke of policy.
>
> 'They keep'em locked up there till they want'em', resumed the little man. 'The effect of that is, you see, to prevent our getting at them; and even if we could, it would be of no use, for they keep them very drunk on purpose. Smart fellow Fizkin's agent-very smart fellow indeed.'
>
> Mr. Pickwick stared, but said nothing.

'We are pretty confident, though', said Mr. Perker, sinking his voice almost to a whisper. 'We had a little tea-party here, last night-five-and-forty women, my dear sir—and gave everyone of'em a green parasol when she went away.'

'A parasol!' said Mr. Pickwick.

'Fact, my dear sir, fact. Five-and-forty green parasols, at seven and six pence a piece. All women like finery,—extraordinary the effects of those parasols. Secured all their husbands, and half their brothers-beats stockings, and flannel, and all that sort of thing hollow. My idea, my dear sir, entirely. Hail, rain, or sunshine, you can't walk half a dozen yards up the street, without encountering half a dozen green parasols.'[8]

The farcical nature of the election campaign is described in *Pickwick Papers*. There is noise and bustle from the morning. The beating of drums, the blowing of horns and trumpets, and shouting of men, and tramping of horses, echoe and re-echoe through the streets from the very dawn. The occasional fight between the light skirmishers of either party has suddenly "enlivened the preparations and agreeably diversified their character".[9]

The use of unfair strategies in the election is described humorously and satirically in *Pickwick Papers*:

> 'Nothin' at all, sir', replied his attendant. 'The night afore the last day o' the last election here, the opposite party bribed the bar-maid at the Town Arms, to hocus the brandy and water of fourteen unpolled electors as was a stoppin' in the house.'

'What do you mean by "hocussing" brandy and water?' inquired Mr. Pickwick.

'Puttin' laud'num in it', replied Sam, 'Blessed if she didn't send'em all to sleep till twelve hours arter the election was over. They took one man up to the booth, in a truck, fast asleep, by way of experiment, but it was no go—they wouldn't poll him; so they brought him back, and put him to bed again.'[10]

The pomp, pageantry and exhibitionism of the parties are satirised humorously in *Pickwick Papers*. The stable-yard shows symptoms of the glory and strength of the Eatanswill Blues. There is a regular army of blue flags. Some are with one handle, and some with two. They exhibit in golden characters four feet high, and stout in proportion. There is a grand band of trumpets, bassoons and drums. There are bodies of constables with blue staves, twenty committee-men with blue scarfs, and a mob of voters with blue cockades. There are electors on horseback and electors on foot. There is an open carriage and four, for the Honourable Samuel Slumkey. There are four carriages and pair, for his friends and supporters. The flags rustle and the band plays. The constables swear and the twenty committee men squabble. The mob shouts and the horses back. The post-boys perspire. Everything is arranged and the whole assembly works for the Honourable Samuel Slumkey, of Slumkey Hall. He is one of the candidates for the representation of the Borough of Eatanswill, in the Commons House of Parliament of the United Kingdom.

The parties, very cleverly, sympathise with the voters to win the election. Perker replies to Samuel Slumkey about the preparation of the husting:

> Nothing has been left undone, my dear sir—nothing whatever. There are twenty washed men at the street door for you to shake hands with; and six children in arms that you're to pat on the head, and inquire the age of; be particular about the children, my dear sir,—it has always a great effect, that sort of thing.[11]

Steven Marcus observes: "An election is an amusing nuisance, and Dickens doesn't regard it as important or offensive enough to be angry about. Politics in this view is discontinuous with the business of life—its meaning, its rationale, is manifest only to those who are professionally implicated in it, the politicians."[12]

In *Bleak House*, Sir Leicester and his group have deteriorated and influences the politics of the country for the gain of his class. He does not hesitate to bully or buy a victory in Parliamentary elections. He is very resentful of the corrupt opposition for making the expensive course necessary. "The 'hundreds of thousands of pounds' required to bring about the truimph of his own party he blames on the 'implacable description' of the opposition and the 'bad spirit' of the people."[13] His cousin, Volumnia, is unable to guess the requirement of this huge money. Sir Leicester retorts her: "It is disgraceful to the electors. But as you, though inadvertently, and without intending so unreasonable a question, asked me 'what for?' let me reply to you. For necessary expenses."[14] Sir Leicester feels that there is a whisper abroad that these necessary expenses are to be connected with bribery in some two hundred election petitions.

The opposition is a rival group contending for the benefits of office. Irrespective of the party winning the election, the country is yet dominated by wealth and privilege that manipulate the political governments. This applies also when the candidates of Mr. Rouncewell, the ironmaster, bag a few seats. This application still holds when they fill the House, despite Sir Leicester's conviction of the destruction of the framework of cohesion in the society. The growing power of the industrialists will "force their way into the coalition of exploitation formed by their predecessors, the landed aristocracy, the lawyers and politicians, the merchants, and the bankers."[15]

Sir Leicester Dedlock's horror that his housekeeper's son has got a seat in Parliament is a very effective satire. Dickens writes in *Bleak House*:

> 'And it is a remarkable example of the confusion into which the present age has fallen; of the obliteration of landmarks, the opening of floodgates, and the uprooting of distinctions', says Sir Leicester, with stately gloom; 'that I have been informed, by Mr. Tulkinghorn, that Mrs. Rouncewell's son has been invited to go into Parliament.'[16]

Dickens, in lighter vein, exposes the political corruption at Chesney Wold in *Bleak House*. The politicians are symbolically referred to as a set of ridiculous rhyming names making a parody of their parliamentary intrigue. The poor people are suffering in abysmal poverty and Lord Boodle, not paying attention to this, comes to tell Sir Leicester that supposing the present Government to be overthrown, the limited choice of the Crown, in the formation of a new Ministry lies between Lord Coodle and Sir Thomas Doodle. Supposing it is impossible for the Duke of Foodle to act with Goodle due to the breach arising out of the affair with Hoodle. Then, giving the Home Department and the Leadership of the House of Commons to Joodle, the Exchequer to Koodle, the Colonies to Loodle, and the Foreign Office to Moodle, which department is to be allocated to Noodle? He cannot be offered the Presidency of the Council; as it is reserved for Poodle. He cannot be kept in the Woods and Forests. The same is not good enough for Quoodle. Then it follows that the country is in great danger because a suitable office cannot be arranged for Noodle. Dickens writes:

> On the other hand, the Right Honourable William Buffy, M.P., contends across the table with someone else, that the shipwreck of the country—about which there is no doubt; it is only the manner of it that is in question—is attributable to Cuffy. If you had done with Cuffy what you ought to have done when he first came into Parliament, and had prevented him from going over to Duffy, you would have got him into alliance with Fuffy, you would have had with you the weight attaching as a smart debater to Guffy, you would have brought to bear upon the elections the wealth of Huffy, you would have got in for three counties Juffy, Kuffy, and Luffy, and you would have strengthened your administration by the official knowledge and the business habits of Muffy. All this, instead of being as you now are, dependent on the mere caprice of Puffy![17]

Noodle is a generic term for a fool and a character in Dickens' favourite play, *Tom Thumb the Great* by Henry Fielding. Boodle is a "slang term for money, especially stolen money; Coodle is a kind of pun on 'coddle'; Doodle is another character in *Tom Thumb* and not only does the word signify the scrawling of meaningless hieroglyphs, but it was a nickname for the incompetent Lord Dudley, Foreign Secretary under Wellington: Foodle puns on 'food'; Goodle suggests hypocrisy; Hoodle, hoodwink and hugger-mugger; Joodle, Judas; Koodle, Kudos; Loodle, loot; Moodle, moodiness; Poodle, a tame and fawning lapdog; Quoodle, quid, quod, quid pro quo. And so Sir Leicester Dedlock is in process of helping to form a coddled Cabinet that robs, scribbles, guzzles, cants, hoodwinks, betrays, jockeys, loots, sulks, fawns, and quacks generally. What a prospect!"[18]

This is a witty parody of the language of political manipulation. The ludicrous rhyming sounds have derogatory implications. Boodle, as a name for a politician, is not auspicious, nor do Noodle and Poodle suggest something good. Dickens recalls "that 'doodle' meant to trifle or to make droning noises. Guffy, Huffy, Muffy and Puffy may also be made to yield derisive associations, and possibly even Buffy, Cuffy, and Luffy."[19]

The conviction of the intelligent and distinct personalities in the selection of a Party to govern the country, Boodle and his retinue and Buffy and his retinue are only choices. These are the great actors. The stage is reserved for them. Other suitable politicians are only stage extras. Only Boodle and Buffy are the first-actors, managers and leaders. No others are supposed to govern the country for ever. The conviction of a few aristocratic families in their sacred right to govern the country—and to exclude all other suitable politicians, is questioned by Dickens. A large number of supernumeraries, are addressed but Boodle and Buffy and their followers and families are England. Implicit in the satire is Dickens' questioning of the right of these people to know and speak for the country. For the people who discuss the condition of the country at Chesney Wold are dandies in religion and in politics and in fashion.

Dickens conveys the political aspects "with a wonderful burlesque brilliance. His description of our party system, with its Coodle, Doodle, Foodle, etc.", writes Bernard Shaw, "has never been surpassed for accuracy and for penetration of superficial pretence". But Shaw's feeling that Dickens "had not dug down to the bedrock of the imposture" is derived from a failure to notice that Dickens portrayed Tom-all-Alone's and the brickmakers as much more than a mere indictment of "individual delinquencies, local plague-spots, negligent authorities".[20]

Dickens satirises the politicians as a gang of duffers seeking to maintain their party game. They had their own technology to manage to do the wrong thing. Dickens describes a General Election and the concern of Sir Leicester Dedlock in *Bleak House*:

> England has been in a dreadful state for some weeks. Lord Coodle would go out, Sir Thomas Doodle wouldn't come in, and there being nobody in Great Britain (to speak of) except Coodle and Doodle, there has been no Government.... Still England has been some weeks in the dismal strait of having no pilot (as was well observed by Sir Leicester Dedlock) to weather the storm; and the marvellous part of the matter is, that England has not appeared to care very much about it, but has gone on eating and drinking and marrying and giving in marriage, as the old world did in the days before the flood. But Coodle knew the danger, and Doodle knew the danger, and all their followers and hangers-on had the clearest possible perception of the danger. At last Sir Thomas Doodle has not only condescended to come in, but has done it handsomely, bringing in with him all his nephews, all his male cousins, and all his brothers-in-law. So, there is hope for the old ship yet.[21]

The intensity of this funny passage arises not merely from "Dickens' contemptuous recognition of one politician being just like another, but more savagely from his awareness of the sheer pointlessness of a system of government that makes no contact with the 'old ship' it is supposed to be steering. That parenthetic 'to speak of' means that for the governors most people are unimportant if not downright unspeakable."[22]

This satire is concerned with a General Election (1852) "one which had as its aftermath the hearing of no fewer than ninety-five petitions against the declared results on the ground of bribery and corrupt practices, as well as more than as many again which were talked of but which did not materialise."[23]

This makes a parody of the chaos following the defeat of Lord John Russell in 1851. The country has been without any government for two weeks. John Russell has formed a weaker administration thereafter. There have been recurrent changes of government during 1852-53. None of them has made much difference to the administration of the country. Dickens has recognised that government has precious little to do with the people. This is not because the Reform Act has "left the vast majority without the vote, nor that, as the events that resulted in 1848 showed, this led to the entrenchment of a deeply anti-democratic form of government; there is also the sheer ignorance of 'England' when it comes to the question of what England actually is."[24]

Dickens has no hope of amelioration and social justice through political methods. He considers the responsibility of these laissez-faire politicians for the downfall of the country.

*Bleak House* discusses that political power in the hands of the politicians is an instrument to gratify their self interests. The pitiable condition of the residents at Tom-all-Alone's and the poor brick makers is caused by the selfishness and power lust of the politicians. "Politics, again, are but a struggle for place, pay, and the means of providing for poor relations at the expense of the country, between Doodle on the one side and Coodle on the other—an affair with which no man of sense and honesty can have any possible concern."[25]

Dickens sardonically comments on the entry to Parliament of the newly rich Mr. Veneering in his novel *Our Mutual Friend*:

> Britannia, sitting, meditating one fine day (perhaps in the attitude in which she is presented on the copper coinage), discovers all of a sudden that she wants Veneering in Parliament. It occurs to her that Veneering is 'a representative man'—which cannot in these times be doubted-and that her Majesty's faithful Commons are incomplete without him. So, Britannia mentions to a legal gentleman of her acquaintance that if Veneering will 'put down' five thousand pounds, he may write a couple of initial letters after his name at the extremely cheap rate of two thousand five hundred per letter. It is clearly understood between Britannia and the legal gentleman that nobody is to take up the five thousand pounds, but that, being put

down, they will disappear by magical conjuration and enchantment.[26]

In the Veneering world, money is highly valued. A man of such world is dehumanised. He values people according to their worth in pounds, shillings and pence. He shows vanity and snobbery and such a man is coming to work for the upliftment of the masses. Mr. Veneering is to become an M.P. after payment. This indicates the corruption in making of a Member of Parliament. Dickens has dug at the current political scene of Parliament.

In *Little Dorrit*, Mr. Merdle is a member of Parliament. All Londoners have taken him as the solid pillar of prosperity. He is based on John Sadleir, M.P. who has represented Irish constituency in Parliament. He has been a Junior Lord of the Treasury in the Government of Lord Aberdeen. He has run wild cat-schemes and the savings of depositors in Irish banks and English investors in railway shares and other ventures has disappeared. He has written in his suicide letter: "I cannot live. I have ruined too many. I could not live and see their agony...I blame no one, but attribute all to my infamous villainy."[27]

Dickens writes of Merdle's suicide in *Little Dorrit*: "Numbers of men in every profession and trade would be blighted by his insolvency; old people who had been in easy circumstances all their lives would have no place of repentance for their trust in him but the workhouse; legions of women and children would have their whole future desolated by the hand of this mighty scoundrel...the greatest Forger and the greatest Thief that ever cheated the gallows."[28] Merdle is the representative of financial corruption and political incompetence. He is congratulated as England's world famous merchant princess and capitalist. But he becomes a swindler. Such people who have no right vision are the members of Parliament working for the betterment of the condition of the masses.

British institutions are not spared the satirical whip. Satirical gibe at Parliament is found in *Martin Chuzzlewit*:

> He heard of Tom Pinch too, and Jonas too, with not a little about himself into the bargain; for though lovers are

> remarkable for leaving a great deal unsaid on all occasions, and very properly desiring to come back and say it, they are remarkable also for a wonderful power of condensation, and can, in one way or other, give utterance to more language—eloquent language—in any given short space of time, than all the six hundred and fifty-eight members in the Commons House of Parliament of the United Kingdom of Great Britain and Ireland; who are strong lovers no doubt, but of their country only, which makes all the difference; for in a passion of that kind (which is not always returned), it is the custom to use as many words as possible, and express nothing whatever.[29]

Dickens laughs at and criticises the politicians with supreme contempt as he has written their speeches and debates as a parliamentary reporter.

He attacks the politicians that they speak much but express nothing. In *Nicholas Nickleby*, Mr. Gregsbury the M.P. "has a tolerable command of sentences with no meaning in them, and, in short, every requisite for a very good member indeed."[30]

Dickens' attack on Parliament as an institution is culminated by a contemporary hatred of red tape. He is very much critical of the political life: "Night after night, I record predictions that never come to pass, professions that are never fulfilled, explanations that are only meant to mystify. I wallow in words. Britannia, that unfortunate female, is always before me, like a trussed fowl: skewered through and through with office-pens, and bound hand and foot with red tape. I am sufficiently behind the scenes to know the worth of political life. I am quite an Infidel about it, and shall never be converted."[31] David finds the debates of Parliament as dreary and monotonous. There is a bitter comment on politician by Dickens: "The inconsistency and recklessness of Traddles were not to be exceeded by any real politician."[32] In *Hard Times*, Parliament is called noisy and dirty machinery where Mr. Gradgrind works for self gain: "He then returned with promptitude to the national cinder-heap, and resumed his sifting for the odds and ends he wanted, and his throwing of the dust about into the eyes of other people who wanted other odds and ends—in fact resumed his parliamentary duties."[33] Dickens dislikes the parliamentarians in *Hard Times*: "The national dustmen, after entertaining one another with a great many noisy little fights among themselves, had dispersed for the present, and Mr. Gradgrind was at home for the vacation."[34]

In *Great Expectations*, Pip refers to Mrs. Gargery's feeble cries after her accident: "But I doubt if they had more meaning in them than an election cry, and I cannot suggest a darker picture of her state of mind."[35] An election cry is not substantial according to Dickens.

The novels of Dickens are filled with satire aimed at parliamentary government. The Parliamentary Barnacles are jeered in *Little Dorrit*, and honourable boards in *Our Mutual Friend* contains bitter satire of Dickens: "When you in the course of your dust shovelling and cinder-raking have piled up a mountain of pretentious failure, you must off with your honourable coats for the removal of it, and fall to the work with the power of all the queen's horses and all the queen's men, or it will come rushing down and bury us alive."[36] Dickens has depicted politicians as foolish, vain, idle, verbose, unreliable, tedious men and insignificant as well as despicable persons.

Dickens has satirised the Chartists in *The Old Curiosity Shop*. The Chartists have believed that universal Manhood suffrage, the secret ballot, limitation of Parliament's life and restrictions on the influence of property in elections would make a free and independent assembly representing the people completely. Dickens has differed to this position: "But two things prevented Dickens's accepting this position—his horror of 'the mob' and (what was closely allied with it) his belief in the infallible virtues of education. In the first of these he was deeply influenced by the events of his time, and was more ready to follow a middle-class scare than to examine the causes of it."[37]

Dickens is very much fearful of chartism. *The Old Curiosity Shop* is a troubled commentary on contemporary affairs, chartism, and the growth, or newly visible energies, of working class politics. The chartist movement is depicted satirically. It is night-time and the spot is dreadful. The smoke changes to fire. Every chimney spirts up its flame. Places shine red hot, with figures moving to and fro within their blazing jaws, and calling to one another with hoarse cries. The noise of every strange machine is aggravated by the darkness. The people near them look wilder and more savage. Bands of unemployed labourers parade on the roads. They are clustered by torchlight round their leaders. The leaders tell them in stern language of their wrongs. They urge them on to frightful cries and threats. The maddened men, armed with sword and firebrand, rush forth on errands of terror and destruction. Some call for bread, and some for drink to drown their cares. Some with tears, and some with staggering feet, and some with blood-shot eyes, goes brooding home. The very night brings no peace, nor quiet, nor signs of blessed sleep. There is only terror of the night. In the Black country, near to Birmingham, the labourer's leaders speak wrong and the language is over heated. The terror of the night is witnessed by the young and innocent girl, Nell when she wanders to the industrial Midlands.

Dickens is extremely pacifist to agitation and so he does not support the militant chartists. He is fearful of the mob in *The Old Curiosity Shop*. He gives a terrifying picture of a working class upheaval. The apprehensive novelist imagines the Black Country "running with blood, plagued with mortal pestilence and with its nights of anguish broken by the screams of orphans and distracted widows and the rumbling of rude coffins".[38]

## COMMERCE

The reproduction of a new brisk, commercial and fashionable London is the banking and trading centre of the world and also the centre of colossal wealth and power and its mediation with its seemy underbelly with a satirist's moral concern is often observed in Dickens' novels. *Dombey and Son* is one such novel. The tone of expansionist and commercial pride evokes the ethos of commercialism—of buying and selling: "Though the offices of Dombey and Son were within the liberties of the City of London, and within hearing of Bow Bells, when their clashing voices were not drowned by the uproar in the streets, yet were there hints of adventurous and romantic story to be observed in some of the adjacent objects. Gog and Magog held their state within ten minutes walk; the Royal Exchange was close at hand; the Bank of England, with its vaults of gold and silver 'down among the dead men' underground, was their magnificent neighbour. Just round the corner stood the rich East India House, teeming with suggestions of precious stuffs and stones, tigers, elephants, howdahs, hookahs, umbrellas, palm trees, palanquins, and gorgeous princes of a brown complexion sitting on carpets, with their slippers very much turned up at the toes. Anywhere in the immediate vicinity there might be seen pictures of ships speeding away full sail to all parts of the world; outfitting warehouses ready to pack off anybody anywhere, fully equipped in half an hour; and little timber midshipmen in obsolete naval uniforms, eternally employed outside the shop doors of nautical instrument-makers in taking observations of the hackney coaches."[39]

Mr. Dombey is a wealthy merchant in London and has the vices of the contemporary industrial and commercial bourgeoisie. He represents the mercantile power of England and his mercantile pride gives him the intoxicating conviction: "The earth was made for Dombey and Son to trade in, and the sun and moon were made to give them light. Rivers and seas were formed to float their ships; rainbows gave them promise of fair weather; winds blew for or against their enterprises; stars and planets circled in their orbits, to preserve inviolate a system of which they were the centre. Common abbreviations took new meanings in his eyes, and had sole reference to them: A.D. had no concern with Anno Domini, but stood for Anno Dombei—and Son."[40]

Mr. Dombey privileges his son Paul over his daughter Florence because a male progeny is considered a sound investment in the patriarchially inscribed world of commerce and business. The inferior status of a girl, in the house of Dombey and Son, is narrated thus: "But what was a girl to Dombey and Son! In the capital of the House's name and dignity, such a child was merely a piece of base coin that couldn't be invested—a bad Boy—nothing more."[41] A.E. Dyson comments: "Who is Dombey? He is The City; he is Export/Import; he is Exchange; he is the Mystery of Equity; he is profit and thrift rolled into one. He is laissez faire, finding his level in the free market, somewhat above the level of most other men."[42]

Mr. Dombey is the symbol of the nineteenth century theory of business enterprise. Even the Lancashire industrialists have not exemplified such a strict devotion to their own profits and power as Dombey exhibits. He is a commercial man and his feeling about his wife's death is significant: "He was not a man of whom it could properly be said that he was ever startled or shocked; but he certainly had a sense within him, that if his wife should sicken and decay, he would be very sorry, and that he would find a something gone from among his plate and furniture, and other household possessions, which was well worth the having, and could not be lost without sincere regret. Though it would be a cool, business-like, gentlemanly, self-possessed regret, no doubt."[43]

Mr. Dombey deplores the very idea of his wife's death in giving birth to his son. To Dombey, money is everything and his wife is just a commodity that can be bought and replaced. In his world of hard commerce, money and items that can be exchanged for money is valourised. It replaces human values, relationships and sentiment. Mr. Dombey is a cold, proud, self-centred business magnate. His wealth has made him arrogant and he has the sole passion of seeing the great shipping and trading firm of Dombey and Son perpetuated once more by a male heir. Mr. Dombey is sure that money can buy everything but not a son. Mr. Dombey is obsessed with his infant heir, Paul and neglects his daughter.

After the death of Mrs. Dombey, Toodle's wife, Polly, is engaged to feed Paul. The relation between Dombey and Toodle is the link between capital and labour. Dombey says to

Polly that he wants to make this engagement a question of mere wages. He provides her a liberal stipend in return for the discharge of duties. He, frankly, tells her that there is an end of all relations between them and the stipend ceases to be paid after the completion of responsibilities. He says that she has children of her own and it is not at all in this bargain that she need become attached to his child, or that his child become attached to her. "When you go away from here, you will have concluded what is a mere matter of bargain and sale, hiring and letting: and will stay away. The child will cease to remember you; and you will cease, if you please, to remember the child."[44] Mr. Dombey just wants to make it a commercial arrangement instead a humane arrangement. The writer uses words such as 'bargain', 'sale', 'hiring' and 'letting'. These words belong to the world of commerce.

With this arrangement, Paul, symbolically, takes his nourishment from lower-class Polly. His very life depends upon her bounty and goodwill. The milk that changes into his blood and muscle lays emphasis on the commonality of rich and poor, their symbiotic relationship. But for Mr. Dombey, placing at Polly's breast is a "degrading necessity, and in order to blur that necessity, he seeks to make the arrangement a mere matter of business. He emphasizes to Polly that her milk is only a commodity; he warns her against forming any attachments to Paul; and he even buys her name, replacing the plebian "Toodle" with the business like "Richards."[45] This is a more "monstrous and startling version of the 'normal' relations of capital and labour under the advanced liberal principles of political economy."[46] Dickens describes the theme of *Dombey and Son* as pride, but Mr. Dombey's pride, is not its dominant principle. The leading principle is the "callous inhumanity of an economic doctrine that strips Mr. Dombey's relations with everyone to an assertion of monetary power".[47]

Dickens's changed conception of business and businessman in Dombey corrodes life. "Mr. Dombey is the spirit of business enterprise."[48] The humbling of Mr. Dombey is done by showing his money ethic deficient in many sorts. Paul asks Mr. Dombey what is money. Mr. Dombey is quite disconcerted. He is "in a difficulty. He would have liked to give him some explanation involving the terms circulating—medium, currency, depreciation of currency, paper, bullion, rates of exchange, value of precious metals in the market, and so forth; but looking down at the little chair, and seeing what a long way down it was, he answered: 'Gold, and silver, and copper. Guineas, shillings, half-pence'."[49] The child is not satisfied with his father's reply. So he puts the question clearly what is money after all and what it can do. Mr. Dombey, then answers, "Money, Paul, can do anything."[50] The child says to his papa that anything means everything and Mr. Dombey affirms that it includes it. Paul asks money could not save his mother. He considers money a cruel thing. Mr. Dombey denies this and opines that a good thing can not be cruel. 'If it's a good thing, and can do anything', said the little fellow,...'I wonder why it didn't save me my mama'.[51] Mr. Dombey expounds to Paul that money is a very potent spirit and never to be disparaged on any account. It cannot keep people alive whose time is come to die. But money causes us to be honoured, feared, respected, courted, and admired, and makes us powerful and glorious in the eyes of all men. It can keep off death, for a long time. For instance, it has secured to his mama the services of Mr. Pilkins. He is often profited himself of the great Doctor Parker Peps. It can do all that can be done. Paul asks, 'It can't make me strong and quite well, either, papa; can it?'[52] Then Mr. Dombey replies his son that he is strong and quite well no doubt. Dickens satirises the money ethic of Mr. Dombey.

Paul, with his queer intuitive insight, perceives what his father should learn through disappointment and suffering. The little boy stresses that money cannot buy life and thus, he foreshadows his own death. The death of Paul is the first overwhelming lesson in Mr. Dombey's education, but "it brings him no closer to Florence, Paul had lavished all his love on his sister, and Paul's death intensifies Mr. Dombey's jealousy of that love and his resentment that his unwanted daughter lives while his son and the plans he had centered upon him perish."[53]

*Dombey and Son* describes the gloom of wealth and its "capacity to petrify or poison human relations, in the family and in society. ...Wealth is an evil, corrupting the heart; prosperity a house built on sand."[54] Little Paul discovers that money can also provide other experts Mrs. Pipchin and the Blimbers for education, old Joey B. in affairs of the heart. "It can bring Walter Gay as a suppliant and beggar, with powers of binding or loosing-powers educatively delegated, on this notable occasion, to Son.... Money, also, brings independence, flattery, self-sufficiency, and emancipation from the needs and solaces of love."[55]

Toots alike Paul fails under the faulty education. He is forced in the great hot-house of Dr. Blimber's very expensive school. He blows before his time: "Unlike Paul, Toots does not die under the rigors of forcing, but like Paul he demonstrates the limits of what money can do. Money cannot buy life, and it cannot produce genius. Though Toots is rich, he will not be powerful or learned or modish. He will go through life good-hearted and simple-minded, his potential withered rather than ripened by money."[56]

The insufficiency of money to replace the fundamental values of life is starkly indicated. Dickens describes the caricatural nature of Dombey's second marriage with Edith in *Dombey and Son*. Mr. Dombey has to visit Edith next day to propose. Edith is alone with her mother who has played the major role for her daughter's marriage. She says to her mother that Mr. Dombey is coming there to-morrow by appointment. 'You know he has bought me',...'Or that he will, to-morrow. He has considered of his bargain; he has shown it to his friend; he is even proud of it; he thinks that it will suit him, and may be had sufficiently cheap; and he will buy to-morrow.'[57]

Edith tells her mother that she has never been a child. She has not enjoyed her childhood as it has not been left to her by her mother. She has been a woman-artful, designing, mercenary, laying snares for men. Her mother has given her birth as a woman. She is in her pride to-night. She has been treated like an object for sale in the market: "There is no slave in a market; there is no horse in a fair: so shown and offered and examined and paraded, mother, as I have been, for ten shameful years, cried Edith, with a burning brow, and the same bitter emphasis on the one word."[58]

The marriage of Mr. Dombey with Edith is a commercial arrangement. Mr. Dombey has bought Edith just as a commodity in the market. She is superior than any object in the market. She is carefully examined by Mr. Dombey before buying Edith. The words 'buy', 'bargain', 'cheap', 'market' are the words taken from the field of commerce. Dickens satirises that marriage is a heavenly union of souls but it has a commercial object in Dombeyian world. Mr. Dombey marries her because she has rank and beauty that can be bought and paid for.

Mr. Dombey, in marrying Edith, purchases a costly commodity in the open market: "He sees me at the auction, and he thinks it well to buy me. Let him! When he came to view me—perhaps to bid—he required to see the roll of my accomplishments. I gave it to him. When he would have me show one of them, to justify his purchase to his men, I require of him to say which he demands, and I exhibit it. I will do no more. He makes the purchase of his own will, and with his own sense of its worth, and the power of his money; and I hope it may never disappoint him. I have not vaunted and pressed the bargain; neither have you, so far as I have been able to prevent you."[59]

Edith says to Mr. Dombey that she has been shamed and steeled. She has been offered and rejected, put up and appraised. Her accomplishment or grace has not been a resource to her. But it has been vended to enhance her value. "I suffered myself to be sold as infamously as any woman with a halter round her neck is sold in any market-place."[60]

Cousin Feenix jokes at the wedding feast of Mr. Dombey and considers their marriage as the marriage of an uncommonly fine girl with a man for whom she does not care even a button. She accepts on account of his immense property. A man meeting Jack in the lobby of the House of Commons asks of the ill-matched couple. Jack opines that they are not so. It is "a perfectly fair and equal transaction. She is regularly bought, and you may take your oath he is as regularly sold!"[61] The words "bought" and "sold" bring us to the heart of Mr. Dombey's view of the world and of the society. His conviction that other people, in fact the "whole universe, exist only for his benefit arise ultimately from his sense of the importance of money."[62]

Mr. Dombey has made necessary changes to receive Edith in his house and Mrs. Skewton praises it. Mrs. Skewton says to Mr. Dombey that the people have carried out every idea hinted to make a perfect palace of the house. The latter responses that it is handsome. He has directed that no expense should be spared and all that money could do, has been done. Cleopatra asks Dombey what it cannot do. "It is powerful, madam", said Mr. Dombey.[63] Dickens' estimation of money is clearly explained.

Having failed to buy life, Mr. Dombey seeks to buy love. He buys Edith, a beautiful woman. She knows that she is being bought and despises the marriage contract. But she accepts it as a fair bargain. Edith is Mr. Dombey's "female counterpart; she is proud, but she is not deluded by her pride as is Mr. Dombey, and it irritates him that she makes no pretense that their marriage is anything other than a commercial arrangement."[64] Mr. Dombey asks about the widowed Edith's fertility, and tests her ability as an artist and a musician.

Mr. Dombey is not pleased with the conduct of Edith. He makes an urge for correction. He understands that she is graced and distinguished by his alliance. He proposes to engage her at Brighton under Mrs. Pipchin. Edith says to Mr. Dombey: "We are a most unhappy pair, in whom, from different causes, every sentiment that blesses marriage, or justifies it, is rooted out; but in the course of time, some friendship, or some fitness for each other, may arise between us. I will try to hope so, if you will make the endeavour too; and I will look forward to a better and a happier use of age than I have made of youth or prime."[65] Mr. Dombey is not able to purchase the absolute subservience of his business subordinates and he is not able to buy the obedience of an aristocratic wife whose beauty is to reflect lustre of his greatness. He does not think that love could not be bought. The marriage degenerates into contest of wills. Edith's position becomes unbearable in the household and she agrees to run off with Carker, Mr. Dombey's manager.

Mr. Dombey governs his domestic establishment and private affairs according to firm business principles. He has acquired "his first wife to breed an heir for the Firm and took a second to display the power of his wealth before his associates in The City and his new circle of seedy-aristocratic acquaintances in the West End. But the wives do not live up to a viable business ethics. They default on their contracts. The first wife dies after delivering a faulty piece of goods called Paul; Edith sells her resplendent self but then quite literally refuses to deliver the merchandise Dombey has paid for."[66]

Mr. Carker has eloped with Edith. Mr. Dombey wants to know about Edith's hideout. He converses with Good Mrs. Brown for secret intelligence. The old woman tells Mr. Dombey that she will positively search Edith's hideout but he will be required to pay for it. Mr. Dombey speaks: 'Money', returned Mr. Dombey, apparently relieved, and reassured by this inquiry, 'will bring about unlikely things, I know. It may turn even means as unexpected and unpromising as these, to account. Yes. For any reliable information I receive, I will pay. But I must have the information first, and judge for myself of its value.'[67] The younger woman, Alice asks Mr. Dombey if he knows something powerful than money and the latter replies that it is not here. Then Alice notes: 'You should know of something that is more powerful elsewhere, as I judge', she returned. 'Do you know nothing of a woman's anger?'[68] It is shown that money is not important over all things. Something is more powerful than money and hence Dombey's money ethic is satirised.

Dickens depicts the pernicious tendencies in the new industrial order and shows its danger and destructiveness. The real villain of Dombey and Son is the soullessness of the new business world. The true embodiment of that world is the "manager Carker—clever, compulsive, ruthless, amoral—the first compelling portrait in the English novel of the new managerial class, of the new anonymous power breed."[69]

Mr. Carker as a manager of Dombey and Son works for his self gain. Due to him, the firm suffers. Many undertakings taken to enhance the reputation of the House lead to ruinous results. Mr. Carker as the manager of the commercial world is deftly satirised. Harriet talks to Morfin about the manager Carker. He is of the opinion that the manager has abused his trust in many ways. He has repeatedly dealt and speculated to advantage for himself rather than for the House. He has led the House to prodigious ventures very often resulting in enormous losses. He has always pampered the vanity and ambition of his employer, when it has been his duty to have held them in check. Undertakings have been entered on, to swell the reputation of the house for vast resources, and to exhibit it in magnificent contrast to other merchant's houses. A few disastrous changes of affairs render them the ruinous consequences. He has resolved to show his employer what has been brought upon him by ministration to his ruling passion. It has been his constant practice "to minister to that passion basely, and to flatter it corruptly, is indubitable. In that, his criminality, as it is connected with the affairs of the House, chiefly consists."[70]

Mr. Dombey's proud world of money and power crumbles. Money has not saved his first wife, preserved his son, restrained his manager, bound his second wife or secured his daughter. The neglected firm of Dombey and Son fails: "One summer afternoon; a year, wanting some odd days, after the marriage in the City church; there was a buzz and whisper upon Change of a great failure. A certain cold proud man, well known there, was not there, nor was he represented there. Next day it was noised abroad that Dombey and Son had stopped, and next night there was a List of Bankrupts published, headed by that name."[71] Mr. Dombey's wealth are auctioned off and his bought servants march out of his house in self-righteous indignation reminding what money can and cannot do. Tortured by the situation, he decides to kill himself but he is saved by his daughter Florence.

It has been the age in which shares have been coveted. Fortunes made out of factories and out of the railways have created immense faith in investment. Dickens despises the idolatory of share in *Our Mutual Friend*: "As is well known to the wise in their generation, traffic in Shares is the one thing to have to do with in this world. Have no antecedents, no established character, no cultivation, no ideas, no manners; have Shares. Have Shares enough to be on Boards of Direction in capital letters, oscillate on mysterious business between London and Paris, and be great. Where does he come from? Shares. Where is he going to? Shares. What are his tastes? Shares. Has he any principles? Shares. What squeezes him into Parliament? Shares. Perhaps he never of himself achieved success in anything, never originated anything, never produced anything? Sufficient answer to all, Shares. Oh, mighty Shares!"[72] In the Veneering world, the values of the society get expression in the recurring emphasis on shares. Share is important character for gaining importance in the society. But Dickens satirises this taste of the Veneering world. Veneerings "emerge from nothing and disappear into nothing, but take in a seat in Parliament on their way, people from nowhere, spreading a sort of doom."[73]

The affect of this money worship is a complete inversion of all values. American commerce is a fraud from beginning to end and it is evident in *Martin Chuzzlewit*, Dickens writes about Major Pawkins: "In commercial affairs he was a bold speculator. In plainer words he had a most distinguished genius for swindling, and could start a bank, or negotiate a loan, or form a land-jobbing company (entailing ruin, pestilence, and death, on hundreds of families), with any gifted creature in the Union. This made him an admirable man of business."[74]

Dickens attacks the money worship of the commercial man in *Martin Chuzzlewit*. People have submitted to money as the sole yardstick of value. All cares, hopes, joys, affections, virtues, and associations of people seem to be fulfilled into dollars. Into the slow cauldron of their talk, they make the gruel thick and slab with dollars. Men are weighed by their dollars. "Make commerce one huge lie and mighty theft. Deface the banner of the nation for an idle rag; pollute it star by star; and cut out stripe by stripe as from the arm of a degraded soldier. Do anything for dollars! What is a flag to them!"[75] Irony is the literary instrument of satire. The satirical aspect of the comic is presented with full force.

The measurement of anything on the basis of its cash-value reduces all things and persons to anonymity. The "uniqueness of personality is erased, and each person is whatever money he has. The use of debased language and the measurement of everything by money operate together to deprive the Americans of individuality. They have become like standardised and interchangeable coins."[76]

The Railways is an integral part of commerce. It has its disruptive effect on the lives of individuals. There is huge upheaval caused by the railways. Like earthquake, the whole neighbourhood is affected by the railways. Houses are knocked down. Streets are broken and stopped. Deep pits and trenches are dug in the ground. Heaps of earth and clay are thrown up. The undermined buildings are propped by great beams of wood. A chaos of carts, overthrown and jumbled together, lay topsy-turvy at the bottom of a steep unnatural hill. Confused treasures of iron soaked and rusted are there. There are bridges everywhere leading to nowhere. Thoroughfares are completely impassable. Incomplete babel towers of chimneys, temporary wooden houses and enclosures, carcases of ragged tenements, and fragments of unfinished walls and arches, and piles of scaffolding, and wildernesses of bricks, and giant forms of cranes, and tripods straddling above nothing are visible. There are a hundred thousand shapes and substances of incompleteness. "Hot springs and fiery eruptions, the usual attendants upon earthquakes, lent their contributions of confusion to the scene. Boiling water hissed and heaved within dilapidated walls; whence, also, the glare and roar of flames came issuing forth; and mounds of ashes blocked up rights of way, and wholly changed the law and custom of the neighbourhood."[77] The Railways is pictured as undermining many walks of life. It becomes a cause of terror and pain.

The Railways is like the remorseless monster Death. It ruins our environment and affects various parts of our social life. The cataclysmic changes are described with elaborate and detailed imagery of death, desolation, atmospheric and auditory invasion: "Louder and louder yet, it shrieks and cries as it comes tearing on resistless to the goal: and now its way, still like the way of Death, is strewn with ashes thickly. Everything around is blackened. There are dark pools of water, muddy lanes, and miserable habitations far below. There are jagged walls and falling houses close at hand, and through the battered roofs and broken windows, wretched rooms are seen, where want and fever hide themselves in many wretched shapes, while smoke and crowded gables, and distorted chimneys, and deformity of brick and mortar penning up deformity of mind and body, choke the murky distance. As Mr. Dombey looks out of his carriage window, it is never in his thoughts that the monster who has brought him there has let the light of day in on these things: not made or caused them. It was the journey's fitting end, and might have been the end of everything; it was so ruinous and dreary."[78] The Railways is the harbinger of fatality. It is thus seen as "destructive, ruthless, an 'impetuous monster', a 'fiery devil'. There is no suggestion of hope of social progress".[79]

## UTILITARIANISM

Utilitarianism is partly a development of eighteenth century rationalism and partly a reaction against the romanticism of the first decade of the nineteenth century which has stressed the importance of instincts, feelings and imagination, of all that is spontaneous, natural and creative in the life of man. James Mill stands against the feelings and believes that rational in man might solve all human problems. A philosophical system developed by Jeremy Bentham, it has been systematised by his disciple John Stuart Mill in *Utilitarianism* (1863). Utilitarianism is beautifully defined in *Oxford Reader's Companion to Dickens*: "In its pure form, utilitarianism is a system of ethics which judges human conduct in relation to the extent to which it conduces to the greatest happiness of the greatest number of people."[80] This philosophy emphasizes the importance of material goods and ignores the moral and spiritual needs of human beings.

Jeremy Bentham (1748-1832) has been a philosopher of law and the founder of a school of thinkers known as Philosophical Radicals. The central idea of Bentham's political and ethical theories is that man is "motivated to increase his pleasure and diminish his pain, that these are calculable quantities and that any act is a moral act which contributes in this, rather than in the reverse direction. It is the greatest happiness of the greatest number that is the measure of right and wrong."[81] To Bentham, pleasure and happiness have the same meaning. The final aim of his philosophy is to manipulate pleasure and pain by a code of laws and a social system in such a way that men would be determined towards virtue. "The idea 'actions are right in proportion as they tend to promote happiness, wrong as they tend to promote the reverse of happiness' is disliked by those who consider that life has a 'nobler' end than pleasure."[82] Some pleasures are more important than others. Some wants the pleasures of the intellect in comparison to the pleasures of the senses. Some prefers the quality of happiness over the quantity of happiness. "It is better to be a human being dissatisfied than a pig satisfied; better to be Socrates dissatisfied than a fool satisfied."[83]

The most remarkable critic of utilitarianism is Thomas Carlyle. He opposes the doctrines and their effects in *Past and Present* because it reduces human relationship mere matter of abstract calculation: "We for the present, with our Mammon Gospel, have come to strange conclusions. We call it a Society: and go about professing openly the totalest separation, isolation. Our life is not a mutual helpfulness; but rather, cloaked under the due laws-of-war, named fair competition and so forth, it is a mutual hostility. We have profoundly forgotten everywhere that cash-payment is not the sole relation of human beings; we think, nothing doubting, that it absolves and liquidates all engagements of man."[84] In Dickens's *Hard Times*, the same material reductionism is evoked. Mr. Gradgrind sats writing in the room with the deadly statistical clock, and proves "that the Good Samaritan was a Bad Economist".[85]

Dickens is an opponent of utilitarian ideas and considers its harmful effect on many aspects of Victorian life. As Carlyle, he looks down on Bentham's utilitarian belief: "What Dickens shared with Carlyle was a hatred of Bentham's doctrine of utility and its social and economic consequences. Contribution to 'the greatest happiness of the greatest number' as the criterion of good, Bentham's most famous dictum, sounded benevolent; but, for Dickens, as for Carlyle, it was the opposite: calculated, determinist, mechanistic. For them, Bentham's followers, the Utilitarians, reduced all relationships to self-interest; and worse, to what Carlyle branded in *Past and Present* as 'Cash payment', the 'cash-nexus'. The main economic consequence of Utilitarianism was laissez-faire economics, a wages system based on statistics and controlled solely by the market: a system, with the near-poverty it brought to many, repugnant to both Dickens and Carlyle."[86]

Utilitarianism influenced all radical thought. It has impacted upon many aspects of practical reform and has worked as a justification for inhuman practices in the workplace. Dickens has gained that utilitarian ideas are operating through society. Paul Schlicke criticizes Jeremy Bentham: "In many of the most natural and strongest feelings of human nature he had no sympathy; from many of its graver experiences he was altogether cut off, and the faculty by which one mind understands a mind different from itself and throws itself into feelings of that other mind, was denied him by his deficiency of the Imagination."[87]

The basis of utilitarianism is Bentham's maxim related to "social legislation: that government should aim towards the greatest happiness of the greatest number of people."[88] But Dickens refuses to assess the qualities of life in terms of quantity as it tend to a mechanistic view of human potential. "Value cannot be decided by majority vote; what is left out of the Bentham-James Mill-Gradgrind formulation is imagination, poetry, sensitivity, discrimination."[89]

Dickens has seen the application of the principle of utility in Education as the major flaw in the social life of the period. In *Hard Times*, he makes a frontal attack on utilitarian doctrine. Thomas Gradgrind is an utilitarian and he belongs to the political party of the Philosophical Radicals. The two of

Gradgrind's children are named Adam Smith and Malthus. During the industrial revolution in England, the teachings of utilitarianism and of philosophical radicalism have been mixed with the teachings of classical economics. In Dickens' time, utilitarian emphasis has been a compound of rationalism and laissez-faire economics. Dickens has attacked the practical combination of rationality and exploitation which dominated life in England creating new types of distress and abuse.

Gradgrind, the utilitarian, is the bosom friend and ally of Bounderby. Bounderby is the brutal and indifferent employer, an individual capitalist. He is a calculating machine. He is a practical utilitarian. He acts completely out of self-interest. He wants not only acquisition of money but power. He represents such self interest in terms of Bentham's 'greatest happiness' principle. The polluting industrial smoke is meat and drink for Bounderby. He says: "It is the healthiest thing in the world in all respects, and particularly for the lungs. If you are one of those who want us to consume it, I differ from you. We are not going to wear the bottoms of our boilers out any faster than we wear'em out now, for all the humbugging sentiment in Great Britain and Ireland...." "Now, you have heard a lot of talk about the work in our mills, no doubt. You have! Very good. I'll state the fact of it to you. It's the pleasantest work there is, and it's the lightest work there is, and it's the best-paid work there is. More than that, we couldn't improve the mills themselves, unless we laid down Turkey carpets on the floors. Which we're not a going to do."[90]

Bounderby's assertion of will involves the deprivation or misery of others. So Bounderby justifies polluting the atmosphere and misusing the Hands. Utilitarianism is a "highly subjective creed and can be used to justify almost anything".[91] Thomas Gradgrind Esquire, Member of Parliament for Coketown, has brought up his children on the lines of John Stuart Mill. His utilitarianism is a theory and there is intellectual disinterestedness in its application. Bounderby is a trader, banker and industrialist. He is concerned with self-assertion and power and material success. He is not interested in ideals or ideas but to be a self-made man.

Dickens observes the affinities and practical tendency of utilitarianism in his presentation of the Gradgrind elementary school. He shows the utilitarian spirit in Victorian education. Thomas Gradgrind delivers a lecture in a schoolroom. He asks the boys and girls of the school to learn only facts. Arguments divested of humanity, amplified by rhetoric construct the parody of utilitarianism in *Hard Times*.

Gradgrind represents the utilitarian educational philosophy and it rejects the children's freedom connected with wonder, imagination and creativity. It, no doubt, throttles the complex inner need of human heart. Gradgrind gets upon the principle of facts and the gross materialism of utilitarianism is his ethics. Dickens, disgusted with the 19th century philosophy of crude utilitarianism of Mill and Bentham, satirically presents Thomas Gradgrind, the unique man of facts and calculation: "Thomas Gradgrind, Sir...peremptorily Thomas—Thomas Gradgrind. With a rule and a pair of scales, and the multiplication table always in his pocket, Sir, ready to weigh and measure any parcel of human nature, and tell you exactly what it comes to. It is a mere question of figures, a case of simple arithmetic."[92] Dickens' imagery of the little earthen pitchers and vessels as well as the mechanical imagery of violence in terms of cannons is organically related with his theory of education. The little vessels are forced to receive imperial gallons of facts. So, Gradgrind is a cannon loaded with facts. He is a grim mechanical machine able to clean the students out of the regions of childhood. Gradgrind asks Sissy Jupe:

"Girl number twenty", said Mr. Gradgrind, squarely pointing with his square forefinger, "I don't know that girl. Who is that girl?"

"Sissy Jupe, Sir", explained number twenty, blushing, standing up, and curtseying.

"Sissy is not a name", said Mr. Gradgrind "Don't call yourself Sissy. Call yourself Cecilia."

"It's father as calls me Sissy, Sir", returned the young girl in a trembling voice, and with another curtsey.

"Then he has no business to do it", said Mr. Gradgrind.

"Tell him he mustn't. Cecilia Jupe. Let me see. What is your father?"

"He belongs to the horse-riding, if you please, Sir."

Mr. Gradgrind frowned, and waved off the objectionable calling with his hand.

"We don't want to know anything about that, here. You mustn't tell us about that, here. Your father breaks horses, don't he?"

"If you please, Sir, when they can get any to break, they do break horses in the ring. Sir."

"You mustn't tell us about the ring, here. Very well, then. Describe your father as a horsebreaker. He doctors sick horses, I dare say?"

"Oh yes, Sir."

"Very well, then. He is a veterinary surgeon, a farrier, and horse breaker."[93]

(Sissy Jupe thrown into the greatest alarm by this demand.)

"Girl number twenty unable to define a horse!" said Mr. Gradgrind, for the general behoof of all the little pitchers.

"Girl number twenty possessed of no facts, in reference to one of the commonest of animals! Some boy's definition of a horse. Bitzer, yours."...

"Bitzer", said Thomas Gradgrind. "Your definition of a horse."

"Quadruped. Graminivorous. Forty teeth, namely, twenty-four grinders, four eye-teeth, and twelve incisive. Sheds coat in the spring; in marshy countries, sheds hoofs, too. Hoofs hard, but requiring to be shod with iron. Age known by marks in mouth."

The utilitarian philosophy of education based on facts is comically shown in Gradgrind's method of teaching. In the Gradgrind's world, only fact and the utilitarian calculus have a place. There is no room in this world for imagination, fancy and emotion. Bitzer's definition of the horse shows the kinds of facts to which Gradgrind attaches the greatest importance and that is the cut and dried facts of intellectual definition. Gradgrind is not concerned with the facts of living and breathing reality which Sissy knows from Sleary's circus and horseriding. He lays stress on facts. He is concerned with the application of utility in education. Lawrence has protested against the harmful tendencies in education. But Dickens' protest is more substantial. Sissy has been brought up among horses, and among people whose livelihood depends upon understanding horses but we are not concerned with such knowledge. Such knowledge isn't real knowledge. Bitzer, the model pupil, on the button's being pressed, promptly vomits up the genuine article. Bitzer's aptness has its evaluative comment in his career. F.R. Leavis observes: "Sissy's incapacity to acquire this kind of 'fact' or formula, her unaptness for education, is manifested to us, on the other hand, as part and parcel of her sovereign and indefeasible humanity: it is the virtue that makes it impossible for her to understand, or acquiesce in, an ethos for which she is 'girl number twenty', or to think of any other human being as a unit for arithmetic."[94]

The government officer, at Gradgrind's model school, asks whether the children will use a carpet having a representation of flowers upon it. The majority of students answer in negative but a few feeble stragglers including Sissy Jupe answer in positive. Then the gentleman asks the 'girl number twenty' whether she will carpet her room—or her husband's room, if she is a grown woman, and owns a husband—with representations of flowers. The girl says that she can do it as she is very fond of flowers. The government officer says that she will put tables and chairs upon them, and people will walk over them with heavy boots then. Sissy replies that it will not crush and wither. They will be the pictures of what is very pretty and pleasant, and she will fancy. The officer repeats that she is never to fancy. The gentleman and Thomas Gradgrind repeat the word 'fact'.

The pupils are asked to imbibe facts and fancy or imagination or poetry or sensitivity is discouraged.

Mr. Gradgrind goes to his utilitarian abode, Stone Lodge, from the utilitarian school room. In the way, he passes the back of a circus booth. He looks at his own metallurgical Louisa peeping through a hole in a deal board and his son mathematical Thomas degrading himself on the ground to catch a hoof of the graceful equestrian Tyrolean flower-act. He goes to the spot and charges his children Louisa and Thomas that they are acting in the name of wonder, idleness and folly. Louisa says to her father that she has wanted to see what it has been like. Mr. Gradgrind is very sorry to find the fact that Thomas, with his education and resources, brings his sister to a scene like this. But Louisa clarifies that she brings her brother to such a scene. Her father is painful to hear this and opines that it makes Thomas no better and it makes Louisa worse. Mr. Gradgrind is amazed to find Thomas in such a degraded position to whom the circle of the sciences is open and who may be said to be replete with facts; who is trained to mathematical exactness. Louisa admits that she has been tired and so she has wanted to enjoy the circus. Dickens shows that Louisa and Thomas are bored in the life of facts and want to see the circus. But Mr. Gradgrind tells them that the circus will make them worse.

*Hard Times* is set in a northern industrial town of Coketown. It is a town of red brick. But due to the smoke and ashes reaching the red brick, it is a town of unnatural red and black like the painted face of a savage. It is a town of machinery and tall chimneys out of which interminable serpents of smoke trail themselves. It owns a black canal in it, and a river that runs purple with ill-smelling dye. In the building full of windows, there is a rattling and a trembling all day where the piston of the steam engine works monotonously up and down like the head of an elephant in a state of melancholy madness. It contains "several large streets all very like one another, and many small streets still more like one another, inhabited by people equally like one another, who all went in and out at the same hours, with the same sound upon the same pavements, to do the same work, and to whom everyday was the same as yesterday and to-morrow, and every year the counterpart of the last and the next."[95]

Coketown is to be seen and felt as a town wihout art. Therefore "all myths and fairytales, all imaginative writing and creation, all fancies strange or consoling, and all mediators of such wares, Dickens included, are exiled from the Gradgrind and Bounderby world. In their place, we have Coketown, a Fact complete and sufficient in its streets and chapels, its suspended smoke serpents, its 'melancholy mad elephants', as in the enslaved and destroyed consciousness of its children, its confines where Stephen Blackpool will live and die."[96] Here, locations of cure and those of penal confinement are interchangeable:

> The jail might have been the infirmary, the infirmary might have been the jail, the town-hall might have been either, or both, or anything else, for anything that appeared to the contrary in the graces of their construction. Fact, fact, fact, everywhere in the material aspect of the town; fact, fact, fact, everywhere in the immaterial.[97]

The Coketown is a world without fancy. There is nothing but fact everywhere in it. Rationality makes a role of a mode of production overriding other values. People are reduced to 'Hands' in Coketown. In the interior fortifications of the ugly citadel, Nature is strongly removal and killing airs and gases are filled in. In the centre of the labyrinth of narrow courts upon courts, and close streets upon streets, where every piece is in a great hurry for somebody's purpose, and the whole has become an unnatural family, shouldering, and trampling, and pressing one another to death; in the last close corner where the chimneys, are built in various fashions of twisted shapes, "among the multitude of Coketown, generically called 'the Hands',—a race who would have found more favour with some people, if Providence had seen fit to make them only hands, or, like the lower creatures of the seashore, only hands and stomachs-lived a certain Stephen Blackpool."[98] The utilitarian industrial civilisation is a condition in which everything is weighed, measured, has its price and emotion is totally out of this world. This is symbolised by the clanking machinery of the Coketown which turns men into 'hands'.

To the factory owners, the only thing real is the statistics of profit and loss, anything else is merely sentimentality, intangible fancy. *Hard Times* analyses and condemns the very ethos of industrialism: "This (says Bernard Shaw) is Karl Marx, Carlyle, Ruskin, Morris, Carpenter, rising up against civilisation itself as a disease, and declaring that it is not our disorder but our order that is horrible; that it is not our criminals but our magnates that are robbing and murdering us; and that it is not merely Tom-all-Alone's that must be demolished and abolished, pulled down, rooted up, and made forever impossible, so that nothing shall remain of it but History's record of its infamy, but our entire social system."[99]

The circus athletes represent human spontaneity and highly developed skill and bring poise, pride and ease. They are always buoyant and like the ballet-dancer. They are of no importance for the utilitarian calculus. They express vital human impulse and serve vital human needs. The Horse-riding is looked down by Gradgrind and Bounderby but brings to the people of Coketown amusement, art and spectacle of triumphant activity. Dickens expresses a reaction to industrialism by presenting the circus. There is dreadful degradation of life in Coketown.

Utilitarianism is confuted in a dialogue between Louisa and her father Mr. Gradgrind about her marriage. The inadequacy of the utilitarian calculus is exposed. Mr. Gradgrind says to Louisa that she is the subject of a proposal of marriage made to him. She answers no word at all. Her father takes it as her preparedness of marriage but she announces that she cannot say about her preparedness or unpreparedness until it is stated to her. Her father takes it as perfectly reasonable and then expresses that Mr. Bounderby has informed him that he has long watched her progress with particular interest and pleasure. He has long hoped that he shall offer her his hand at a suitable time. Feeling the arrival of that time, Mr. Bounderby has made his proposal of marriage to him and has entreated him to make it known to her and to express his hope that she will take it into her favourable consideration. Louisa asks her father several questions. Once she asks whether he thinks she loves

Mr. Bounderby. Mr. Gradgrind is extremely discomfited by this unexpected question. Secondly, she asks whether he asks her to love Mr. Bounderby. Thirdly, she asks 'whether Mr. Bounderby asks her to love him'. Her father explains to her daughter that Mr. Bounderby does not do her the injustice and does not do himself the injustice of pretending to anything 'fanciful', 'fantastic' or 'sentimental'. Louisa asks her father's advice. Mr. Gradgrind replies her on the basis of his utilitarian principle:

> I would advise you (since you ask me) to consider this question, as you have been accustomed to consider every other question, simply as one of tangible Fact. The ignorant and the giddy may embarrass such subjects with irrelevant fancies, and other absurdities that have no existence, properly viewed—really no existence—but it is no compliment to you to say, that you know better. Now, what are the Facts of this case? You are, we will say in round numbers, twenty years of age; Mr. Bounderby is, we will say in round numbers, fifty. There is some disparity in your respective years, but in your means and positions there is none; on the contrary, there is a great suitability. Then the question arises—Is this one disparity sufficient to operate as a bar to such a marriage? In considering this question, it is not unimportant to take into account the statistics of marriage, so far as they have yet been obtained, in England and Wales. I find, on reference to the figures, that a large proportion of these marriages are contracted between parties of very unequal ages, and that the elder of these contracting parties is, in rather more than three-fourths of these instances, the bridegroom. It is remarkable as showing the wide prevalence of this law, that among the natives of the British possessions in India, also in a considerable part of China, and among the Calmucks of Tartary, the best means of computation yet furnished us by travellers, yield similar results. The disparity I have mentioned, therefore, almost ceases to be disparity, and (virtually) all but disappears.[100]

Louisa asks her father of his recommendation. And Mr. Gradgrind replies: "Confining yourself rigidly to Fact, the question of Fact you state to yourself is: Does Mr. Bounderby ask me to marry him? Yes, he does. The sole remaining question then is: Shall I marry him? I think nothing can be plainer than that?"[101]

When Louisa asks her father whether she will marry Bounderby. Then Mr. Gradgrind utters: "Precisely. And it is satisfactory to me, as your father, my dear Louisa, to know that you do not come to the consideration of that question with the previous habits of mind, and habits of life, that belong to many young women."[102]

The conversation between Mr. Gradgrind and Louisa, concerning marriage of Louisa and 55 year old Bounderby, is quite important. The arguments put forward to convince Louisa reveal a mind dried up by its worship of a systematic theory of facts. Mr. Gradgrind quotes statistics to prove to his daughter that she need not take into consideration the disparity of years between Mr. Bounderby and herself. In this context, he declares love irrelevant and considers it as 'misplaced expression'. The issues are reduced to "algebraic formulation they are patently emptied of all real meaning. The instinct-free rationality of the emotionless Houyhnhnms is a void. Louisa proceeds to try and make him understand that she is a living creature and therefore no Houyhnhnm, but in vain (to see it, he must have overleaped at a bound the artificial barriers he had for many years been erecting between himself and all those subtle essences of humanity which will elude the utmost cunning of algebra, until the last trumpet ever to be sounded will blow even algebra to wreck)."[103]

Louisa sits so long looking silently towards the town. Her father reacts: "Are you consulting the chimneys of the Coketown works, Louisa?"[104] She answers: 'There seems to be nothing there but languid and monotonous smoke. Yet, when the night comes, Fire bursts out, father!'[105] Mr. Gradgrind does not feel his error until he ruins the lives of his children. When he conveys to his "daughter Louisa a proposal of marriage from the odious Bounderby, she gazes on the fumes of the factory chimneys and muses aloud that they seem to be nothing but languid and monotonous smoke. But the obtuse, well meaning father misses all her yearning for sympathy and understanding, even the allusion to those fires of human passion that burst out in the dark night of despair, and Louisa goes to her doom."[106]

Louisa thinks and says to her father that life is very short. But her father replies that "the average duration of human life is proved to have increased of late years. The calculations of various life assurance and annuity offices, among other figures which cannot go wrong, have established the fact."[107] Louisa tells her father that she speaks of her own life and Mr. Gradgrind replies that life's longevity is considered in aggregate. She wishes to do little as she thinks herself little fit for something. Finally, she is satisfied to accept the proposal of marriage since Mr. Bounderby likes to take her.

The dependence on reason is liberating, no doubt, "but as the instrument of a class which was both reforming and aggressive it became, in a real history, an alienation, in which the calculation of interest was separated from all other human impulses and ties."[108] In the case of Bitzer, rationalising is important: "His only reasonable transaction in that commodity would have been to buy it for as little as he could possibly give, and sell it for as much as he could possibly get; it having been clearly ascertained by philosophers that in this is comprised the whole duty of man-not a part of man's duty, but the whole."[109]

The utilitarian uses statistics and arithmetic to rationalise an economic system. Sissy Jupe says: "Then Mr. M'Choakumchild said he would try me again. And he said, This schoolroom is an immense town, and in it there are a million of inhabitants, and only five-and twenty are starved to death in the streets, in the course of a year. What is your remark on that proportion? And my remark was—for I couldn't think of a better one—that I thought it must be just as hard upon those who were starved, whether the others were a million, or a million million. And that was wrong, too."[110]

Louisa has no outlet for her emotional life except in her love for her brother Tom. She lives for him and marries Bounderby for his sake. But she is responsive to Mr. James

Harthouse. His statement in *Hard Times*, is an intelligent criticism of the Gradgrind philosophy: "The only difference between us and the professors of virtue or benevolence, or philanthropy—never mind the name—is, that we know it is all meaningless, and say so; while they know it equally and will never say so."[111]

Louisa arrives back to her father's house, fleeing from temptation of Mr. Harthouse and she speaks to her father that it has been her task from infancy to strive against every natural prompting that has arisen in her heart. But there has lingered in her breast, sensibilities, affections, weaknesses capable of being cherished into strength, defying all the calculations made by man. She has not been known to his arithmetic but to Creator. She asks her father whether he would have given her to Mr. Bounderby, the husband she hates, after knowing those natural impulses. She, again, asks whether he would have robbed her of the immaterial part of her life, her refuge from sordid and bad in the real things around her, her school in which she should have learned to be more humble and more trusting with them, and to hope in her little sphere to make them better.

Louisa reveals that a new acquaintance has been thrown into her way by chance, light, polished and real. He has read her thoughts and he has been very communicative to her. She says: "There seemed to be a near affinity between us. I only wondered it should be worth his while, who cared for nothing else, to care so much for me."[112] Louisa says again that he has gained her confidence and has known the story of her marriage. But she insists that she has not disgraced herself but plainly speaking she loves him. This utilitarian system is greatly shocked. Dickens dramatises the failure of the system satirically as the fallacy of the system is calamitously demonstrated. Now, Mr. Gradgrind is more concerned with his daughter than his system. He has wanted to do great things in measuring fathomless deeps with his little mean excise rod, and in walking over the universe with his rusty stiff-legged compasses. Within the limits of his short tether he has tumbled about "annihilating the flowers of existence with greater singleness of purpose than many of the blatant personages whose company he kept."[113]

Tom, Mr. Gradgrind's son, has his descent to debt and commits a bank robbery. He escapes from justice to the circus where he is in the form of a Negro servant. The non-utilitarian Mr. Sleary gives him an opportunity to disguise: "In a preposterous coat, like a beadle's, with cuffs and flaps exaggerated to an unspeakable extent; in an immense waistcoat, knee breeches, buckled shoes, and a mad cocked hat; with nothing fitting him, and everything of coarse material, moth-eaten and full of holes; with seams in his black face, where fear and heat had started through the greasy composition daubed all over it; anything so grimly, detestably, ridiculously shameful as the whelp in his comic livery, Mr. Gradgrind never could by any other means have believed in, weighable and measurable fact though it was. And one of his model children had come to this!"[114]

Mr. Gradgrind asks his son of the robbery and the whelp replies that he has forced the safe himself overnight and shut it up. He has had the key that has been found made long before. He has dropped it that morning that it might be supposed to have been used. He has not taken the money all at once. He has pretended to put his balance away every night but he has not done. Mr. Gradgrind is very shocked to hear this.

The ironic satiric discomfiture of the utilitarian philosopher is caused by the rebound of his own theory upon himself. Dickens has belief in Greek idea of Nemesis. Evil turns upon itself and so it comes to Gradgrind. Bitzer, the real successful and truimph of the system arrives to intercept Tom's flight. He holds his son by the collar.

Mr. Gradgrind is emotionally broken down and makes, frantically, an appeal to Bitzer to save his son, Tom, from the processes of justice for bank robbery. He has the sentiments of a father and so he talks of human heart. He is transformed from the hardened ideologue of facts to sensitivity. He asks Bitzer whether he has a heart and his utilitarian student replies:

> 'The circulation, Sir', returned Bitzer, smiling at the oddity of the question; 'couldn't be carried on without one. No man, Sir, acquainted with the facts established by Harvey relating to the circulation of the blood, can doubt that I have a heart.'[115]

Mr. Gradgrind asks his pupil whether his heart is accessible to compassion. But his student denies and says that it is accessible to Reason. He asks Bitzer his motive in reason for preventing the escape of this wretched youth. Bitzer speaks in a very business-like and logical manner. He is going to take young Mr. Tom back to Coketown in order to deliver him over to Mr. Bounderby, and he will then promote him to young Mr. Tom's situation. Mr. Gradgrind says that this is solely a question of self-interest with you:

> 'I beg your pardon for interrupting you, Sir,' returned Bitzer; 'but I am sure you know that the whole social system is a question of self-interest. What you must always appeal to, is a person's self-interest. It's your only hold. We are so constituted. I was brought up in that catechism when I was very young, Sir, as you are aware.'[116]

Mr. Gradgrind offers money against Bitzer's expected promotion. But Bitzer goes over the calculations in his mind and refuses the offer for his improved prospects in the Bank. As a last measure to soften Bitzer, Mr. Gradgrind recalls his many years at his school. He reminds the pains bestowed upon him and asks to persuade himself to disregard the present interest and release his son. But Bitzer affirms: 'I really wonder, Sir', rejoined the old pupil in an argumentative manner, 'to find you taking a position so untenable. My schooling was paid for; it was a bargain; and when I came away, the bargain ended.'[117]

It is the major constituent of Gradgrind's ethics that everything is to be paid for. Nobody is to be given anything or render help without purchase. Gratitude and other virtuous feelings are sentimental humbug and thus to be abolished. The complete chain of human existence from birth to death is a bargain no doubt. Social living and social behaviour are mere matters of self interest and not a structure of humane attachments. Bitzer's reply to Gradgrind is refutation of his long cherished utilitarian principle:

> 'I don't deny', added Bitzer, 'that my schooling was cheap. But that comes right, Sir. I was made in the cheapest market, and have to dispose of myself in the dearest.'[118]

Tom's escape is carried out successfully by Mr. Sleary. Mr. Gradgrind admires the animals and takes shelter in the world of imagination. Mr. Sleary says that a dog is a wonderful animal and Mr. Gradgrind praises his instinct. He also admires his scent.

Dickens attacks the Benthamites on the very ground Mill attacks them in his Autobiography. "Mill had to discover poetry in order to recover from the ravages of the Benthamite education imposed on him by his father; and the ultimate deficiency of the Gradgrind system, too, is that it ignores or condemns the imagination."[119] Dickens' view is opposite to Bentham's, and *Hard Times* pursues its monstrous logical conclusion the "consequences of a philosophy of self-interest carried into practice."[120] The system (or all institutions) is systematically attacked. "The only positive values are personal, outside the system: where a repressed humanity asserts itself in personal love and care and responsibility, or breaks out in the fanciful and eccentric play of the Horseriding."[121] Dickens arranges to make the struggling human feelings defeat the system. He adds a politic warning: "Utilitarian economists, skeletons of schoolmasters, Commissioners of Fact, genteel and used-up infidels, gabblers of many little dog's—feared creeds, the poor you will have always with you. Cultivate in them, while there is yet time, the utmost graces of the fancies and affections, to adorn their lives so much in need of ornament; or, in the day of your triumph, when romance is utterly driven out of their souls, and they and a bare existence stand face to face, Reality will take a wolfish turn, and make an end of you."[122]

## NOTES

1. Ivor Brown, *Dickens in His Times*, Thomas Nelson & Sons Ltd., London, 1963, p. 22.

2. Humphry House, *The Dickens World*, Oxford University Press, London, New York, Toronto, 1942, p. 172.
3. *Ibid.*, pp. 177-78.
4. Michael Slater, *Charles Dickens, American Notes Pictures from Italy*, 'Everyman,' J.M. Dent, London, Charles E. Tuttle, Vermont, 1997, p. 127.
5. Introduction and notes by David Ellis, *The Pickwick Papers, Charles Dickens*, Wordsworth Classics, Hertfordshire, 2000, p. 155.
6. Martin Price, *Dickens: A Collection of Critical Essays*, Prentice Hall, Englewood, Cliffs, N.J., 1967, p. 77.
7. David Ellis, *op. cit.*, p. 156.
8. *Ibid.*, p. 158.
9. *Ibid.*, p. 162.
10. *Ibid.*, p. 163.
11. *Ibid.*, p. 165.
12. Steven Marcus, *Dickens from Pickwick to Dombey*, Chatto and Windus, London, 1965, p. 46.
13. Jacob Korg, *Twentieth Century Interpretations of Bleak House*, Prentice Hall, Englewood Cliffs, N.J., 1968, p. 25.
14. Andrew Sanders, *Charles Dickens, Bleak House, Everyman*, J.M. Dent, London, Charles E. Tuttle, Vermont, 1994, p. 517.
15. Jacob Korg, *op. cit.*, p. 26.
16. Andrew Sanders, *op. cit.*, pp. 357-58.
17. *Ibid.*, p. 147.
18. Philip Hobsbaum, *A Readers' Guide to Charles Dickens*, Thames and Hudson, London, 1972, pp. 156-57.
19. Jacob Korg, *op. cit.*, p. 27.
20. *Ibid.*, p. 26.
21. Andrew Sanders, *op. cit.*, p. 511.
22. John Lucas, *The Melancholy Man*, Methuen & Co. Ltd., London, 1970, p. 212.
23. T.A. Jackson, *Charles Dickens: The Progress of a Radical*, People's Publishing House, New Delhi, 1990, p. 33.
24. John Lucas, *Charles Dickens: The Major Novels*, Penguin Books, Harmondsworth, Middlesex, 1992, p. 93.
25. Philip Collins, *Dickens: The Critical Heritage*, Routledge and Kegan Paul, London, 1971, p. 498.
26. *Our Mutual Friend*, Charles Dickens, Wordsworth Classics, Hertfordshire, 1997, p. 229.

27. Ivor Brown, *op. cit.*, p. 19.
28. *Little Dorrit*, Charles Dickens, Wordsworth Classics, Hertfordshire, 1996, p. 638.
29. Chuzzlewit Martin, *Charles Dickens*, Wordsworth Classics, Hertfordshire, 1994, pp. 616-17.
30. Introduction and notes by Dr. Tim Cook, *Nicholas Nickleby, Charles Dickens*, Wordsworth Classics, Hertfordshire, 1995, p. 184.
31. Adrienne E. Gavin, *David Copperfield, Charles Dickens*, Wordsworth Classics, Hertfordshire, 2000, p. 533.
32. *Ibid.*, p. 467.
33. Philip Collins, *Charles Dickens, Hard Times*, Everyman's Library J.M. Dent and Sons Ltd., London, 1978, p. 184.
34. *Ibid.*, p. 192.
35. Margaret Cardwell, *Charles Dickens, Great Expectations*, Oxford University Press, New York, 1993, p. 141.
36. *Our Mutual Friend, Charles Dickens*, Wordsworth Classics, Hertfordshire, 1997, p. 476.
37. Humphry House, *op. cit.*, p. 179.
38. Ivor Brown, *op. cit.*, p. 27.
39. Valerie Purton, *Charles Dickens, Dombey and Son, Everyman*, J.M. Dent, London, Charles E. Tuttle, Vermont, 1997, p. 34.
40. *Ibid.*, p. 4.
41. *Ibid.*, p. 5.
42. A.E. Dyson, *The Inimitable Dickens*, Macmillan, London, New York, St. Martin's Press, 1970, p. 102.
43. Valerie Purton, *op. cit.*, p. 7.
44. *Ibid.*, p. 18.
45. Harry Stone, *Dickens and the Invisible World*, Macmillan, London, 1980, p. 151.
46. A.O.J. Cockshut, *The Imagination of Charles Dickens*, Collins, St. James Place, London, 1961, p. 99.
47. Alan Shelston, *Charles Dickens, Dombey and Son, and Little Dorrit*, Macmillan, Basingstoke, Hampshire, 1985, p. 69.
48. Edgar Johnson, *Charles Dickens, His Tragedy and Triumph*, Penguin Books, New York, London, 1986, p. 317.
49. Valerie Purton, *op. cit.*, p. 92.
50. *Ibid.*
51. *Ibid.*

52. *Ibid.*, p. 93.
53. Harry Stone, *op. cit.*, p. 148.
54. Kathleen Tillotson, *Novels of the Eighteen Forties*, Oxford: Clarendon Press, 1954, p. 196.
55. A.E. Dyson, *op. cit.*, p. 103.
56. Harry Stone, *op. cit.*, p. 159.
57. Valerie Purton, *op. cit.*, pp. 380-81.
58. *Ibid.*, p. 381.
59. *Ibid.*, p. 382.
60. *Ibid.*, p. 731.
61. *Ibid.*, p. 495.
62. Grahame Smith, *Dickens, Money and Society*, University of California Press, Berkeley and Los Angeles, 1968, p. 107.
63. Valerie Purton, *op. cit.*, p. 482.
64. Harry Stone, *op. cit.*, p. 148.
65. Valerie Purton, *op. cit.*, p. 547.
66. John Gross and Pearson Gabriel, *Dickens and the Twentieth Century*, Routledge and Kegan Paul, London, 1962, p. 123.
67. Valerie Purton, *op. cit.*, p. 697.
68. *Ibid.*
69. Harry Stone, *op. cit.*, p. 149.
70. Valerie Purton, *op. cit.*, p. 720.
71. *Ibid.*, p. 780.
72. *Our Mutual Friend*, *Charles Dickens*, Wordsworth Classics, Hertfordshire, 1997, p. 107.
73. *Page Norman*, *Dickens'*, *Hard Times, Great Expectations* and *Our Mutual Friend*, Macmillan, London, 1979, p. 166.
74. Chuzzlewit Martin, *Charles Dickens*, Wordsworth Classics, Hertfordshire, 1994, pp. 248-49.
75. *Ibid.*, p. 254.
76. J.H. Miller, *Charles Dickens*: *The World of His Novels*, Harvard University Press, Cambridge, Massachussetts, London, Oxford University Press, London, 1959, p. 133.
77. Valerie Purton, *op. cit.*, p. 64.
78. *Ibid.*, pp. 273-74.
79. Kathleen Tillotson, *op. cit.*, p. 200.

80. Paul Schlicke, *Oxford Reader's Companion to Dickens*, Oxford: The University Press, 1999, p. 581.
81. Allan Grant, *A Preface to Dickens*, Longman, London and New York, 1984, p. 61.
82. Basil Willey, *Nineteenth Century Studies*, Chatto and Windus, London, 1955, p. 171.
83. *Ibid.*
84. Allan Grant, *op. cit.*, pp. 61-62.
85. Introduction by Philip Collins, *Charles Dickens, Hard Times*, Everyman's Library, Dent and Sons Ltd., London, p. 192.
86. Graham Storey, *Charles Dickens, Bleak House*, Cambridge University Press, 1987, p. 12.
87. Paul Schlicke, *op. cit.*, p. 582.
88. Philip Hobsbaum, *A Reader's Guide to Charles Dickens*, Thames and Hudson, London, 1972, p. 175.
89. *Ibid.*
90. Philip Collins, *op. cit.*, pp. 112-13.
91. Philip Hobsbaum, *op. cit.*, p. 181.
92. Philip Collins, *op. cit.*, p. 2.
93. *Ibid.*, pp. 2-4.
94. F.R. Leavis, *The Great Tradition*, Penguin Books, Harmondsworth, Middlesex, 1962, p. 252.
95. Philip Collins, *op. cit.*, p. 19.
96. A.E. Dyson, *The Inimitable Dickens*, Macmillan, London, New York, St. Martin's Press, 1970, p. 187.
97. Philip Collins, *op. cit.*, p. 20.
98. *Ibid.*, p. 56.
99. Edgar Johnson, *Charles Dickens, His Tragedy and Triumph*, Penguin Books, New York, London, 1986, p. 406.
100. Philip Collins, *op. cit.*, pp. 87-88.
101. *Ibid.*, p. 88.
102. *Ibid.*
103. F.R. Leavis, *op. cit.*, pp. 262-63.
104. Philip Collins, *op. cit.*, p. 89.
105. *Ibid.*
106. Edgar Johnson, *op. cit.*, p. 407.
107. Philip Collins, *op. cit.*, p. 89.

108. Slater Michael, *Dickens, 1970*, Chapman and Hall, 1970, pp. 90-91.
109. Philip Collins, *op. cit.*, p. 103.
110. *Ibid.*, p. 51.
111. *Ibid.*, pp. 148-49.
112. *Ibid.*, p. 196.
113. *Ibid.*, p. 199.
114. *Ibid.*, p. 254.
115. *Ibid.*, p. 257.
116. *Ibid.*, p. 258.
117. *Ibid.*
118. *Ibid.*
119. Monroe Engel, *The Maturity of Dickens*, Harvard University Press, Cambridge, Massachussetts, 1967, p. 173.
120. Joseph Gold, *Charles Dickens, Radical Moralist*, University of Minnesota Press, Minneapolis, 1972, p. 198.
121. Michael Slater, *op. cit.*, p. 92.
122. Philip Collins, *op. cit.*, p. 146.

# Education

# 5

The Yorkshire schools were an important component of English social life. They were notorious for negligence, cruelty and pedagogical incompetence. Robert Southey's *Letters from England* noted that the boys were a source of cheap labour on their master's farm. John Abernethy complained that his clothes were taken away after his arrival in the institution. Richard Cobden remembered that he was ill-fed and ill-taught. Sir Joshua Walmsley described a parent who refused to pay fees for his son when the boy came back home ill from malnutrition. The schools were spartan, harsh and cruel. Many of them advertised 'no vacations', 'no extra charges' and were used as a "depository for orphans, bastards and other unwanted children".[1]

The philosophy of laissez faire, unchecked private greed, indifference of the state and gullibility of the public led to make this wicked system of child torture under the mask of school education: "Traders in the avarice, indifference, or imbecility of parents, and the helplessness of children; ignorant, sordid, brutal men, to whom few considerate persons would have entrusted the board and lodging of a horse or a dog; they formed the worthy cornerstone of a structure, which, for absurdity and a magnificent high-minded laissez-aller neglect has rarely been exceeded in the world."[2]

Dickens, during his childhood at Catham, had met a boy from one of the Yorkshire schools who had been operated upon for an abscess by his Yorkshire guide, philosopher and friend with a penknife. Hearing of the brutalities of the Yorkshire schools sitting as a boy near Rochester Castle, Dickens's childish imagination had been haunted by a vision of the "dirty schoolroom as a hideous dungeon and the school-master as an ogre torturing little boys."[3]

Discussing Yorkshire schools, Philip Collins refers to Southey's *Letters From England* that Bowes was the cheapest part of England and tradesman and other higher class parents sent their children from the great towns to the schools established here. At sixteen pounds a year, "the schools were run 'upon the most economical plan', the food being rough, the beds sheetless, and the formal education meagre. The boys washed their own clothes, and supplied the labour for their masters' harvest-fields."[4] Since travelling was slow and expensive, the families of the boys could not visit the boys and it was very much difficult for boys to go home in London. These added in making the schools attractive to the patrons. Some renunciated their children. The patrons sent their boys to Yorkshire with a quarter's fees in advance and became oblivious of the child.

Dickens had the first hand experience of Yorkshire schools. In January 1838, Charles Dickens and Hablot Browne went to Yorkshire on a trip. Their destination was the small Yorkshire village of Bowes. It was on the moors, near the River Greta. It was importantly the site of a school or 'Academy' run by William Shaw. Dickens noted in his diary that evening: "Shaw the schoolmaster we saw to-day, is the man in whose school several boys went blind sometime since, from gross neglect."[5]

Two cases were brought against Shaw in 1823 by parents of blinded boys. During the trial, it proved that the boys were given maggoty food and slept in overcrowded, flea-infested beds and ten boys had lost the vision before. Shaw paid three hundred pounds damages for each case. His academy was affected by an epidemic of Opthalmia. He neglected the victims but being panic-stricken brought them to a London specialist for three hundred guineas. His school was very much profitable to him although it was cheap. He was not responsible to the boarders and behaved harshly to them. The food, the washing and sleeping facilities were miserable. Sick boys were kept in a damp stone-floored house. Doctors were not called for them and they spent two or three months untreated in the washhouse. Boys having disreputable clothes or missing them were asked to hide under the table to escape the eyes of visitors. Diseases spread and became deadly through gross neglect and bad living conditions. Shaw was an inefficient teacher but a harsh profiteer. During his visit to Bowes, Dickens wandered around the local churchyard and found the graves of thirty-four boys approximately who had died attending the cheap school of the district.

Similar schools were spread in other parts of Yorkshire. They took pupils on the charge of twenty guineas a year. The mushroom growth of private schools and the total neglect of education by the state created Yorkshire schoolmasters. Dickens, as a social analyst, is very much pained to find large groups of such imposters, least qualified and trained to impart education to children.

Dickens condemns this system brutally in his Preface to *Nicholas Nickleby*. A man unfit for any other occupation in life, "was free, without examination or qualification, to open a school anywhere; although, preparation for the functions he undertook, was required in the whole round of crafts and trades, the schoolmaster excepted."[6]

In the 1848 Preface to *Nicholas Nickleby*, Dickens writes that he had gone under a pseudonym to collect secret information of land. He was urged by a local man never to send a boy to one of these schoolmasters 'while there's a harse to hoold in a Lunnun, or a gootther to lie asleep in.' A lady sent him an anecdote about a vicious Yorkshire teacher. Dickens replied to her: "Depen upon it that the rascalities of those Yorkshire schoolmasters cannot easily be exaggerated and that I have kept down the strong truth and thrown as much comicality over it as I could, rather than disgust the reader with its fouler aspects."[7]

Dickens spoke fiercely against the Wellington House Academy in a speech on education in November 1857 at a charity banquet at London Tavern on behalf of The Warehouseman and Clerk's school:

> I don't like the sort of school to which I once went myself [he said], the respected proprietor of which was by far the

> most ignorant man I have ever had the pleasure to know, who was one of the worst-tempered man perhaps that ever lived, whose business it was to make as much out of us and to put as little into us as possible....
>
> I don't like that sort of school, because I don't see what business the master had to be at the top of it instead of the bottom, and because I never could understand the wholesomeness of the moral preached by the abject appearance and degraded condition of the teachers....
>
> I do not like that sort of school, because I have never yet lost my ancient suspicion touching that curious coincidence that the boy with four brothers to come always got the prizes. In fact, and in short, I do not like that sort of school, which is a pernicious and abominable humbug altogether.[8]

His Yorkshire schools experiences and his Wellington House Academy's experiences mixed to form a hatred of the system of education of the time and finds reflection in his novels.

Dickens satirises some educational practices of his time. He detests cruelty, inefficiency, cramming and repression in education. There were charity schools along the streets to churches under the escort of a beadle. They were in leather breeches and with mortified straw baskets for bonnets. These schools did much harm by marking off their pupils as the recipients of charity. Robin Toodle in *Dombey and Son* is Dickens' satiric thrust on these institutions. Mr. Dombey prizes Mrs. Toodle's services as Paul's wet nurse by nominating her son to the Charitable Grinders. These institutions were financed by subscription entitling donors to nominate candidates. Dickens disliked this system and had objection because the system was humiliating to candidates who were required to canvass for votes and there was an embarrassment to the subscribers who were approached frequently by letters and visits from the desiring suppliants. Robins' education to such a school is satirised:

> Now it happened that poor Biler's life had been, since yesterday morning, rendered weary by the costume of the

Charitable Grinders. The youth of the streets could not endure it. No young vagabond could be brought to bear its contemplation for a moment, without throwing himself upon the unoffending wearer, and doing him a mischief. His social existence had been more like that of an early Christian, than an innocent child of the nineteenth century. He had been stoned in the streets. He had been overthrown into gutters; bespattered with mud; violently flattened against posts. Entire strangers to his person had lifted his yellow cap off his head and cast it to the winds. His legs had not only undergone verbal criticisms and revilings, but had been handled and pinched. That very morning, he had received a perfectly unsolicited black eye on his way to the Grinders' establishment, and had been punished for it by the master: A superannuated old Grinder of savage dispositon, who had been appointed schoolmaster because he didn't know anything, and wasn't fit for anything, and for whose cruel cane all chubby little boys had a perfect fascination.[9]

Robin is 'Number 147'. In his noticeable school uniform (yellow cap and leather small clothes), Robin is tormented in the streets by the mischievous boys. He is the victim of the brutal schoolmaster. The teacher knows nothing and uses corporal punishment freely. Dickens was against the cruelty to students and the incompetency of teachers. He observes: "If it was my ungrateful case", said Mrs. Chick, solemnly, "and I had your reflections, Richards, I should feel as if the Charitable Grinders' dress would blight my child, and the education choke him."[10]

Such is the reason that even society's charities and generosities fail of their stated objectives. They are not really directed toward human welfare, but are "instruments of ostentation and keeping the poor in their place".[11] The charitable Grinders' school also is not beneficial for human beings. Robin Toodle suffers much terror in his journey to school. He receives ritual flogging and starts on his career of 'waging' or truancy and he is brought to bad ways and companionship. He turns out a liar and a sneak. His schooling is the root of his corruption.

Honour is not taught at the Grinders' School. The system encourages hypocrisy. His father is distressed as Robin goes bad. He regrets to his benefactor that Robin was huffed and cuffed, and flogged and badged. He was taught as parrots by a brute schoolmaster acting as a hound. Dickens comments in *Dombey and Son* on the failures of the Grinders' system. Many of the friends and masters of past Grinders dislike this system of education for the common people. But the governing powers of the Grinders' Company pick out a few boys well turned of the system as examples of good produce which settled the "business of those objectors out of hand, and established the glory of the Grinders' Institution."[12]

Dickens' own experiences and minute observations of the English schools enabled him to infer that these institutions crippled the innocent children. He makes a humorous but critical attack on many shortcomings of the Ragged School system in *Our Mutual Friend*. He finds the ragged schools 'a slight and ineffectual palliative of an enormous evil'. In this ragged school, Charley Hexam first learns the alphabet. The great preparatory Establishment is a miserable loft in an unsavoury yard. Its atmosphere is oppressive and disagreeable. It is crowded, noisy and confusing. Half of the pupils drop asleep or fall into a state of waking stupefaction. The teachers possess no idea of execution and their efforts are muddle.

It is a school for all ages and for both sexes. The two sexes are kept apart and the students are partitioned off into square assortments. The place wears a grimly ludicrous pretence that every pupil is childish and innocent. This pretence, enhanced by the lady visitors, leads to the ghastliest absurdities. Young women, with their vices, are expected to profess themselves captivated by the immoral book, *The Adventures of Little Margery*. The adult pupils are taught to read out of the New Testament. They stumble over the syllables and keep their bewildered eyes on the particular syllables. They are absolutely ignorant of the sublime history. The unfortunate infants are handed over to the prosiest and worst of all the teachers with good intentions. The teacher repeats the word sepulchre five hundred times and "never hinting what it meant; the conventional boy smoothing away right and left as an infallible commentary; the whole hotbed of flushed and exhausted infants exchanging measles, rashes, whooping cough, fever, and stomach disorders, as if they were assembled in High Market for the purpose".[13]

Dickens' objection to the ragged school is shaped in a brutally comic manner. Sleeping infants, yawning infants, restless infants, whimpering infants are darted and smoothed. They are taught but do not learn the meaning. The pupils are affected by measles, rashes, whooping cough, fever and stomach disorders. The jocosity and pomposity of religious preaching is shown in the school system. It is satirically comic to find that the religious preaching is performed in the very jumble of the school by the worst teacher. The preaching paragon of a teacher, the Chief Executive, is assisted by a volunteer boy as the assistant of the executioners. The volunteer boy darts and hits the sleepy little infants:

> It was the function of the chief executioner to hold forth, and it was the function of the acolyte to dart at sleeping infants, yawning infants, restless infants, whimpering infants, and smooth their wretched faces; sometimes with one hand, as if he were anointing them for a whisker; sometimes with both hands, applied after the fashion of blinkers.[14]

Dickens did not share with the ragged school supporters who wanted to protect their evangelical commitment and party machinery at the cost of educational progress. He considered the ragged school movement as a prelude to comprehensive educational and social progress.

The public school-curriculum is elaborately narrated mediating the satirised real perception: the world constituted through the writer's observation with that of the implied attainable ideal in *Bleak House*. Richard Carstone had been at Winchester. He learns for eight years at a public school. He learns to make Latin Verses of several sorts admirably. It is nobody's business to know his natural bent or to notice his failings or to adapt any kind of knowledge to him. He is adapted to the verses, and knows the art of making them to perfection. Esther Summerson observes: "Although I had no doubt that they were very beautiful, and very improving, and very sufficient for a great many purposes of life,...I did doubt whether Richard would not have profited by some one studying him a little, instead of his studying them quite so much."[15]

Dickens comments that Richard was only administered Latin Verse education without any respect to natural inclination and aptitude. This was the defect in the school curriculum and the comic satirist satirises this. Winchester is blamed to ruin Richard's prospect of life. Dickens recalls Sydney Smith's horrible accounts that he was forced to make 10,000 Latin Verses in his school days.

At Thomas Gradgrind's school, at Coketown, the children are crammed with Facts. Dickens dislikes such a new educational method. The entire educational construct is starkly utilitarian, a kind of totalitarian hegemonistic ritual that banishes sensibility and humanity, reducing human beings to mechanical devices in the body politic of the state:

> Now, what I want is, Facts. Teach these boys and girls nothing but Facts. Facts alone are wanted in life. Plant nothing else, and root out everything else. You can only form the minds of reasoning animals upon Facts: nothing else will ever be of any service to them. This is the principle on which I bring up my own children, and this is the principle on which I bring up these children. Stick to Facts, Sir![16]

Thomas Gradgrind stresses that only facts should be taught to the pupils. Dickens' sense of the outrage of the wretched old-time method is depicted. Richard Burton observes: "He was continually satirising the older view, embodied in Mr. Gradgrind of doleful memory, wherein the impartation of 'facts' was the sole aim, and browbeating discipline the sole way of inculcation."[17] Gradgrind represents the dangers of "doctrine, dogma and absolutism, in this case Rationalism, in education, yet education by definition is resistant to the evils of its forms, for, except in a totalitarian state (and even there education for the state is to some extent self-defeating) education is the most disinterested social activity. It is always, relatively speaking, liberating and for this reason Dickens places much value and emphasis on it."[18]

Mr. Gradgrind's questions are a parody of object lesson in *Hard Times*. Gradgrind asks Sissy to define a horse. But she (girl number twenty) is unable to define a horse. Mr. Gradgrind comments that she possesses no facts and asks Bitzer to define the horse, a common animal. The boy defines it as quadruped and graminivorous. He tells that it prossesses forty teeth (twenty-four grinders, four eye-teeth and twelve incisive). He adds that it sheds coat in the spring and sheds hoofs in marshy countries. He is of the view that its hard hoofs are shod with iron and its age is known by marks in mouth. This episode presents contrast between the verbalised head knowledge and the knowledge of the senses and heart. Bitzer has verbalised head knowledge. He answers only facts. Dickens "saw that to do the child justice you must develop its self-activity, and not bear down on merely an imitation. Bitzer was purely imitative when he defined a horse. Imitation turns out that sickening parrot-like unthinking use of words and of memory which, if persisted in, will put a successful quietus on any real exercise of the reasoning faculty."[19]

Mr. Gradgrind's companion, the government officer, takes over and asks children to answer some questions. He asks the girls and boys whether they will paper a room with representations of horses. Some students say that they will paper the room with representations of horses and some are of the opinion that it cannot be done. One corpulent slow boy answers that he will paint it and will not paper the room. But the gentleman and Thomas Gradgrind ask them that they are required to paper the room positively. The government officer makes it crystal clear that they will not paper a room with representations of horses as they never see horses walking up and down the sides of rooms in reality. He emphasises that they are not to see anywhere that they do not see in fact. They are not to have anywhere that they do not have in fact. Taste is the second name for Fact.

He stresses that they are to be regulated and governed in all things by fact. The word Fancy is to be discarded. They are not to have, in any object of use or ornament, that is a contradiction in fact. They do not walk upon flowers in fact so they cannot be allowed to walk upon flowers in carpets. They never meet with quadrupeds going up and down walls. Hence they must not have quadrupeds represented upon walls. They must use "for all these purposes, combinations and modifications (in primary colours) of mathematical figures which are susceptible of proof and demonstration. This is the new discovery. This is fact. This is taste."[20]

This model school is conducted on the principle of fact and the pupils are asked to imbibe facts. But there is complete failure of the perfect system of hard headed utilitarian Manchester school. The total force of this satire is evident when Gradgrind, who stands "as sponsor for such a conception of the child as a sort of little human hopper into which to throw facts, to be ground out by the educational mill and the result dubbed 'education' when he applies this principle to his own household, makes a terrible wreck of his domestic happiness".[21]

The personal and social manifestations of such an educational system is filled with disastrous consequences. There is a total breakdown of the system. Louisa, Gradgrind's daughter, comes back from her husband and she complains to her father, Mr. Gradgrind, that she should have been a million times wiser, happier, more loving, more contented, more innocent and human if she had groped her way by her sense of touch being free, when she knew the shapes and surfaces of things and exercised fancy. This night her husband being away, her lover was with her. This minute he expects her. She is not ashamed and says to her father that his philosophy and his teaching will not save her. He holds her but she falls on the ground and the pride of his heart and the triumph of his system lies an insensible heap at his feet. Dickens lashes heavily the crumbling of the system based on facts. Louisa is very much harmed by this philosophy. Barbara Hardy comments: "Gradgrind's redeeming opposite is Sissy, the pupil who teaches her master that the truth of the reason, and he can learn her lesson only when faced by the sterile fruits of his teaching in another pupil, his daughter."[22]

Gradgrind's son Tom, the product of the same school commits theft in the bank. Gradgrind is worried about this robbery and asks Tom. Tom replies that so many people are employed in conditions of trust. So many people out of so many will be dishonest. Its being a law, his son asks him to comfort himself. When Tom tries to escape the justice, he is intercepted by Bitzer. Gradgrind asks Bitzer to release his son. He reminds his years at the model school. He remembers the pains bestowed on him and asks his pupil to disregard the present interest and release his son. But Bitzer refuses as he says that his schooling was paid for, it was a bargain and the bargain ended when he left the school. Bitzer is the product of the Gradgrind's school and he is not helpful to Gradgrind. Tom is saved in a circus by Mr. Sleary. *Hard Times* shows that if a child is brought up in a circus it is a prodigy of virtue but when he is sent to a model school he can grow to rob a bank or make a prostituted marriage. The anatomy of a heartless education and heartless industrialism, connected by the criterion of efficiency concludes with a sad and sober appraisal:

> Herself again a wife—a mother-lovingly watchful of her children, even careful that they should have a childhood of the mind no less than a childhood of the body, as knowing it to be even a more beautiful thing, and a possession, any hoarded scrap of which is a blessing and happiness to the wisest? Did Louisa see this? Such a thing was never to be.[23]

The radical disaster of education is that it defines class-consciousness and destroys individual worth. Education is the badge of a class or station. The iron-master tells Sir Leicester that Rosa should be better educated if she is to marry his son. Dickens observes:

> 'Are you aware, sir, that this young woman whom my Lady —my Lady—has placed near her person, was brought up at the village school outside the gates?'

'Sir Leicester, I am quite aware of it. A very good school it is, and handsomely supported by this family.'

Then, Mr. Rouncewell, returns Sir Leicester, 'the application of what you have said is, to me incomprehensible.'

'Will it be more comprehensible, Sir Leicester, if I say', the iron-master is reddening a little, 'that I do not regard the village school as teaching everything desirable to be known by my son's wife?'[24]

Sir Leicester discovers in Rouncewell's observation an evidence that people are liking "to educate other 'people out of their stations, and so [are] obliterating the landmarks, and opening the floodgates, and all the rest of it'. In other words, for his far more than for Rouncewell, education is a way of creating or confirming class-consciousness. Rouncewell's request has a proper reasonableness about it. There is no reason to suppose that the education that the village school has to offer is much good. Even so, we are meant to feel, I think, that what he plans for Rosa may have perhaps less to do with consideration for her than for her future social position."[25]

Rick in *Bleak House* has great expectations because he is the product of a certain class of education. In *Dombey and Son*, Rob is sent by Dombey to a charity school for the sake of class-consciousness. Dombey's determination to educate Rob is in the interests of ensuring that "the inferior classes should continue to be taught to know their position."[26] Education played a vital role in nineteenth-century England in stabilising class-consciousness. Thus Miss Tox admires that the nursery school to which Paul is to be sent is 'exclusion' itself. For Paul is not to know the inferior classes.

Krook teaches himself to read and write so that he is not taught wrong by others. Mr. Jarndyce asks Krook of his learning. The latter replies that it is slow as it is hard at his time of life. Mr. Jarndyce advises him to be taught by someone. But the oldman is very conscious and denies to be taught by someone as they may teach him wrong. Dickens satirises such a system which creates suspicion in others. John Lucas comments on Dickens's concern with education in *Bleak House*: "Education may and probably does teach wrongs, it imposes a way of seeing, and in suggesting as much, Dickens denies all the liberal suggestions about education as a process of disinterested enlightenment."[27]

In *Our Mutual Friend*, the values imbibed by Charley Hexam are part of his education. They make him socially contemptuous of Lizzie and her friends and he becomes infected with anti-working class attitudes and the idea of 'getting up in the world'.

The first batch of Queen's scholars, enlisted as pupil teachers under Kay-Shuttleworth's 1846 Minutes, emerged from the training colleges in 1853. Dickens presents these new certificated teachers as industrial produce characterised by monotonous homogeneity of dispensation of information but hardly qualifying as humanely recognisable educator. Of Mr. M'Choakumchild, Dickens writes:

> He and some one hundred and forty other schoolmasters, had been lately turned at the same time, in the same factory, on the same principles, like so many pianoforte legs. He had been put through an immense variety of paces, and had answered volumes of head-breaking questions. Orthography, etymology, syntax, and prosody, biography, astronomy, geo-graphy, and general cosmography, the sciences of compound proportion, algebra, land-surveying and levelling, vocal music, and drawing from models, were all at the ends of his ten chilled fingers. He had worked his stony way into Her Majesty's most Honourable Privy Council's Schedule B, and had taken the bloom off the higher branches of mathematics and physical science, French, German, Latin, and Greek. He knew all about all the Water Sheds of all the world (whatever they are), and all the histories of all the peoples, and all the names of all the rivers and mountains, and all the productions, manners, and customs of all the countries, and all their boundaries and bearings on the two-and-thirty points of the compass. Ah, rather overdone, M'Choakumchild. If he had only learnt a little less, how infinitely better he might have taught much more![28]

Dickens satirically points out that M'Choakumchild is overloaded with knowledge of all the branches. As a school teacher, he has succeeded in indoctrinating his young pupils in the principles of practicality. He has stimulated them to think in terms of "nothing but fact and use. For this reason M'Choakumchild specialists in subjects related to the world of facts and figures."[29] He is engaged in killing the innocents. He denies them the right of childhood and suppresses their imagination and individuality. He goes to work in the preparatory lesson, not "unlike Morgiana in the Forty Thieves: Looking into all the vessels ranged before him, one after another, to see what they contained.... When from thy boiling store, thou shalt fill each jar brim full by-and-by, dost thou think that thou wilt always kill outright the robber Fancy lurking within—or sometimes only maim him and distort him!"[30] M'Choakumchild surveys the inclined plane of little vessels arranged in order, ready to have imperial gallons of facts poured into them to the brim. Dickens indicts him as he destroys the human identity of his students with his terrible and overpowering scholarship. His revered facts about geography, economics, statistics are comparable to the facts of classical grammar stuffed to the sons of the prosperous merchants.

Dickens presents the stipendiary schoolmaster Bradley Headstone. He has his decent blackcoat and waistcoat, decent pantaloons and decent hairguard round his neck but suffers from a definite 'stiffness of manners'. The dead uniformity of the school system has destroyed his spontaneity. He performs in an involuntary mechanical motion. Dickens unfolds his criticism of the training college regime in the character of Bradley Headstone in *Our Mutual Friend*:

> He had acquired mechanically a great store of teacher's knowledge. He could do mental arithmetic mechanically, sing at sight mechanically, blow various wind instruments mechanically, even play the great Church organ mechanically. From his early childhood up, his mind had been a place of mechanical storage. The arrangement of his wholesale warehouse, so that it might be always ready to

> meet the demands of retail dealers—history here, geography there, astronomy to the right, political economy to the left—natural history, the physical sciences, figures, music, the lower mathematics, and what not, all in their several places—this care had imparted to his countenance a look of care; while the habit of questioning and being questioned had given him a suspicious manner, or a manner that would be better described as one of lying in wait.... He always seemed to be uneasy lest anything should be missing from his mental warehouse, and taking stock to assure himself.[31]

The intellectual insecurity of Headstone replaces the relentless confidence of M'Choakumchild. This educational system is connected with the processes of capitalist economy. Headstone's personal neuroses are connected organically with the socio-intellectual system of which he is a cog, a system which is revealed "as inhuman not only in its underlying values—commercial and mechanical—but in its division of knowledge and experience into isolated compartments".[32] Dickens is producing a deep humanist critical analysis of the modern British educational system.

There was an anarchy of religious sectarian schooling for the poorer classes as the sects were intolerant to one another and shamefully at discord. There was a scanty supply of amateurish dame school teaching in home-premises for meagre fees. Dickens portrays an utterly incompetent teacher, Mr. Wopsle's great-aunt, in *Great Expectations.* He satirises the dame schools in general as they were extremely faulty and criticised by official and unofficial observers. The amateur dame school of Mr. Wopsle's great aunt has the characteristic faults. This school is attended by Pip and educational operations are conducted for an hour or so by the lady after closing her little village shop. Dickens caricatures:

> Mr. Wopsle's great-aunt kept an evening school in the village; that is to say, she was a ridiculous old woman of limited means and unlimited infirmity, who used to go to sleep from six to seven every evening, in the society of youth who paid twopence per week each, for the improving

> opportunity of seeing her do it. She rented a small cottage, and Mr. Wopsle had the room up-stairs, where we students used to overhear him reading aloud in a most dignified and terrific manner, and occasionally bumping on the ceiling. There was a fiction that Mr. Wopsle "examined" the scholars, once a quarter. What he did on those occasions, was to turn up his cuffs, stick up his hair, and give us Mark Antony's oration over the body of Caesar.[33]

Mr. Wopsle's great aunt is the victim of inertia and she has no good academic activity but Pip, somehow, learned to read and write. The educational scheme or course was set up by Mr. Wopsle's great-aunt. The pupils eat apples and put straws up one another's backs. Then Mr. Wopsle's great-aunt makes an indiscriminate totter at them with a birch-rod. The pupils form in line and buzzingly pass a ragged book from hand to hand. The book contains an alphabet in it, some figures and tables, and a little spelling. In the meanwhile, Mr. Wopsle's great-aunt falls into a state of coma originating from sleep or a rheumatic paroxysm. The pupils, then, enter among themselves upon a competitive examination on the subject of Boots. The competition is meant to ascertain who could tread the hardest upon whose toes. Then Biddy rushes at them and distributes three defaced Bibles. Bibles are illegibly printed and are speckled all over with ironmould and contain specimens of the insect world smashed between their leaves. The course is usually lightened by several single combats between Biddy and refractory students. Then Biddy gives out the number of a page and all read aloud. Biddy leads with a high shrill monotonous voice. None of students possess notion of, or reverence for, this reading. Due to this horrible din, Mr. Wopsle's great-aunt awakes. She staggers at a boy fortuitously and pulls his ears. This is a sign to terminate the course for the evening. The students emerge into the air with shrieks of intellectual victory. There is no prohibition to students to entertain himself with a slate or even with the ink. It is difficult to pursue that branch of study in the winter season as the little general shop in which the classes are held is also Mr. Wopsle's great-aunt's sitting-room and bed-chamber-being but "faintly illuminated through the agency of one low-spirited dip-candle and no snuffers".[34]

Dickens gives a hilarious description of Mr. Wopsle's great-aunt. She frightens the indisciplined students. She is cruel too. The students and Biddy have no reverence for the Bible. They possess moral depravity. There is no serious endeavour for education and everything is light and comic. This amusing account is based on Reports on elementary education, from the Manchester Statistical Society's in 1834-35 to the New Castle Commission's in 1859. They all "dwell upon the Dames' infirmity and illiteracy (the simplicity of childhood is taught by ignorance, and often imbecility), the dirty, ill-lit and unventilated rooms in which they taught, often using them at the same time for cooking and other household chores ('more than half of them are used as dwelling, dormitory, and schoolroom'), the general inadequacy and sometimes complete absence of books ('five only out of...65; appearing to be tolerably well provided'), the frequent failure to teach writing 'even in the most elementary form', the lack of discipline both intellectual and moral".[35]

Dickens was of the view that little teaching was going on in some schools. Pecksniff ensnares parents and guardians and pockets premiums. He works little to justify by instructing his pupils in architecture.

In *David Copperfield*, Murdstone marries David's mother and the boy suffers much in the name of education. David's lessons are presided over nominally by his mother but really by Mr. Murdstone and his sister. He was natural and good at lessons with his mother. He learnt the alphabet at her knee. To this day, when he looks upon the fat black letters in the primer, they remind no feeling of disgust or reluctance. On the other hand, he seems to have walked along a path of flowers as far as the crocodile book. He is cheered by the gentleness of his mother's voice and manner all the way. But David was miserable and restless when hard lessons were given and supervised by Murdstone. But these "solemn lessons which succeeded those, I remember as the death-blow at my peace, and a grievous daily drudgery and misery. They were very long, very numerous, very hard...and I was generally as much bewildered by them as I believe my poor mother was herself."[36] The Murdstones stand for firmness and tyranny. Murdstone administers David terrifying lessons. He introduces a 'lithi' and 'limber cane'. He warns David to be more careful today and begins his lessons. David is much fearful and he is unsuccessful at lessons.

At the outset, the lesson is a good freshner to his presence of mind. Later he feels the words of his lessons slipping off by the entire page. He tries to lay hold of them. But they seemed to have put skates on and they skim away from him with a smoothness. There is no checking. Dickens writes: "We began badly, and went on worse. I had come in with an idea of distinguishing myself rather, conceiving that I was very well prepared; but it turned out to be quite a mistake."[37] David is frightened and he cannot remember his lessons. Dickens is very critical of the tyranny administered to pupils as this is very harmful. David funks his lessons and he is beaten for his failures. Dickens knows that physical cruelty is lesser permanently injurious cruelty than authority inflicts. "Mr. Murdstone is the revolting ogre that he is because alongwith his carefully wax-ended cane he knows how to wield the weapon of mental cruelty too."[38]

Miss Monflathers belongs to Boarding and Day Establishment. She is made of warped gentility, snobbery, bad temper and soured virginity. She epitomises the bourgeoisie belief of propriety in the education of the young women.

Mrs. Pipchin is the owner of the special infantine boarding house to which Paul Dombey is sent at Brighton. Dickens writes of Mrs. Pipchin: "This celebrated Mrs. Pipchin was a marvellous ill-favoured, ill conditioned old lady, of a stooping figure, with a mottled face, like bad marble, a hook nose, and a hard grey eye, that looked as if it might have been hammered at on an anvil without sustaining any injury. Forty years at least had elapsed since the Peruvian mines had been the death of Mr. Pipchin; but his relict still wore black bombazeen, of such a lustreless, deep, dead, sombre shade, that gas itself couldn't light her up after dark, and her presence was a quencher to any number of candles."[39] Mrs. Pipchin was a great manager of children. The secret of her management was to give them everything that they did not like and nothing that they did. At noon she presides over some Early Readings: "It being a part of Mrs. Pipchin's system not to encourage a child's mind to develop and expand itself like a young flower, but to open it by force like an oyster, the moral of these lessons was usually of a violent and stunning character: the hero—a naughty boy—seldom, in the mildest catastrophe, being finished off by anything less than a lion, or a bear."[40]

Mrs. Pipchin is a bitter old lady of remarkable firmness. The development of mind of a pupil should be natural but Mrs. Pipchin wants to develop it by force. She is a lady of devastating character and the moral of her lessons is violent too. Dickens effects a caricature to laugh at the oddities of the cruelty practised in the name of education. Mrs. Pipchin possesses a special variety of cruelty inflicted on children. She uses a 'dungeon', an empty apartment, in which delinquents are imprisoned in solitude. When Paul Dombey arrives, Miss Pankey had been brought to the castle-dungeon for having sniffed three times in the presence of visitors. Master Bitherstone is filliped and is treated with salt water. Mrs. Pipchin's system of management is nearly the system of Murdstone.

The deserted school at Salem House is based on Wellington House Academy. Dickens describes the room of this school in *David Copperfield*. The place is extremely forlorn and desolate. The long room contains three long rows of desks and six of forms and bristles all round with pegs for hats and slates. The school is filled with squalor. Scraps of old copy-books and exercises are scattered on the dirty floor. Some silkworms' houses, are dispersed on the desks. Two miserable little white mice, run up and down in a fusty castle made of pasteboard and wire. A bird, in a cage, is in a melancholy state and makes a mournful rattle now and then in hopping on his perch. There is a "strange unwholesome smell upon the room, like mildewed corduroys, sweet apples wanting air, and rotten books. There could not well be more ink splashed about it, if it had been roofless from its first construction, and the skies had rained, snowed, hailed, and blown ink through the varying seasons of the year."[41]

Dickens satirically presents the school room that it is not hygienic and has not a happy atmosphere about it. Ivor Brown observes: "The squalid, ink-splashed, smelly school-room could be an exaggerated version of the premises at Wellington House."[42] Dickens hits at this establishment in particular and at bad schools in general in his portrait of Salem House. Salem House is the magnified reproduction of a degrading institution in the first half of the 19th century England. The place wears a gloomy and terrific look. It is heavily covered with dust and so David sneezes very much. It seems that Salem House is a great snuff box. The snug garden of the school looks like a very small desert. This school is homely only for a camel or a dromedary.

The students of this school show low spirit. The second master is shabby and epileptic. The first master wears a wig. The porter Gungay possesses a wooden leg and the headmaster has no voice. Dickens paints the creepy figure of Mr. Creakle: "Mr. Creakle's face was fiery, and his eyes were small, and deep in his head; he had thick veins in his forehead, a little nose, and a large chin. He was bald on the top and back of his head, and had some thin wet-looking hair that was just turning grey, brushed across each temple, so that the two sides interlaced on his forehead. But the circumstance about him which impressed me most, was, that he had no voice, but spoke in a whisper. The exertion this cost him, or the consciousness of talking in that feeble way, made his angry face so much more angry, and his thick veins so much thicker, when he spoke, that I am not surprised, on looking back, at this peculiarity striking me as his chief one."[43] The caricature is built upon the exaggeration of oppositional characteristics of an ideal perception. Such a picture is created through physiology, mannerism and attitudinal details.

Dickens describes through Creakle many features of mid-nineteenth century private schools. Mr. Creakle has not the natural inclination for teaching. He has little education and enlightenment. He has come to teaching when he is a failure in trade: "I heard all kinds of things about the school and all belonging to it. I heard that Mr. Creakle had not preferred his claim to being a Tartar without reason; that he was the sternest and most severe of masters; that he laid about him, right and left, every day of his life, charging in among the boys like a trooper, and slashing away, unmercifully. That he knew nothing himself, but the art of slashing, being more ignorant (J. Steerforth said) than the lowest boy in the school; that he had been, a good many years ago, a small hop-dealer in the Borough, and had taken to the schooling business after being bankrupt in hops, and making away with Mrs. Creakle's money."[44] Mr. Creakle is a bully and mean. Knowing only the art of slashing, he comes to teaching when he is bankrupt in hop dealing.

Dickens lashes Mr. Creakle as a schoolmaster. He states:

> Mr. Creakle came to where I sat, and told me that if I were famous for biting, he was famous for biting, too. He then showed me the cane, and asked me what I thought of that, for a tooth? Was it a sharp tooth, hey? Was it a double tooth, hey? Had it a deep prong, hey? Did it bite, hey? At every question he gave me a fleshy cut with it that made me writhe.[45]

Mr. Creakle asks the students to come fresh up to the lesson as he comes fresh upto the punishment. This shows his diabolical nature. The students become silent by his mere presence. He looks at them like a giant surveying his prisoners. He declares his diabolical creed: 'My flesh and blood'...'when it rises against me, is not my flesh and blood'.[46]

Mr. Creakle's credentials for the teaching profession expose the state of contemporary school education. He is coarse and ignorant. He regarded teaching and thrashing as identical. Dickens writes of Creakle focalised through David:

> I should think there never can have been a man who enjoyed his profession more than Mr. Creakle did. He had a delight in cutting at the boys, which was like the satisfaction of a craving appetite. I am confident that he couldn't resist a chubby boy, especially; that there was a

> fascination in such a subject, which made him restless in his mind, until he had scored and marked him for the day. I was chubby myself, and ought to know. I am sure when I think of the fellow now, my blood rises against him with the disinterested indignation I should feel if I could have known all about him without having ever been in his power; but it rises hotly, because I know him to have been an incapable brute, who had no more right to be possessed of the great trust he held than to be Lord High Admiral, or Commander-in-chief; in either of which capacities, it is probable that he would have done infinitely less mischief.[47]

Mr. Creakle had special inclination for the chubby boy. Dickens shows that Mr. Creakle is a brute. Another victim is beaten by him and he is making an effort to wipe the sting with a pocket handkerchief. A pupil with imperfect exercise is also thrashed by him: "When the unwashed, illiterate Squeers leaps upon one of his ragged, starveling victims and lashes him in brutal fury the cruelty and injustice of sheer bestiality. When the sadistic sycophant Creakle (whom Dickens, by a stroke of murderous satire, depicts as finishing his career as a Middlesex Magistrate, childishly vain of his 'model' prison—in which transparent hypocrites and humbugs get favours and an esteem denied to honest men in civil life)—when this Creakle, sneaks behind an unfortunate boy bent over a desk, and gives him a wealing cut with his cane just for the sheer pleasure of seeing his victim writhe in agony, this is, from its purposeless perversity, seen as an even more unforgivable outrage than is the brutality of Squeers."[48]

Mr. Creakle is the representation of Mr. Jones, the school teacher at Wellington House Academy: "Mr. Jones, like Mr. Creakle—as many of his pupils had cause to remember was very free both with his cane and with a bloated mahogany ruler."[49] He used the latter to rule ciphering books and also to smit the palms of his pupils. He had certainly love of the cane. Jones and the cane were inseparable and he lashed the boarders with it indiscriminately. Once he was particularly savage and his pupil threw an inkpot at his head. His students had no respect for him. He had a habit of drawing the pair of pantaloons of his pupil tight with one hand and caning him with the other.

David recalls his own school that it is carried on by sheer cruelty, "whether it is presided over by a dunce or not, there is not likely to be much learnt. I believe our boys were, generally, as ignorant a set as any schoolboys in existence; they were too much troubled and knocked about to learn; they could no more do that to advantage, than anyone can do anything to advantage in a life of constant misfortune, torment, and worry."[50]

Dickens shows that the school is for the administration of cruelty rather than learning. Mr. Creakle has the fault of social vanity. He considers Mr. Sharp, Mr. Mell, the junior masters as his subordinates and behaves in a disrespectful manner. They are miserably paid and are discriminated in food. Mr. Mell is dismissed on the ground of his low parentage and that his mother is dependent on charity in an almhouse. These all reflect Mr. Creakle's snobbery. Much of the "haphazard, desultory teaching, poor discipline punctuated by the headmaster's sadistic brutality, the seedy ushers and general rundown atmosphere, are embodied in Mr. Creakle's Establishment in *David Copperfield* (one of Dickens's better names, with its overtones of a creaky, ramshackle business)."[51]

In *Nicholas Nickleby*, Dickens describes the notorious and dungeon like boarding-schools in Yorkshire. He has heard the painful cruelties inflicted on the young boarders of the Yorkshire institutions since his childhood. In the preface to the first edition of the novel, he writes: "There are upon record trials at law in which damages have been sought as a poor recompense for lasting agonies and disfigurements inflicted upon children by the treatment of the master in these places."[52] Dickens applies his biting satire in the description of Mr. Squeers and his establishment. Comedy is often 'blended with pathos and grotesque horror' in the characters "of the Squeers family, and in some of the educational dialogue, but the Squeers' school room is like an inferno, often unrelieved by humour and particularized by hideous physical detail, like Bolder's wart-covered hands, and the boys' 'foul appearance of dirt, disorder, and disease'."[53]

Dickens describes the sight of the schoolroom full of stunted, hopeless and vicious boys in *Nicholas Nickleby*. Nicholas sees an image of every reject that a cruel society can collect for the purpose of their slow elimination. The children are pale and haggard faces, lank and bony figures, in the school. They wear the countenances of old men. They are emaciated and shackled with deformities with irons upon their limbs. There are the boys of stunted growth. Theirs long meagre legs are not able to bear their stooping bodies. There are the bleared eyes, the harelips, the crooked feet. Every ugliness or distortion represents the cruelty and neglect offered to the boys from the earliest dawn of infancy. There are little faces which should have been handsome. They are darkened with the scowl of sullen dogged suffering. The light of childhood is quenched. Its beauty has gone. Its helplessness alone remains with them. The vicious-faced boys brood with leaden eyes. There are young creatures on whom the sins of their frail parents have descended. They weep even for the mercenary nurses and they are lonesome even in their loneliness. With "every kindly sympathy and affection blasted in its birth, with every young and healthy feeling flogged and starved down, with every revengeful passion that can fester in swollen hearts, eating its evil way to their core in silence, what an incipient Hell was breeding here!"[54] Dickens produces this with a tone similar to Macaulay discussing the sieze of Derry of Marx on the subject of Working Day. It has strong emotional pressure and power of observation. When Nicholas observes the scene, he is hopeless. The sheer harshness of the school system dehumanises the boys and they become mentally and physically crippled. They are not the orphans of *Oliver Twist* and they are more positively rejected. They are the outcasts of a society whose values are dehumanised totally.

Mr. Wackford Squeers, the proprietor of torturing Dotheboys Hall is the symbolic representation of monstrosity in cruelty, hypocrisy, guile and greed. He is the representative of a class. His physiology, his business hypocrisy and his treatment to children are given graphic representation of existing facts to bring our attention to a group of Yorkshire schoolmasters. Dickens writes:

> Mr. Squeers's appearance was not prepossessing. He had but one eye, and the popular prejudice runs in favour of two. The eye he had was unquestionably useful, but decidedly not ornamental, being of a greenish grey, and in shape resembling the fanlight of a street door. The blank side of his face was much wrinkled and puckered up, which gave him a very sinister appearance, especially when he smiled, at which times his expression bordered closely on the villainous. His hair was very flat and shiny, save at the ends, where it was brushed stiffly up from a low protruding forehead, which assorted well with his harsh voice and coarse manner.[55]

So Squeers has repulsive look. The ridiculous incongruity of his dress multiplies the incongruity of his moral being:

> He was about two or three and fifty, and a trifle below the middle size; he wore a white neckerchief with long ends, and a suit of scholastic black, but his coat sleeves being a great deal too long, and his trousers a great deal too short, he appeared ill at ease in his clothes, and as if he were in a perpetual state of astonishment at finding himself so respectable.[56]

The grotesque description of Squeers' methods of teaching of Dotheboys Hall is a parody of the method employed in certain establishments. It contains the Jonsonian humour of the school master's hypocrisy. Squeers asks of the first boy. The temporary head of the philosophical class reports that he is cleaning the back parlour window. Then Squeers reacts to Nickleby that he runs the practical mode of teaching, the regular education system. C-l-e-a-n, clean, verb active, to make bright, to scour. W-i-n, win, d-e-r, der, winder, a casement. The boy knows this out of book, he goes and does it. It is just the same principle as the use of the globes. Squeers asks of the second boy and he gets the reply that he weeds the garden. B-o-t, bot, t-i-n, tin, n-e-y, bottiney, noun substantive, a knowledge of plants. The boy learns that bottiney means a knowledge of plants, he goes and knows then. Squeers says to Nickleby that this is his system of imparting knowledge but it is noted that he gets stuck in the pronunciation of word 'Botany'. Squeers, exercising teaching catechism, asks the third boy 'what's a horse'. The boy replies 'a beast'. In the manner of utilitarian school of Gradgrind, Squeers terms the horse as 'quadruped'. Then he asks the boy to go and look after his horse and rub him. Such educational system sucks out the very vitality of the students. Nicholas sees that boys are silent. There is no noise, no clamour of the schoolroom, no boisterous play or hearty mirth at Dotheboys Hall. The children shiver and lack the spirit of life.

The drunken Squeers taps at the door of Mrs. Sliderskew with a tipsy profundity. He is ridiculously presented as a grammarian with his conjugation of verbs and exposition of morphological and phonological features of English vowels and consonants. He introduces himself to Mrs. Sliderskew:

> Ah! it is me, and me's the first person singular, nominative case, agreeing with the verb 'it's', and governed by Squeers understood, as a acorn, a hour; but when the h is sounded, the a only is to be used, as a Land, a heart, a highway', replied Mr. Squeers, quoting at random, from the grammar.[57]

Squeers shows to be knowledgeable in English spelling. But his knowledge is of a misleading and dubious nature. He is credited with bottomless ignorance. His chief purpose is to make money. Smacking, boxing and flogging are other ingredients of Squeers' torture to children like starvation. Squeers beating Smike is a horrible picture:

> "Spare me, sir!," cried Smike.
>
> "Oh! that's all, is it?" said Squeers, "Yes, I'll flog you within an inch of your life, and spare you that."[58]

Mrs. Squeers takes Smike's head under her arm and gives many blows calling him a nasty, ungrateful, pig-headed, brutish, obstinated, sneaking dog.

Mr. Squeers uses cruelty to children as a matter of mere likings. The children are given in the care of Squeers, a sadist in power who is the living embodiment of cruelty and savagery. Dickens writes: "Much vexed by this reflection, Mr. Squeers looked at the little boy to see whether he was doing anything he could beat him for. As he happened not to be doing anything at all, he merely boxed his ears, and told him not to do it again."[59]

The two diabolical dimensions of his personality are his inhuman treatment of his boarders and his hypocrisy to cover it up with moral precepts on system and discipline. It is evident when Squeers with Nicholas and five other pupils is to make a journey to Yorkshire. He enjoys a sumptuous breakfast and leaves the children hungry with warm water. He asks the hungry children to 'conquer' their passion and he consumes a large quantity of milk and cold beef. He moralises:

> Conquer your passions, boys, and don't be eager after vittles'. As he uttered this moral precept, Mr. Squeers took a large bite out of the cold beef, and recognised Nichoas.[60]

Squeers calmly continues with his breakfast. He asks the boys to subdue their appetites and thus conquer human nature. He, with his mouth full of beef and toast, speaks to Mr. Nickleby that this is the method to inculcate strength of mind.

The cruelty of the Yorkshire schools is very shocking. Dickens describes the same sort of cruelty in *Nicholas Nickleby*: "Mrs. Squeers, sir, replied the proprietor of Dotheboys, 'is as she always is—a mother to them lads, and a blessing, and a comfort, and a joy to all them as knows her. One of our boys—gorging his-self with vittles, and then turning ill; that's their way-got a abscess on him last week. To see how she operated upon him with a penknife! Oh Lor!' said Squeers, heaving a sigh, and nodding his head a great many times, 'what a member of society that woman is'!"[61] Mrs. Squeers operates on the abscess of the boy with a penknife. Dickens shows the utter negligence attended to the boys at Dotheboys Hall.

An epidemic of scarlet fever breaks out in Squeers' school. He reaches London over some bothering law business connected with an action for inhuman neglect of a boy. His glib to Ralph

Nickleby of his care of his boarders reveals his own bestiality: 'Grazing', said Squeers, raising his voice, under the impression that as Ralph failed to comprehend him, he must be deaf. 'When a boy gets weak and ill and don't relish his meals, we give him a change of diet—turn him out for an hour or so everyday into a neighbour's turnip field, or sometimes, if it's a delicate case, a turnip field and a piece of carrots alternately, and let him eat as many as he likes. There an't better land in the country than this perwerse lad grazed on, and yet he goes and catches cold and indigestion and what not, and then his friends brings a law-suit against me.[62] He practised animal husbandry on the model of Manchester school. The animal imagery leads to the imagery of disease and dissolution. It indicates the rottenness. Squeers regards the boys as less valuable than the domestic animals. Dickens observes:

> "How is my Squeery?" said this lady in a playful manner, and a very hoarse voice.
>
> "Quite well, my love," replied Squeers. "How's the cows?"
>
> "All right, every one of' em', answered the lady."
>
> "And the pigs?", said Squeers.
>
> "As well as they were when you went away."
>
> "Come; that's a blessing", said Squeers, pulling off his great-coat. "The boys are all as they were, I suppose?"
>
> "Oh, yes, they're well enough", replied Mrs. Squeers, snappishly. "That young Pitcher's had a fever."[63]

Not only Squeers is brutal, he covers his real nature under an affected jocosity. When he tastes the milk meant for the boarders, he smacks his lips and comments that richness is here.

In his preface to *Nicholas Nickleby*, Dickens writes: "Mr. Squeers and his school are faint and feeble pictures of an existing reality, purposely subdued and kept down, lest they should be deemed impossible."[64] He looks upon the imposture, ignorance and brutal cupidity of Squeers not an individual aberrations but the common vices of a group. He launches an attack upon the cold-blooded cruelty and ridiculous ignorance of the education system.

Squeers is treated "not as the study of a human being, but the representative, pure and simple, of a vile institution."[65] In *Nicholas Nickleby*, the school is a societal institution whose purpose is to spread civilisation and promote humanity, "becomes by application of this same rule of enlightened self-interest, an instrument of de-educating children, turning boys into savages. Dotheboys Hall is a Hobbesian inferno, where the students and teachers exist in a state of open warfare."[66]

Creakle is a weaker villain than Squeers. His wife opposes his harshness and he is to operate his terror through an assistant Tungway. Creakle and Tungway oppress the boys but the boys find refuge and protection in Creakle's wife and daughter. Salem House pretends to respectability whereas Squeers keeps his tongue in his cheek. Creakle, a nasty does not achieve the mythological stature of Squeers.

In *Dombey and Son*, Dickens presents his comprehensive vision of the unscientific and antichild psychological foundations of 19th century school education. Dr. Blimbers Establishment imparts classical education through forcing and cramming Dickens describes this school as a 'hot house' in terms of the horticultural imagery. Here, unnatural processes are used to produce classical scholars out of the little masters. Like Gradgrind system in *Hard Times*, children are crammed with facts in the Blimber system.

The Blimber system is a much more refined system of cruelty. The Doctor only undertakes the charge of ten young gentlemen. But he is always ready to supply learning for a hundred. The business and delight of his life is to gorge the unhappy ten with it. In *Dombey and Son*, Dickens acknowledges that education is created by and feeds the corruption. There is a forcing apparatus incessantly at work at the Blimber's school. All the boys blow before their time. Mental green peas are produced at Christmas and intellectual asparagus are produced all the year round. Mathematical gooseberries are common at untimely seasons under Doctor Blimber's cultivation. Every Greek and Latin vegetable is produced of the driest twigs of boys during the frostiest times. Nature is of no value at all.

Irrespective of a young gentleman's intention to bear, Doctor Blimber makes him bear to pattern. Dickens notes two charges against Blimber. He forces on his boys prematurely and he makes no allowance for their individual difference in ability and interests.

The system of forcing is attended with its disadvantages. There is not the right taste about the premature productions and they do not keep well. Moreover, one young gentleman, with a "swollen nose and an excessively large head (the oldest of the ten who had 'gone through' everything), suddenly left off blowing one day, and remained in the establishment a mere stalk. And people did say that the Doctor had rather overdone it with young Toots, and that when he began to have whiskers he left off having brains."[67] Toots is a symbolic representation of the perils of a wrong system of education.

Dr. Blimber system has harmful and destructive kind of unnatural change. The system's unnaturalness is indicated through the agony of the little children who are engaged in the relentless grind of soulless teaching. This system produces adults with warped minds instead of gentleman. Dickens' satiric genius is applied to point out the monstrosity of the system.

Blimber's forcing results in not growth but stultification. A young gentleman's spirit is destroyed in three weeks. He bears all the cares of the world on his head in three months. He conceives bitter sentiments against his parents or guardians in four. He becomes an old misanthrope in five months. He envies curtius that blesses refuge in the earth, in six months; and at the "end of the first twelvemonth had arrived at the conclusion, from which he never afterwards departed, that all the fancies of the poets, and lessons of the sages, were a mere collection of words and grammar, and had no other meaning in the world."[68] Boys are disabled for life under this system. They are impaired in their capacities for growth. Each boy changes to worse but Toots is affected dangerously. He is maimed in his manhood and intellect. Dickens, with his satiric technique, points out Blimber's denial of the reality of change, of natural growth and organic development.

When Paul is taken to Dr. Blimber, he is interviewed and left alone in the Doctor's study and his father Mr. Dombey is taken to see the school. The condition of Paul is described with images of dehumanised discomfort: "And there, with an aching void in his young heart, and all outside so cold, and bare, and strange, Paul sat as if he had taken life unfurnished, and the upholsterer were never coming."[69] Paul looses his spirits under the determined forcing of the Blimber establishment. His death is caused or accelerated by this regime. An unfurnished life provided by Blimber is "stuffed with academic aridity and empty of warmth and imagination."[70]

Dickens sketches Dr. Blimber with contempt. His physical feature forms an impression of hideousness: "The Doctor was a portly gentleman in a suit of black, with strings at his knees, and stockings below them. He had a bald head, highly polished; a deep voice; and a chin so very double, that it was a wonder how he ever managed to shave into the creases. He had likewise a pair of little eyes that were always half shut up, and a mouth that was always half expanded into a grin."[71]

Mrs. Blimber pretends to be a scholar. She claims: "If I could have known Cicero, and been his friend, and talked with him in his retirement at Tusculum (beautiful Tusculum!), I could have died contented."[72] Paul is under care of Miss Blimber and he considers her "as a kind of learned Guy Faux, or artificial Bogle, stuffed full of scholastic straw."[73] She is dry and sandy with working in the graves of dead languages. Mr. Feeder, B.A., is a kind of a "barrel-organ, with a little list of tunes at which he was continually working, over and over again, without any variation".[74]

Dickens brings out the cold blooded, unimpassioned dull and dreary mindset of the teachers at Dr. Blimber's establishment through their blown up false rhetoric. When Paul comes to this school, Dr. Blimber calls him a young person making a pilgrimage to Parnassu's and he shows him the areas of the half asleep god. Mrs. Blimber indulges in inane rhetoric, an art of denigration or self ridicule. Mr. Dombey is welcomed to the garden of chosen flowers by her:

"Like a bee, Sir," said Mrs. Blimber, with uplifted eyes, "about to plunge into a garden of the choicest flowers, and sip the sweets for the first time. Virgil, Horace, Ovid, Terence, Plautus, Cicero. What a world of honey have we here."[75]

At the Blimber Academy classics are excessively and wrongly taught. The students are busy in the pursuit of hard verbs, severe noun-substantives, inflexible syntactic passages and exercises that haunt their minds. A boy concludes that all the fancies of the poets and teachings of the sages are only collection of words and grammar, nothing else. The boys consider the Romans as very bad people, their virtual enemies. In this way, "young Tozer, 'ridden by his lesson as a nightmare', would talk in his sleep 'unknown tongues, or scraps of Greek and Latin—it was all one to Paul—which, in the silence of night, had an inexpressibly wicked and guilty effect' (a stroke which Edward Fitzerald thought 'as terrible as Macbeth')."[76] Classical education prevailed in many public schools of the time and Dickens hates the mechanical education.

Childhood fancy is suppressed at Dr. Blimber's Academy. The description of the Victorian violence stands in stark contrast to the educator's emphasis on creativity, affection and the joy of the learning process. At Dr. Blimber's establishment, nothing takes place as vulgar as play. The holidays starts with a dispersal but 'breaking-up' is severe and rude an expression to the academy: "The young gentlemen oozed away, semi-annually, to their own homes; but they never broke up. They would have scorned the action."[77] Paul Dombey is not a cheerful boy by nature. Still, he finds this regime gloomy and joyless. He misses his sister and an old sailor named Glubb whose tales of sea-voyages stir his imagination. He describes to Mrs. Blimber: "He's a very nice old man, ma'am', he said. He used to draw my couch. He knows all about the deep sea, and the fish that are in it, and the great monsters that come and lie on rocks in the sun, and dive into the water again why they're startled, blowing and splashing so, that they can be heard for miles."[78] Mrs. Blimber considers these outpourings of Paul as bad but she is confident that his study at the academy will improve him.

Paul Dombey is the victim of the 'pygmy theory' of child development in Wordsworth's words and the children are denied in it the "uniqueness of their vision and considered to be merely, in Mr. Dombey's words, 'little people'."[79] Susan Nipper denounces the errors of the Blimber system and becomes an enemy of Mrs. Pipchin but society admires them. Dickens attacks an educational vice more insidious than Yorkshire schools. In *Dombey and Son*, the pervading uneasiness about the contemporary society replaces an intermittent concern with particular social inadequacies. Blimber system bears this pattern and produces disastrous results. Squeers' peoples had no parents but Blimber's select ten young gentlemen reflect 'glory and reputation' on the master. The parents destroy their children to see that they gain a place in the world. Dickens condemns the type of education Paul receives at Doctor Blimber Academy as it obstructs the normal child growth of Paul.

Squeers' victims are the victims of cruelty and selfish greed. Creakle's victims are the victims of a cruel sycophant. They are the victim of an evil educational tradition. Miss Monflathers' and Mr. Pipchin's are the victims of snobbery, ill-tempered egoism. They are the victim of an evil tradition of parental discipline. Dr. Blimber's victims are the victims of more evil educational tradition—"the tradition of classicism-plus parental vanity, the desire to be parents of a prodigy of miscalled 'learning'".[80]

Comparing those representations, Allan Grant writes: "Of inadequate schools, whether brutal like Dotheboys Hall, and Doctor Creakle's Academy, or totally misguided like Doctor Blimber's or Mr. Gradgrind's establishments, are among his most savage and memorable satirical attacks on what he took to be inhuman aspects of nineteenth century English life. Schooling equals denial and repression, whether systematic or terroristic, and what is denial is the child's world of imagination."[81]

In Dotheboys, Dickens attacks not only the cold blooded cruelty but the block headed ignorance. In Dr. Blimber's establishment, genial ridicule suffices for its condemnation. Dickens traced the evil consequences of gross neglect or mistaken zeal common in every household. He found that the vices of society can be traced in these bad beginnings. All his specimen teachers are bad. Squeers, a blatant rogue and impostor, is aware of his own rapacity. Other bad teachers are more complicated cases of educational wickedness. But Dr. Blimber, Mr. M'Choakumchild and Mr. Headstone are all competent, well-meaning, respectable but disastrous mentors of youth. Mrs. Pipchin is mean, unloving and selfish. Squeers, Mr. Murdstone and Creakle are all brutes, with a relish for inflicting pain on the child victims. Squeers' savagery is due to his uncouth and illiterate barbarity of his nature. Mr. Murdstone is a polished brute, an outcome of the industrial revolution. In Blimber system, there is no starvation and brutal physical infliction of the Squeers system, and none of the petulant, snobbish arrogance and spiritual desolation of the Monflathers-cum-Pipchin system. In this gentle system, the food is good and unstinted in quality. But there is a refined cruelty in Blimber system. With no stimulus to the imagination, the Blimber system is more perverse, the most irrational, the most cruel and unjust system of all. Like Gradgrind system, Blimber system regards the child as a passive subject and nature and imagination of no value at all.

Mr. Murdstone consists all the features of the evils of an education system. "He is, beneath all his veneer—his gentility, his glossy black whiskers, his gleaming teeth, and his fine linen —as greedily savage and as savagely greedy as Squeers; he is as sadistically delighted at a chance to use the cane as Creakle, whom he chooses as a fit agent for carrying out his designs; he is as pettily malignant as Miss Monflathers and as much of a snob; he is as egotistically and as ignorantly tyrannical as Mrs. Pipchin; and as much disposed to the forcing system as Dr. Blimber—without the Doctors' excuse of infatuate classicality."[82]

## NOTES

1. Philip Collins, *Dickens and Education*, Macmillan & Co. Ltd., London, 1963, p. 100.
2. Joseph Gold, *Charles Dickens: Radical Moralist*, University of Minnesota Press, Minneapolis, 1972, p. 73.
3. Edgar Johnson, *Charles Dickens: His Tragedy and Triumph*, Penguin Books, New York, London, 1986, p. 25.
4. Philip Collins, *op. cit.*, p. 100.
5. Peter Ackroyd, *Introduction to Dickens*, Mandarin Paperbacks, London, 1992, p. 56.
6. Philip Collins, *op. cit.*, p. 94.
7. *Ibid.*, pp. 99-100.
8. Christopher Hibbert, *The Making of Charles Dickens*, Longman, London, 1967, p. 86.
9. Valerie Purton, *Charles Dickens, Dombey and Son, Everyman,* J.M. Dent, London, Charles E. Tuttle, Vermont, London, 1997, pp. 68-69.
10. *Ibid.*, p. 82.
11. Alan Shelston, *Charles Dickens, Dombey and Son* and *Little Dorrit*, Macmillan, Houndmills, Basingstoke, Hampshire, 1985, p. 74.
12. Valerie Purton, *op. cit.*, p. 522.
13. *Our Mutual Friend, Charles Dickens*, Wordsworth Classics, Hertfordshire, 1997, p. 202.
14. *Ibid.*
15. Andrew Sanders, *Charles Dickens, Bleak House, Everyman*, J.M. Dent, London, Charles E. Tuttle, Vermont, London, 1994, pp. 152-53.
16. Philip Collins, *Charles Dickens, Hard Times, Dent*, London and Melbourne, Everyman's Library, London, 1978, p. 1.
17. Richard Burton, *Charles Dickens*, Folcroft Library Edition, Folcroft P.A., 1977, p. 274.
18. Joseph Gold, *op. cit.*, p. 200.
19. Richard Burton, *op. cit.*, p. 278.
20. Philip Collins, *op. cit.*, p. 6.
21. Richard Burton, *op. cit.*, p. 274.
22. Martin Price, *Dickens: A Collection of Critical Essays*, Prentice Hall, Inc. Englewood Cliffs, N.J., 1980, p. 49.
23. Philip Collins, *op. cit.*, p. 267.
24. Andrew Sanders, *op. cit.*, pp. 361-62.

25. John Lucas, *The Melancholy Man*, Methuen, London, 1970, p. 220.
26. *Ibid.*, p. 159.
27. *Ibid.*, p. 218.
28. Philip Collins, *op. cit.*, p. 7.
29. Debiprasad Bhattacharya, *The Middle Class in Dickens*, Minerva Associates, Kolkata, 2000, p. 92.
30. Philip Collins, *op. cit.*, p. 7.
31. Marcus Stone, *op. cit.*, p. 204.
32. Norman Page, *Dickens, Hard Times, Great Expectations* and *Our Mutual Friend*, Macmillan, Houndmills, Basingstoke, Hampshire, 1979, p. 163.
33. Margaret Cardwell, *Charles Dickens, Great Expectations*, Oxford University Press, New York, 1993, pp. 43-44.
34. *Ibid.*, p. 72.
35. Philip Collins, *op. cit.*, p. 96.
36. Adrienne E. Gavin, *David Copperfield, Charles Dickens*, Wordsworth Classics, Hertfordshire, 2000, p. 49.
37. *Ibid.*, p. 52.
38. T.A. Jackson, *Charles Dickens, The Progress of a Radical*, People's Publishing House, New Delhi, 1990, p. 37.
39. Valerie Purton, *op. cit.*, p. 98.
40. *Ibid.*, p. 101.
41. Adrienne E. Gavin, *op. cit.*, p. 71.
42. Ivor Brown, *Dickens in His Time*, Thomas Nelson & Sons Ltd., London, 1963, p. 156.
43. Adrienne E. Gavin, *op. cit.*, p. 74.
44. *Ibid.*, p. 77.
45. *Ibid.*, p. 79.
46. *Ibid.*, p. 74.
47. *Ibid.*, p. 80.
48. T.A. Jackson, *op. cit.*, p. 42.
49. Christopher Hibbert, *op. cit.*, pp. 85-86.
50. Adrienne E. Gavin, *op. cit.*, p. 84.
51. Angus Wilson, *The World of Charles Dickens*, Martin Secker & Warburg, London, 1970, p. 61.
52. Debiprasad Bhattacharya, *op. cit.*, p. 49.

53. Barbara Hardy, *Charles Dickens: The Writer and His Work*, Profile Books Ltd., Windsor, Berkshire, England, 1983, p. 43.
54. *Charles Dickens, Nicholas Nickleby, Hard Times, A Christmas Carol*, Octopus Books Ltd., London, 1983, p. 70.
55. *Ibid.*, p. 32.
56. *Ibid.*, pp. 33-34.
57. *Ibid.*, p. 503.
58. *Ibid.*, pp. 112-13.
59. *Ibid.*, p. 33.
60. *Ibid.*, p. 42.
61. *Ibid.*, p. 297.
62. *Ibid.*, p. 298.
63. *Ibid.*, p. 63.
64. Monod Sylvere, *Dickens the Novelist*, University of Oklahoma Press, Norman, 1967, p. 144.
65. K.J. Fielding, *Charles Dickens: A Critical Introduction*, Longman, Green and Co., London, New York and Toronto, 1958, p. 39.
66. F.S. Schwarzbach, *Dickens and the City*, University of London, The Athlone Press, London, 1986, p. 65.
67. Valerie Purton, *op. cit.*, p. 139.
68. *Ibid.*, p. 141.
69. *Ibid.*, p. 147.
70. Allan Grant, *A Preface to Dickens*, Longman, London and New York, 1984, p. 107.
71. Valerie Purton, *op. cit.*, pp. 139-40.
72. *Ibid.*, p. 144.
73. *Ibid.*, p. 159.
74. *Ibid.*, p. 140.
75. *Ibid.*, p. 144.
76. *Ibid.*, p. 143.
77. *Ibid.*, p. 177.
78. *Ibid.*, p. 148.
79. Garret Stewart, *Dickens and the Trial of Imagination*, Harvard University Press, Cambridge, Massachussetts, 1974, p. 162.
80. T.A. Jackson, *op. cit.*, p. 43.
81. Allan Grant, *op. cit.*, p. 95.
82. T.A. Jackson, *op. cit.*, p. 44.

# Conclusion

From the legendary Archilocus to contemporary times, satire as a literary mode mediates between the ideal perception and the real. The differential perspective sets up suggestions for correction. This may apply to individuals, systems and institutions. Dickens' satiric vision which manifests as a literary equivalent of the pictorial caricature consistently focuses on institutions as a contested site for recruitment and resistance. It is the institution that is an organ of the ruling class and which maintains with subtleties and doughty resilience status quo in power relations. In doing so, it represents unequal relationships which are paraded as common sense and labelled as normal or natural. Ordinary individuals are really aware that they are being recruited into what appears to be a consensual mental framework that is actually manufactured by such apparatus. To this Althusser gives a name of the ideological state apparatus. In the process 'interpellation', an individual becomes a willing accomplice to once own subordination. Although Althusser differentiates between 'ideological' and 'repressive', Dickens injects bits of repression and wide exploitation with the ideological apparatus. These are clearly seen in his depiction of administration, judiciary, religion, politics, commerce, utilitarianism and education.

Dickens expresses serious concern over the inefficient and loose administration of Victorian England represented through alarming situation of crime prevalent in English social life. He exposes child kidnapping and stealing of clothes of children in *Dombey and Son* and pick-pocketing and theft in *Oliver Twist*. There were gross inadequacies in administration due to shortcomings in the police forces. In *Great Expectations* and

*Oliver Twist*, Dickens exposes the failures and inefficiency of the police. Bucket, the inspector, in *Bleak House*, is ridiculed for his compromised moral position.

Dickens satirises Lord Mayor's inaction and cowardice in controlling the mobs. In *Martin Chuzzlewit*, he ridicules the worthless and careless magistrates for failing to squelch the mob by firm action and to act with right decision.

In *Oliver Twist*, Dickens jeers at the evils of the New Poor Law by satirising the workhouses. The inhumanity, cruelty and the indifference of the workhouse authorities to the sufferings of the paupers are subjected to Dickens' bitter satire. The sparseness of diet offered to inmates of the workhouse is ridiculed. Bumble, the corrupt bureaucrat of the workhouse is laughed at to indicate the tyranny of the system. Robert Gissing remarks that though it is proved demonstratively "that tenderness of heart led him astray in his bitterness against the new Poor Law; we see, of course, that herein he pursued his humane task, seeking in all possible ways to mitigate the harshness of institutions which pressed hardly upon the poor and weak. He could not away with those who held—or spoke as if they held—that a man had no duty to his fellows beyond the strict letter of the law."[1]

*Bleak House* satirizes the poor sanitation, the pollution and the creeping moisture creating diseases. Bad drainage, contaminated water, nauseous air and the bad smell of graveyard are significantly investigated causing diseases and deaths. In *Oliver Twist*, the prevalence of measles, the filthy place of London and Jacob's Island are ridiculed. In *David Copperfield*, Dickens satirises the dirty building and bad ventilation. He writes these inadequacies to arouse the interests of Victorians in sanitary question. In a new Preface to *Oliver Twist*, he insists on the necessity to improve slum condition: "I have always been convinced that this reform must precede all other Social Reforms; that it must prepare the way for Education, even for Religion; and that, without it, those classes of the people which increase the fastest must become so desperate, and be made so miserable, as to bear within themselves the certain seeds of ruin to the whole community."[2]

From 1849 onwards, sanitary reform was a principal subject of his public speeches and journalism, 'the most momentous of all earthly questions'; Dickens described this in "his address 'To Working Men' published in *Household Words* on 7 October, 1854".[3]

Dickens presents a severe institutional satire on English administration in the depiction of Circumlocution Office in *Little Dorrit*. He shows how Tite Barnacle and his family ruled the governments' departments on the sound principle of 'How Not To Do It'. The inefficiency, inaction and favouritism of the Civil Service are exposed. In his attack on the Civil Service, there is exaggeration, burlesque and calculated caricature but it is prompted by genuine indignation. His satire is eventual contribution to humane reform. Rare is something done better in English Literature than the immortal exposure of the methods of Red Tape and Place-Making, and of the policy, not 'merely of Letting Things be, but of Hindering Things From Being Better', which acted as an obstacle in the British progress. If Dickens might offer any apology for such an exaggerated fiction as the Barnacles and the Circumlocution office, he "would seek it in the common experience of an Englishman, without presuming to mention the unimportant fact of my having done that violence to good manners, in the days of a Russian War, and of a Court of Enquiry at Chelsea".[4]

Dickens does not recommend a better bureaucratic organisation. He has firm belief in the office's capacity for extinguishing action in a blanket of minutes, memoranda and letters of instruction. He considers the evils of the bureaucratic organisation as removable. "Radicalism may strengthen public administration by breaking the monopoly of office-holding, but it also strives to minimise administrative authority in the name of public opinion."[5]

The faulty, expensive and delayed administration of justice of the Court of Chancery are satirised in *Bleak House*. Tom Jarndyce was fed up with his case in the same court and blew his brains out. Richard depends a lot on the verdict of Jarndyce vs. Jarndyce and pays heavy penalty for it. The frustrated Miss Flite goes mad. The Court of Chancery leads to the ruin of half-insane Krook—the victim of the legal system. Gridley becomes violent and fires shots to keep his wits together.

The monumental suit Jarndyce vs. Jarndyce comes to close as the property in dispute has been consumed in legal costs and so it is of no value to the wards in the case. "The purely legal abuses of Chancery, its interminable delays and prohibitive costs, were equally perversion of its original purpose. It had originated in the Middle ages, as a means of speeding and mitigating the King's justice as it were to cut 'red-tape'."[6]

The gross corruption of the Court of Chancery will bring about its own destruction. It is shown in the demise of Chancery: "If all the injustice it has committed, and all the misery it has caused, could only be locked up with it, and the whole burnt away in a great funeral pyre-why, so much the better."[7]

Dickens' vision goes far beyond legal reform. He could accomplish what he wanted by burning away of the court 'in a great funeral pyre'. On a symbolic plane, the disintegration of Krook is the disintegration of Chancery. In Krook's Spontaneous Combustion, Dickens views the explosion of the entire legal system:

> The Lord Chancellor of that court, true to his title in his last act, has died the death of all Lord Chancellors in all courts, and of all authorities in all places under all names soever, where false pretences are made, and where injustice is done.... It is the same death eternally-inborn, inbred, engendered in the corrupted humours of the vicious body itself—and that only—Spontaneous Combustion, and none other of all the deaths than can be died.[8]

Dickens offers a slight hint in Krook's Spontaneous Combustion that moral justice will exist in some vague, apocalyptic future.

In Bardell vs. Pickwick case in *Pickwick Papers*, Dickens ridicules the pompous procedures of the court trial. Mr. Justice Stareleigh's manners and appearance expose the distortion and monstrosity of the judicial system. Witnesses are bullied in by sly solicitors. "Pickwick withdraws first by refusing to pay the damages after the suit is decided against him. His refusal to take part in the unjust proceedings of the law makes him a kind of Thoreau. Pickwick too believes that there are times when the only place for a good man is behind bars. The institutions of organised society are corrupt, and when there is a choice between one's own inner knowledge of what is right, and obedience to an unjust decision, there is only one choice to make. One chooses to be true to oneself, though this means passive resistance to the law of the land."[9]

Mr. Nupkins, the judicial magistrate, is ridiculed for his negligency of the procedure of criminal prosecution. Mr. Fang, the police court magistrate is jeered for his vicious stupidity.

The Sergeants Inn—the court for obtaining the legal document—is satirised for its naturalisation of perjury in the legal system. Insolvent Court is dealt with sarcasm. In *David Copperfield*, Dickens attacks the hypocrisy of proctorship and considers it a theatrical performance. The iniquity of the criminal law, made for their own benefit by the privileged class is attacked in *Great Expectations*.

Lawyers are presented by Dickens as corrupt and dishonest. They twist the case in such a way that the original merit of the case disappears. Mr. Vholes is greedy and his sole delight is to exploit his clients. Mr. Tulkinghorn is the agent of destruction. Mr. Buzfuz is little interested in the factual content of the case. He makes it believe of a lie by his powerful oratory. Dodson and Fogg practice organised dodging and planned obfuscation or confusion of reality and plunder gullible people. Mr. Perker is dodging and fogging agent of legal chicanery. Mr. Snubbin is dishonest and he is a legal quibbler. Sampson Brass is obsequious, rapacious, double-dealers, perjurers and suborners of evidence. Sally Brass is involved in such crimes as perjury and false evidence. Mr. Spenlow describes the nature of his professional business that in the litigation of a disputed will of thirty or forty thousand pounds the advocate could make significant gain through a series of evidence of interrogatory and counter interrogatory sessions.

The Fleet Prison in *Pickwick Papers* is the epitome of sheer inhumanity. The compassionate spirit of Pickwick does not endure the wretchedness in the spirit and so he locks himself in his room. Steven Marcus observes: "Pickwick can allay his insulted sense of justice by arraigning Dodson and Fogg, or he can withdraw from the dismal reality of the Fleet by locking himself in his room, disposing, ultimately, of whatever he cannot reform by removing it from sight."[10]

In *Great Expectations*, the Newgate Prison is shown as a vile place where debauchery and villainy are practised. In *Little Dorrit*, Marseilles prison possesses unventilated darkness. It is gloomy and contains despairing humanity inside.

Dickens dislikes intolerance, exclusiveness and positive religion. He believes in an ideal of toleration and reasonableness in religion derived from the tradition of Milton and Locke, champions of the free religious conscience. 'Positive religion' shows a sterile reliance upon the doctrinal element in belief. Dickens' opposition to this originates from a Romantic sense of Christianity as a religion of heart, a religion based upon deep feelings about man, nature and God. These feelings surpass denominational barriers, and offer a unifying rather than divisive faith. Dickens takes part in a Romantic tradition of flexible Christianity and follows a 'reiterated conviction of the irrelevance of religious forms'.

Special sort of chapel going and sermonising are shown ludicrous in Dickens' fiction. The religious spirit is represented as hypocritical and self-seeking rather than being genuine spiritual communion. Puseyism, the workings of the Calvinist Conscience and an attempt to indoctrinate somebody with stern views of man's immoral nature are detested. Dickens, heartily, detests the serious evangelising aspects of early nineteenth century religion. The perversion of true religious spirit among the Methodists and Evangelists is satirised in *Pickwick Papers* as is Sabbatarianism in *Little Dorrit* and *Nicholas Nickleby*. Dickens' satiric portraits of evangelical clergymen (Non-Conformists) indicate his dislike of their attitudes and a disagreement with their doctrine. He finds their extreme adherents extremely amusing. In the manner of Carlyle,

Dickens holds the radically Protestant view that nothing interfered more with 'true' religion than the contemporary fetishism of 'Rituals, Liturgies, Creeds, Hierarchies', "which obscured the divinely ordained duty to act righteously and serve one's fellow man".[11]

Dickens shows the failure of Christianity to act as a Social Gospel by exposing the religious hypocrisy of Victorian Society in *Oliver Twist*. He discovers the soulless ritualism of the religious practices of the English society. He presents the inadequacy of Church to fulfil the saving role of the religious institution. Dickens' opposition to institutional official Christendom is expressed with uncompromising strength of feeling in *Dexter Letters*: "As to the Church, my friend, he wrote de Carjat on 5 October, 1864, I am sick of it. The spectacle presented by the indecent squabbles of priests of most denominations, and the exemplary unfairness and rancour with which they conduct their differences, utterly repel me."[12]

Dickens hates other types of religious practices—Ritualist fopperies and Roman Catholic Priestcraft. He ridicules the sectarian intolerance in *Barnaby Rudge*. He dislikes religious bigotry and attacks overenthusiasts to form a counteracting force sustaining reason and common sense. He satirises Little Bethelism, the narrow and cheerless religion in *The Old Curiosity Shop*.

Dickens' most energetic satire is directed against practitioners of religion such ecclesiastical figures as Chadband in *Bleak House*, Reverend Mr. Stiggins in *Pickwick Papers*, Melchisedech Howler in *Dombey and Son*. He casts his satirical net in Murdstone in *David Copperfield*, Pecksniff in *Martin Chuzzlewit* and Mrs. Varden and Miss Miggs in *Barnaby Rudge*.

Dickens shows the pseudo benevolence of the false philanthropic missions of religious missionaries by ridiculing Mrs. Jellyby and Mrs. Pardiggle in *Bleak House*. In brief, he demolishes not religion but the cant and perversion of religion.

Dickens is very much dissatisfied with the politics of his time. He detests the working of parliamentary democracy of contemporary England. In *Pickwick Papers*, he decries the pomp and show, the absurd rivalry of the political parties, the fare election campaign and the unfair elections. In *Bleak House*, he attacks the use of bribery to win the election, the political corruption, the parliamentary intrigue and the party game of the politicians. In *Martin Chuzzlewit* and *Nicholas Nickleby*, he attacks the incompetent politicians. In *Little Dorrit*, he ridicules the corrupt politicians acting as swindlers. In *Our Mutual Friend*, he digs at the foolish and vainglorious politicians. He satirises the terrific upheaval of the Chartists in *The Old Curiosity Shop*.

In Politics, the choice is between the Dandies, the Coodles and Doodles—'the Governing class who do not govern'—as Carlyle called them in *Past and Present* and the extreme opposite, Chartism, the working class movement campaigning with threats of physical violence. Dickens is doubtful of Parliament and at the same time frightened off 'the mob' to support the Chartists. In letters and speeches, he does not support 'physical force Chartism' although he feels sympathy for the People's Charter. He trusts in 'the common sense and senses of common people', rather than in political parties or doctrines.

Chesterton likes to compare Dickens with Cobbett. He asserts that both are alike. There is a genuine affinity between the two men and they are possibly to assume that the real conduct of politics is not important and there is no loss to the world when its practice is abandoned completely. "For, both of them, politics, especially in its institutional aspects, frequently, looked like nothing more than complicated and extravagant ceremony, and both firmly supposed that whatever the substantial issues of politics might be, and whatever issues of life might fall within its ill-defined province, they were at bottom simple and could be relieved by simple, moralistic means."[13]

Dickens ridicules the nineteenth century theory of business enterprise. In the field of commerce, money replaces human values, relationships and sentiments. In *Dombey and Son*, Mr. Dombey's ideas that money can buy anything and human relations are conducted on the sound principles of hard commerce, are jeered. Dickens exposes that money is deficient as it cannot buy life. It poisons human relations. Wealth corrupts our heart. Money does not save his first wife. The commercial marriage of Edith and Dombey degenerates as money cannot replace the fundamental values of life. She does not live to the business ethics of Mr. Dombey and runs off with Carker. His relation with his daughter is not congenial. Money, even, cannot produce genius. Toots and Paul are rich but their potential is withered by money. The power of money of Mr. Dombey crumbles and his neglected firm of Dombey and Son fails. Mr. Carker, the manager of the business sector is ridiculed as he works for his self-gain. "Love, not business, is the only basis for human relationships, but actually not even business itself can be conducted as Dombey conducts Dombey and Son without disaster. For Dombey values a dignified appearance equally over the real situation of his marriage and the solvency of the firm. The attack in *Dombey and Son* is not really on business at all, but on a poor out moded kind of business mentality that carries its standards over into areas where they are even less useful and more ruinous than they are in business."[14]

In *Our Mutual Friend*, Dickens satirises the taste of the Veneering world regarding shares. In *Martin Chuzzlewit*, he ridicules people who recognise money as the only yardstick of value. The measurement of things by its cash value denigrates all things and persons to nothingness. The Railways is satirised in *Dombey and Son* as it has disrupted the lives of individuals. It is the cause of terror and pain.

The main tenets of utilitarianism include the exposure of all institutions to the tests of rational utility in the interests of the greatest happiness of the greatest number. It also consists an objective ethics in which the judgement of right and wrong actions is dependent on calculation of the amount of pleasure or pain produced by those actions. *Hard Times* is set in Coketown, an industrial city without fancy or emotion. Dickens dislikes many aspects of the industrial world. He is not anti-industrialist but he attacks the industrialist's mistaken philosophy the suppression of imagination. He wants any change motivated by humanitarian concerns. The novel unmasks the heartless scheme of values behind institutions that stunt love, imagination and life. Thomas Gradgrind is an utilitarian and his ally Bounderby is utilitarian in practice. The former brings up his children on the lines of John Stuart Mill and he discourages in them natural impulses and sensitivity. He arranges his daughter, Louisa's, marriage with Bounderby. She is not happy with him and the marriage fails. She returns to her father and charges him for this breakdown. His son, Tom, commits bank robbery and tries to escape from justice. Gradgrind's utilitarian pupil, Bitzer, intercepts him. Gradgrind makes an appeal to his pupil to save his son's life but Bitzer insists on self-interest. At last, his son takes refuge in Sleary's circus. "Mill had to discover poetry in order to recover from the ravages of Benthamite education imposed on him by his father, and the ultimate deficiency of the Gradgrind system, too, is that it ignores or condemns the imagination."[15]

Dickens surpasses even Carlyle in burning denunciation of the dismal science of classical economic theory or the heartlessness of the cash nexus as the only link between man and man. He utters a prophetic warning to utilitarian economists, schoolmasters and commissioners of Fact. He asks them to develop in the poor the greatest graces of the fancies and affections. Otherwise, Reality takes its revenge.

Dickens satirises some educational practices of his time. He detests cruelty, inefficiency and repression in education. In *Dombey and Son*, he laughs at the Charity schools as the student is tormented by people and the teacher. Mrs. Pipchin practices cruelty in the name of education. Dickens satirises the unscientific and anti-child psychological foundations of the nineteenth century school education. Blimber system is devastatingly cruel and its forcing system results in the stultification of students. Dr. Blimber, Miss Blimber and Mr. Feeder, B. A. are all epitome of cruel teachers. Dombey possesses a superb description of the overcramming Educator's system "worth whole volumes of essays on the subject if Bigotry would believe that laughs may tell truth".[16] Future scholarship will be grateful to Dickens for his temperate but yet severe rebuke of all attempts to overtask a child's intellect in the classical institution.

In *Bleak House*, Dickens attacks the public school curriculum as it does not cater to the natural bent of the student. He ridicules the class-consciousness created by education. In *Hard Times*, he satirises the utilitarian system of education in which the inculcation of facts is the sole aim and imagination is suppressed. He also mocks the trained teacher M'Choakumchild overloaded with verbalised knowledge murdering the innocents. *Hard Times* emphasises, with the whole Dickens' power and skill, that this is not merely a "rhetorical antithesis: that mere fact, or logic, that leaves half of our lives out of account—any method of ruling conduct or affairs that lacks sympathy, love and understanding between human beings—is, in the end, not merely sterile, but bitterly destructive of all the moral virtues, beauty, and everything that is best; that a sound life cannot exist without happiness; and that the proper education of children must take into account their moral development, which it should foster through their fancy and love of life."[17]

In *Our Mutual Friend*, Dickens attacks the ragged school system. He shows the facetousness and pomposity of religious preaching in such an oppressive and noisy set up. He also ridicules Bradley Headstone, a mechanical teacher and thus lashes the modern British educationl system. In *Great Expectations*, he satirises the bad academic activity of the amateurish dame school and its incompetent and tyrannical teacher, Mr. Wopsle's great aunt. In *David Copperfield*, Murdstone uses cruelty to teach David. Salem House represents the degrading institution of the nineteenth century England. He ridicules the school teacher, Mr. Creakle, who is cruel, incompetent and hypocritical. In *Nicholas Nickleby*, Dickens jeers Dotheboys Hall keeping stunted, hopeless and vicious boys. Squeers, a teacher of this school, is hypocritical, guile and greedy, ignorant and torturing. *Nicholas Nickleby*, strongly, assaults on the iniquities of the Yorkshire schools. It is aimed, primarily, at those cheap seminaries where "starvation is taught gratis, and which we fear were too common throughout

England; and we rejoice to hear that the exposure has already put down many infant bastilles."[18]

Dickens' writings stirred the contemporary social consciousness as hardly ever before. "Parents were ashamed, that were never ashamed before, until the kind satirist laughed at them; relatives were frightened, scores of little scholars were taken away; poor schoolmasters had to shut their shops; every pedagogue was voted a Squeers, and many suffered, no doubt unjustly, but afterward school boys' backs were not so much caned; school boys' meat was less tough and more plentiful; and school boys' milk was not sky blue."[19]

It ought to be acknowledged that Dickens has done much social good in satirising the institution of education. "He should be immortalised, if only for the putting down the school tyrannies, exposing and crushing school pretensions, and doubtless saving many a fair intellect from withering blight and perversion."[20]

Dr. Strong's school is depicted as an attainable ideal. The scholastic curriculum is endowed with goodwill. There is plenty of liberty and noble games are arranged. The students are 'studiously engaged at their books'. The head boy 'very affable and good-humoured' greets the new boy and introduces him to the masters 'in a gentlemanly way'. The headmaster, a clergyman, is a classicist and his Dictionary of Greek roots is his only intellectual interest and a student grows 'great in Latin verses'. He possesses sweet amiability, enduring simplicity and 'the least suspicious of mankind'. Philip Collins remarks: "Doctor Strong's was an excellent school, as different from Mr. Creakle's as good is from evil. It was very gravely and decorously ordered; and on a sound system; with an appeal, in everything, to the honour and good faith of the boys, and an avowed intention to rely on their possessions of those qualities unless they proved themselves unworthy of it, which worked wonders."[21]

Dickens is interested in the spirit in which the school is conducted. He endorses the humane and liberal methods characteristics of Arnold's reforms at Rugby and Hawtrey's at Eton. Boys must be trusted and should be given much liberty. They must be treated with respect and affection. Dickens' ideal is a public school: "I believe there is not in England (he said a few years before his death), any institution so socially liberal as a public school.... As far as I know, nowhere in this country is there so complete an absence of servility to mere rank, to mere position, to mere riches as in a public school. A boy there is always what his abilities or his personal qualities make him. We may differ about the curriculum and other matters, but of the frank, free, manly, independent spirit preserved in our public schools, I apprehend there can be no kind of question."[22]

In *Pickwick Papers*, the grotesque people are the subject of satire. The hypocritical Stiggins takes pineapple brandy but praises tea and temperance. The magistrate Nupkins intimidates court officials and prisoners with an impartial ignorance of the law. The learned members of the legal profession twist the very truth for their self gain. The rival newspapers editors Pott and Slurk inflict insults on one another. The parliamentary candidates Fizkin and Slumkey possess political abuse.

In *Oliver Twist*, Dickens has scathing remarks about the new Poor Law and London's criminal slums. Bumble, the workhouse beadle, is subjected to vindictive ferocity. *Nicholas Nickleby* describes the infamous Yorkshire schools—brutal boarding schools. The students are not properly educated, nurtured, housed or clothed. These cheap seminaries created spectres of hunger, cold and injustice. *Bleak House* discusses institutions from government and law to philanthropy, religion and rotting tenements of Tom-all-Alone's. It also consists Mrs. Jellyby's philanthropic mission and the parliamentary satire on Coodle and Doodle. These all represent the corrupt and entangled web of vested interests and power. Dickens dwells much on the droll and cruel slowness of the Court of Chancery. Edgar Johnson writes: "The key institution of the book is the court of Chancery, the key image the fog pervading the atmosphere of the entire story with an oppressive heaviness.

But both law and fog are fundamentally symbols of all the murky forces that suffocate the creative energies of mankind, the entanglement of vested interests and archaic traditions protecting greed, fettering action, and beclouding man's vision. *Bleak House* is thus an indictment not merely of the law, but of the whole dark muddle of organised society."[23]

*Hard Times* exposes the cold-hearted rationalisation of political economy and the industrial greed that applies 'economic laws' to justify its cruel exploitation of the labouring classes. K.J. Fielding writes: "The novel was thus a protest not merely against certain characteristics of Victorian Society, but against all repression of the human spirit by the letter of the classroom, the constitution, the law and the so-called principles of political economy. Dickens' purpose was not just to strike at utilitarianism, but all kinds of social abuses which he thought ran counter to human life and happiness because they were framed according to supposed 'facts' while they ignored obvious human needs."[24]

*David Copperfield* discusses the cruel, gloomy religion of the Murdstones and the predatory formulas of the courts of Doctors' Commons. These all stress on society's insensitiveness to human welfare and its worship of blind eyes and brutal idols. In *Little Dorrit*, the Marshal sea, Mrs. Clennam's grim theology, the circumlocution office and the great financial swindler, Merdle are unmasked. In *Our Mutual Friend*, Veneerings and Podsnaps are jeered whose values are in dust heaps symbolising material ambitions.

Dickens strikes at the follies or abuses in every sphere of society with remarkable vigour and precision. The system of English jurisprudence, the machinery of civil administration and the principles of political economy seem worthless or mischievous to his eyes. Dickens is a social novelist and his comedy tries to subvert the established order by unmasking the corruption. But some critics views that the corrupt order is spiritually disordered. Therefore the novelist is only able to measure human worth against inherent spiritual disorder.

Dickens' satire, primarily, heightens human worth and leaves the social muddle 'unpurged'. But it eludes correction. A caricaturist and satirist stands in a "mundane and moral daylight with Voltaire and Aristophanes, directing his missiles cruel or gay at the stupidities, the pretensions, the evil practices of his less enlightened fellows, and thereby wins them to greater sanity".[25]

The very purpose of Dickens' institutional satire is to excite our sympathy for the aggrieved and suffering in all sections of society. He directs our attention to the helpless victims of untoward circumstances or a vicious system—to the imprisoned debtor—the orphan pauper—the parish apprentice—the juvenile criminal—and to the tyranny exercised with impunity in schools under the combination of parental neglect with the mercenary brutality of a pedagogue.

The volume and extent of the social evils are very much alarming during Victorian age. With a reformist zeal, Dickens attacks the harshness and the lack of sympathy of the law and the cruel treatment practised to the children. He intends to draw the attention of the administrators of the country to redress and solve those evils. Dickens' institutional satire regarding politics is intended to cure the evils in our parliamentary system of government. The novelist satirises politicians to make them honest, self-sacrificing and better upholders of the causes of the masses. He wants to make parliament apt enough to redress the grievances of the people.

## NOTES

1. George Robert Gissing, *Charles Dickens: A Critical Study*, Blackie, Bombay, 1928, p. 110.
2. Graham Storey, *Charles Dickens: Bleak House*, Cambridge, Cambridge University Press, 1987, p. 7.
3. *Ibid.*, p. 6.
4. Alan Shelston, *Charles Dickens, Dombey and Son* and *Little Dorrit*, Macmillan, Basingstoke, Hampshire, 1985, p. 132.
5. Alexander Welsh, *The City of Dickens*, Clarendon Press, Oxford, 1971, p. 45.

6. F.S. Schwarzbach, *Dickens and the City*, University of London, The Athlone Press, London, 1986, p. 134.
7. Andrew Sanders, *Charles Dickens, Bleak House*, 'Everyman,' J.M. Dent, London, Charles E. Tuttle, Vermont, 1994, p. 8.
8. *Ibid.*, p. 414.
9. J.H. Miller, *Charles Dickens: The World of His Novels*, Oxford University Press, London, 1959, p. 30.
10. Steven Marcus, *Dickens from Pickwick to Dombey*, Chatto and Windus, London, 1985, p. 48.
11. Dennis Walder, *Dickens and Religion*, George Allen and Unwin, London, 1981, p. 10.
12. *Ibid.*, p. 209.
13. Steven Marcus, *op. cit.*, p. 46.
14. Monroe Engel, *The Maturity of Dickens*, Harvard University Press, Cambridge, Massachussetts, 1967, p. 112.
15. *Ibid.*, p. 173.
16. Philip Collins, *Dickens the Critical Heritage*, Routledge and Kegan Paul, London, 1971, p. 219.
17. K.J. Fielding, *Charles Dickens: A Critical Introduction*, Longman, Green and Co., London, 1958, p. 132.
18. Philip Collins, *op. cit.*, p. 84.
19. *Ibid.*, p. 354.
20. *Ibid.*, p. 231.
21. *Ibid.*, p. 116.
22. Christopher Hibbert, *The Making of Charles Dickens*, Longman, London, 1967, p. 89.
23. Edgar Johnson, *Charles Dickens: His Tragedy and Triumph*, Penguin Books, New York, London, 1986, p. 387.
24. K.J. Fielding, *op. cit.*, p. 133.
25. A.E. Dyson, *Dickens: Modern Judgements*, Macmillan, London, 1968, p. 262.

# Bibliography

## Dickens' Novels


1. *Charles Dickens, The Pickwick Papers*, Introduction and notes by David Ellis, Wordsworth Classics, Hertfordshire, 2000.
2. *Charles Dickens, Oliver Twist*, Introduction and notes by Ella Westland, Wordsworth Classics, Hertfordshire, 2000.
3. *Charles Dickens, Nicholas Nickleby, Hard Times, A Christmas Carol*, Octopus Books Ltd., London, 1983.
4. *Charles Dickens, Barnaby Rudge*, Editor Hawes Donald, Everyman, J.M. Dent, London, Charles E. Tuttle, Vermont, 1996.
5. *Charles Dickens, Dombey and Son*, Editor Purton Valerie, Everyman, London, Vermont, 1997.
6. *Charles Dickens, David Copperfield*, Introduction and notes by Adrienne E. Gavin, Wordsworth Classics, Hertfordshire, 2000.
7. *Charles Dickens, Bleak House*, Editor Sanders Andrew, Everyman, J.M. Dent, London, Charles E. Tuttle, Vermont, 1994.
8. *Charles Dickens, Hard Times*, Introduction by Philip Collins, Everyman's Library, Dent, London, 1978.
9. *Charles Dickens, Little Dorrit*, Editor Sucksmith Harvey Peter, At the Clarendon Press, Oxford, 1979.
10. *Charles Dickens, Great Expectations*, Editor Cardwell Margaret, Oxford University Press, New York, 1994.

11. *Charles Dickens, Our Mutual Friend*, Wordsworth Classics, Hertfordshire, 1997.
12. *Charles Dickens, The Old Curiosity Shop*, Wordsworth Classics, Hertfordshire, 1995.
13. *Charles Dickens, Martin Chuzzlewit*, Wordsworth Classics, Hertfordshire, 1994.
14. *Charles Dickens, Little Dorrit*, Wordsworth Classics, Hertfordshire, 1996.
15. *Charles Dickens, Nicholas Nickleby*, Introduction and notes by Dr. Tim Cook, Wordsworth Classics, Hertfordshire, 1995.

## Critical Books

Ackroyd, Peter, *Introduction to Dickens*, Mandarin, London, 1992.

——, *Dickens' London: An Imaginative Vision*, Headline, London, 1987.

Allen, Walter, *The English Novel*, Penguin Books, Harmondsworth, Middlesex, 1991.

Burton, Richard, *Charles Dickens*, Folcroft Library, Folcroft, PA, 1977.

Brown, Ivor, *Dickens in His Time*, Thomas Nelson and Sons Ltd., London, 1963.

Bhattacharya, Debiprasad, *The Middle Class in Dickens*, Minerva Associates, Kolkata, 2000.

Cockshut, Anthony Oliver John, *The Imagination of Charles Dickens*, Collins, St. James Place, London, 1961.

Collins, Philip, *Dickens: The Critical Heritage*, Routledge and Kegan Paul, London, 1971.

——, *Dickens and Crime*, Macmillan & Co. Ltd., London, New York, St. Martin's Press, 1962.

——, *Dickens and Education*, Macmillan & Co. Ltd., London, 1963.

Dyson, A.E., *Dickens: Modern Judgements*, Macmillan, London, 1968.

——, *Dickens, Bleak House*, Macmillan, London, 1969.

——, *The Inimitable Dickens*, Macmillan, London, St. Martin's Press, New York, 1970.

Engel, Monroe, *The Maturity of Dickens*, Harvard University Press, Cambridge, Massachussetts, 1967.

Fielding, K.J., *Charles Dickens: A Critical Introduction*, Longman, Green and Co., London, New York and Toronto, 1958.

Flint, Kate, *Dickens*, The Harvester Press, Brighton, Sussex, 1986.

Gissing, George Robert, *Charles Dickens: A Critical Study*, Blackie, Bombay, 1928.

Gold, Joseph, *Charles Dickens: Radical Moralist*, University of Minnesota Press, Minneapolis, 1972.

Grant, Allan, *A Preface to Dickens*, Longman, London, New York, 1984.

Gross, John and Gabriel Pearson, *Dickens and the Twentieth Century*, Routledge and Kegan Paul, London, 1962.

Hardy, Barbara, *Charles Dickens: The Writer and His Work*, Profile Books Ltd., Windsor, Berkshire, England, 1983.

——, *The Moral Art of Dickens*, The Athlone Press of the University of London, London, 1970.

Hibbert, Christopher, *The Making of Charles Dickens*, Longmans, London, 1967.

Hobsbaum, Philip, *A Reader's Guide to Charles Dickens*, Thames and Hudson, London, 1972.

House, Humphry, *The Dickens World*, Oxford University Press, London, New York, Toronto, 1942.

Jackson, T.A., *Charles Dickens: The Progress of a Radical*, People's Publishing House, New Delhi, 1990.

Jane, Vogel, *Allegory in Dickens*, The University of Alabama Press, University of Alabama, 1977.

Johnson, Edgar, *Charles Dickens: His Tragedy and Triumph*, Penguin Books, New York, London, 1986.

Korg, Jacob, *Twentieth Century Interpretations of Bleak House*, Prentice Hall, Englewood Cliffs, N.J., 1968.

Larson, Janet L., *Dickens and the Broken Scripture*, The University of Georgia Press, Athens, 1985.

Leavis, F.R. and Q.D. Leavis, *Dickens the Novelist*, Chatto & Windus, London, 1970.

Leavis, F.R., *The Great Tradition*, Penguin Books, Harmondsworth, Middlesex, 1962.

Lucas, John, *Charles Dickens: The Major Novels*, Penguin Books, Harmondsworth, Middlesex, 1992.

——, *The Melancholy Man*, Methuen & Co. Ltd., London, 1970.

Marcus, Steven, *Dickens from Pickwick to Dombey*, Chatto & Windus, London, 1965.

Miller, Joseph Hillis, *Charles Dickens: The World of His Novels*, Harvard University Press, Cambridge, Massachussetts, Oxford University Press, London, 1959.

Monod, Sylvere, *Dickens the Novelist*, University of Oklahoma Press, Norman, 1967.

——, *Martin Chuzzlewit*, George Allen & Unwin, London, 1985.

Nisbet, Ada and Blake Nevius, *Dickens Centennial Essays*, University of California Press, Berkeley, 1971.

Page, Norman, *Dickens, Hard Times, Great Expectations* and *Our Mutual Friend*, Macmillan, London, 1979.

Pope, Norris, *Dickens and Charity*, Macmillan, London, 1978.

Price, Martin, *Dickens: A Collection of Critical Essays*, Prentice Hall, Englewood Cliffs, N.J., 1967.

Reid, J.C., *Charles Dickens: Little Dorrit*, Edward Arnold, London, 1967.

Sadrin, Anny, *Great Expectations*, Unwin Hyman, London, 1988.

Sanders, Andrew, *Charles Dickens: Resurrectionist*, Macmillan, London, 1982.

Schlicke, Paul, *Dickens and Popular Entertainment*, Unwin Hyman, London, Boston, Sydney, Wellington, 1985.

——, *Oxford Reader's Companion to Dickens*, Oxford, The University Press, 1999.

Schwarzbach, F.S., *Dickens and the City*, University of London, The Athlone Press, London, 1979.

Shelston, Alan, *Charles Dickens, Dombey and Son* and *Little Dorrit*, Macmillan, Basingstoke, Hampshire, England, 1985.

Slater, Michael, *Dickens, 1970*, Chapman and Hall, London, 1970.

Smith, Grahame, *Dickens: Money and Society*, University of California Press, Berkeley and Los Angeles, 1968.

Spilka, Mark, *Dickens and Kafka: A Mutual Interpretation*, Dennis Dobson, London, 1963.

Stewart, Garrett, *Dickens and the Trials of Imagination*, Harvard University Press, Cambridge, Massachussetts, 1974.

Stone, Harry, *Dickens and the Invisible World*, Macmillan, London, 1980.

Storey, Graham, *Charles Dickens, Bleak House*, Cambridge University Press, 1987.

*The Times Literary Supplement*, TSL Education Ltd., London, Feb. 4, 2000.

Tillotson, Kathleen, *Novels of the Eighteen Forties*, Oxford, The Clarendon Press, 1954.

Tomlin, E.W.F., *Charles Dickens 1812-1870: A Centenary Volume*, Weidenfeld and Nicholson, London, 1969.

Trevelyan, G.M., *English Social History*, Orient Longman, Bombay, 1968.

Walder, Dennis, *Dickens and Religion*, George Allen & Unwin, London, Boston, Sydney, 1981.

Welsh, Alexander, *The City of Dickens*, Clarendon Press, Oxford, 1971.

Willey, Basil, *Nineteenth Century Studies*, Chatto and Windus, London, 1955.